"Deborah Deneaux ... is unforgettable. Her story... is so layered and rich ... This book doesn't flinch from ... real, personal, intimate pain ... And yet, somehow, the story doesn't drown in that sorrow. It balances on the thin line between despair and redemption ..."

~ *Literary Titan (5-star review)*

"...a journey defined by elegance and raw emotion ... The author's attention to cultural detail ... is a valuable aspect of this novel ... I joined Pauline and DeeDee, admiring this powerful expression of feminine resilience. ... subtle delights embedded in a well-told story ..."

~ *Janice P. Kehler, Wisconsin Writers Association*

"Peters' writing features ... lovely passages, ... The characters are well-rounded and distinct; ...The novel handles weighty themes frankly and with nuance ... A moving story of friendship, family, and recovery."

~ *Kirkus Reviews (starred review)*

"The Dancer and the Swan is a beautifully executed book ... (it) oozes charm and inspired storytelling .... Captivating and incredibly moving, this is a five-star read, no question."

~ *Alice Bennett, Reedsy (five-star review)*

ALSO BY JAMES L. PETERS

Shrugging
Turntable
Fortune Falls

VISIT THE WEBSITE:

JamesLPeters.com

FOLLOW ON FACEBOOK:

facebook.com/James.L.Peters.Author/

The Dancer and the Swan

James L. Peters

Six by 9 Publishing

First Edition

LIBRARY OF CONGRESS
CATALOGING-IN-PUBLICATION DATA:

Peters, James L.

The Dancer and the Swan / James L. Peters

ISBN 979-8-9985884-0-2

Cover Design: Lori Chilefone

Dedicated to the Grandmother
I never knew,
Grace Mabel Peters,

and the Grandmother
I should have known better,
Susan Genevieve Cronce

CHAPTER ONE

The Death Nurse

Two months ago, I buried my father. The last of my immediate family—of anyone that had still dangled from the threads of my life.

Father joined Mother in eternal rest at Crowder Cemetery right here in Leland Grove, Illinois. A spot waits for me next to them, before an imposing slab of upright stone, gothic letters chiseled across the front declaring our family name: SWANSON. For the first part of my life, it's where I knew I would end up, and absolutely not where my remains will reside.

It's been over thirty years since I buried my daughter, whose small, modest tombstone stands amid a field of stones over two hundred miles away, the years 1995-1995 etched into the marble. My place is next to her.

I like the idea of cremation. It's not very Catholic of me, but there's something lyrical and poetic about returning to dust instead of my body being embalmed. Burned to ash, carried by the wind across distant lands. I will dust the dreams of lovers, be a mote in the eyes of those who hate, grit the icy walkways to steady slippery steps, and choke the voices that lie and slander.

But no, my body needs to lie beside Kaiya. I feel I'd be abandoning her otherwise. Instead, my organs will be removed, my blood drained, body filled with formaldehyde, and I'll be boxed up like a time capsule. No poetic ending for Pauline Swanson. Nor do I deserve one.

Last month, my body turned fifty-three. My brain, however, holds fast to its mental age of thirty. Meanwhile, my parched and brittle soul often feels a thousand years old.

I've survived my parents, my offspring, several failed relationships, and lately I can't help but feel like the walking dead.

I just started volunteering for St. John's Hospice. I'd already been caring for my father for the last two years of his life while he slowly withered away from colon cancer. I need something else to fill that time, something to feel good about, and helping others makes me feel good.

As a volunteer, I won't be prescribing medications. I won't diagnose or treat. I'm simply a companion, someone to be present and aware in between those times when healthcare professionals are called for. We volunteers make it possible for someone to remain at home in the final stages of their life. I'm eager to feel comfortable and competent in this role as a companion and support. Admittedly, I don't yet. As is usually the case, I'll have to rely upon my false sense of confidence to get me through. Historically, that has served me about as well as a coin flip, yet it is the social crutch I put all my weight on.

I earned my driver's license only ten years ago and applaud my achievement at this level of independence and control, but I'm still anxious behind the wheel of such a large and potentially dangerous machine. I know I annoy other drivers by my overly cautious speed and attention. At intersections I look both ways three times. I count out a full four seconds at every stop sign. I drive exactly the speed limit. Maybe I'm overcompensating for a less-than-cautious younger life, but no tailgating, honking or fist waving will deter my zealous approach to safe driving.

I pull into the River Bend Senior Living Apartments parking lot. The two-story facility spreads wide, occupying a significant portion of the block it sits on. It's a cozy, almost Victorian vibe with a hint of Howard Johnson's from the outside. It looks modestly upscale, the kind of place where someone of means would reside in her final days. I could age gracefully and content in such a place, though my bartending salary couldn't afford it.

I have my big handbag stuffed full of goodies—Scrabble, a deck of cards, a well-leafed copy of *The Scarlet Letter*, cheese, cashews, dark chocolate, and a forty-five-year-old Catholic missal given to me for my first communion. Add to that my travel-everywhere bottle filled with aspirin, Ibuprofen, antacid, and gas pills—my little pharmacy I take wherever I go since hitting my fifties. The bag is left over from my past life as a librarian. Decorated with quills and scripted quotes from Shakespeare, its vinyl is cracked and has duct tape running across its bottom where it split years ago.

I park my ten-year-old Jetta up against the building by the main entrance. It runs like a dream with 190,000 miles from previous owners and 2,403 from me. I don't travel, don't drive much, and still rely on public transport whenever it's convenient. Bag over my shoulder, I head toward the main door with a tight, wide grin stretched across my face. Almost more a grimace. I do that when I'm nervous or stressed—grin like a fool. I suppose it's my equivalent of the old western tough guys biting down on a leather bit while someone digs a bullet out of their arm.

Here's my six-foot-one, one-hundred-ninety-five-pound

middle-aged frame strutting down the hall of River Bend Senior Living, ready to meet a dying woman while wearing a big, tight grin under a blaze of wild mahogany hair streaked with silver. Anyone strolling the halls of the apartment complex might just turn around and walk the other way.

My father dead only two months and I'm already diving into volunteer hospice care. It seemed a good idea at the time. I started the process only a few days after I buried him, trained and shadowed for a month after being vetted by the program. That doesn't prevent me from feeling completely unprepared.

I walk the long first-floor hallway through a complicated mix of odors that bring to mind potpourri, greasy food, and hospitals. Door after door displays welcome wreaths, fake flower swags, and other decorative hangings hand-made by elderly hands, young grandchildren, or some retired housewife peddling her crafts at a fair. Some look as if they've been here for a long time. On this summer morning, one door still displays a big, knitted Christmas wreath with pictures of young children as ornaments. Most are more seasonally relevant, patriotic, or vaguely spiritual.

I take a left, and apartment 1134 is the second on the right. Hanging from a nail in the door is a fancy black metal frame that seven white ceramic tiles are slid into, each one with a fancy calligraphic letter wrapped with vines and flowers. All together, they spell out, "DENEAUX." Behind the door, the faint moan of a saxophone and soft thump of bass.

Deborah Deneaux. Seventy-six years old. Never married. Born in New Orleans. Went to college in San Francisco. Moved to Chicago in the eighties. Ran a successful national advertising firm. Retired to a life of philanthropy. Ended up here in Springfield, Illinois. Enrolled in the St. John's Hospice Program with stage four sarcoidosis. Has a son and a granddaughter who live in the area.

That's all I know as I take in a breath. Hold it. Knock.

She should be expecting me. My watch says I'm seven minutes late. After twenty seconds, my knuckles are about to connect with wood again when the door opens to reveal a vision I wasn't expecting.

Ms. Deneaux is stunning. Her faux-wrap Caribbean print dress in royal purple patterning drapes over her lithe body in a way no dress has ever looked on me. She wears her hair short in a loose afro of elegant gray. The shine of her brown eyes under stark drawn eyebrows questions me intently. If not for the few small, reddish lesions poking out from her brow line and hiding behind the curl of sideburn, her brown skin would be flawless and radiant. Long, red polished nails curl around the door frame as she holds the door defensively ajar.

"Yes?"

"Ms. Deneaux. It's wonderful to meet you. Sorry I'm late. I'm Pauline with St. John's Hospice."

Those eyes travel up and down my figure. "Yes. My son set this up, but this isn't necessary."

"Oh, I'm sorry if there's been any misunderstanding."

"The misunderstanding is between me and my son." Burgundy lips frown, and our eyes connect again. Hers might be apologetic or annoyed. "I'm afraid you're just caught in the middle of it."

Perhaps I should go, but I resist giving up so easily. "Are you not interested in hospice care?"

Her smile is polite, but barbed. "I don't need any death nurse, dawlin'." The words gently roll between her lips. They softly slide and swirl with a seductive hint of French, but accented by an off-beat cadence.

I smile. "That's good, because I'm an end-of-*life* volunteer—emphasis on life." I lean in just a bit. "I'll let nature and God tend to your death."

She's quiet for a moment, and I don't know if I've offended. Her lips purse and her smooth brow furrows, the consternation of wrinkles more closely suggesting her age.

"Well, might as well come inside. No sense airing out my life to neighbors."

She opens the door and, after a few seconds' hesitation, I follow her inside.

A short half-wall and closet are all that make up the entryway to a very comfortable living room adorned with over a half century of life and culture. It's very apparent that Ms. Deneaux has lived. Black and white family pictures on the wall suggest a fairly prosperous young family from where I assume is New Orleans, where she grew up. In one photo, a tall, broad-shouldered and burly man in pin-striped suit and fedora stands proud next to a slim woman in white dress with long curls under a woman's white derby. Two young boys and a little girl pose before them in front of a storefront window calling out, "Deneaux Haberdashery." Below that photo on a shelf sits a picture of a young girl frozen in dance pose. On a lower shelf, a sophisticated young woman in a sharp tan business suit shaking hands with a large man while having her arm around an elderly gentleman in front of an old-time McDonalds. Further down on the wall hangs a framed landscape photo of a stage filled with a diverse mix of children and adults holding a banner that proclaims, "Thank You, DeeDee!" and a plaque declaring, "To Deborah Deneaux, In recognition of 12 years of support and service – The American Dance Theatre of Chicago."

Canvassed artwork on the walls, vivid colors drenched in night-life shadow, of Black jazz musicians, of old building facades and lamp posts of what must be New Orleans, and of svelte silhouettes frozen in dance. Ornate ebony pottery and sleek, sensual sculptures of bodies in motion command the spaces where they are displayed on shelves and end tables.

Despite the stale Berber carpeting and crinoline walls, Ms. Deneaux's living room is rich and dark and textured. There are layers of story here.

"Have a seat, dear. But don't think you'll be staying long." She sits a bit heavily on a plush black suede couch against the wall under a large oil painting—almost as wide as the couch—of four jazz musicians in a dark, smoky night club.

I'm entranced. My steps are cautious and slow, eyes lingering over everything as I move through the room.

"What a symphony of life…"

"Pardon?"

My cheeks get hot. I didn't mean to say that out loud. "I'm sorry." My eyes stick to every artifact and element of history, art and culture suggested by Ms. Deneaux's room. I point to a picture. "Your family?"

She nods. "Papa and Maman. My two older brothers and me."

"New Orleans, isn't it?"

Ms. Deneaux reaches for a clear loop of hose sitting beside an oxygen tank and slips it around her head and under her nose. "Yes." She turns the valve at top of the tank and settles back into the couch. "Papa's shop on Claiborne Avenue. He was a very well-respected businessman. Fitted some of the most important men in and around the Seventh Ward in the finest suits."

"And this is you?" I point to the picture of the young girl dancing.

She nods. "My first recital at Municipal Auditorium."

"You were a dancer?"

Ms. Deneaux sits straighter, rolls back her shoulders. "I was a student of Tony Bevinetto."

I politely shake my head.

"My dear. He was a famous choreographer of stage and screen. He chose me as one of the John Pela dancers on Channel 4." She rounds her words in a poetic lilt.

"That's wonderful. When was that?"

Her head tilts up, eyes looking beyond this place and time. "Oh, that would have been…1967? No, '68. I was seventeen."

I move to the picture in front of the old-timey McDonalds with the two men. "And this is you as well?"

When I turn to her, I can see her patience faltering. Pursed lips and eyes squeezed narrow. "Yes. Now, sit down, dawlin'. You're making me nervous."

I take a seat against the wall across from her in a velvety, red-upholstered Queen Anne-style chair, its cabriole legs and frame a deep mahogany.

"Listen here," she says, pulling the hose out from below her nose to let it sit under her chin. "I appreciate your interest in me. I'm sure you mean well, but there's really no reason to waste more of your time. I'm sorry you came all this way for nothing. As I said, I've no need for a death nurse. Not yet."

"Hospice volunteer."

"Whatever."

"Ms. Deneaux. My visit has already been worth it just sharing these few moments with you."

"Yes, well, mind you. I've nothing against you, dear, but I didn't request your services. Raymond just likes to feel he's being useful, when actually he just becomes a bother."

"Raymond," I say. "Your son?"

"Yes. He doesn't so much try to mean well, as he likes to *feel* as if he tries to mean well." A wink. "If you know what I mean." She snorts a sharp laugh and hacks into her hand.

"I'm sure he is feeling a little lost and helpless as you approach your end of life."

She bristles to that, shakes her head and ties up her arms. "End of life. People telling me I'm at the end of my life. Let God decide that for me. I'm just living day to day. Don't need any death nurse helping me through my so-called 'end of life.'"

8

"Hospice volunteer," I correct. "And I agree. But, also understand, Ms. Deneaux. From the day we're born, we need to be guided through our end of life. Our life begins to end from our very first breath. Feel free to let your life go on another thirty years. I'm just offering to be here and share in a little part of it."

Once again, she's struck silent, a reaction I'm used to. I don't mean to, but I put people off-balance. I can turn them on or turn them off—rarely anything in-between. By the scrutiny of squinted eye, it seems Ms. Deneaux is still teetering between two extremes of opinion.

"Girl, something different about you, isn't there? Hmm." She shakes her head and laughs out loud, and I'm realizing just how much I'm enjoying this woman. "You are an odd one!"

"You wouldn't be the first to notice," I say and smile.

Ms. Deneaux sighs, shakes her head, then gives me a puzzled grin. "Well, the time I've left is too precious to waste on boring people. And they've overwhelmed my days. The doctors, the nurses." She waves a hand around her. "So many of these sad souls in this building, dealing out their remaining days with solitaire and coffee klatches. I have no opinion on the weather, and I don't wish to talk about my bodily functions, and I certainly don't want to hear about theirs!"

I bark laughter. My cheeks flare red again from my loud burst.

"Something tells me you just might be a bit more colorful company, and I suppose I could use the company, at least for today."

Hand to my heart. "Well, I would be honored to be that company."

She nestles back into the couch. "What's your name again, dawlin'?"

"Pauline."

"Your full name. Good to know, in case we're related." She winks.

"Swanson. Pauline Swanson."

"Married name?"

"Most certainly not."

Ms. Deneaux grins and nods. "Well, see, already we share something in common." Hands slap down on her lap. "So, tell me about yourself."

That's not a question I'm ever comfortable with, and I feel like I'm taking far too long to answer. "Not much to tell, really. I was born here in Springfield. Well, Leland Grove. I studied library science at Northwestern University. Got my first library job in Skokie and lived there for a while. Moved around a bit for a few years. Came back here ten years ago after my mother died to look after my father. He was diagnosed with cancer two years ago, and I became his primary caregiver until he died two months ago."

Her mouth crimps sideways. "Well, wasn't that an interesting list of details you've just recited. Now, how about telling me about *you*?"

I chuckle to that. "Ah, you wish to know about the mysteries of Pauline. Well, those are not so easily revealed. But, seeing as you let me in to this wonderful place of yours, I will indulge you just a little. I am a Catholic girl, a book lover, and a recovering alcoholic that tends bar at a downtown hotel."

She laughs and brings a hand down on the arm of the couch. "Ooo, child! Now you're talking tea. Tell me more."

"Oh, no. That's all you get for now, I'm afraid."

"You are a tease, dawlin'."

"I'm selfish. I suspect yours is a far more interesting story, Ms. Deneaux. And I'm all ears."

CHAPTER TWO

Wrath of God & Man

"It would be wonderful to hear about growing up in New Orleans."

"It was wonderful to grow up in New Orleans."

"What about that television show you mentioned. Tell me about your dancing."

The music played. The TV cameras dollied and tracked. And DeeDee danced with five other girls on a Saturday afternoon in 1968 to Tommy James and the Shondells while thousands of teenagers watched at home on Channel 4.

Ten years of dance instruction culminated on that point. Exhaustive training— two years at Kelly School of Dance, followed by four years at NORD and over two years at Tony Bevinetto's Studio. Handpicked by Mr. Tony to be spotlighted that week as one of John Pela's Tony Bevinetto Dancers.

And DeeDee wanted to be anywhere but there.

She wasn't naïve. She knew all about what it meant to be Black. Papa and Maman educated her in the challenges and roadblocks. That's why they sent her to Saint Mary's Academy for girls. That's why they enrolled her in dance school at age six.

"You're Black in America," Papa would say. "You don't have the luxury for childish things. No loafing or lolling about your days. You have to be graceful and smart. You need to work three times as hard to earn half as much. But you're also Creole. We helped build this city. And we Deneauxs work hard and don't abide excuses."

They had Creole neighbors who white passed, leaning on their fair skin and straight hair, but the Deneaux's bloodline was only lightly thinned by French blood. DeeDee's paternal grandparents were born in Haiti, brought over by their parents, whose ancestors were freighted over in chains from West Africa via the Transatlantic Slave Trade.

The Seventh Ward was her entire world, so New Orleans had always been a welcome home for her, and DeeDee felt the pulse of its heartbeat. There was never any question that the city was hers and she belonged there.

Dancing on that bright, decorated sound stage with five White girls and a White television crew and mostly White high schoolers watching her mash potato and twist her way through choreographed steps, she felt out of place for the very first time.

That must have been how Ruby Bridges had felt at six years old being escorted into the all-White classroom of William J. Frantz Elementary School for the first time. Ruby had been a hero of hers growing up. Three years younger, but she seemed so much braver. Inspired by Ruby and the three other Black girls who were integrated into the other public school—McDonogh No. 19—DeeDee started to resent going to her all-Black, all-girl private school. She hated wearing the blue, woolen A-line pleated skirt and those black and white saddle oxfords. She wanted to do something heroic, and heroes didn't wear clown shoes.

Although most of the White parents pulled their kids from classes with the Black girls, and even the teachers resisted, Ruby stuck it out at W.J. Frantz Elementary. The McDonogh Three stayed for a couple years at McDonogh, then they were moved to different schools to integrate. Ultimately, after facing horrendous abuse and severe bullying, their parents ended up putting them in Black-segregated schools.

And now, here was Deborah Deneaux, a Black Tony Bevinetto Dancer on the *John Pela Show*, a show that itself had only recently allowed any Black high school dancers a few years prior. DeeDee was finally following in Ruby's steps and realizing how little it felt heroic and how much it just felt humiliating.

But DeeDee danced like she never had before, in perfect coordination with five girls who barely acknowledged her existence otherwise.

Growing up in the Seventh Ward, an A-student at St. Mary's Academy, it was easy to be spared the hostilities of the world. She had lived mostly isolated among those who were like her. And New Orleans had always seemed different. It wasn't Alabama, where just a few years prior, hundreds of people tried to cross the Edmund Pettus Bridge in Selma for their right to vote and were met instead by police batons and water cannons. It wasn't Mississippi with its flames of racial hostility. New Orleans wasn't even really Louisiana. It was its own world, where its Cajun and Creole, African and Central American populations were an integral part of its culture and development. During her childhood, there had been a relative and long-standing harmony among all races and peoples in New Orleans, even if there wasn't equality. But things started to change as the civil rights movement spread across the land. Papa and Maman would talk about it sometimes. They warned DeeDee's brothers, three and six years older, to take care, that the winds of change were blowing. And, although George and Alfred were both in Black-only schools, they were young boys, full of piss and vinegar, and more prone to trouble, especially Alfred. The White culture of New Orleans felt threatened and was starting to push back hard against the gale force of integration and equal rights. They may not have minded their Black folk giving the city some color and culture, and they may have abided a certain amount of success and limited freedoms unlike other southern territories—but not while sharing the same spaces.

And so, on that Saturday afternoon, in a live broadcast on WWL-TV Channel Four, Deborah Deneaux danced. But, really for the first time, she was dancing solely as a Black girl in a White world.

The Tremé neighborhood around Claiborne Avenue had been, more than any plot of New Orleans land, most comfortably and naturally her home. It was where DeeDee belonged. How many days over the summer months did she help out at the Haberdashery, to sweep the front walkway and say hello to Mr. Bajolière, the Barber next door who always sat outside his shop in-between snips and trims and smoked his Pall Malls. How many afternoons did she stroll with Maman or friends under the lush canopy of oaks that ran down the middle of Claiborne, window shopping all the Black-owned storefronts and dreaming of a dress or stylish hat or new pair of shoes. It was their thriving community. A Creole world and its boulevard of prosperity.

But a monster encroached. And Papa was intent on stopping it.

The great concrete serpent was winding its way across the southern states. Birthed in California, its belly slithered across Texas and writhed through Louisiana, and it had its eyes on the downtown. The question was, through which neighborhoods would it cut its path?

The Interstate 10 viper turned its head to the French Quarter, but that historic White district was fighting back hard, so that serpent tongue gave the Seventh Ward a taste. The alternate path was planned right through Claiborne Avenue and the heart of the Seventh Ward. City officials kept it quiet for as long as they could. When Papa found out, he went into full resistance mode.

Sitting at the dinner table, a fourteen-year-old DeeDee watched Papa ignore his supper while he railed against his fellow Tremé neighborhood business and homeowners. "Damn fools, they are. All but Charbonnet and a few others. Telling me, 'More important things to be thinkin' 'bout, Georges.'"

"*Calme-toi*, Father," Maman had said, smiling to DeeDee and Alfred.

"What's more important? This is about our home. Our livelihood. Our way of life. *Mon Dieu*!"

"Shoosh, now. Eat your food 'fore it gets cold."

Seventeen-year-old Alfred shook his head and stabbed at a piece of chicken-fried steak. "Lost cause, Pop."

Papa dropped his fork and knife with a clatter. "What do you mean, 'lost cause?'"

Maman glared at Alfred. "Don't now…"

"Does this mean we have to move?" a nervous DeeDee interrupted.

"Beating the Whites? Making them give up their French Quarter?" Alfred said. "No way, no how."

"So, we're just supposed to roll over? That how I raised you?" Papa scowled.

"You raised us to survive and thrive—" Alfred said.

Papa nodded sharply. "*Vivi et prospère*. That's right. What I've always told you all. Not enough for us to just survive—"

Alfred: "Can't do that sinking in a lost cause."

DeeDee: "Will we, Maman?"

"Please, all of you," Maman's voice pitched up.

Papa and Alfred gave her their attention. Alfred's shoulders slumped and his eyes fell to his plate.

"Not over dinner, please," Maman said. "Lord blessed us with this meal, let's honor that. Plenty of evening for discussion."

DeeDee looked over to the empty chair across from her. "Why haven't we heard from George?"

Maman's eyes glanced at the empty chair, then kept her attention to her plate. "Girl, don't you know he's at war? He can't be sending messages every day."

"But it's been a month."

Knife through her battered steak, she held up and scrutinized the skewered piece of meat. "Twenty-seven days." Maman took a thoughtful bite.

"He hasn't gone so long before without—"

Maman's hand slapped against the tabletop. "Can we please just eat our dinner in peace?" The silence following her strained composure hung thick in the room.

Alfred leaned into DeeDee. "Girl…" The suspended word an inflected warning.

George Jr. was the oldest, a man of twenty, and groomed to be the successor to Deneaux's Haberdashery. George, tall and lanky and bookish, already ran most of the business's backend for Papa. George was smart. Savvy. He had coerced Papa into some local advertising that was coming back to them in spades. Even after Hurricane Betsy came through in '65 to cause all that store damage to the front window and door—water coming through the ceiling to soak clothes—they were having their best year ever. Good enough that it guaranteed DeeDee's enrollment in Tony Bevinetto's Dance Studio that year.

Then George Jr. got his name picked, like over 200,000 other young men, to be sent off to Vietnam. Maman had been almost inconsolable. "They're taking my boy away! They're making him fight their war!"

That had been the cry of many a Black mother, who were more likely to see their son off to war than others. For Aurelia Deneaux, the irony was not misplaced that, only a hundred years prior, most Blacks weren't allowed to fight for their own freedom in the country they lived in. Now they were being sent to die for it.

The bulldozers came in early '66. Papa met them, like St. George against the dragon, along with a small handful of business owners and residents. Unable to stop their approach, they merely became an audience to two-hundred-year-old oaks being plowed down by progress. But not progress the Tremé Neighborhood would ever see. DeeDee had never seen her father look so feeble, so defeated.

Alfred just got angrier. Her brother's volatility shifted into higher and higher gears. The lack of aid after Hurricane Betsy in their districts. George's conscription into the army of a country that recognized them as less than second-class citizens. And now, as almost a physical manifestation of Whites' attitude toward them, they plowed down and destroyed so much of what represented their success and prosperity. He stopped going to church and started attending marches. They saw less and less of him and feared more and more for him.

Through all of this, Papa, Maman, and DeeDee went to mass and prayed. They read from the Bible and prayed. They honored the Lord's Day and prayed.

The Lord responded loud and clear in 1968. He responded with Martin Luther King Jr's assassination, and Bobby Kennedy's just two months later. He responded with the I-10 overpass nearing completion as it cut the Seventh Ward Tremé neighborhood in two and decimated her beloved Claiborne Avenue. And

He responded with the visit from the United States Army telling them that George Deneaux, beloved brother and son, had been killed in the line of their country's duty in Vietnam.

And DeeDee danced in front of those television cameras that fall of 1968, performing to an unseen New Orleans audience while still reeling from the loss of her brother, her neighborhood, and the illusion of comfort and belonging.

It was her last time dancing as a student of Tony Bevinetto.

When it seemed like nothing could get any worse, in the following summer, Hurricane Camille like the breath of God spun past them and took away their porch, a portion of their roof, and any hope that things would get better for them.

DeeDee wondered how her prayers could have offended God so strongly.

CHAPTER THREE

Weapon of Flesh

I drive home four hours later, and I'm having trouble grounding myself in this time, this world. In the few hours of one afternoon with a dying woman, I am raging with the emotions of a rebellious youth.

I hardly spoke a word, barely drew a breath, as Ms. Deneaux shared parts of her childhood.

"Call me DeeDee," she had said at one point after I had asked her something trivial.

I couldn't. But after that, I did start calling her Ms. Deborah. For me, that is more comfortable, respectful, and affectionate.

At one point, I asked her, "How did you survive the racism, the prejudice, the attack on your culture…"

She gave me a gentle, patronizing smile. "Getting a kick out of your past-tense there, dawlin'." Wink. "Listen, when the storms come, when the lightning and thunder bears down on you, when nature lets you know you aren't in control any more, what do you do?"

I had no idea. "Take shelter, I suppose? You just thank God you've survived and climb out to clean up any mess."

"And just maybe you build back a little stronger in preparation for next time. I got used to the Weather Channel of my life, where every day calls for developing storms."

Recalling Ms. Deborah speaking of her early years, fragments of my childhood resurface, even if I don't want them to.

Like Ms. Deborah's Seventh Ward, our neighborhood in Leland Grove was prosperous and thriving. Unlike her, I had no siblings. Until I was nineteen years old, I thought I was the reason why. Father said my size had damaged Mother's cervix during birth, resulting in her infertility. He was keen on reminding me that, "God have mercy, Pauline, you literally broke the mold." I came to learn that abnormalities of the cervix or negligence by medical staff were the most likely cause. Yet, despite that knowledge, after believing I was the reason I had no brothers or sisters for so long, I could never shake the debilitating unworthiness I felt, nor escape the weight of wholly unobtainable expectations on me.

A staunch and zealous Catholic man, Father had the fervor of a preacher and the savvy of a Wall Street broker. Mother, on the other hand, was quiet and withdrawn. A healthy woman, yet never vibrant. She was no run-of-the-mill midwestern Catholic. Her fear of God drove her fundamental faith. She possessed a mostly liberal heart that voted conservative because abortion and homosexuality were the sins of all sins. She softened a bit in her later years. If not accepting of, she became more forgiving of those who transgressed God's words. The gays, the atheists, they would be judged by God—most certainly by my father—but not by her.

Ms. Deborah's lilting voice expressed a connection and belonging to the neighborhood of her youth that I never experienced. The children in my neighborhood, and at my school, constantly reminded me of that. Fortunately, I was mostly ignored, though certainly I received my share of abuse due to my height, my build, and my posture. "Bigfoot," and "Ape Girl" were two of the many references I had to endure. And I just wore a big grin and walked on by every time.

It was maybe my painful, nervous, strained grin that so endeared me to adults. They saw this big, awkward, sweet, sad young girl smiling her way along the travails of life, and it warmed the cockles of their hearts.

And then there was Father Edward. I certainly seemed to warm his cockles.

At age eleven, I loved only one person. Jesus. I could endure any slight, any insult, any discomfort, because of that love, and I felt the radiance of His pure love for me. It was a warmth akin to coming in from the cold to huddle by a crackling fire. That's what my smile was. That's what let me survive all the ridicule and debasement that otherwise would have crushed me. So, of course, I wanted to do whatever would show my love for Him, to support His mission any way possible.

I joined the Catholic Youth Organization and worked with other young people to bring them closer to a relationship with our Lord. During those years, I spent a lot of time with Father Edward. He brought me with him to guide the at-risk youth on exercises and Scriptures to bring them into the light. Sometimes we'd just play games with wayward teenagers to keep them off the street and out of trouble. Father Edward—all the kids called him Father Eddie—had a youthful charm, despite his middle age, that made it easy to laugh with him but also a sage presence that gave his every word weight. To his constituents, his enthusiasm and charm was a welcome deviation from the stodgy, withered, and humorless pre-Vatican II priests that had hung around too long in our parish. To the troubled youth he worked with, he was slick and cool.

My father, of course, hated him. Saw Father Edward as brash and slick—too clever for clergy. That just attracted me to him even more.

I spent several afternoons a week with Father Edward, helping him plan activities and prepare the chapel for early morning mass. I was shy and demur before him. I felt clumsy and ugly and feared he didn't like me. He would comfort my insecurities with a hand around my shoulder. He would ease my lack of confidence by rubbing my back. He would soothe my trepidations by caressing my thigh.

At eleven, despite my discomfort, he flattered me with his interest. I reveled in each moment with this important adult I respected who gave me such positive attention when all my peers did nothing but make me feel like a creature.

It wasn't long before Father Edward was introducing me to feelings I would not feel again until college. I started to feel dirty and sinful. And yet, he made me feel mature and powerful. At eleven, I didn't condemn what was happening. Despite my discomfort, and in lieu of my pleasure, Father Edward introduced me to a power, a weapon I could wield.

For two years, I spent those afternoons with Father Edward. For two years, an important and respected person in the community, in our parish, loved me. And then, one day, he was just gone. Like he had never been a part of our congregation.

The whispers of parishioners weren't privy to a thirteen-year-old, but I could still catch a word or phrase, and years later heard the more open talk that made it fairly apparent I hadn't been the only one—just a silent one. The Diocese had shipped him off to another parish, another state, and washed their hands of it, just as Pilate had taught them.

I've never told anyone. Forty years later and I still don't fully understand the damage that was done to me. It was Jack, beautiful, mysterious Mr. Jack, who breezed into and stormed out of my life for good or ill all those years ago, who was my first step in recognizing the extent of the damage. He somehow disarmed me, made me understand that the weapon I wielded only managed to wound me. There are times that I curse the day Jack ever came into my life, but despite how lost and troubled he was, and whether intentional or not, because of him, I was put on a path toward health and healing. But he, like so many other broken pieces of my past, is best left buried and forgotten.

Back home at my apartment, I go online and find some sixties jazz to play. I don't want to let go of Ms. Deborah's world. Beyond the hardship and challenges, she conveyed a certain warmth and strength of family, and the inner child lost inside myself stirs.

But whatever remains of that child still cowers in a corner and won't come out. Hasn't come out for over forty years. Maybe longer.

I am thankful for the final years I had with my father. After decades of not speaking, to rebuild a relationship with him, to end up being his primary caregiver, was a blessing I cannot express in words. I was a daughter to him again, and he accepted it, even welcomed it, after a time.

Nine years. Thinking about it now, it honestly rattles me a bit. The time slipped by so fast, and yet it was almost a decade of my life stagnating. I existed for him. I gave up a dream job at the St. Louis Central Library to work eight to ten hours Tuesday through Saturday behind the bar of the Long 9 Lounge at the Crown Plaza Convention Center, and the rest of the time devoted to Father—cooking, cleaning, doing his laundry, playing cribbage and scrabble with him, reading Bible passages to him. And, in those final months, feeding him, bathing him, and cleaning him when he soiled himself. It was only in these past two months that I realized how much of the last decade was not my own.

If I'm to be honest, I had desperately hoped for Father to give me something during that time. I'm still reconciling with the fact that I will never receive it from him.

He never gave his forgiveness.

He never said those words to me. And now, I'll never know if somewhere inside of him he ever did or could forgive me. This haunts me.

Had I cared for him solely for the purpose of receiving his forgiveness? I try to avoid thinking about that—tell myself that I was simply fulfilling the role of a Christian daughter—but yet, there is this part of me that, I cannot deny, is unfulfilled and disappointed.

Mother's forgiveness was really the catalyst to me reclaiming my life. I had all but given up on it. Especially after Jack left me—the one relationship that, as swift as it was, still managed to fill my head with absurdly unrealistic expectations. When he turned his back on me, I was prepared to go off the rails. Drinking? Sex? Debauchery? Everything was on the table at that point. Part of me was excited to dive into my inhibitions once again and lose my everlasting soul in a gluttony of carnal sins. I was aloft in an emotional windstorm.

But mother reached out to me, told me she missed me, that she loved me, and was concerned about me. She told me she forgave me and was there if I needed her. She was the tether to pull me back and down to ground level. She ended up sending me to a place of reflection and spiritual healing.

We emailed each other. We spoke on the phone. Eventually, we shared our lives through pictures and memes on Facebook. Mother kept telling me to come home, but I wasn't ready. I couldn't face him—certainly not without an invitation from Father. I refused to ask, and it was clear to me he wouldn't give one.

If Mother had suffered a long, slow disease—a cancer or some muscular or neurological disease—I would have gone to her. I would have faced Father down. Her sudden, fatal heart attack was a shock. I was struck dumb, as was my father, who for the first time in twenty-two years was forced to contact me and communicate. It was horrifically uncomfortable, but an important first step to rebuilding our relationship.

In that first contact with him, I also realized that our separation was, to some degree, as much my fault as his. Our embargo on contact was mutual and completely inferred but never actually established by either of us.

I had done something unthinkable, and we both assumed that our relationship was irreconcilable.

I sit now in my recliner, the music softening my mood. As the late summer evening creeps in, my living room darkens while the mellow melancholy of Miles Davis's horn hangs in the air. In the fading embers of twilight, I once again find myself unearthing a past I thought I could leave buried in regret.

James L. Peters

.

CHAPTER FOUR

Looking the Demon in the Eye

Monday night and I'm in a little community room in downtown Springfield, standing in front of a podium before two dozen people who are drinking too much coffee out of small Styrofoam cups, most of them jittery for a smoke. In my hand is something that means almost as much to me as my faith—a fancy silver coin, blue-plated with the number fifteen inside a pyramid. Each side of the pyramid has a different word: Unity, Service, Recovery. And around the edge of the coin, the most important credo that has guided me to this point: ONE DAY AT A TIME.

Into the microphone, I say what I have said so many times that it should have lost all its meaning, but somehow manages to bear the same weight as the first time I uttered it to a group of people a lifetime ago.

"My name is Pauline, and I am an alcoholic."

I've told the story so many times, but it still hurts. It's no longer a personal pain. The story I share doesn't exactly feel like me anymore. It feels like I'm telling someone about an imaginary sister who I love so much and feel so very bad for.

"I was a good girl growing up. Devout and innocent. I loved my God and my parents. But I was also awkward. I was picked on. Never had many friends. My parents, meanwhile, couldn't quite relate to this little girl who spent so much time alone, who wrote poems to Jesus and who held funerals for road kill. My father, especially, was a rigid man. Faith to him was measured like a credit score.

"Anyway, I didn't realize it at the time, but when I finally got to college, I was ready to burst out of the tiny, constricting shell of my world.

"Before I knew it, I was making friends with the kinds of people I never knew existed. I was a liberal arts major, and the people I was associating with were artistic and flamboyant, expressive and dramatic. I loved their vivacity and energy. They were passionate and intense.

"And they drank. Some did drugs. They shared the bottle, pipe, and pill while they shared their pains and their intimacies.

"Belonging wasn't even a conscious decision. As much as these people were antithesis to every aspect of my previous life, I also recognized that they were everything missing from my life.

"So, of course I partook in the drugs and the drinking. I expressed my longings. I opened up about my inhibitions. And they embraced and encouraged.

"In no time, I found myself finishing off bottles of vodka each week. I was having regular encounters with college men. I was getting extra, extra credit with a professor. I was doing so many things that my faith made me ashamed of doing—but the drinking dulled that shame and increased the power I felt when I let men think they were taking advantage of me."

"By the end of my junior year, I was drunk all the time, and a target for anyone looking to get their jollies off quick and easy."

I often pause at this point. One day, I might even convince myself to share the whole story. But I've always skipped over my biggest, unforgiveable sin.

"Rock bottom was when I lost all my friends, my reputation, my relationship with my parents, and any semblance of respect I had for myself. To this day I don't remember the last quarter of my senior year or how I had managed to graduate. I just remember waking up one morning in graduation cap and gown, my mouth still around the cock of some guy I didn't know who was lying in either my or his vomit."

Long pause. All addicts have that one moment, the gratuitous, horrible, disgusting moment that becomes the fulcrum to their recovery. I've heard too many to remember them all. Most involve vomit or blood. Too many involve dead bodies. After a few years in AA, you start to anticipate them, rate the horror stories. Mine sits at about a six out of ten. There's so many sevens and eights. The nines, though uncommon, will keep you up at night. I've only heard one ten. She didn't last two months before she killed herself from an overdose. I can't even bring myself to speak her story out loud.

It's a good pause. Enough time for the room to smell and taste the experience. I take a deep breath before continuing.

"Since joining AA and the twelve-step program, I've only fallen off the wagon once. That was twenty years ago today. At the time, I thought it was because of a guy. But now I'm not sure if that's completely true. There were demons I hadn't faced, and those demons were thirsty. I'm proud to say that I haven't allowed them one drop for two decades now, and, with God's help, those devils will stay parched for another forty if I have anything to say about it. Thank you."

The applause is polite. Thunderous applause doesn't happen in AA, at least not any meetings that I've attended. We're too tempered by our abstinence to abide wild swings of mood and enthusiasm. But the approval is warm and genuine, and it always feels rewarding.

Harold, our chapter leader, rises from his chair in the front row and approaches me.

"Pauline, you've inspired so many who have come through our doors, many of them still here today. Some who have been with you from the beginning. On behalf of all of us, we congratulate you on earning this next step in sobriety—your twenty-year chip."

Harold puts out his hand, the maroon coin face up, that embossed "20" glinting in the overhead lights.

I hesitate. I'm overcome with a complexity of feelings. There's pride at making it twenty years sober. There's some sadness thinking about those I know who never made it to this point, who succumbed to their dry devils. There's also shame, or anger, or some combination of both, that I ever did all the things I did that led me to needing to earn that chip in the first place. What about the chips to represent the years of degradation and vice, of lewdness and overindulgence? And then there's the humility of knowing that I never had the strength of will to do this on my own. The chip doesn't belong to me. My faith, my God, gave me the strength I lacked to pull me out of the darkness.

But, more than anything, I think about the fact that I may have told a six-point story, but that's not what I lived. As I accept the twenty-year-chip in my hand, hold it tight in clenched fist, I hold on to my stomach. I think of Kaiya, and I wonder if I will ever shake free of that demon.

"Old-fashioned sweet," I say and put the glass in front of the man in the suit coat and button-up collared shirt. "Enjoy."

He nods and keeps plowing through his story of winning a lawsuit against some employee suing for wrongful termination to the two women and one man who look like they're trying to maintain interest.

I move to the next stool. "What can I pour for you?" It's a woman in a floral top and big, frizzy hair. The Long 9 Lounge is busier than normal for a Wednesday night—early attendees to a Thursday Healthcare Philanthropy conference. Not an open seat at the bar counter, and the couches and chairs beyond are all occupied with chattering professionals.

"Vodka Gimlet," she says, not looking at me. Her eyes are scanning the room. I notice the slight impression on her naked ring finger. Maybe she's one of those—the married person looking to get lucky, who sees a work conference as being an absolution from the sin of adultery. Or, simply a woman whose husband left her and she has finally shed the pain and heartbreak of his memory by taking the ring off.

I get to work, running the cocktail shaker through the ice chest, then adding the vodka, simple syrup, and lime juice. Slamming a pint glass over the silver mixing cup, I shake it like a fiend over my head, then crack it open and screen the highball into a martini glass. Garnish with a lime, and serve it up.

For a decade, I've been staring down my personal demon as a bartender at the Long 9. One of my AA sponsors actually quit on me because they were certain it was the worst possible thing I could do. For me, though? It was the best possible job. It constantly reminds about how stupid people can get when imbibing the demon juice. I can testify before God that I am less likely to fall off the wagon now than when I first took this job.

I can also, occasionally, identify someone who is in a seriously dark place. Unlike some bartenders who will serve and serve despite what our license regulates, I try my best to intervene and support. At first, I was a little nervous about losing my job, but despite the couple of times people threatened to complain to management because I refused to serve, I either recognized them as a lost cause and served them, or I used my AA experiences to connect with them and perhaps get a reading on their demon, help them take that first step to exorcising it.

It doesn't happen often. I can maybe count on one hand the number of times I might have made a real difference. But even one success makes being here worthwhile. And, more than anything, it keeps me on the wagon and heading down the right path.

Don't get me wrong. I miss being a librarian in the worst way. Who knows? Maybe I'll get back to it someday. But, those positions are thinning out quickly, so I'm not actually sure there was ever a future in it. Addiction? Depression? Now there's a growth industry.

"Hey, how'd your first day volunteering go?" Margie buzzes past me to pour some sweet vermouth into a Negroni mix. She's been a bartender here for six months. I like her a lot. She's young and pretty and gets all the attention and tips. I don't mind. Besides, she'll move on in another year. They all do. I've outlasted just about everyone. Walt was the only long-hauler I've ever worked with. He was here decades before I started, and lasted until two years ago when he finally retired at sixty-nine.

"Good. Great, actually. She's a really amazing woman. I'm looking forward to learning more about her."

"Great! But, she's, like, dying, right? That's the whole deal?"

I smile at Margie. "Oh, we're all dying, my dear. You're just too young to realize it yet."

CHAPTER FIVE

Mass for the Dead

S unday morning at church. I hopped around parishes for a time when I first returned to Springfield, trying to find the right one. I'm tough to please. I love the older, gothic churches with hard wooden pews, the churches that still make you kneel during the Consecration and glow with beautiful stained-glass windows depicting the saints and sacraments. Detailed, carved reliefs along the wall showing each Stage of the Cross. Yet, a more modern mass with contemporary music can be inviting and joyful. It's hard to find an old church with a young soul.

But St. James the Greater was my church since childhood, and the parish of my parents. Its tall spires loom over me, and the Roman arch around huge, ornate oak doors at the top of wide stone stairs gives me a thrill every Sunday as I approach. Inside, the nave showcases dramatic rows of Corinthian columns leading to the shiny ornate mosaic tilework of the apse radiating the glory of the resurrection behind the crucifixion of our Lord. I always enter penitent and awestruck.

The mass itself is a bit dry, but there's a younger priest, Father Tom, who I really enjoy. He has an angelic voice as he sings the Consecration, and his homilies are funny, heartwarming, and inspirational.

But oh my Lord in Heaven, that withered woman poking away at the ancient organ in the balcony is like listening to a sad animal bleating out its last breaths.

Sometimes, it's worth going the extra miles to attend the Ecumenical Center on the University Campus. They hold a later Catholic Mass—at 11:30am—and the building is very antiseptic, the interior a drab room of wooden chairs, burgundy carpeting, with a plain wooden cross at front and two podiums beside an unadorned marble alter. Seasonal banners are the only hints of color and life.

The musicians, however, kick some serious butt for the Lord. Five singers, a guitarist, pianist, bass player, and a djembe-player performing all of Michael Joncas's biggest hits. Their priests are like a revolving door, but they have a Deacon who's a regular, and he may not have the gravitas of some of the better priests I've seen, but has a sweet sincerity that, along with the music, warms the otherwise dull and cold church.

Sunday mass is the foundation upon which my week is built. Without it, I would be adrift among the tick and tock of transient time, of meaningless hours, lost in a lack of purpose and meaning. I do wonder sometimes, however, how much of that has become its own addiction of a kind.

I step into one of the back pews of St. James, drop the minimally cushioned kneeler and get on my knees to pray. Today, I'm distracted. Instead of a prayer, I offer up to my Maker what Ms. Deneaux had shared with me—her bitterness toward the God she had believed in so fervently. One she may not believe in anymore. I ask God questions I've been asking since before

I can remember, why he allows floods to destroy lives, why he allows wars to kill sons and daughters, why he lets good people be persecuted at the hands of bad.

I ask God why he would allow one of his servants to do what Father Edward did to me for two years.

What possible purpose could all this pain and suffering in the world serve?

Of course, no answer comes. And when I look up, see Christ on that cross in St. James Church, I suspect He himself asked similar questions of His Father. Jack certainly thought he had an answer to the mystery of life.

Stop that. Jack is distant past. A momentary blip in my life. There's no reason to think about him now.

Somehow, I still believe. My faith is strong. If I were to be completely honest, it is not because I hold my faith as an absolute truth. That conviction died with me many years ago. No, my conviction now is more the desperate clinging to the edge of a chasm, to avoid falling into the abyss I know would devour me.

Without my faith, my belief, I am lost. Therefore, I must believe, or I will perish.

I simply do not have the strength or the will to face the alternative.

Leaving Mass, I am spiritually rejuvenated, as always. I discount my negative thoughts and cling to the inspirations of the liturgy and the communal celebration of a congregation of faith that fills me with hope and direction and a way to survive until Sunday next, when the battery of my soul will be recharged once again.

It's a little bit before noon now, and I head over for my second visit with Ms. Deneaux. I've been looking forward to this almost as much as Sunday mass.

Once at River Bend Senior Living and strutting down the hall to her apartment, I turn the corner to see a man just leaving her room. He is tall—taller even than I—with a lean, but not lanky, frame. He's dressed sharply in blue chino pants, athletic black polo, shaved head and black goatee with a salting of gray. He has his mother's milk chocolate skin and narrow mouth, but unlike his mother, his brow and eyes express a heaviness and worry, despite high cheek bones that would accommodate a broad smile, and an angled chin that would accentuate the smile he doesn't wear.

The apartment door closes with enough force that the ceramic-tiled sign clatters against the wood. He expels a heavy breath, eyes to the floor.

I'm uncertain how to begin any exchange, so I simply say, "Hello?"

The man looks up. "What?"

That blunt reaction puts me immediately off-guard. "I'm sorry..."

"Sorry for what?"

"What?"

"Huh?"

I shake my head. This entire interaction has derailed. "I'm a volunteer with St. Joseph's Hospice. I'm here to see Ms. Deneaux."

His scowl remains for another moment, then washes away, replaced by the warmth of the smile his features had suggested all along. "Oh, I am so, so sorry. It's wonderful to meet you. I'm Raymond, her son." He puts his hand out.

I grab it and shake it vigorously. From his expression, I can see he wasn't expecting the intensity of response, which I admit is nervous and overreactive. I'm known for fist-crushing hand-shakes. It's just who I am.

"Mr. Deneaux! Oh, it's wonderful to meet you."

"Raymond, please."

I'm still pumping his fist. I know it, and I can't stop.

"Your mother is…"

"..a handful…"

"…amazing. What a tremendous woman."

Raymond has dropped his gaze to his hand being pulverized by my grasp. I let go and he discreetly runs it down the thigh of his pant leg.

"Well, thank you for being here for her. I honestly wasn't sure she'd even allow anyone from your organization to help her."

I smile and give him a wink. "I can be pretty irresistible when I try."

He smiles politely, nods, and we look at each other in awkward silence until his expression stretches with a sudden realization. "I actually didn't catch your name?"

"Pauline." I put out my hand again. Stupid, since we already shook. "Pauline Swanson."

He looks at my hand, holds up his and smiles. "I kind of need this hand to function, so maybe I'll pass on the…"

His head nods to my outstretched gesture and I cough out a loud laugh and withdraw my hand. "Sorry. I don't know my own strength."

It's his turn to wink. "Oh, I suspect you might." He glances at his Apple watch on his wrist, which lights up five after noon. "I have to fly. Sorry…um…"

"Pauline."

"Right. Pauline. Great to meet you. Don't let her majesty take advantage of you."

"I'll gladly take anything I can get from her," I say and hold his gaze just long enough for his to fall.

"Have a nice day," he says as he walks past me. My eyes follow his departure around the corner of the corridor.

"Huh," I say to no one at all, and I knock on Ms. Deborah's door.

"Sit yourself down, now," Ms. Deborah tells me, patting the cushion of the black suede couch next to her. "It's good to see you."

I take a seat next to her. She is in a loose, flowing white cotton V-neck two-piece with a big, looping necklace of obsidian and coral. Her legs are crossed, and her sandaled feet tap to the beat of the quiet jazz playing in the background. In the air, I smell a caramelly sweetness, and I see a tray of baked goods on the coffee table.

Ms. Deborah holds out the tray to me. "Would you like one, dear? Freshly baked pralines, just for you."

The small brown confections are tiny puddles of buttery sweetness, each surrounding a pecan. I take one and try it. They are soft and creamy. Even the pecans seem to melt in my mouth, leaving behind the rich caramel sweetness of dark brown sugar.

"I've just discovered the eighth deadly sin," I say, and Ms. Deborah laughs lightly.

"Please, help yourself." She sets the plate down. "Would you like something to drink?"

"Thank you, I'm fine."

She nods, reaches for the loop of oxygen tube and slips it under her nose.

"Is there anything I can get or do for you? Anything from the store? Laundry to be done? Cleaning?"

"Goodness, girl. You're not my maid. Stop that, now. Tell me about your day. What did you do?"

I can't help the grin that spreads across my face. "Well, I just met your son."

Ms. Deborah rolls her eyes. "Oh, dear Lord. I suppose you did. What did Raymond have to say to you? Nothing good about me, I'm sure."

I wave her comment away and reach for another praline. Those are going to be a problem for me, I know it. "No, no. He was very nice. For the minute of time we spent with each other."

Ms. Deborah inhales deeply through her nose, eyes closed with a small shake of head. "That boy. He insists on being nothing but a burden to me."

"How could such a fine and proper-looking son be a burden visiting his mother?"

Her pursed lips send a ripple of wrinkles across her cheeks, and she draws another deep breath. "That, dawlin', is a story long in the telling, and I've no desire or energy for it today. What about you? You seem to me like you were the sweetheart of your parents. Tell me a little more about yourself. I prattled on all day last time."

I feel myself stiffen and draw back. I try to relax and not show any discomfort, but pleasant moments of my childhood are few and far between, and I don't feel like dampening the mood so early. I quickly try to recall a pleasant memory.

"Well, let's see. My father was a banker, and my mother was a retired nurse and homemaker."

"Brothers or sisters?"

"No, it was only me. Well, me and my Alaskan Husky, Oscar."

"Oh, beautiful animal!"

I nod. "Yes, and imaginary. My father didn't like animals. 'Beasts of the earth don't belong in the home,' he'd say. He found it uncouth. When I was still quite young, I'd occasionally find a dead animal on the road in front of our house and bring it to our back yard to bury it. I had a little cemetery right on the border of our land against a small crop of trees. My father had a conniption when he discovered it. Thought it sacrilegious. Told me to stop playing with filthy dead things. But I remember one day, my mother discovered me digging a hole in the back yard, this poor flattened squirrel beside me that I was about to bury.

Mother came over to me, put a hand on my shoulder and said, 'Pauline, what in the world are you doing?'

"'Sending the squirrel home to God,' I said.

"'That's awfully thoughtful of you,' mother said.

"When I laid the dead squirrel to rest and covered it with dirt, Mother asked, 'Do you have words?'

"I remember trying, but the words didn't come. I had started to cry, thinking I was doing it all wrong.

"Mother patted my back and told me to calm down. 'How about you let me say the words you are feeling?'"

"I nodded, and she said this wonderful prayer that I don't remember exactly, but was something like, 'Lord, receive the compassion of this child, who mourns for the loss of this creature which You created, and who loves Thee which resides within every living thing.'"

"And then, she looked down at me, kissed my forehead, and said, 'Your father need not know. Our little secret.'"

Ms. Deborah lays her hand over mine and looks at me warmly. "What a wonderful story. Your mother sounds delightful. Is she still with us?"

I shake my head.

"I'm sorry."

I nod, run a finger across my eye. "I am, too."

CHAPTER SIX

Where the lines Are Drawn

"How are you feeling? You look tired."

"I'm fine, dawlin', just winded from the baking. Some days, my breath outruns me and I have to catch it. Just need the oxygen more often now. Have another praline."

"I've had enough, thank you very much."

"I'll take that as a compliment."

"That picture on the shelf. That's you at the Golden Gate bridge, right?"

"M-hmm."

"You lived there for quite a while?"

"A decade, thereabouts. Got my MBA at San Francisco State."

"Whatever could have made you leave New Orleans?"

Nineteen sixty-eight was a hard year.

George killed in action in Vietnam. Two assassinations of social and political leaders a mere two months apart. Rioting in Washington D.C., Chicago, Baltimore, Cincinnati, and all across the land. A country slowly coming apart at the seams.

She watched the Tremé neighborhood get gutted. Over five hundred homes gone, and where beautiful oak trees once stood all along Claiborne Avenue, now huge concrete columns held up a six-lane behemoth. The beauty, vibrancy, and life of her home had been essentially destroyed, the Seventh Ward split in two. Their family business, now in the ruins of a wasted downtown, was soon to follow.

DeeDee was left emotionally uprooted.

After her performance on the *John Pela Show*, she pulled out of Tony's dance school. She didn't have the heart for it anymore, and more importantly, with the expected demise of Deneaux Haberdashery, her family could no longer afford such luxuries.

In 1969, a very different DeeDee Deneaux emerged from the rubble of her tragedies, an eighteen-year-old woman, carefree and ne'er-do-well, with some rebellion in her blood and adventure in her heart. She spent less time around the funerary somberness of their home. Father a beaten man, Mother still mourning her oldest son who was taken from her. DeeDee's parents trudged doggedly within the mire of life while DeeDee and Alfred stormed through it.

DeeDee didn't see much of her brother during that time. Alfred had joined in with a group of young Black men who had liberty and freedom on their minds and anger in their hearts. Often, he didn't come home until one or two in the morning. Sometimes, he didn't come home at all. She worried for him, for all of them, but she was also quietly impelled by what she imagined he schemed and did every night.

DeeDee, meanwhile, embraced the nightlife. She and her friends, most who, like her, had just graduated from St. Mary's that summer, celebrated their freedom from academia by hitting the area bars and clubs. For DeeDee, it was a summer of firsts.

She had her first drink at the Rockery Inn on the corner of Canal and Robert E. Lee. She had never been there before. The sign outside the stone building said "Famous for Fried Chicken" and "Cocktails," but the "and" was inferred. When DeeDee went up to the counter, she said, "Give me one of your famous fried chicken cocktails!" She and all the girls hollered laughter while the bartender rolled his eyes.

She had her first kiss at Lenfants, the car hop on Canal. It was with suave and smooth-talking Anthony Johnson, the older brother of her friend Hazel. He came out with them sometimes along with a couple of his friends. One night, Anthony drove her, Hazel, and Sally to Lenfants where they met up with Joe and Leroy, two of his buddies. Anthony stuck to DeeDee like glue that night.

Anthony Johnson was a slick dresser in black slacks, white short-sleeved button-up, yellow suspenders, and yellow fedora. He had this hairline mustache that looked so debonaire and yet so adorable to DeeDee. He told her how good she looked in her white summer dress and how she had turned into a fine young woman. He bought her a burger and shake, and they fed each other french fries at a booth inside. Hand diving into his pin-striped slacks, he pulled out a fistful of dimes and dropped them into the jukebox to play Marvin Gaye and Aretha Franklin.

While Hazel and Joe stayed inside, Sally and Leroy went for a stroll outside. DeeDee joined Anthony in the back of his 1956 Buick Skylark.

"I'm gonna squeeze one out of you, DeeDee Deneaux," he said, leaning in for the kiss he threatened with toothy grin.

"Excuse me, mister?" DeeDee chuckled, clicked a loud "Tsk" and shook her head. "I'm not that kind of lady."

"Well, little miss DeeDee, would you allow Anthony Jackson the honor of making you into one of those ladies?" His widening grin was contagious.

DeeDee flushed hot. "I might entertain that notion," she said, turning to him, "with the proper invitation of—"

The kiss was abrupt, sloppy and fleeting, but she felt it down to her toes.

Their brief time in the back seat ended when the others returned and catcalled their groping intimacies. She would see Anthony Johnson a few more times that summer, but Hurricane Camille ended whatever opportunities and fun the summer of '69 had to offer.

That summer also introduced DeeDee to night clubs, live music, and moving her body to jazz and blues beats. Not the choreographed dancing she spent so many years training at— just smooth, easy, free gyrations that made her feel sexy and made mens' eyes turn her way.

Of all the clubs, The Dew Drop Inn was the place to be. "The South's Swankiest Night Spot," The Dew Drop Inn was on La Salle Street in the Garden District just south of the Seventh Ward. Frank Painia, a Black businessman, ran the place since 1945. He was a legend not just in those parts, but to so many Black musicians for giving them room and board during hard times while they performed at the Dew Drop. He also saw himself hauled off to jail more than once for occasionally letting a few jazz- and blues-loving White folk mix in with his colored crowd.

Every night at the Dew Drop was wild and exhilarating. Depending on the night, the evening's emcee might be Mr. Google Eyes, a well-known local blues singer, or the flamboyant female impersonator going by the name Patsy Vidalia. DeeDee and friends watched vaudeville shows and comedy acts, heard dramatic readings, and best of all, got to watch performers like

Little Richard and Ray Charles, Duke Ellington and Count Bassie, make the room go wild with their music. Little Richard himself (he was just Richard Penniman back then) even wrote a song about The Dew Drop Inn.

Other times, when DeeDee and friends were feeling more daring and adventurous, they'd wander into the French Quarter and Bourbon Street. Jim Crow had just keeled over and died a few years back, but his memory and the fondness for him by southern Whites remained, especially in the French Quarter. That neighborhood still had few clubs that welcomed Blacks, even though the White clubs had been enjoying Black musicians for decades. Whenever DeeDee walked through the more accessible areas of the French Quarter, she always thought about that concrete behemoth crushing the soul of her Tremé neighborhood and how it originally had its eyes on that *vieux carré*.

The very last time DeeDee ever visited the French Quarter was early August of '69, just before the hurricane sidled past New Orleans and left it windswept and under water. What happened that night would be a catalyst to changing the direction of her life forever.

It had been the usual crowd of girlfriends, club hopping through the Garden District. By eleven o'clock, most of the girls had headed home, leaving only DeeDee and Hazel.

"Let's hit Bourbon Steet," DeeDee suggested.

Hazel didn't look enthusiastic. "No, DeeDee. Not just the two of us. Let's head back to the Dew Drop."

"Come on. That blues band we like is playing at The Diamond Club tonight."

"Which band?"

"The one with that oh-so-fine bass player. You know the one!"

Hazel smiled. "Oh, *that* one!" He had winked at Hazel and given her looks when they had seen them play at the Dew Drop a few weeks ago.

The two of them headed north and into the French Quarter. Strolling down Bourbon Street, DeeDee spotted the dark blue door of The Diamond Club and they slipped inside.

Beyond the small, dark lobby, both of them were stopped in their tracks. They stood before a large room, stage in front, with a big black curtain splitting the room in two. Each side of the room was clearly distinguished by its patronage—a large audience of White folk sitting at tables on the right, and a standing-room only area sparsely filled with Colored folk on the left. A large, older White man sat on a barstool in front of the curtain, sweat running off his bald head.

"Let's get out of here, Dee," Hazel whispered in DeeDee's ear and yanked on her arm.

The old, sweaty guy looked up, tossed a thumb to the left and said, "You're over there."

DeeDee stood for a moment and looked at the two sides of the room. The side with the White audience was packed and sitting at their tables, talking, drinking and laughing as they mostly ignored the Black band members playing. On the "Colored" side, the Black patrons were sparse and reserved as they stood and listened, moving in a cautious groove to the beat. George suddenly came to mind, her big brother who spent almost two years halfway round the world fighting a war he had no stake in, and no right to be in. Is this what he died for?

Something boiled inside of her. She got warm and her head felt light, like it was pulling away from her shoulders, a tethered balloon.

"No. Let's go in."

Hazel gave a determined, insistent shake of the head. "No, Dee. I don't want to."

DeeDee grabbed Hazel by the elbow. "Come on, now. It's a free country, ain't it?"

"No, ma'am. It sure ain't!" Hazel said while yanked by DeeDee into the designated area to mingle with the other Black patrons on the left side of the room.

They went to the corner where a small wet bar and an older Black bartender in white shirt and black bow tie was selling drinks. DeeDee ordered a bourbon neat and slapped two bits down on the counter. She'd never had it before, but Anthony ordered it that way when they went out. It sounded like a drinker's drink. The bartender grinned at her and tilted the bottle twice into a tumbler and handed it over. DeeDee raised the glass to him, tilted it back and took it all at once. The burn hit her throat and wrung it tight like a rag. She almost coughed it out, but shut her eyes and held tight. She ordered another and knocked that back as well.

"What are you doing, girl?" Hazel's eyes were wide. "Are you insane?"

DeeDee smiled. "I'm having a night out on *my* town. Listening to *my* band." She slipped past Hazel. "Excuse me, dawlin'. I need room to groove."

The band was playing some driving twelve-bar blues. DeeDee joined two other women and moved to the beat with them. Hazel kept in the corner near the bar and sipped a spritzer, distractedly swinging her hips while her nervous eyes darted around the room.

By the second song, DeeDee's body became looser, unrestricted. Her hands ran down her hips to her thighs, glided back up and crossed her body to hug her rolling shoulders. Her bottom shimmied and her head swayed to the rhythm of the music and the changing mood of the night. She felt light and suspended in the moment.

It didn't take long for several gentlemen to move closer to her and swing in time, pumping their fists and moving their hips, eyes ogling her up and down over hungry smiles. They offered her drinks, which she poured down her throat, rivulets of golden booze running down the corners of her mouth, round her cheeks, onto her neck and down the valley of her burgeoning cleavage.

The band picked up on the growing energy on that side of the room, and they got louder and livelier. The guitar player and singer took special notice of DeeDee, recognizing her as the battery charging the crowd, and he called out to her in his deep-throated lilt. "That's right, now. Oh, yeah. There you go," DeeDee's groove and grind intensified, and she twirled about the room, whipping her short skirt bottom about.

This was no Bevinetto White girl Hollywood dance. This wasn't being a spectacle on some Saturday teen dance hour show. This was a DeeDee who had watched the bold, mature, confident Black women at the Dew Drop express themselves— their bodies, their spirit, their femininity. How they took owner- ship of themselves with sultry moves that caressed and flowed like water over their men.

For the first time, DeeDee danced as herself.

She moved closer to the curtain as she gyrated, her eyes drilling into it. A raunchy guitar solo took over the lyrics and she hooted and cheered, raising her arms and swinging round and round. At the curtain, she gave it a bump with her behind. The curtain fluttered and rippled. She bumped it again. A couple of men around her laughed and clapped. A quick glance at Hazel to see a dropped jaw and wide eyes.

DeeDee thrust her hip against the curtain, again and again, each time ruffling the curtain a little more. She twirled a toe underneath a loop of linen, turned and gave the clapping men a lustful leer. Their eyes and mouths shot open, shook their heads as their smiles widened—a mix of dare and warning, of excite- ment and disbelief.

Toe hooked under the curtain, she kicked her foot up and caught the curtain bottom in the air. She hoisted the fabric around her waist, treated the curtain like a dress bottom and raised her knees in a can-can as she shouted out and laughed.

From the other end of the curtain, a loud shout: "Keep to your side, nigger!" A brutal shove by several sets of hands, one which caught her lip and split it open. She fell back and to the ground, hitting her head hard enough that she saw dots of light like fireflies twinkle before her vision.

Vice grip hands around both of her upper arms forcefully yanked her off the floor as two large White men violently escorted her toward the exit.

From behind her, several men shouting. "Hey, man. Let her go!"

"Put her down!"

"Son of a bitch!"

The curtain fell in a cascade of fabric as several White men from the other side charged through, red-faced with fists raised. "What in the Sam Hell's going on, boy?"

"Uppity Goddamn darkies!"

"Back off!"

"We weren't doing anything!"

"Get your Black asses outta here!"

But all that faded away, beyond her now, as she was dumped to the curb and kicked in her side before the front door to the club slapped shut. DeeDee laid on her back, staring up at the stars as blood ran from her lip and down her cheek, her head pounding and her side throbbing.

In little time, the door opened again. For a moment, DeeDee heard a loud kerfuffle of shouts and scuffling before the door swung closed and Hazel scrambled to her.

"What did you *do*? *Why*?" She grabbed DeeDee's arm and tried to pull her upright. "We've got to get out of here *now*."

DeeDee's head still swam. She was upright, but not ready to stand.

"Get *up*!" Hazel almost screamed and yanked harder.

DeeDee managed to get to her feet, wobbling in place.

"If you don't get moving right now, I'm leaving you!"

DeeDee looked at the door of the club, then the street, then to the sidewalk. "Go on, then. Leave."

Hazel stood there. "What?"

DeeDee snapped to attention, head suddenly clear, and glared at Hazel. "GO!"

Hazel stood there for a moment more, looked as if she was going to say something, then shook her head and ran off.

DeeDee wiped at the blood on her face. She brushed the dirt soiling her dress, straightened it out the best she could, and started walking. Queerly, she felt as if she had just woken up from a dream. What just happened? She had no clear idea, only raw emotion.

All she did know was that this wasn't home anymore. Not for her. She didn't belong, wasn't welcome, and she wasn't going to live her entire life feeling this way.

CHAPTER SEVEN

Rummaging Through the Past

I head over to my parent's place early the next morning, tired from a long night racing around to serve up every kind of traditional and trendy highball to nonprofit healthcare fund-raisers. My back is sore and my legs ache, but I need to get done what I should have finished weeks ago.

My parents had been in good shape financially. The best gift they could have left me was no debt, no mortgage, and all their financials in order. As an only daughter, the burden of settling their estate fell completely on me, though I received generous help and guidance from my father's financial advisor. He, in turn, had received substantial instruction from my father before his health had really taken a downturn.

The house was left to me, as well as a tidy little sum of $25,000 that I rolled into my meager 401K. Most of their money was gifted to the church. In fact, in the next month or two, the three holy water fonts just before the nave of St. James the Greater will each bear a large bronze plaque on their pedestals with etched words that say, "*In Memory of Bert and Emma Swanson.*" It will be a strange day the first time I dip three fingers into one of their memorialized fonts—to see their names when I make the sign the cross, a reminder of my own baptism when they had presented me before the priest to be anointed and have my original sin absolved 53 years ago.

Both Mother and Father died in this house. Even if I could afford the property taxes (which I can't), I would never live in this house. It's not merely that there is no sense of welcome or belonging in this place. Even when I'm here by myself for half a day sorting through everything that needs to be thrown out, packed up or auctioned off, I feel haunted by whatever Earthly residue of their spirit or soul hangs upon the air of this empty home.

Meanwhile, I continue to put off thinking about what could be a significant life-changing event for me. Selling this two-story, four-bedroom and three-bath home with finished basement in a fairly wealthy suburb will bring in a significant amount of money. Rolling it into my 401K would ensure a comfortable retirement in twelve years. Or, I could spend the next decade of my life doing pretty much whatever I want, going wherever I want, and having the true walkabout I've always dreamed of but never had the means, let alone the courage, to do.

But the home isn't even on the market yet, which is why I need to get down to business and finish clearing everything out.

The auction house was hired by the Parish since my parents left all items not claimed by me to be left to the church. They want everything in two weeks so they can fully appraise the items being auctioned and promote the sale, which is one month from now. All the furniture, the appliances, and Father's tools are going. Everything in the garage is going. I'm even letting them have the car. I'm barely comfortable driving my little VW which feels huge to me. I refuse to put myself behind the wheel of an SUV. St. James Parish will probably gain an additional fifty to one hundred thousand dollars out of the auction. That's fine. I don't want to be bothered trying to sell it. Maybe they can invest in a good PA system, find some decent musicians and retire that morbid organ.

I don't plan to keep much. I have already taken some pieces of art that hung on the wall—nothing that is worth a lot other than in sentiment. I always loved the contemporary and stylized Madonna and Child painting that hung in their bedroom. It's just a limited-edition print by an unknown artist and probably not worth much, especially as a reproduction, but the oak frame is beautiful and the swirling blues of Mary's dress and the glittery gold of her and baby Jesus's halos convey such a peaceful and spiritual maternal love.

I kept several pieces of Father's art. A man of numbers and calculations, his only creative outlet was a brief period in his life that he did some woodworking. His first piece was a beautiful wooden crucifix that hung in the living room. Several contrasting woods laid out in geometric patterns form the upright and the crossbeam. With a jigsaw, he cut out the silhouette of Christ, emptiness of arms outstretched, a reflection of both death and resurrection. Finally, he soaked buckthorn twigs in water until supple and wrapped them into a crown of thorns to hang around the top of the cross.

His most complicated and popular work was a reproduction of a piece he saw when out of town and visiting a Christian gift shop. It was an abstract three-dimensional representation of the last supper done in cherry, walnut and pine. He scribbled out a quick but detailed sketch of it on a receipt he had in his pocket. For the better part of a month he poked away at it, cutting, sanding, staining, and gluing it together. Once finished, it found a special place on our dining room wall. He received more comments and compliments about it than anything else he had ever made. He created several more for family members and friends who had shown a particular admiration for it. These became cherished items in their homes.

Shortly after Father died, I had been in his basement workroom wondering how I would even begin to sort through all the wood, tools, and equipment. Inside a large workbench drawer, I found the rough beginnings of another last supper reproduction next to an updated sketch of the planned final piece on graph paper. On the paper, he had written, "For Pauline."

I never knew that he had intended to make one of his last suppers special for me. Likely, he abandoned the project when we stopped speaking. In fact, I'm not sure he ever built anything after that.

Sorting out all these remnants of my two lives here—the life before I left for college, the life when I returned ten years ago—I need to remind myself that, just because I don't have a lot of good memories here, doesn't mean I had bad memories here, either. The fact is, my father was not a mean man, simply stern and serious. Certainly not one who could relate to a sensitive and emotional little girl—and even less equipped to deal with an emotional, sensitive and awkward teenaged girl.

As I fill a garbage bag with the minutia and detritus of my parents' everyday life, moving from kitchen to living room to bedroom, I'm still reflecting on my last visit with Ms. Deborah and her astounding story. A spark glows inside of me that smolders against my insides and threatens to turn to a flame of inspiration.

I had choked out a laugh after she finished her story about being thrown out of the night club. No humor in it, only shock and respect. I told her she had the heart of a warrior.

She smiled and looked away, either embarrassed or modest. Her chest heaved a bit. "Unfortunately, back then—" She inhaled deep through her nose, "I was as impetuous and thickheaded as one, too."

"But do you really expect me to believe," I said and leaned

in close to her, "you didn't have your first kiss until eighteen years old?"

She put a hand to her heart. "It's true! I came from a strict, Christian family, just like you. Went to an all-girl private Catholic school. Tell me, where was I going to find any smooching?" She chuckled, which turned into a juicy cough.

"Where you'd least expect it, I've found," I said and smiled.

"Oh, but I would like to get out of this apartment, to hear live music again. To dance."

I gasped. "Oh, Ms. Deborah. You might just die if you tried!"

"But at least I'd be living before I die." Her fist went to her mouth as she broke down into a bout of wet, bronchial coughing. She recovered, but her breath was thin.

I drew back, suddenly concerned. Until now, I had focused on Ms. Deborah's strong and healthy spirit and mind. I hadn't been paying attention to her body.

The fact is, I was already forgetting my place as a hospice volunteer and just becoming a fan of this woman. It's been easy to forget that she is dying from an advanced stage of sarcoidosis. I fear that is partly due to her refusal to respect that fact, and partly due to my fervent wish that it wasn't true.

I rested a hand on her knee. "Ms. Deborah, I fear I've become too enrapt in your story and not enough in your well-being. While you share your wonderful story, you're neglecting your oxygen."

I suggested to her that, from now on, whenever she talks for a length of time, I'll put my hand up as a signal reminding her to breathe in through her nose a few times. She thought me silly, but agreed.

Her recollections of Anthony Johnson and her first kiss brings to mind the first time I ever kissed a boy.

At fourteen, I already felt a certain amount of experience—

albeit experience I couldn't share with anyone. But it gave tall, big-boned and awkward Pauline a leg up on all the other girls in the CYO. Father Edward had already shown me how I could turn a boy into putty in my hands, and I used that to my advantage.

Jeremy Kindless wasn't the most popular boy in the Christian Youth Organization, but he was cute in a quiet, bookish kind of way, and he was generally liked by all the other kids in the organization. When we were partnered up for an upcoming Bible study event, I found myself attracted to him. He was very nice and sweet to me, which I wasn't used to, and perhaps a big reason why I became so enamored with him. One afternoon when we were finding passages to help teenagers avoid lust and sexuality, we were working through 2 Corinthians 10:4-6 when I reached over and put a hand on Jeremy's inner thigh. He jumped noticeably, and I was terrified he would chastise me, call me names and make me feel horrible. But instead, he flushed a glowing, vibrant red and looked at me with a shocked, yet willing expression. My hand moved further until it rested upon a fast-growing bulge. I squeezed and released, moved my hand back and forth over that hard lump. He squirmed in his seat, and it didn't take long until his face twisted, his eyes clamped shut and he moaned. The crotch of his pants darkened, he slowly opened his eyes and turned to me. I kept my eyes locked onto his. And then, he moved in, and he kissed me. It was the first time since Father Edward that I felt attractive and desirable. That I had any worth.

Jeremy and I fooled around several times after that, but in the end, nothing emotional ever came from those occurrences, just a carnal sexuality. One I controlled and manipulated.

Thinking now about Ms. Deborah's story at the segregated club, I realize that, whereas at eighteen she was tearing down the curtains that were barriers to her potential, during my teenage years, I was putting up my own emotional curtains. By college, they were smothering me.

CHAPTER EIGHT

Picking at Old Wounds

On the northeast corner of Springfield, Laverna Road stretches through cornfields and flatlands of manicured lawns and towering oaks on the way to the Motherhouse—well, what used to be the Motherhouse until it was turned over to the Diocese of Springfield. Now, less than two dozen Hospital Sisters of St. Francis remain at what had been their convent and church in the States since 1917.

Their order was established in 1844 by Father Christopher Bernsmeyer in Westphallia, Germany. He had witnessed a group of women in Our Lady of Grace Chapel tending to the sick and poor with utter dedication and devotion. They inspired him to begin the Congregation of the Hospital Sisters of St. Francis.

Their order grew, and by 1875, Bishop Peter Joseph Baltes of Alton, Illinois wrote to the Hospital Sisters in need of the nuns' ministrations to their ailing population. In response, twenty Sisters took a perilous six-month journey across the ocean, with few belongings among them, and arrived in the United States to establish their Motherhouse in Springfield, Illinois. Thus began their ministry, which at its peak was home to over 700 nuns and resulted in 15 Catholic nonprofit hospitals across Illinois and Wisconsin.

As I drive through the 300-acre compound of sprawling trees that shade the grassy flatland, I see the impressive Chiara Center, comprised of St. Francis of Assisi Church and the surrounding complex, ahead and to the left. The church presents a modest brick façade emboldened by arched Romanesque doorway and windows, two tall bell towers, and its glorious stained-glass rose window. Until a few years ago, the rest of the buildings had served as living quarters for the Sisters, and areas for meeting, dining, meditation, and administration.

To my immediate right is the Mission Outreach Center—where I'm headed at the moment—but first, I deviate and turn onto Franciscan Road that runs straight behind Chiara and through low-lying farmland on one side that many years ago was still used by the Sisters, and a gently undulating rise of trees and grass on the other side where the old convent still resides, now more of a rest home. Continuing straight, I come to acres of plain white granite markers spread out across cemetery grounds, well over one thousand Hospital Sisters who have been laid to eternal rest over the last century and looking like the fallen of a world war. It overwhelms me every time I see it. I knew a few of those nuns. They took me in long ago when I was lost and alone.

My current connection to the Motherhouse and the Hospital Sisters is only via the St. John's Hospice Program through what had been their hospital here in Springfield. My past connection to the Hospital Sisters, however, runs much deeper.

I stop the car, step out into the pure, cleansing early morning sun. Into this field where these servants of Christ lie—sown like the seeds of faith—I kneel before them, unworthy. I ask for their blessing, thank them for their devotion, and praise God for guiding their path and receiving them into His house.

In front of the Mission Outreach Center, I grab the large box from the back of my VW and head to the entrance, fumbling a bit with the door as I balance the box on my knee.

Inside is a huge, nondescript warehouse with many white eight-foot folding tables set up in stations where volunteers sort through supplies donated by medical centers. Against the walls are storage areas for gauze, medical utensils, salves, medical tape, masks, gloves, and every other kind of supply that is abundantly available at any hospital in the United States, but precious and scarce to third-world and war-torn countries.

I spent a lot of time in this room sorting through the perfectly good medical equipment and supplies deemed unsuitable for our health care, but desperately wanted and needed in other parts of the world.

In the empty room, I call out, "Anyone here?"

From a side office, Tamara steps out and sees me. "Pauline! Is that you? Good God, girl! It's been ages! It's so good to see you!"

Tamara is casually dressed in skirt, simple cotton pullover, and plain white comfortable shoes. A full six inches shorter than me, twice as wide, and three times as cheerful, she reaches her arms out to me. I put the box down just in time to receive her big, tight hug I have missed so much. "Hello, Tamara. It's wonderful to see you again."

She looks up at me with her big, bulging eyes. "What brings you here, sweety?"

"Oh, just stopping by to drop some items off. My father passed about two months ago—"

"I'm so sorry, honey."

"Thank you. I've been cleaning out my parent's house, and I gathered up all the remaining medical supplies that still seemed usable."

I hand over the box.

"You are so thoughtful. Yes, of course, I'm sure we can add this to our inventory." She sorts through the gauze, oxygen hose and mask, latex gloves, and other items in the box. "This is wonderful."

"Glad if any of it can go to good use." I look around the place, see it as it is when twenty or thirty volunteers are working through a truckload of supplies donated by hospitals all over the Midwest. My box seems so meager and ineffective.

"Slow morning," Tamara says, seeing me look around the empty space. "We'll have a full crew here in a few hours. Big shipment coming in. Did you know we hit the one hundred mark a few years ago? Over one hundred countries supplied by Mission Outreach."

"That's incredible," I say.

Tamara looks me up and down. "Damnation, but it's been so long. We've missed you! What's happening in your life?"

I attempt a grin, but unsure if I succeed. "I wish I had stories to tell, but up until recently, I was just working and caring for my father full time. It's the main reason I stopped volunteering."

"Goodness, but that's totally understandable."

"Oh, but I did just start volunteering at St. John's Hospice."

Tamara's face lights up. "You did? Oh, that's wonderful. Good for you!"

I nod. "Figured I did it enough for my father these last years, I could put that experience to good use."

"Preach it, girl. That's great."

"How about you, Tamara? How're those three boys of yours?"

She laughs while shaking her head. "Sammy just hit college—going to Madison. Mikey's a junior in high school and causing nothing but trouble. Jared's still my innocent little sweetheart because he don't know any better yet!"

I laugh with her. Tamara started as a volunteer here about fifteen years ago and, after seven years, when a supervisory position opened up, she took it. Three years after that, she was promoted to director when her predecessor retired.

"I wish I could stay longer and catch up, Tamara, but I have to get to work in a bit, and I still want to stop over and see if I might be able to say hi to Sister Gene."

Tamara puts hands to hips and huffs. "Oh, that little bitty is still around! She sure was one to ruffle a lot of feathers! God love her, she was a handful!"

Yes she was. But then again, so was I.

Twenty years ago, after six years of sobriety, I fell back off the wagon. My head and my heart all messed up over Jack, a guy who had only existed in my world for less than a month and who I had only spent a few days with. It's not every day, however, you meet a guy who believes he has the power to literally think the world away.

I'm not sure exactly why learning about him via that silly website of his captured my attention, but as we began to correspond via email, every message from him intrigued me, and early on in our communications, I found it so easy to take control, to manipulate. His continued responses and attention fed the flames of my curiosity and interest.

When we finally met, he was so lost, and I naturally fell into the role of dominant seductress. I thought I could control him, to overpower him like I had so many before. His vulnerabilities, however, put me off course. His honesty put me on-guard.

When I discovered just how troubled he was, the crazy ideas of his which he believed so completely, I became uneasy, and my control continued to slip. My life was complicated enough.

I didn't need or want all his honesty of emotion, sincerity of words, let alone his delusions. I was a recovering alcoholic with more than enough regrets, emotional scars, and psychological hang-ups of my own.

So, I tried to scare him away. I let him see the me that, at that time, was as raw and real as it got. I exposed myself to him, certain he would flee. Instead, he simply showed tenderness and concern.

I didn't know how to deal with someone like him. Someone who might possibly accept me for who I was, want to be with me, perhaps even have an attraction to me. Me, as myself, outside of fulfilling any carnal need.

To regain control, things needed to make sense again, to be simple and predictable, so I activated my own power. I seduced him, forced myself upon him, expecting him to succumb like every other man. But Jack's reaction was different—demur and passive at first, then responding with sensitivity. As I groped and straddled him, forced myself upon him, he parried with gentleness. For the first time, I felt overly aggressive, abusive, and foolish.

Confused and overwhelmed, I broke away from him. That ended our evening.

The next day, we had a wonderful time together despite a few rocky moments. I had never enjoyed the company of a man in this way before—to simply be, and have that be enough. To enjoy spending time with someone and have them seem to enjoy spending it with me. The experience completely disarmed me, and I found myself at the edge of a dangerous and terrifying precipice, with the risk of slipping over the edge and falling in love.

I will never forget that evening. No powerplays, no mind games or sexual manipulation. That night was the purest intimacy I had—and have—ever experienced.

And it would devastate me.

The next day, he left me. In the end, he was still nothing but damaged goods, just like me. He had his own demons he was running from, or running to.

Unfortunately, his harsh and abrupt departure led my own personal demons back to me with a vengeance.

I fell off the wagon. Hard. Frankly, I was ready to fall off the edge of the Earth. Jack, meanwhile, returned a few days later, finding me at Kaiya's grave. In that moment, I told him about her, shared with him that deepest secret, the wound that still won't heal. He said he came to apologize, that was all, and then he left.

For him to so suddenly return, and so immediately leave me forever, only deepened that festering wound. When I found out he had tried to kill himself, it was as if he had chosen nothing over me. Of course, who am I to judge him in the end? He had a mental condition—some kind of epilepsy, apparently, that made him think and do all those things.

That is no excuse, however, for what he did to me the next time we met five years later.

Looking back upon those fleeting events now, I realize how little Jack actually had to do with my emotional collapse. The structure of my life had already been condemned by the time he stepped into it—he simply became my wrecking ball and brought it all crumbling down upon its foundation.

I think about all of this now, of course, because those are the events that led me to the Hospital Sisters and their Motherhouse.

As religious as I am, I don't tend to think about God as this warm father-figure who is looking over me personally and interested in every aspect of my life. First and foremost, as a Catholic, I do believe strongly in the concept of good works and personal accountability. God helps those who help themselves.

I am too insignificant for God to take personal interest in me. Yes, he may care for the lowliest sparrow. That doesn't mean He protects that sparrow from every misfortune. Sparrows get eaten. They crash into windows and break their necks. They are prey to cats, and they are shot by some nasty little boy with a BB gun. If someone believes God is looking out for them, that any prayer or entreaty to Him is going to have some impact on their life—good for them. They are a far more important person than I. When I see the vast amount of suffering in this world, it is obvious to me that God is not going to care if I get that job I want, or help get a medical bill paid. He's not going to get me out of a jam, or cure any sickness that I or a loved one is facing, no matter how much I pray.

That being said, I indulge my faith in the idea that God had a hand in nudging my mother, who I had not spoken with for almost ten years, to reach out to me a few days after Jack abandoned me.

Because Mother quite possibly saved my life. And she did it by offering me her forgiveness and telling me to go to the Sisters.

How is that not God intervening upon a fallen sparrow?

If I had not heard those specific words from my mother, "Of course I forgive you. I love you," I would have likely never spoke to her again. Not because I didn't love and miss and long for her, but because I felt so ashamed of my life.

We talked for hours, and I shared so much of my heartache and loss, my addictions and my self-loathing. Even so, I still kept so many of my sins from her.

Hearing the ruined state of my spirit, she made a suggestion. "Go to the Sisters. Go to the Motherhouse."

Mother had been a pediatric nurse at St. John's Hospital for many years before marrying Father, and she remained a nurse until a few months before having me. She had been to the Motherhouse several times, both as a volunteer at Mission Outreach, and on retreats.

"I don't understand. What are they going to do, Mother? I don't think they make a habit of taking in wayward women."

"Pauline." Mother's voice was stern. "You can no longer trust yourself or your decisions. All that is left is to trust in God. And if you want to get His attention, there's no better place to do it."

And so, I left a final phone message for Jack, telling him to have a good life, packed up my essentials, abandoned my apartment, and left Skokie, Illinois where I had been living. I hopped on a bus and took the four-hour trip to Springfield.

Mother met me at the bus depot and drove me to the Motherhouse. It was late afternoon, and she left me at the steps of the Chapel entrance of Chiara.

The doors were open, so I entered the church. In the vestibule, there was a receiving desk, but it was unoccupied. I walked beyond, into the dark stillness of the nave. The emptiness of that large house of God made my stomach tumble. The weight and atmosphere of the church suggested an unearthly presence, as if God Himself stood waiting for me at the altar. The majesty of the ceiling high overhead shimmered in blue mosaic tile speckled with twinkling gold stars. Towering, marbled pillars held that ceiling up. At the front, winged gold angels framed the gilded sacristy. My legs weakened before such opulent glory and magnificence. I stumbled into the nearest pew and fell to my knees. Folding my hands tightly, I prayed to God and begged Him to have mercy on this sinner. I asked Him how I could ever be forgiven, how I could free myself from the taint of my sins.

I don't know how long it was—a minute or an hour—but a voice with heavy east-European accent cut through the cathedral of silence.

"May I help you?"

I startled to the sudden presence of a gnomish woman in black and white standing in the aisle looking at me quizzically with her steel-bearing eyes and downturned mouth.

I turned to her, tried to speak, and broke down in a spasm of tears.

She huffed and jammed hands to her hips. "Well, it appears I will need to." She sat down beside me and put a hand on my shaking shoulder. "I'm Sister Iphegenia. You will come with me."

✤

For the next month, I was Sister Iphegenia's servant. She would use me in the most mundane and trivial ways. She seemed to enjoy it.

"Pauline! Tea!"

"Pauline! Calendar!"

"Pauline! My notes!"

And I would dutifully fulfill her every command. As much as Sister Iphegenia sent me about with trivial errands, among all those duties was the spiritual guidance I desperately needed.

To Sister Gene, I was a stray brought in from the cold. To most of the other Sisters, however, I needed more help than they could provide. I was a distraction to their mission, a lumbering force of nature moving through the Motherhouse like a storm. They didn't understand my presence any more than I did. Sister Gene held her ground with them, and regardless of how they felt about my being there, their guidance as much as Sister Gene's was a rope lowered into the abyss for me to climb out of. And I certainly didn't make it easy for them.

There was my first day making coffee in the big urn for the Sisters. I put in far too many grounds, and the coffee came out like a black sludge. Teary-eyed, I apologized to the nuns.

"God must need us to be more alert today," Sister Georgette said, smiling through a bitter wince. "Thank you, Pauline, for heeding His guidance."

There was the terrible time I lost Sister Gene's notes for a speech she was to give before the visiting Sisters coming from over twenty different countries.

"I don't know what to say," I stammered. "I swore I put them right here. I'm so sorry!"

Sister Gene put a hand on my shoulder. "It appears the Lord wishes me to be off script tonight." Sister Gene smiled her impish grin. "I just hope God is ready for Sister Iphegenia unchained!" She winked at me, and I wept laughter and relief.

I burned whatever side dish the kitchen staff would assign to me. I knocked a San Damiano Cross off the wall while dusting and chipped it. I disrupted a meditation with a badly timed question. All that, and these nuns were unphased. Everything was God's will.

Over time, I realized that these Sisters in no way believed that God had brought me to them as some kind of planned and purposeful chaos. They weren't prisoners of predestination. They simply saw every circumstance, either of apparent ill or good, as a blessing, a reminder of the miracle of life. These women refused to be deterred by setbacks, inconvenience, discomfort, or ills.

"Pauline," Sister Gene snapped at me one day as I dusted the leaves of a rubber tree plant in the corner of the hallway. "You're moping again. I've told you. Don't mope about. We don't need any self-pity here. It's not allowed."

"Sorry, Sister." Said without conviction. I was tired of being reprimanded about this.

"Proclaim one reason, right now, to thank God."

"I—" Nothing came to me, hard as I tried.

"Now!" The little old woman had her fists balled at her sides and looked almost raving with frustration.

"I'm—I'm thankful that you're late for your meeting so you won't be able to yell at me more."

Sister Iphegenia gave me a hard, glaring gaze, then looked at her watch. "You're darn tootin' you should be thankful for that," she said, and her legs whisked her forward. The echoes of her laughter carried down the hall.

As the days passed, Sister Gene brought me to the Mission Outreach center where she handed me off to Tamara.

"Tamara, this is Pauline. Put this lost soul to work."

"Why, certainly!" Tamara was all smiles. "Welcome to Mission Outreach, honey. You're about to help us save a lot of lives!"

After being there a month, I could sense my time at the Motherhouse was drawing to a close. How the Hospital Sisters interacted with me shifted. I had more free time because they were giving me fewer tasks. Even Sister Gene spoke less to me.

One early evening, as I sat in my one chair by my one nightstand in my tiny room, I heard a rap on my door.

"Come in."

Sister Gene looked at me with those forged eyes. "Why are you still here?"

The question caught me by surprise. "I'm sorry?"

"Ah," she said, nodding as she stepped further into my tiny room. "Is that why? Because you're sorry? Sorry for what?"

My head shook. "No, no. Sorry, I just didn't understand—"

"Sorry. Right. I get it. No need to say it again. But sorry for what?"

"No, no. I'm not *sorry*, I was just looking for clarification on your question—"

Sister Gene sat down on the corner of my bed. "Excuse me? You're not sorry for what you've done?"

I dropped my book to my lap. "Wait. What I've done? What am I supposed to be—"

Sister Gene put a hand over mine. "Cut the bull, Pauline. You are here. I found you alone in the back pew of the chapel. When I asked if you needed help, you sobbed. You are a sorrowful woman—either because of things you've done, or because of things done to you. You've been here a month, a guest of my indulgence and patience."

"And I thank you."

"But you burn things, which annoys the kitchen staff. And you break things, which annoys the janitorial staff. And you darken our halls with your sullen mood, which annoys my fellow Sisters. I am tired of constantly taking responsibility for your presence."

"I'm so sorry, Sister."

"See? Again, you are sorry. Yet, you do not heal. You have been in God's house for a month, and still have not allowed Him into your heart. He wants to forgive you, Pauline. He is waiting for you to accept his absolution, no matter your transgressions. Yet your heart continues to refuse him. Why?"

I couldn't hold it back. I wept in that chair, feeling as alone as I ever had.

"Why, Pauline? Why do you not accept God's forgiveness?"

I heaved heavy sobs as I looked up at Sister Gene. "Because I don't want to be forgiven, Sister. I just don't think I could live with that."

Sister Iphegenia shook her head. "That's not up to you, Pauline. That's up to God."

"But how does one go before God with such guilt and regret?"

Sister Gene reached out to me, drew me into her small frame and held me tight. "My sweet girl. It is those who deny their guilt and refuse remorse who live outside of God's light. For you, the repentant, He is eager and ready to give His love and forgiveness."

I held her tight and wept into her shoulder. She patted my back. "If you are ever ready, I am here to listen to your confession, and God will forgive you."

I nodded and took in heavy, hitching breaths.

"Good. Progress. I like that. And, in the meantime," Sister Iphegenia said, "perhaps we can put more effort into your kitchen abilities, okay?"

Much of the old convent has been torn down, but what is left now serves as assisted living for the few sisters that remain. A lovely old nun welcomes me and brings me inside to where Sister Iphegenia sits in the common room, a knitted blanket over her legs as she stares out the window at the row upon row of simple white tombstones spread across the acres of land.

I approach her slowly. She is 93 now, so small and frail. She makes no eye contact, has no awareness of my presence. The shine of those keen eyes is gone.

"Sister Gene? It's me. Pauline."

She stares. It isn't exactly a vacant stare, but fixated. Her eyes gaze upon something that is well beyond this life and time.

I crouch down in front of her, gently put my hands upon her dry, bony ones. "I had to stop by, to see you. To thank you."

She stares ahead, her small, gnomish face wrinkled and slack.

"You did so much for me, I can never thank you enough. And I want you to know, I realize now. I understand."

Sister Iphegenia's gaze is undeterred.

"I know now. God's forgiveness is not something that must be deserved. It's something granted each and every day to a heart willing to accept it."

I move closer to her, put hands lightly on her shoulders and give the most gentle hug. "I try, Sister Gene. Every day, I try to accept it. It's still hard, but I try."

CHAPTER NINE

Dirty Laundry

I t's been some time since I woke up looking forward to something. These last few months have required a fair amount of acclimation to a routine that no longer includes cooking up oatmeal for Father's breakfast, helping him wash and dress himself, and dosing him three times a day with morphine, haloperidol, lorazepam, prochlorperazine, and bisacodyl—of which all were to make his dying easier, not his living longer. After Father passed, I was not only confused by the contradictions of grief, relief, and regret, but also afflicted by much more spare time that only managed to aggravate my battling emotions.

In those prior years, upon once again becoming his daughter and trying to fill the void that Mother's death had left in his life, I lost any of the exuberance that life had—even at my worst—injected in me. All that remained was duty and honor. Guilt and regret. It was hard to tell any of those apart, and they resulted in the same narrow focus and driving motivation that left my head uncluttered by passion or desires. I cooked and cleaned, I fetched his paper and shopped for his groceries. I searched for the remote control he lost almost daily, and every noon I sat down at the kitchen table as he broke out the cribbage board and shuffled his Bicycles.

We spoke so little to each other over those years. I'd ask what he needed from the store, or tell him that breakfast was ready or that dinner was in the fridge. He'd announce when he was out of toilet paper or ask me to make the egg salad Mother used to make with the extra relish. Otherwise, we grew comfortable in each other's silences. Sometimes, when I was vacuuming or dusting or straightening up the house, or even if I was just sitting and reading a book, I would look up and catch him staring at me, his lips slightly apart, as if he intended to say something. When our eyes connected, his mouth would shut and his gaze would drop to his crossword or his funnies. I always said a silent prayer of thanks that Father never said anything, for fear of what bitter words might have clung to the tip of his tongue. It was only after he was gone that I lamented his silence and wondered if perhaps it was forgiveness that had sat upon his lips.

This morning, upon awakening, a little of my earlier vibrant life before being shackled by the duty to my father, the one that craved excitement and new experiences, surges back. The anticipation of being with Ms. Deborah again makes my legs swing over the edge of my bed and puts me upright. Over to the window, open it wide, look out and down from three stories up in my little apartment over the law offices of Andrew, Jacobs and McCoy, to the drone of morning traffic and sidewalk of bustling pedestrians. I stick my head out, take in a deep breath of cool late summer morning air, and exhale into the breeze.

A grin draws tight against my cheeks, and I laugh. "Oh, that's the stuff."

As I'm about to knock on Ms. Deborah's door, from inside her apartment I hear talking, the giggle of a female voice, and Ms. Deborah's lilting laughter. She has visitors, maybe her son and granddaughter. Perhaps they are having a private discussion, a family moment. I hesitate for fear of intruding.

But, it's 11:03am, and Ms. Deborah is expecting me. I wouldn't want her to think me disrespectful of my position and her time, so I give the door a few gentle raps. Faintly, bubbling up from the other side of the door, that same youthful voice says, "I'll get it!"

The door flies open fast enough to startle me, and I cough out a loud laugh. The beaming smile of a younger woman— could be seventeen, could be twenty-five—looks up to greet me. Rosy cheeks glow from her smooth, brown complexion as the elegant weave of her braids loop and fall past slim naked shoulders that peek out from a frilly blouse top. For a moment, I imagine I've travelled back in time to watch a DeeDee Deneaux who flirted with the segregation of black curtain and seduced ogling men with seductive sways of hips to the wail of Bourbon Street blues. Perhaps it's the eyes, the proud cheek bones, the buoyancy of spirit in the girl's smile that makes it apparent this must be Ms. Deborah's granddaughter.

"Hi! You must be Pauline!" Said with absolute certainty and exuberance.

"True indeed, I must. I've tried otherwise, but remain stubbornly Pauline."

The young woman scrutinizes me with a sideways stare. "Grann said you grooved to a different tune." She grins.

I lean in closer. "Same tune. Just humming the harmony." My wink produces a laugh from her.

She puts out her hand. "I'm Julienne—everyone calls me Jules."

We shake. Her grip rubs my knucklebones together—firm— and I like that. This one has the boldness of her grandmother.

"I can see why Grann likes you." She turns, tugging on my arm and pulling me inside. "Come in. Dad and Grann are expecting you."

That gives me a moment of pause, but there's no reason to be nervous. Still, my only encounter with Raymond Deneaux was fleeting and awkward. Of course, my encounters with others are rarely anything else.

Towed into the living room by the tug of Jules, I'm released in the center of the room and feel on display for Ms. Deborah who sits on the left side of her black couch, and Raymond, who hugs close to the arm of the couch's right side. Ms. Deborah beams at me in a silken black wrap with a flourish of deep red and rose pattern. Raymond looks sharp in a pair of creased navy-blue slacks and tan, striped sport jacket. My audience is far too fashionable and trendy for my comfort. My 'frumpé couture' flowered skirt and long, loose ribbed top is a stark contrast to this stylish room.

Raymond springs upright, smiles and offers his hand. I laugh my nervous laugh.

"I'll be gentle." My grip is still firm, but I back it off a measure of force.

His smirk is good-natured, though perhaps thinned by slight embarrassment. "Good to see you again, Pauline." He takes his hand back and gestures to one of the chairs against the opposite wall. "Please, have a seat."

"Thank you." I sit in the Queen Ann chair, and Jules plops down comfortably on the floor beside me, young limber legs knotting together like a pretzel, face alight with enthusiasm as she rocks in place.

Ms. Deborah's warm, inviting attention falls on me. "And what have you been up to these last few days?"

I explain about getting my parent's belongings ready for auction and home prepared for sale. "There's still a lot to do, but I'm making good progress."

"Any brothers and sisters to help?" Raymond asks as he brings a coffee cup to his lips, then pauses. "I'm sorry, I should have offered. Coffee? Water?"

"Thank you, no. And no, no immediate family. I had an aunt and uncle in the area, but my uncle died many years ago and shortly after my aunt moved to Florida to be with her children. What remaining family there is—I've never really been close to."

What I don't share is that I self-exiled myself from my extended family for too long to ever find a comfortable way back in. Even long before that, my shy discomfort kept me from building any kind of relationship with cousins or other kin.

"And you've lived here your whole life?" Raymond sips his coffee.

My knees are drawn tight together, my back rigid and upright. "Much of it. I left home for college and moved to Skokie."

Raymond's brow raises. "Northwestern?"

I nod. "And a job working at the public library after."

"I'm just getting ready to head to UChicago," Jules says.

Ms. Deborah raises her fists. "Go, Maroons!"

I give Jules a confused look.

"Our mascot. I'm on a basketball scholarship."

"Impressive," I say. "What are you studying?"

"I'm just starting freshman year. I haven't declared yet."

"But you want to get into psychology," Raymond says.

Jules grabs her thighs as she sits, shoulders rolling forward into an offensive stance. "Psychiatry. And no, I said I was thinking about it."

I watch her and Raymond stare at each other, eyebrows now transmitting some silent argument. Finally, after pinching tight the glare she gives him, Julienne looks back at me with raw enthusiasm. "I'm actually really interested in their social work program."

I put up a hand and circle it before her, as if to read her

aura. "I do sense some powerful empathetic energy radiating off of you." I wink at her, and she cracks a stiff laugh.

"See, Dad? She knows!"

"You'll be great whatever you decide, Jules," Ms. Deborah says as she looks at Raymond. "And you'll be the wonderful father who supports her, won't you, Raymond?" She pats his knee and his expression sours.

"Well, we should be moving along." Raymond stands, straightens his pant legs with a brisk tug. "Julienne needs to finish packing and then we have a long drive north to drop her off."

I stand up with Raymond.

"Pauline, would there be any chance you could take care of my mother's laundry?"

"Raymond!" Ms. Deborah scowls at him and sputters a cough.

He glances at her quickly, then looks back at me. "The laundry is just down the hall. It would really help her a lot."

"Pauline is *not* my servant, Raymond, nor does she work for you."

He sighs, his eyes keeping just off his mother but glaring in her direction. "It's why she's here, Mother." He returns attention to me. "And maybe wash her dishes?"

"Enough, Raymond!"

He rolls his eyes to me, puts up his hands in surrender and backs away closer to the door.

I bow to Raymond. "You can count on me to do whatever is within my capacity to attend to Ms. Deborah's needs."

Raymond gives a slight nod of head and his attention retreats to the pictures on the wall.

Jules stands and moves over to Ms. Deborah. "Goodbye, Grann." She bends over, wraps arms around her grandmother and doesn't let go.

"Oh, I'm going to miss you, *Chéri*," Ms. Deborah says, eyes squeezed shut and arms tight around her granddaughter.

"I love you. I'll come visit often."

"That would be wonderful. You be good and do good, you hear?"

"I will."

They part. Ms. Deborah coughs and takes a deep inhale of oxygen. She looks up at Raymond and he is looking down at her.

"Goodbye, Mother. You take it easy, you hear me?"

"Yes, Raymond."

His arms cross. "No more walks to the corner store for things you don't need."

"Mmmm."

"Promise?"

"Mmmm."

Raymond points to me and then to the door. I point to the door and then to myself with a quizzical look. He nods, prods Jules with a gentle nudge of her shoulder and they leave.

"Give me just a second, Ms. Deborah. I'll be right back."

"Call me DeeDee, dear."

I follow Raymond and Jules outside and close the door quietly behind me. Raymond is right there waiting for me while Jules walks away down the hall. We are nearly eye to eye, and that makes me more comfortable and confident.

"What can I do for you, Mr. Deneaux?"

"Raymond, please," he says with forced congeniality and combing his goatee with the fingers of his left hand.

I nod. "How can I help you?"

"Not me. I need you to help my mother."

"That's what I'm here for."

He runs a hand over his smooth, brown pate and looks uncomfortable. He's making me uncomfortable and that makes my grin widen.

"Listen, my mother is just coming out of a short remission, but the fact is, just a month ago we didn't even know if she would make it. She's a very sick woman. But she's also a very stubborn woman. She refuses to abide by her doctor's orders to not exert herself. We just really need someone to help her with chores and make sure she keeps rested."

My smile is splitting my face in two. I'm not angry, and I'm not offended, even though Raymond seems to have different expectations of me. Giving him the benefit of the doubt, I refuse to believe he's trying to take advantage of St. John's Hospice, to avoid paying for a housekeeper or doing it himself. His concern is focused on his mother's well-being and his limitations being able to be there for her more often himself. I tell myself that and try very hard to believe it.

"Mr. Deneaux—"

"Raymond—"

"—As I said inside, I will do whatever is within my capacity to meet your mother's needs. That includes your mother's wishes. If she would like me to do those chores for her, I will happily comply."

Raymond slaps a hand against the door frame and leans with a huff. "But that's what I'm trying to tell you—"

"Actually, you're not trying to tell me anything. You are successfully ordering me to disregard your mother's wishes so you can feel better."

"Now hold on—"

"My apologies, but I think you should hold on, because what I'm going to say can be a hard thing to accept. The fact is—this is your *mother's* end of life, not *yours*. She gets to decide how she wants to live her final days. She won't get another chance. If she wants to do her dishes and her laundry until she can't anymore, that's up to her. It's my job to make her comfortable and as satisfied as possible with what life she has left."

Raymond stands erect again, mouth open and ready to counter my words.

"And, coming from someone who just recently lost her father and had every opportunity but didn't say things that needed to be said, this is your last chance to make sure *you* can be as comfortable and satisfied as possible with your relationship with your mother."

His mouth hangs open a moment more, then clamps shut. He squints, looks away, and then back at me.

"Fine. Can you at least try to convince her that she could use a little help?"

I drop a hand of heavy sympathy on his shoulder. "Of that I can solemnly promise."

James L. Peters

CHAPTER TEN

The Serpent's Tail

"*Ignore my poor Raymond, dear.*" Cough. "*He's overcompensating for being an angry boy who hated his mother. Now he's a resentful man swallowing his obligation like medicine.*"

"*I hope you don't mind my asking, but, you never married, correct?*"

"*Mm-hmm. That's right.*"

"*And you raised Raymond alone?*"

"*Yes I did. I did, indeed.*"

Pause. "*Did you know the father?*"

"*I had to know him enough to make Raymond, dawlin'!*"

"*Touché.*" Pause. "*Was this when you moved to San Francisco?*"

Nod.

"*I've always dreamed of going to San Francisco. Tell me about it. What was it like?*"

"*Well now, not sure you're ready to hear all that.*"

"*Of course I am.*"

"*Some of it might change your opinion of me.*"

"*Only in the best way possible.*"

"Mmm. We'll see."

Hurricane Camille had swept away the Deneaux front porch, where once they sat sipping iced tea in the late afternoons and weekend mornings, and waving to neighbors who passed by either on their way to Claiborne Avenue or strolling the neighborhood. The porch was where, so often, they had enjoyed time chatting casually as they entertained company. The porch served as an access point to the Tremé neighborhood, the Seventh Ward, and to their world.

Interstate 10 cleaved their world like a concrete axe falling. Somehow, the loss of the porch was the final insult to removing them entirely from a community they once loved. Father said he would rebuild, but even by summer of 1970—almost two years since the hurricane—the front of their home remained in ruins.

One morning as DeeDee passed the partially open door to Alfred's room, she caught his short, broad frame hastily packing a suitcase that lay open on his bed. She stopped in her tracks and stepped inside his doorway.

"What are you doing?"

"What does it look like?"

"Are you going somewhere?"

He expelled a sigh as he tossed socks, underwear, and another shirt into the case. "What. Does it. Look like?" Alfred had been in a perpetual, undeclared war his entire life, and DeeDee often found herself on the wrong side of his battle lines.

She rarely entered his room, and certainly only by invitation. It was relatively sparse. Beyond the twin bed and nightstand with lamp and alarm clock, his dresser displayed a wrestling trophy and a small bookshelf held a few books—from James Baldwin, Richard Wright, Alex Haley and Ralph Ellison to Robert Heinlein and Isaac Asimov. His walls were mostly bare other than a framed picture of Martin Luther King to the right side of his bed and Malcolm X on the left side. The picture of King showed him with hand raised against the backdrop of hundreds of thousands who had amassed while he gave his speech on the steps of the Lincoln Memorial. The photo of Malcolm was a profile of him in glasses, finger against his temple while his intense stare cut right through to the soul.

"Where?" DeeDee's casual tone attempted to diffuse his aggression.

He looked up at her then, moved around her to the door and shut it. "A few of us are heading to San Fran. Join up with the Black Panthers there." He hissed and balled his meaty fists. "No one's serious about anything here. Nothin' getting done. But the shit is going down in San Fran and I want to be a part of it."

Sudden notions spun and tumbled around in DeeDee's thoughts. The sense of entrapment here in New Orleans. Her desperation to experience the larger world. She snatched at the first impulse. "Take me with you?"

Alfred's heavy brow lowered, and he laughed without any humor. "You crazy, girl? I'm not taking you anywhere. Shut up about stuff like that." He darted back to his dresser, pulled out a pair of pants and tossed them into the suitcase.

"But—"

He swung around and jabbed a finger at her. "And don't you go telling mom and pop about this, you hear?"

"You mean you're just going to leave and not tell them?"

Alfred fell momentarily silent and motionless, as if it was the first time realizing what he was intending. "They wouldn't understand." He dove back into his dresser, grabbing more shirts and another pair of pants. "I'll tell them, but only with a suitcase in hand and a car waiting."

DeeDee charged her brother, grabbed his arm and squeezed tight enough to make him jump and stop packing. "Don't you leave me here. I need to get out of this place. I hate this place, I hate everything about it. It hates *me*. Do you understand? Please!"

Alfred dropped the remaining clothes in his hand, turned to face her with hard scrutiny. It was the first time DeeDee could remember being this close to her brother when they were face to face. She took a step back.

"Jesus, girl. You ain't any little girl anymore, are you? How did I miss you growing up?"

DeeDee looked up at him with hard eyes. "Last couple of years put a lot of extra growing on me."

Alfred nodded slow and almost smiled. "That they did, Dee. For all of us." He looked out the window, down at his suitcase, then back to her. "It'll kill Mom and Pop for you to leave. You know that, right?"

"They're already dying inside. I can't hang around and watch that happen anymore."

He mulled it over for a bit. "You're really serious? You really want to come with?"

"Yes. Absolutely."

"You get that there ain't any place waiting for you. No one to take care of you."

She nodded.

"By the time we get there, it'll be too late for regret. You'll be stuck there, on your own. Hear what I'm saying?"

"I do."

He shrugged. Nodded. "Not sure you know what you're getting yourself into but...Go. Pack your things. We head out tomorrow. You hear me, though, right? You're on your own when we get there. I'm not babysitting you."

As she dashed out the door and into her room, her mind already travelled a long road to a golden bridge and a welcoming community against a mist-covered bay where all the opportunities she didn't have in New Orleans awaited.

That evening, the Deneaux Family all sat at the dinner table. Maman and Papa were quiet, as usual. Alfred was present, which wasn't usual lately, and DeeDee was nervous and jittery, which wasn't at all normal.

Maman set her sausage gumbo on the table alongside a bowl of steaming rice, then eased herself into her chair. Papa's motions were methodical, mechanical as he took his plate and assembled his meal—spooning rice and ladling gumbo over the top.

Maman reached for the serving spoon in the rice, but her hand froze as her eyes targeted first Alfred, then DeeDee.

"What's with you two?"

Alfred gave her the quizzical look of someone who knew exactly why a question was asked.

DeeDee's eyes widened with guilt. "Huh?"

"Don't, 'Huh,' me, girl. You're twitching up a storm, and your brother actually made himself present for dinner. Now I'd like to know what about today has you jumpin' like a bean and your brother pretending like he still cares about this family."

Alfred winced. "Ma—"

She shot a stern glance at him. "Come, now. You haven't graced us with your presence more than once this past month."

Papa simply forked gumbo into his mouth and stared ahead.

DeeDee looked at Papa, then turned to Alfred, who glared at her with a silent, blaring threat. When she finally looked to Maman, DeeDee couldn't hold it back any longer.

"We're leaving."

Their mother finished serving herself rice and gently placed the spoon back in the bowl. She folded her hands before her, briefly glancing at Papa who finally looked up from his dinner to meet her gaze.

"Leaving? Where?"

"Dee, what in the—" Alfred seethed through clenched teeth as he fisted his fork upright in hand.

"San Francisco," DeeDee said. "We're leaving tomorrow."

Maman picked up her napkin and stretched it out over her lap. "Tomorrow? Really? Just like that?"

"Ma—" Alfred started.

"You'd desert our family, just like that?"

"No, Maman," DeeDee said.

"Do you have jobs? A place to stay? What are you going to do?"

DeeDee looked to Alfred and her brother just shook his head.

"On a whim, you just decide to up and quit your job at the sugar factory?"

"That job's going nowhere," Alfred said. "I'm almost twenty-two, Ma. You can't expect me to be around forever."

DeeDee felt tears well up in her eyes. She absolutely did not want to abandon her parents. She still felt the comfort and safety of their presence. Memories from her childhood flooded in, of Maman consoling her when she scraped a knee, or when she felt the sting of a denigrating or depreciative word. Papa's hand of encouragement on her shoulder, his protective reassurance in her bedroom at night when she feared the terror lurking under her bed. Yet, over the last couple years, she had felt so abandoned by them, and by this entire city. How could she explain that to them?

"Go."

Her father's voice was barely discernable from the end of the table, but reverberated as it carried across the room. Maman, Alfred, and DeeDee all stared at him with varying surprise and shock.

"Georges?" Maman said.

Papa looked up from his plate, first to his wife, then to Alfred and DeeDee. "Go. See if it's any better than here. If it isn't, go somewhere else. There must be someplace better, at this time, at this moment." He drifted back to his plate. "There must. Find it."

"Georges, how can you say that?" Maman cried. "How can you tell them to leave?"

Papa looked so tired, so defeated. His sad eyes drooped toward Maman. "They're adults now, Aurelia. And it's only going to get harder for us. Business failing. This whole area dying. Better for all of us if they look for opportunity instead of adding to our struggle."

Alfred had tears in his eyes as he looked at his father. "Pop—"

Papa looked at him and smiled. "Thrive, my son. Find some place where you both can."

DeeDee followed her Papa's gaze to Alfred, whose razor stare was keenly sincere and resolute. "We will, Papa. I promise."

That morning, DeeDee stood beside Alfred with suitcase and handbag in her hands, ready to move forward on the adventure of her life. Alfred's stance was stolid, his short, bullish frame looking ready to shoulder through any wall blocking his way. Papa and Maman stood before them in the small kitchen. Behind them, the back door that led to the alleyway and to the car that would take them to another world.

"Is there nothing I can say—" Maman started, eyes flitting between DeeDee and Alfred.

Papa put an arm around her while he looked upon his two remaining children. "It's time, Aurelia. They need to cut a path of their own."

DeeDee dropped her bags beside her and ran into her mother's arms. "Maman!"

"Oh, *ma petite fille*," she sobbed and held DeeDee tight.

"Don't forget about your Maman, will you?"

"Never!" DeeDee cried and held her tighter.

Father put his hand out to Alfred and Alfred took it. "You look after your sister, you hear me, boy?"

"I will, Pop."

"Be a better man than I."

Alfred's eyes welled. "I could only ever hope to be as good, Pop." He drew his father in and they embraced, slapping each other's backs.

As a family, they held on to each other for long seconds. DeeDee regretted not doing this more often. Knowing that they were putting over 2,200 miles between them, she realized more than ever how important her parents were to her, how she wanted them to remain in her life.

DeeDee finally pulled away from Maman and Alfred from Papa, and they swapped places. The embraces were just as tight and just as desperate.

At last, it was time.

They stepped out to where a cherry red Plymouth Valiant idled in the alleyway. Alfred's friend Russell commanded the driver's seat, big afro squashed against the car roof, shoulders broad and dark against a white tank top, elbow on the car window ledge and bicep flexed. Mousy Cole with close-shaved head and pinched eyes, rode shotgun.

"Toss your shit in the trunk and let's motor," Russell said.

Alfred hoisted his suitcase into the trunk, then raised a hand to his parents who stood on the stoop of the back door.

DeeDee waved frantically at them. "Bye! I love you!" She tossed her suitcase and handbag in the trunk.

"Write!" Maman said. "And be safe!"

The two got into the back of the Valiant and the doors creaked shut with a loud, rattly thunk. The engine revved, the gears ground, and the red Plymouth sped off down the alley.

DeeDee's eyes were glued to the right-side passenger window as they drove past the bayous and swamplands, the southern pine forests, and the plains of the American south. As they travelled west down Interstate 10 on their way to California, DeeDee was caught in a storm of emotions. The trepidation of leaving her parents behind. The excitement of leaving New Orleans and Louisiana for the first time in her life. The irony of using the very interstate that had destroyed her home, but allowed them the most direct and fastest path to their destination. They drove through San Antonio and El Paso, Texas; Tucson and Phoenix, Arizona; and onward to Los Angeles, California.

It was five days of driving, averaging five hundred miles each day. They stopped rarely, using Russell's copy of *The Negro Motorist Green Book* as a guide for safe places to eat, rest, and gas up. Every mile made her rash decision to accompany these three boys on their adventure seem all the more outrageous. As exhilarating as it was to be heading to the almost mythical west coast, she was equally filled with panic and constantly swallowing back the urge to ask that they turn around and bring her home.

In the rashness of her decision, she realized she never even had a chance to say goodbye to Anthony Johnson, or to Hazel for that matter. Just what exactly was she thinking? Why had she jumped onto Alfred's plan so quickly without thought?

But she remembered clearly how the last few years had been in New Orleans, smothered by her parents' mourning of their oldest son and their livelihood, and incensed by her growing impression that a significant portion of New Orleans didn't want her or her family there. She had become a kind of insubstantial spirit, a ghost anchored to the tragedy of a broken home and confined to haunt her decimated community.

The mystique of the west coast offered opportunity and social change. So much was happening there and driving American society as a whole. Alfred and his friends insisted on being a part of that social change. DeeDee intended to reap the benefits of it.

On the fifth day, they hit the tail end of the I-10 in Los Angeles. Even from inside the car, DeeDee was unsettled by the magnitude of the west coast metropolis and the sheer amount of traffic on the sprawling stretch of concrete. They headed northbound, first on the new Interstate 5, then finishing on the 101 that took them into San Francisco.

The sun had set by the time they entered into the City by the Bay. They were supposed to meet up with Russell's cousin, Joe, in the Fillmore District. They drove north up the 101, passing through the bright lights and shiny new developments standing tall in the Produce Market, the flamboyant Latino Mission District, the psychedelic and schizophrenic life of the Lower Haight. DeeDee would learn the names and personalities of these neighborhoods over time. At that moment driving through each area, her eyes were simply wide with excitement at the architecture, diversity, and vibrancy of the San Francisco landscape.

When they reached the Fillmore District, her excitement turned to dread.

Empty lots. Torn down or abandoned homes and businesses. Boarded up buildings. All shrouded in the darkness of night. They turned west off the 101 and onto Geary Boulevard, a six-lane monstrosity running through the northern edge of the Fillmore District. Further north lie what DeeDee would later learn was the prosperity of the Pacific Heights area. South of Geary, the devastation caused by decades of urban renewal initiated by the San Francisco Redevelopment Agency.

A few remaining derelict Victorians and some abandoned or failing storefronts stood amid empty rubble-strewn lots where homes and businesses had once been. A spattering of people occupied the sidewalks, mostly Blacks and a couple elderly Japanese. They sat crumpled on cement stoops, leaned against poles or huddled on the ground. A few staggered down the sidewalk, looking half out of their minds. Some walked with a menacing strut and eyes that scoped their surroundings for a hustle or a fight, or maybe to deter either. DeeDee's mind flashed with images of her devasted Claiborne Avenue and Tremé neighborhood. Russell had talked like this was a thriving Black district. Instead, it looked as if the neighborhood was under siege.

Her heart beat faster and her excitement turned to foreboding. Was this the hope and promise they had come here for?

Joe lived on a side street off Geary Boulevard in an apartment he shared with two others. Each of them were members of the Black Panther Party for Self-Defense, which was headquartered in Oakland and supposedly had an office somewhere in Fillmore. Joe told Russell he had a place for all of them to stay until they got settled, and that he would get him, Cole, and Alfred into the BPP.

"Eighteen sixty-four…eighteen sixty-two…" Russell pulled over and cut the engine. "Eighteen sixty should be right here." Russell pointed out his open window to an empty lot and pile of debris.

"You sure that's the address?" Alfred looked at Russell from the back seat through the rear-view mirror.

"Yup."

"And this is the right street?"

"Damn straight." Russell ran a hand over his tall, round afro, shaking his head as he looked at the empty lot.

They sat there in the still car, impotent of action, and DeeDee felt helplessly lost in a current of confusion and indecision. She had joined this wayward group of boys on an adventure thinking they would arrive at a magical location where opportunity would be at every corner. Where they would see society evolving, prosperity budding upon the branches, and fortune hanging like ripe fruit ready for picking. Instead, they had sat now for the better part of five minutes curbside to an area whose roots have rotted and leaves have withered and fallen. There was nothing here to reap but gloom and despair.

"When'd you talk to Joe last?" Cole's voice finally squeaked as he picked at his lip.

"About a month ago. Things were all set."

"You got his number?" Alfred asked.

Russell tossed a thumb at the lot and snorted. "You think that's going to do us any good, bro? Shit."

They continued to sit with no discussion, no plans, no action. DeeDee was getting nervous and restless. It was night, and anyone who had been outside had either retreated to their apartments or moved on. The unlit sidewalks were abandoned, every remaining building amid the dilapidated neighborhood was dark.

"What do we do now?" Her voice cut through the silence, more pinched and thin than she intended to sound. Reality drenched her thoughts—where would she sleep, when would she eat next, how could she keep herself safe? Why had none of these questions filled her head before she decided to leave the comfort of home?

"Just shut up and let me think," Russell said.

From her spot in the back seat, DeeDee turned her head, having noticed movement outside from behind. Through the rear window, she watched a tall figure move toward the car, the stranger's eyes locked on the Valiant, one hand grasping something stuffed into the front of his pants.

"Hey—" she said.

"I said shut up," Russell said. "I need to think."

"Man, don't tell my sister to shut up, okay?"

"Alfred, man, would you—"

DeeDee raised her voice. "Someone's coming," She watched this tall, imposing man approaching at a trot, a dozen steps from the back of the car. He pulled something out from his pant waistline that glinted in the moonlight.

"What?" Russell looked at her in the rear-view mirror.

"Shit, man, she's right," Cole said, turning around, voice strained.

"Get moving," Alfred told Russell.

A hard, metallic rap on the back window right next to DeeDee's head. She yelled out as a man with a wiry beard stared through the window at her and waved a gun.

Russell started the car and floored it, tires squealing as he pulled away from the curb. Just as quickly, everyone was thrown forward as the car came to a sudden, screeching halt. When DeeDee looked up, another man in rough jeans and ratty denim jacket stood blocking the front of the car. He had the snub-nosed muzzle of a gun pointed right at Russell through the windshield.

"Just drive over him, man!" Cole cried.

"With that gun right on me, man?" Russel sneered. "You fucking crazy?"

Behind them, the large man in short peacoat and scraggly beard who had rapped on the window stepped up from behind the car, came around to the side and pointed his gun directly at DeeDee. His gun tap-tap-tapped aggressively against the glass.

Russell put his hands up. "Holy shit."

Alfred did likewise. "Mother fuck."

Cole whimpered and put his hands on his head.

DeeDee was struck mute, muscles tense and joints locked. She sat there, mouth hanging open, yet feeling like she could get no oxygen.

The man in the denim jacket stepped around to the driver's side and aimed his gun directly at Russell. "Welcome to San Francisco. You comin' from Louisiana, huh?"

Russell nodded and kept his eyes forward.

"Well, we're the visitor's bureau. We just need to collect an entrance fee from you all."

Russell kept his eyes straight ahead. "That so?"

"Then you lovely folk can be on your way."

"How much?"

"Whatever you got, brother."

Russell slowly moved his hand down and into his back pocket. As he did so, the gun pressed against his cheek. Slowly, he pulled his wallet out and handed over three twenties, a five and two ones.

"That all?"

Russell kept his eyes ahead. "It's all I've got..." and he turned to lock eyes on the assailant, "*brother.*"

The man wadded up the money and stuffed it in his pant pocket. "All *you* got, sure." He waved the gun in the direction of the other passengers. "Now the rest of you."

Alfred and Cole dug in their pockets and pulled out another forty-two dollars between the two of them. They handed it to Russell who passed it on to the armed man.

The bearded man wrapped harder on DeeDee's window. She gasped and went rigid.

"You too, honey," the guy up front said. "Roll it down and give it up."

DeeDee couldn't talk, couldn't move. Her body trembled and her forehead felt feverish. She was having a hard time catching her breath. She had never been so scared.

"She doesn't have shit, man," Alfred said.

"Bullshit. Give it up."

"No bullshit, man. Just take our money and go."

The guy at the driver-side window stood upright and looked

over to his partner. "If she can't pay with cash—"

Alfred's eyes were fierce as he slowly shook his head, hand resting on the door handle. "Don't even, man."

Through the rearview mirror, Russell caught Alfred's eyes, and mouthed, "Be cool." He turned to the man at his window. "You got all you're going to get without any trouble. We're gonna leave now, brother."

A pause. Casual swirl of the gun. "Yeah, fine. Go on, then. Hope you enjoy your stay here in lovely San Francisco!"

"Right." Russell slammed his foot on the gas pedal. The cackle of the jeans jacket mugger echoed across the street for a block.

Russell's driving was aimless, travelling straight for a few blocks, turning right, then straight for another couple blocks, then turning left. He didn't seem to know or care where to go.

"Jesus H. Christ what do we do now?" Cole said. "We got no money and nowhere to go!"

"Settle down, man," Russell said. "Shit, you got a tendency to whine, you know that?"

"Wha—why—" Cole was stammering. "How the fuck could you not talk to Joe for a month and drive us all the fuck up here like this, man?"

"Shut the fuck up, Cole."

Alfred shook his head. "Cole's right, though. We're in a fix. What's the plan?"

Russell looked around. "Don't know. Just keep driving round 'til something comes to mind. Too late to talk with anyone at the Black Panther chapter. We can connect with them tomorrow. Maybe they can help us. Maybe Joe will be there. I don't fucking know."

DeeDee was still rigid with shock and fear. Her hands squeezed her lap so tightly her nails drew blood just above her knees below the hem of her summer dress. What a terrible mistake she made. What a nightmare she was in. She held back tears pushing behind her eyes, but she wasn't able to hold back the brimming despair that kept her mute and immobilized in her seat.

When they turned off Eddy Street and onto Fillmore, they approached a row of storefronts, all closed. One of them had a big sign, black writing against white over the door that said, "Black Panther Party" with smaller writing above stating, "We Serve the People." The side window was covered with posters and signs, but it was too hard to read them on the unlit street. The small office was dark like every other business on the block.

"Maybe we just hang out here. Wait for them to come," Alfred said.

"What, all night?" Cole's voice pitched up higher. "Sleep in the car?"

"Got a better idea, asshole?" Russell sneered.

DeeDee felt Alfred's hand lay on her thigh. "Dee? You doing alright?"

She turned to her brother, certain she would erupt into sobs. It was like a force inside of her raging to get out. She held it in, driving fingernails deeper into the flesh of her legs. "It's no different. Not here. Not anywhere, is it?"

Alfred lifted his hand and placed it on her shoulder. "Hey, now. Don't you worry. Things'll get better. This is just a rough spot. Trust me, we'll be okay. Get me?"

DeeDee nodded, even though she didn't believe a word of it. She was angry—at herself for believing San Francisco would be any better than New Orleans; at Alfred, for always looking to be part of the solution and so often only exacerbating the problem; at Russell for making them believe he had everything under control.

Mostly, though, her fury raged at some nebulous, omnipresent threat. More and more, she could sense it overhead, like the beating of huge wings, casting the gloom of a predatory shadow over her, ready to dive and attack every time she tried to change direction. Sitting in the back seat of the car on this desolate street, she felt compelled to duck and cover.

DeeDee tried to sleep, but the fright that shivered her muscles, the discomfort of the back seat, the awkwardness of being next to her snoring brother, and the unease being in close quarters with two other men she hardly knew, kept her wide awake. Add to that the restlessness of Cole body-slamming the back of his chair in front of her every time he shifted, and she was ready to leap out of the car and face whatever next disaster awaited her.

Strobing red and blue lights suddenly splashed the inside of the car and her stomach lurched. She jabbed Alfred in the side. He snorted and shifted, eyes remaining shut.

"Alfred," she hissed. "We're in trouble."

A loud, short whoop of siren stirred all three guys awake.

Russell turned and looked behind him. "Aw, shit, man."

Cole's eyes went wide and white. "We're cooked."

Alfred looked at DeeDee, serious and calm. "Just stay cool. Hear me?"

DeeDee could only reply with a slow nod of utter despair.

The rolling red and blue lights around them fluttered as two police officers approached from either side of the car. One walked over to the driver's-side window while the other hung back, talking into his CB.

"What's going on here?" The officer looked to be in his thirties, with bushy mustache. His hand rested on the butt of his gun, one finger on the hammer.

"Nothing," Russell said. "Just parked."

"Parked for what?"

"Just parked."

The officer scanned the dark, empty street. "You meeting someone?"

"No."

The policeman's eyes raised to the Panther office. "Grab me some ID."

"Yes, sir." Russell went for his pocket.

"Easy now," the officer said, grip tightening on his gun.

Slowly, for the second time that hour, Russell grabbed his wallet from his pant pocket. He slid out his driver's license and held it up for the policeman, who snatched it from his hand.

"Russell Turner. New Orleans. Long way from home. What brings you here, Russell Turner?"

"Supposed to meet my cousin."

"Supposed to?"

"Can't find him."

The officer nodded, glanced back at the Black Panther Office. "So, you just happen to park in front of this here building, huh?"

Russell looked at the office, then looked straight ahead again.

"Step out of the car."

DeeDee's stomach dropped.

"Why—?"

Russell was cut off by the squeal of old metal as the driver-side door was yanked open. "Get out of the car."

Russell looked up at the officer. "Did we do some—"

The officer grabbed Russell by the back of the neck, getting a fistful of skin and hair, and dragged Russell out of the car where he floundered on the ground. "Hey, man! What the fuck? Let me go!"

Cole started to whine. "Oh, man, oh shit oh man oh shit."

Alfred grabbed the handle of his door. DeeDee's eyes flared at him. She shook her head vigorously. Alfred paused, but kept his hand on the door handle.

"Stand up, damn it!" the officer commanded and yanked

Russell mostly upright. Russell tried to pull away from him, to get even footing, but the police officer shoved him against the car hard and spun him around. "Spread 'em!" He kicked Russell's legs apart.

"This is bullshit, man! We didn't do anything!"

Alfred opened his door but stayed seated. "Hey, man. This ain't necessary."

The large policeman behind them walked around and jabbed his nightstick at Alfred. "You shut that fucking door now." The officer, with slicked back gray hair and high forehead kicked the door shut hard, slamming it into Alfred's arm. He yelped. "Fuck you!" he screamed, holding his wrist to his chest.

Russell shouted out when the officer on him jammed a nightstick into his back, forcing him over the hood of the car. The officer shoved Russell's head down against the hood. "You lookin' to put on a black beret, boy? Leather jacket? That what's going on here?"

Through clenched teeth, "None of your damn business, man."

"It's our damn business when you filthy hoodlums obstruct the law. It's our damn business when you fucking criminals start targeting police officers."

"We weren't doing anything, goddamn it!" Russell tried to worm out from under the officer's fist and stick. The nightstick rose up and came down hard right between Russell's shoulder blades. DeeDee screamed.

Alfred threw his door open, hard enough to put the other officer standing by it off-balance. He jumped out just before the officer regained his standing and lunged at him. Alfred sidestepped and kneed him in the gut. The officer grunted, but it wasn't enough to stop him, and Alfred got a hard and fast shoulder in the sternum that threw him back against the car. He tried to push the large man away, but the officer rebounded quickly, grabbed Alfred's arm and twisted it around and behind his back, throwing him into the side of the car.

"No, please, let him go!" DeeDee cried.

From further down the street, the racing engines of two cars as they roared into view. Tires squealed as a Ford and Chevy sedan came to a halt some distance from the commotion. The officers snapped their attention to the vehicles as they held Russell and Alfred to the car.

The four doors of each sedan flew open and out stepped ten very serious men in black berets and black leather jackets. In their hands, a mixture of rifles, shotguns, and handguns all pointing up. In fast, organized steps, they formed a circular perimeter in an arc around the scene, approximately one hundred feet from the officers. They stood rigid, shoulders straight and back, and one by one, they lowered their guns, slowly swept the scene with them, and aimed the guns skyward again.

The officer twisting Alfred's arm behind his back looked over at the armed group. "Disperse, you fucking punks."

One of the ten took one step forward. "What's the charge, pig? Or is this just police harassment?"

"You ain't the goddamn law!" the officer leaning on Russell shouted.

"You ain't either, pig. You're supposed to uphold the law. We're here to watch. Make sure you do it."

The one officer released Alfred's arm and looked at his partner. "Tom. Not worth it, man. Let's go." Alfred stumbled back away from the officer, massaged his shoulder and rubbed his wrist.

Officer Tom kept hold of Russell for another moment. Finally, he gave Russell's head one last, quick shove and let him go. Russell flew upright and turned to face the officer, fist raised.

"That's right, boy. Give me a reason."

Russell slowly lowered his fist. He scowled at the officer. "We didn't do nothing, man. Nothing."

Officer Tom moved in closer with a thin grin. "Not yet you

didn't. But you will. Won't you?" He looked to his partner. "Let's go, Wayne."

Officer Tom and Officer Wayne walked back to their car. "You all be good now, you hear?"

They slipped into the patrol car. The lights shut off and the black and white slowly pulled away.

DeeDee thought back to that evening late last summer at the nightclub, when she had stood tall, bruised and battered, full of strength and defiance. At that time, Hazel's panic and fear disgusted DeeDee. As she cowered in the back seat, she could feel that shadow spreading over her, of some threat swooping down upon her. She understood now what she hadn't then. Poor Hazel had fallen under that shadow, had looked up into the cold, yellow eyes of a predatorial threat. Of course she had run away. That's all DeeDee wanted to do now.

One of the black-clad and beret-wearing men stepped forward. "You good, my brothers?"

Russell laughed out loud. "Yeah, man. We're good now. Where in the hell you all come from?"

The lead man, rifle at his side, pointed up at the apartments. "Neighborhood watch, man. We were on patrol in the area, and someone radioed to us about the pigs hassling you."

Russell put out a hand. "Thanks, brother. Thank you all."

The man shook it. "We are here to protect the people, brother." In response, the other nine men, standing tall, raised their fists into the air.

And that was how Alfred, Russell, Cole, and DeeDee first met the Black Panthers.

James L. Peters.

CHAPTER ELEVEN

Ghosts of the Past

espite a long night at the bar, I wake up early, hop in the shower and get ready for the day. I sit down at the computer with a cup of coffee and dive into some research.

Yesterday, despite reminding her to take breaks and get plenty of oxygen, Ms. Deborah fell into a bout of coughing that scared me. As she bent over in a spasm of bronchial fits, I noticed for the first time how lesions were spreading over the nape of her neck and up the back of her scalp through her thinning hairline. Mr. Raymond's words from the hallway reverberate now in my head, and once again I worry that I'm not doing what I should for her. But that will change now.

I type, "pulmonary sarcoidosis" into the internet search.

St. John's Hospice had given me some paperwork about the disease and I had skimmed over all of it, but it's now past time to take this disease and my role seriously.

Throughout the morning, I read about the condition, watch

videos about it, and learn a lot.

The lesions on her scalp are granulomas, the clumping of white blood cells due to her hyperactive immune system. Those same granulomas are spreading through her lungs and likely her liver and kidneys.

Sarcoidosis is especially prevalent in the Black community—Black women are up to 18 times more likely to die from it than White women. Yet, two-thirds of people who contract sarcoidosis will find that the condition resolves itself.

Not, unfortunately, for Ms. Deborah.

As she progresses, she will face ever-increasing shortness of breath, coughing, elevated calcium levels, the further spread of lesions and thinning hair, fatigue, and weight loss. Being in hospice, she is no longer receiving treatments to combat the sarcoidosis but is still receiving anti-inflammatories to keep her as comfortable as possible.

For whatever reason, going into this volunteer position and understanding that I am not there to minister to the dying but rather be a companion to the living, it didn't seem important to know much about whatever the person was dying from. Now, as much as my core responsibility is to help her be at peace with her life and, if she wishes it, help her find spiritual peace as she reaches her end, it's becoming clear how much this disease is, inevitably and unavoidably, an integral part of her final days.

It's just past noon by the time I shut off my computer. Over the past four hours I have gained a far deeper understanding of the disease, a far greater respect for Ms. Deborah's condition, and much more sympathy for Raymond's overzealous reaction to his mother's condition. It's time to be the best hospice volunteer I can possibly be.

Before work, I head over to my parents' house. In a few hours, I make steady progress. I dig around in the closets of each room, sifting through racks of clothing to take to King's Closet, a Christian nonprofit clothing store that provides to the disadvantaged and homeless. As I look through all my mother's dresses—the casual sun dresses she wore around the house and her elegant Sunday dresses she wore to mass, and formal gowns she wore to parties, weddings and funerals—I wish once again for her lithe shape so I could take some of these home with me. I have fond memories of my mother in her summer dresses and her high-necked angora winter sweaters.

As a child, I hugged and snuggled up against these articles of clothing. In my early teens, I shielded myself from my father behind these fabrics. By my late teens, it was those same articles that tried to calm me, to settle me down, as I began to rage and rebel against all those who either didn't understand me or didn't respect me. Yes, it is odd, yet so telling, that in all those memories of my mother, I recall the pattern and texture of her dresses and blouses and knitted sweaters more than I do her visage or her words. It's not that she was distant or aloof. She was not a cold woman, but as much as she was able to embrace me when scared or sad and be a buffer between myself and my father in my later teen years, she was always simply a dependable expectation. A reliable fixture for consolation. Although always there to comfort with an embrace, every year I grew older we spoke less.

As much as she loved me, each year that passed, I became more of a mystery to her. She, a prom queen, a debutante, little miss popularity who constantly but modestly reflected on her school days, simply did not know how to relate to this awkward, emotional girl other than try to fix her while sympathizing with her. To lend the soft, cozy commiseration of cotton, silk, or cashmere to a sad, confused, and broken girl. Only after hitting rock bottom as an adult did she find me again, pull me out of the depths. Though the physical distance remained, whether by phone or email or online, I could still emotionally snuggle up against the warm and comfortable memory of those clothes. I could almost smell her clean, lavender scent.

Knowing that I am older than my mother was when she was raising me, my heart breaks for her now, because it's obvious just how much she was unable to fully relate to my father in the same way she couldn't relate to me. She was a peck on his cheek, a squeeze of his hand, the polite laugh to his joke, and the blush of modesty to his compliment. I don't remember ever coming upon my parents and witnessing them being anything other than what their dutiful roles required. They didn't enjoy each other; they were simply compatible, comfortable.

And who am I to begrudge them that relationship? For me, at 53 years old? There's no need for the lust of my teens, the eroticism of my twenties, and the passion of my thirties. At this moment, at my age, I desire nothing less than the hope that in this latter part of my life I might find someone who, above all else, is simply, tolerably, compatible.

I am no spinster, though I imagine some might mistake me for such. Admittedly, I do not spend much time on my appearance. I do not prowl the bars and night clubs looking to hook up with anyone. I do not subscribe to any online dating services. Based on my job, however, there are plenty of opportunities to meet and interact with men—men who are on the road, lonely, and bored. There appears to be an odd mystique about being a female bartender—especially a mature one. I'm not sure if it is the slightly masculine attire I wear (they gave me the option of a skirt and blouse, but I go with the black slacks, white button-up collared shirt with bow tie, black vest and a red, paper rose in the lapel.) The gender reversal, when combined with my red lips and full hips, my long wild hair and dark eye liner, can trigger a carnal attraction in a certain type of man.

I've had men twenty years younger and men twenty years older ask me to join them after bar close. Sometimes I will, as long as I have any kind of genuine interest in them. Most of those encounters aren't intimate, and rarely end up in their room.

Tonight, for example. I've been serving light beers to this one guy at the corner of the bar for the last couple of hours. He looks about forty, maybe just shy of that. Full head of dishwater blond, wavy hair, combed straight back. He has the shadow of a full beard, piercing blue eyes, and cute little nub of a nose. He's lacking a chin, which drops him from the rank of Greek god to being just an above-average Joe, but he's friendly and he's funny, and I'm doing what I do too often—focusing on one customer while tending to the others almost as an irritation. It's a problem I constantly work on.

Will and I (his name is Will and he's from Madison, Wisconsin, works for a PR firm and is here on business) have gone beyond all the small talk (he's divorced and has two teenaged kids). We've moved on to movies and music, and now we've just shifted into books (unfortunately Will likes horror, but he says he has also enjoyed Jonathan Saffron Foer). I'm realizing I'm just a bit smitten with this one, and he seems genuinely lonely and/or desperate enough to settle for me tonight. I keep cool and wait for his play.

"So, any plans for tonight?" He has experience, I can tell, because the question is very straight-forward with full eye-contact.

"Nothing I'm committed to," I reply, and that's as close to a lie as I can make. I planned on going home and going to bed, but no, I'm not committed to doing that alone. "What about you?"

He blows out a heavy sigh. "I have nothing to do until my flight leaves tomorrow in the early afternoon. Any ideas how I could kill some time and have some fun in Springfield?"

I could honestly gobble up the smile he's giving me. I haven't felt the stir in my loins Will is causing for a very long time. An extra Act of Contrition may be required at my next confession at church.

My elbows plant in front of him on the bar top and I lean in close. "As a citizen of Springfield, I have a civic duty to ensure any visitor looking for ways to enjoy our great city is given every opportunity."

Will smirks and moves in just a small bit closer to me. I can almost feel electricity popping between us. "Well, then, I call upon you to serve your municipality appropriately and within your complete capacity. What time do you get off?"

"Depends on how good you are."

He laughs and I blush. Oh my goodness, I'm out of control with this guy.

"How about you meet me back here at midnight?" I say, trying to be more sensible.

Will slaps two twenties down on the counter and stands. "Pauline. I will see you back here in—" He looks at his watch. "—just under two hours."

My face is beaming, I can feel it. I'm hot and flushed. This might very well end up being a memorable night.

I rinse out the cocktail shaker that I had just used to make another Aviation for a tipsy woman two seats down chatting away with her quasi-interested husband. I start grabbing pint glasses out of the dishwasher and stacking them up against the wall. Out of my periphery, I see someone approach the bar just as I grab two more glasses. I turn and face the person.

"Hello, Pauline."

I stop. The glasses slip out of my hand and shatter on the ground. My eyes are wide, and the person in front of me just smiles a sympathetic smile.

I stammer a moment, stare, and only two words slip from my lips, like a curse. "Mr. Jack."

James L. Peters

CHAPTER TWELVE

Sifting Through the Ruins

In the following years after leaving the Motherhouse, through much of 2007 and 2008, I travelled. I didn't have a lot of money nor a lot of resources, so my attempt at walkabout was restricted to the Midwest. I mostly journeyed by bus, though I also hitchhiked more than I probably should have. That little adventure took me through Indianapolis, Indiana; Cincinnati, Ohio; Louisville, Kentucky; and finally St. Louis, Missouri, where I settled down for the next eight years working at the best job I ever had in the public library.

In each city, the first thing I did was hunt down a local Alcoholics Anonymous chapter. From there, I would hit the closest Catholic church for evening or Sunday mass. Between those two resources, I could usually learn about a halfway house or other services that might be available to me. If needed, I'd also do some volunteer work for the church while there. Between the museums or minor attractions I could see for free, I'd make a stop at the local libraries, sit and enjoy a cup of coffee or chai tea at any little café I could find. The libraries and cafés were sanctuaries, places of comfort and safety that kept me centered and at ease when otherwise panic might set in if I didn't know what to do or where to go next, which was almost a daily anxiety.

When I had no idea where to sleep, the couch of an AA sponsor was often available until I could land my own place to stay. On a few occasions, a park bench or the alcove of a business had to suffice.

I was usually able to find some form of temporary income, enough to keep me in an area for at least a couple months. From gas station convenience stores to waitress to office janitorial, I did it all. None of those jobs bothered me; in fact, they were usually fun because they weren't permanent.

Those couple of years might have been a sad excuse for the global Walkabout I had dreamed of since college, but it was the closest I could manage, and it helped to cleanse my spirit and renew my soul. I could have settled in any of those locations had opportunity arose, but fortune led me to the St. Louis Central library just when one of their librarians had retired. I ended up blissfully wading through the Dewey Decimal System for the next eight years. I was happy there. I loved my job, the people I worked with, and I enjoyed the tired, rundown pretention of St. Louis. It was there that I was able to slowly rebuild my life.

In the summer of 2012, I found myself back in Skokie, Illinois for an extended weekend. That's where I had lived throughout my college years and for a rough decade after. My close friend Jasmine was getting married, and she asked me to be a bridesmaid. I didn't know what to say at first. Me, a bridesmaid? The mere thought was both hysterical and terrifying.

I agreed, though. There was no way I could let Jazz down. I went to a local bridal shop and had them measure me. It's the first and only time I've had my measurements taken, and no, those confidential numbers will never be shared with anyone.

Returning to Skokie was a shock. So many of my worst days were left behind in Skokie. My alcoholic years filled with debauchery and vice. The miserable year after college getting myself dry. Skokie was also where I made the worst mistake of my life—the one I still regret to this day and am unable to forgive. Kaiya's tombstone stands there in a cemetery as a marker to my regret.

But Skokie also had good memories, as fleeting as they were. Working at Capos & Cantos, the downtown corner café, a hangout for hipsters, beatniks, and other Bohemians to sip expensive coffee drinks, listen to folk artists, and attend poetry slams. That's where I first met Jasmine, who started there a few months after me. It's also where I ended up finding my studio apartment above the café.

It was during that time in Skokie that threw me into a three-day whirlwind relationship with Jack Cross, a man who sincerely believed he could somehow end the world just by thinking it away. He never did, though he certainly almost ended himself when he attempted suicide after abandoning me. Not because of me, of course. In fact, it was more in spite of me in some strange way. How someone who existed within such a tiny fragment of my life could have such an impact on me—both positive and negative—is hard to explain, let alone understand.

Returning to Skokie certainly brought Jack back into my thoughts, and it only got worse during the bachelorette party, since we started at Capos & Cantos, where Jazz was now a manager. That happened to be the first place I had brought Jack after he arrived.

Seeing Jazz again was fantastic, though. We had stayed in contact by phone and email, but it was the first time seeing her in five years. Our friendship had layers that ran deep. We developed a close friendship within the first couple months of working together. For a short time after that, we became more than just friends and became intimate, both of us exploring our sexualities. After years of promiscuity with college men and professors, I had lost the taste of the male gender—figuratively and literally. I had been new to experiencing the touch and passion of a woman. Jazz was not. She was a good teacher.

In the end, our sexual relationship didn't last, but we remained intimate friends. To this day, Jazz and I share a passion and closeness that I have never experienced since. And, though Jazz was a special person and a unique experience in my life, I realized that I was completely and totally heterosexual.

Jazz ended up finding her perfect mate in a realtor named Janice McElroy, and after five years of being together, Janice popped the question during a downtown Chicago carriage ride and Jasmine enthusiastically said yes. I couldn't be happier for her.

Fortunately, the bridal party only assembled briefly at Capos and Cantos and we quickly hopped on a party bus. We motored off to some of the livelier night clubs in Skokie. As the bus took us from place to place, it became a tremendous test to remain sober among all the younger partiers—especially the lesbian partiers, who could drink as much and as hard as I ever could. I was on the phone to my sponsor two times that night, and begged God for strength the entire evening.

The ceremony on Saturday was beautiful. They chose the Emily Oaks Nature Center for the ceremony and had a woman minister from the United Church of Christ officiating. It was a small ceremony with only about fifty of their closest friends and family attending.

The reception was held at a converted barn that hosted events, a charming location with strings of old-style lights looping along the rafters, silver and gold balloon bouquets, and bottom-lit fluttering silk sheets dressing the walls. They had a DJ spinning a mix of saccharine seventies love songs, 80s punk, and 90s grunge. The evening was like a dream.

Jasmine and Janice were having their dance. Halfway

through, the bridal party was told to join. I was paired with Jasmine's brother Francis, and we were rocking back and forth to "Longer," by Dan Fogelberg. Most of the bridal party leaked tears to the music as they watched Jazz and Janice lovingly hold each other.

When the song was done, Francis, who was only nineteen and completely uncomfortable around me, pulled away and returned to his seat. I went to the wet bar and ordered a seltzer water. As I sipped my drink at a high top near the bar and watched the rest of the guests step onto the floor and start dancing to The Clash's "London Calling," my attention turned to the silhouette of someone tentatively stepping in from the barn entrance, looking not quite at ease. It was a man, and he hung by the door, looking about him, until he seemed to look at me. He stepped forward and a cone of light illuminated his face.

I hadn't seen that face in five years. Until I laid eyes on him, I had convinced myself I was over him.

Jack Cross.

Mr. Jack.

The world-ender.

I stood, frozen in place. His hand raised in a meek greeting as he approached, wearing dress pants, white button-up shirt, suspenders, and tie. He looked really, really good, and he was the last person I wanted to see. But there he was, and in a few seconds, he was at my high-top table looking right at me, his brown eyes wide yet still somehow sad, his brown hair longer and bushier, but still with those adorable, unmanageable curls. He had a few extra pounds on him, which suited him well.

"I finally found you," he said.

"Are you kidding me?" I replied.

He paused a moment. "You may not remember, but I don't have much of a sense of humor."

I laughed. "Oh, I remember."

"Well. Good. Glad you remember some part of me, at least."

I sipped seltzer. "Oh, do I ever. I certainly remember you leaving me standing in the cold at the cemetery, never to see you again." I gave him a big smile.

He shrugged, head downturned, and gave me an angled glance with a smirk. "Had a few things going on at that time."

"Did you."

"And I deeply regret how our last meeting went."

"Do you?"

"Yes. You got my letter, didn't you?"

I puked laughter in his face. "Oh, you mean the one that essentially implied you were killing yourself?"

His smile froze, his eyes fell to his hands that seemed to try and find something to do with themselves on the table top, but instead just twitched and fiddled about. "Maybe we should just slow down a moment."

I looked about the room. "Should we ignore the fact that you are, right now, crashing a wedding reception?"

A hand went to his face, pinched his mouth as he looked about nervously. "I don't intend to take advantage of Jazz's wedding reception. Happy for her, by the way."

I uprighted myself, standing a good three inches over him, and finished my drink, slamming the empty glass down on the small round table top. "What in the world are you doing here, Jack? How did you possibly find me?"

Jack's shoulders dropped as he took one step back. "Listen, do you mind if I get a drink? It would really help to settle my nerves."

"Your nerves?" I couldn't help but laugh again. "Sure thing, Mr. Jack. You go get yourself some liquid courage, then come back here and tell me everything that led you to find me after five years." I laughed louder. "Order yourself a double!"

Those sad brown eyes of his. What was it about them that

could be so disarming? My smile withered. I put up a hand and nodded. He gave a single nod back and went to the bar.

Part of me simply wanted to leave right then. In fact, to this day, I think that might have been the best option. But I didn't. How could I? Five years ago, this guy evacuated from my life after coming into it like a wrecking ball. I couldn't help but wonder what he's been doing, and why he stayed away for so long.

He came back with a pint glass of dark beer. No surprise there. He never seemed to be into liquor. He took a sip, then put his gaze deep onto me. "You look really good."

I laughed.

"Jesus, I mean it."

"Watch your language, please."

"Oh, right. Sorry. I forgot."

"I think you forgot many things, Mr. Jack."

His look was penetrating. "I never forgot you, Pauline. I looked for you, you know."

I pulled back, unable to swallow what he just said.

"I'm serious. For over a year, I tried to find you. You weren't in Skokie. No one knew where you were. You were off the grid."

"I was on Walkabout."

Jack slapped at his chest. "Me, too! To find you!"

My expression clearly conveyed that I thought he was bull-shitting me.

"No, seriously! I came back to Skokie, then I went to Spring-field. I found out from some of your library coworkers that you were from there originally. I actually met your father."

"You...what?"

"I spoke with your father. I hunted down all the Swansons in the phone book."

That dumbfounded me. "You didn't. You couldn't."

"I did. He was very nice. You know, he had a lot of regrets over you."

My head started to shake. "Don't."

Jack put up his hands. "But he didn't know where you were. Meanwhile, I was running out of ideas, and the path was cold. I stopped by that nun's place, what's it called?"

My eyes just about popped out of my head. "The Hospital Sisters? The Motherhouse?"

"Yeah, that's it. They remembered you, but had no idea where you were."

My gaze narrowed on Jack. "You really spent all that time looking for me? Why?"

His hand reached out to mine. I pulled my hand away, leaving his at the center of the table, abandoned. "Do I really have to explain it?"

I nodded. "Yes. You absolutely do."

He drew his hand back slowly. "I—I thought maybe— I really believed you might be a part of my new life. Part of my recovery."

"You believed I might be, or you wanted me to be?"

His nods were small, almost a palsy. "Wanted. To be."

"Oh, Jack." I didn't know what else to say. All this time, I thought he had just written me off. Of course, hearing his story then, I realized how I hadn't been accessible. It made perfect sense that he wouldn't have been able to find me. And in reality, I guess I just never presumed to think he would have ever looked for me.

I reached a hand out toward his. "And what, exactly, brings you here now?"

His hand cautiously grazed mine. "I happened to see a social media post that referenced Jasmine's wedding. Friend of a friend of a friend of a friend. It made me think of you, and I realized you might likely be at the wedding."

"So you stalked Jazz's nuptials to find me?"

He shrugged. "Pretty much."

"Amazing."

I let him take my hand in his. "It's amazing that I finally found you."

I gave a slow nod. My head was a little dizzy, as if I wasn't drinking seltzer water. "So. What now?"

We left the wedding early. I had him wait outside while I went to Jasmine and told her I wasn't feeling well. She was very gracious, although disappointed. Had she known the real reason, she would have tried to stop me. She never approved of Jack.

Jack and I took off in his car. He suggested a restaurant for us to sit and chat. I told him to take me to his hotel.

My thoughts floated somewhere above me. I was with a man I hadn't seen for five years, who had somehow overwhelmed my emotions in the course of a handful of emails followed by a few days together. He was back, and I no longer felt in control of what would happen next.

We started in the hotel restaurant because he hadn't had anything to eat all day. I just had an iced tea and a side of fries to nibble on. We caught up on the last five years. He talked about his mother, who after a serious health threat, was doing much better since moving to the Seattle area near his oldest sister. He mentioned his other sister, Liz, and how after floundering in LA for a couple years, she somehow managed to land a gig booking bands for a heavy metal night club. Jack suspected it was because she was sleeping with the manager of the place. Mr. Jack, meanwhile, was back at it in marketing and advertising, doing graphic design and copywriting for a small tech company in west-central Wisconsin. He wasn't particularly happy there, but he said it paid the bills.

I filled him in on some of my story, including my time at the Motherhouse, and then my midwestern wanderings that led me to St. Louis and back in the library system. He was genuinely happy for me.

"Skokie was my first stop back once I had recovered. I really did want to find you."

"So, the whole thing with your head—your belief in that thing you had—about ending the world—?"

"The Shrug—" Almost spoken with embarrassment.

"Right. That was all just part of some kind of epilepsy?"

He rolled his shoulders. "That's what they say."

"But you don't believe it?"

His head shook, but without conviction. "I'm not saying that. But it's out of my head, regardless. That's all that matters."

"I'm glad for that. I really am."

He reached over to my side of the table, ran a finger across my forearm. "You were the only person who knew about my—condition. My belief. It meant a lot to me that I could share it with someone else."

I nodded but couldn't look directly at him. "I know."

"Well, I'm not sure you completely do. I strongly suspect that most people in this world would have written me off as crazy and got as far away from me as possible. You didn't."

"I tried."

He frowned with silent questioning.

"You think that night at the poetry slam I was trying to lure you in? I was trying to scare you off." Boy did I. I had put on my most outlandish, risqué outfit and wildly dramatic makeup. Mr. Jack's jaw just about hit his chest. At the slam, I read my most lewd and lurid poem, and he did not hold back on how uncomfortable it made him to hear me share graphic examples of my lascivious escapades.

He looked dubious at first to my statement, then his eyes widened, and he laughed. 'Oh. Oh my God. That makes so much sense, now."

I nodded. "Well, don't get me wrong. I wasn't making anything up. I just thought, at the time, if I dropped all my camouflage and showed you the real me, you'd high tail it out of there." I smiled. "But you didn't."

"No, I didn't."

"Why not?"

The pause was thoughtful, and I didn't press it. Finally, he said, "I guess, at the time, I recognized a similar vulnerability to mine. I saw the façade you were showing others, hiding some pain or darkness you carried, just like I was."

"Huh. I guess that isn't too-far removed from the truth."

We continued our light banter for almost two hours until I finally leaned forward with direct eye contact. "Time to move up to your room?"

Momentarily shocked, Jack gave an earnest nod. We stood, and I followed him to the elevator and then to his room. We didn't speak the entire way there. My heart was racing.

Jack swiped his key card and opened the door. He entered first and held the door for me. "Sorry for the mess." he rushed into the room to clear away dirty socks and a pair of pajama bottoms on the floor. He moved a suitcase off the bed.

"No need to present airs, Mr. Jack," I said and laughed.

"Have a seat. Can I get you something? I think the minibar has soft drinks."

I sat down in the chair at the small table by the window. "I'm fine."

"Oh, great." Jack sat on the edge of the bed. Neither of us said anything for half a minute. We simply looked at each other.

"So," Jack said.

"So," I answered, amused. I could tell he was nervous and unable to move the moment forward. "You're still terrible at small talk." I got up and sat down next to him on the bed, my thigh making contact with his, my shoulder against his shoulder. I laid a hand on his leg. "What's the plan, Mr. Jack?"

"Plan?"

"Shall we continue to be uncomfortable with each other and fumble our words? Dodge our intentions? Keep treading the murky waters of our past? Or, do we take a deep breath and dive right in?"

Jack smiled. "Now there's the Pauline I know." He smiled and moved in close. Our lips touched, delicate and cautious. That gentle brush of our mouths quickly became the hard and forceful push of aggressive kissing. His hand came around to the back of my head and pulled me in tight. I wrapped my arms around his waist. Quickly, we were trying very hard to occupy the same space, moving heads and bodies as we held more tightly to each other. One or the other of us pulled us down toward the bed and we fell into a lateral position, legs over the edge, hands groping. He maneuvered on top of me, rolling me to a supine position as he kissed my chin, my neck, my chest. My hands pulled out his tucked-in shirt and slipped under the cotton fabric to touch and caress his flesh. His head kept moving down as he started to shimmy my bridesmaid gown up and over my stomach. He nuzzled the peach panties over my groin with his nose as I squirmed, feeling a charge in my loins that ran up my spine.

"I recognize this tattoo," he mumbled as he kissed my stomach.

"Mmmm," I said, eyes closed and feeling warm and restless. I didn't want to think about that tattoo on my stomach. I didn't want to think about anything.

"I hope you've forgiven yourself—ow!"

My legs scissored his hips.

"Pauline—I can't breathe!" He pushed at my legs, trying to squirm out of my hold.

"Stop," I said. "Don't."

"Jesus! Fine, just let go!"

"And don't take His name in vain, damn it."

He was fighting hard now, enough to squeeze out of my leg

lock. "Shit! What the hell? What did I say?"

I propped myself up by my elbows and looked hard at him. "You sure know how to ruin a mood, Mr. Jack."

He held my knees, hands softly caressing. "I'm sorry. I—I just saw the tattoo and—I couldn't help but think about—Forget it. I shouldn't have said anything."

I raised myself back up to a sitting position, facing him squarely. "Poor Mr. Jack. You really do know just how to say the wrong thing at the right time."

His cheeks reddened and he turned his face away from me. "I don't mean to."

I put a hand against his face. "I know. No harm done."

He gave me a hopeful look. "You sure?"

"Yes. But you'll need to shut up now."

"I—"

I placed a finger to his lips. "Stifle, please." I kissed his lips. "Don't ruin this." I kissed him again, this time with my tongue sneaking through his lips. He met it with his. We fell back against the bed. In little time, our clothing was off and we managed to do what we'd been waiting over five years for.

I woke up that next morning alone in Jack's hotel bed. Jack was just finishing getting dressed. The clock said 7:17am.

"Going somewhere?" I said through sleepy eyes and sluggish mouth.

He stepped over to bedside, reached down and kissed me. "Good morning."

"Amazing evening," I said and smiled.

"Long overdue." His eyes broke from mine quickly.

I scooted myself upright against the headboard, drawing covers up to my chest. "Breakfast?"

His look was apologetic, and I was already getting a bad feeling. "Sorry. I can't. I need to get back."

I gave a confused nod. "Back where?"

"Home," he said.

"Wisconsin?"

"Yeah."

Something about his tone, his delivery, was slippery, keeping certain information from me. Nothing I could nail down definitively, yet I sensed it clearly.

"Something you need to share with me?" I was all smiles as I said it.

He turned away to look in the mirror as he buttoned up his shirt. "What do you mean?"

I threw the covers off me, stood up and faced him, completely naked. His eyes darted at and away from me through the mirror as he rolled up the cuffs of his sleeves. "What aren't you telling me, Jack?"

He finished rolling up his left sleeve. "Pauline, things are complicated right now."

My hands went to my sides. "Oh, you think?"

Jack reached for the white hotel robe hanging on a hook next to the small closet and handed it to me. "Yes, I do. More than you realize."

I grabbed the robe and threw it on, but didn't bother to swaddle or tie it. "Why don't you explain it to me, please."

He turned to me then, and those big sad brown eyes really started to piss me off.

"Listen. Things are kind of a mess right now. I'm—I'm actually engaged."

There it was. I knew something was wrong, but I would never have guessed that Jack would pull something this low. The Jack I knew was the most innocent, naïve person I had ever met. "You're fucking kidding me," I said.

He put his hands up. "Wait. Just listen."

"Oh, I'm all ears."

His hands slowly fell. "Okay. Now just give me a second. See, I met this woman a couple years ago. We got on pretty well. This was after all that time I spent looking for you. She was how I was able to kind of get over you."

"Oh, good for her," I said.

"Come on, settle down. Just listen."

I cupped my hand behind my right ear.

"We've been together now for a little over two years, but our relationship has been off and on the whole time. She was the one to propose, sort of. Not me. It was a few weeks ago." He paused, looked anxiously at me as if waiting for some response. I gave an annoyed nod, not of agreement, but rather of frustration for him to continue.

"I haven't given her an answer yet. I told her I needed time."

I looked smugly at him. "Ah, I see. So, you hunted me down to get a latent piece of ass before you got married!"

"No! Oh, come on, now. Give me a break."

I shook my head. "Oh, Jack. Nothing about this is good."

He sat down on the bed and put his hands around my waist as I stood over him. "Listen. Please. I came here because it was my last chance to find you, to find a reason why Rachel and I aren't meant to be."

"I didn't want to know her name," I said.

"Sorry." He rubbed at my sides. "But do you at least understand?"

I looked down at him. "Mr. Jack. I'm sure there may have been some decent way to present this to me in a manner that was honest and sincere and fair to both Rachel and to me."

He nodded at me.

"This was not that way."

His head dropped as he held on to me.

"You decided to conceal vital information so you could get in my pants."

Jack's head shot up. "No! Pauline, that's totally—"

I shook my head at him. "Sorry, Jack. Too late. Whatever your true intentions, they are permanently mired by dishonesty and mistrust."

Jack stood, his hands falling to his side. "Pauline, don't you understand? I haven't stopped thinking about you. I haven't stopped loving you."

I acknowledged his words with a sympathetic nod. "It's time for us to say goodbye, Jack. This isn't right. It's not fair to me, it's not fair to her. How dare you try to make me the other woman that cancels your wedding."

Jack stood before me, shoulders wilting. His head slowly moved back and forth. "I never meant to hurt you, Pauline. I was ready to be with you. I wanted to be with you."

"Not this way, Jack. I'm sorry." I grabbed my bridesmaid gown and slipped it on.

"What if I told you I was leaving her?" he said with some desperation.

"Lucky her," I said, snatched my underwear and bra from the floor, and headed for the door. "Take care of yourself, Mr. Jack."

I left him there, and I truly believed I would never see him again.

CHAPTER THIRTEEN

Clearing the Rubble

"Jesus Christ."

He looks at me with utter shock. "What did you say?"

"I was praying. Asking Jesus to please, for the love of God, keep you away from me." I grab a broom and start to sweep the broken glass into a pile.

The last time I saw Jack Cross, I was 38 years old. Fifteen years ago. My brain simply cannot comprehend that I am seeing him again, right here, in my bar.

"I can go if you want me to." His expression sags and I can tell he is hurt, but not necessarily surprised.

Words barely even begin to come. I don't know how to feel about seeing him. Annoyed by his presence, shocked at his change in appearance. His widow's peak is prominent, and he has a beard now, which shows a fair amount of gray. He looks about thirty pounds heavier—which doesn't necessarily suit him well. Above all, he looks tired and worn. Seeing him like this makes me feel old and past my prime. I certainly don't need this reminder on top of everything else I'm facing.

"Why?" It's all I can manage to say, but that one word conveys so much. I go around the corner, grab the long-handled dustpan and sweep the pieces of glass into it.

He gives me a half-assed grin steeped in apology. "Believe it or not, I'm here on business."

"Really?" I dump the glass into the garbage.

"God's honest truth. My company put me up here." He puts up his hand. "I swear, I did not know you'd be here until I stepped into the bar."

I shake my head. "I don't believe it. I can't believe it."

He shrugs. "I know. But it's true. Crazy world, huh?"

I nod. "Crazy world."

We stare at each other for a very long time. Finally, I toss a Long 9 Lounge coaster in front of him. "What can I get you?"

"Considering how this night is developing? I'll take a bourbon. Neat. Buffalo Trace if you've got it."

I turn. "Coming right up." Apparently, Jack has acquired a taste for liquor.

I grab the bottle from the top shelf and pour it into a crystal tumbler. I give it an extra tip of the bottle. Least I can do.

"Here you go," I say and hand it over.

"Thanks." He takes a pull and savors it. Setting the glass down, he looks up at me. "So, um, you're a *bartender?* How does that work?"

I smile glibly. "Pretty well, actually."

"Really? Kinda like Sam Malone from *Cheers?*"

I don't understand the reference at all. "Sorry?"

"You know, the TV show, Cheers?"

"I never watched much TV, Jack."

He looks disappointed. "Oh. Well, it was a popular show from the eighties. About a bar. The bartender was a recovering alco—" He cuts short. "Never mind."

I dump the shattered glass into the garbage can. "In that case, I suppose it's like that."

He nods. Stares ahead. Takes another sip of bourbon.

"So," he says.

I lean down toward him on the bar counter and smile a little too big. "So!" I say it louder than intended and he recoils slightly. "How are you, Jack?" His name cracks from the whip of my tongue.

"I'm good." He grabs the tumbler and knocks back half the drink.

"Did you ever marry what's-her-face? Rhonda?"

He grins. "Rachel."

I flick a finger at him. "That's her."

"I did."

I try very hard not to grimace. "That's wonderful."

"Thank you."

I grab a towel and wipe down an area of the bar. "Kids?"

"No, it never worked out."

I pause, unsure how to react. "Sorry."

"Don't be."

I tell myself not to be hostile to him. It's been fifteen years. Water under the bridge, as they say. There's no reason to be bitter about the ancient past, and certainly no reason to be angry about his sudden appearance, especially if what he says is true and it is simply happenstance. Hard as that is to believe, I can't hold that against him.

I move on to take care of several other customers, mix their drinks and serve them up. I check back with them, one by one, avoiding Jack as I do it. I chat for a bit with the woman nursing the Aviation as she disparages the healthcare system and its lack of support of women's health. I laugh with the gentleman at the center of the bar who shares a joke about the west coast that

I don't get. I can see that Jack's glass is almost empty, and he's just staring ahead, but I'm hesitant to approach him. I'm still struggling with whether I'm happy to see him or want nothing to do with him.

"So, how long have you been in Springfield?" He asks it as I walk past, even though I'm avoiding eye contact. He finishes off his drink.

I pull out some remaining glasses from the dishwasher. "A little over ten years now."

He spins his empty glass on the bar top. "How are your parents?"

"Both have passed," I say.

"Oh. I'm sorry."

"Mom back in 2017. That's what brought me back here. To help with my father."

"When did he pass?"

"Just a few months ago."

He looks thoughtful. I move on and get some prep done for tomorrow.

"Listen, I'm sorry. I realize this is uncomfortable. The moment I recognized you, I should have turned around."

"Don't be silly." I point to his empty glass. "Let me get you another drink. On the house."

He gives me a hard stare. "You sure?"

I grab the bottle of Buffalo Trace and give it four tilts. "Absolutely. Here you go." I drop the glass in front of him.

"Well. Thank you."

"Absolutely."

He takes a drink, and I start slicing limes. The lounge is emptying out, just one man left at the bar and two people chatting on a couch.

He takes a breath and I reflexively tense.

"Listen, I feel I need to explain about—"

"Stop. Don't. It's in the past, Jack. No reason to drudge it all up now."

His mouth scrunches up. "I just feel I should—"

I slam the paring knife down on the cutting board. "Stop. Please. I really don't want to talk about it." I look right at him. "Okay? It's all good. It's fine. Let it go. Okay?" The last came out as a desperate plea. I'm getting angry, and I don't want to.

There's a heavy silence between us. He drinks with a certain frustration, not looking at me. I keep myself occupied with slicing and move on to some general cleaning. He finishes off his bourbon quickly and pulls two twenties out of his wallet. "I'm sorry for intruding on you like this." He slaps the cash on the table. "Goodbye, Pauline."

He stands up, turns around, and walks out of the bar.

"Wait, Jack—" But he's already at the elevators and either out of earshot or not willing to respond.

I turn back to the bar and start to load dirty glasses into the washing machine. From the center of the bar, I hear the gentleman who shared the joke about the west coast declare, "That seemed tense."

I turn and look over to him. "You have no idea."

I hang around the bar until 1:15am, a good hour past close. Will is a no-show.

I didn't need that tonight. I'm feeling miserable and worthless enough. I don't even understand why. Because of Jack? Seriously? He didn't turn me down when we were last together. I walked away from him. Why would his return make me feel any less about myself?

I get up, turn off the only light left on in the bar. Surrounded by darkness other than emergency lighting, I walk out of the

Long 9 and take the elevator down to the first floor. Say good-night to the overnight desk clerk and step into the quiet evening.

The bastard is happily married. Despite our encounter, our love making, he drove home to her, accepted her proposal, and married her.

What an asshole.

And yet, I'm feeling like I made the mistake. I let the opportunity pass. Had I wrongly played the noble card? Did I feign righteousness thinking he'd come back for me? Why didn't I just accept his fawning love and say to hell with Renee or Rhoda or whatever her name is?

I try to convince myself that I don't need anyone—don't want anyone mucking up my life. Tonight, however, I'm not buying it. I wanted Will to show up. I wanted someone to remind me that in some strange way, I can be desirable. Appealing. Wanted.

Because tonight, I don't feel that way. Not at all.

"Ah, hello, *mon chanson du cygne*," Ms. Deneaux says. "Come in."

I step inside the apartment and take my normal seat in that scarlet-cushioned Queen Anne chair against the wall. Her steps are more careful, slower, as she approaches the couch. She eases herself down and loops the oxygen tube around her head and under her nose.

"What did you call me? 'Shan-sun du-seena'?"

"*Chanson du cygne*. It basically means 'swan song.'" She smiles.

I smile back at her, and it tastes bittersweet as my mind travels back thirty years in my past. "Oh my goodness. You know, that was my nickname all through college and for many years after."

Ms. Deborah nods. "It doesn't surprise me. Because of your last name, obviously, but also something about your manner. Your presentation. You can be very dramatic, like it might be your last performance and you want to end with a flourish."

I laugh loudly at that. No one has ever dissected me in such a fashion. Not since Jack. It is inarguably an apt description. "You are an absolute joy to be around, Ms. Deborah."

She smiles. "You must call me DeeDee."

"How are you feeling today?"

She gives me a cautious but serious look. "I feel wonderful."

She doesn't look wonderful. I'm seeing her differently now since my conversation with Raymond and my deeper dive into pulmonary sarcoidosis. I notice how thin she is, I hear the tightness of her breathing, see the lesions against her scalp and poking up from her V-neck blouse. I've been too enamored with her life, her presence, to notice. Now, it is clear just how sick she really is.

I get up and sit down beside her on the couch, a position I haven't taken until now, but feel comfortable at this point getting closer to her. "How about we practice some belly breathing today?"

She wears a confused look. "Do what, now?"

"Belly breathing. Surely, they showed you this in rehab?"

"Dear, I haven't been to rehab in over two months."

"Well listen, diaphragmatic breathing—" I put my hand on my stomach "—breathing from down here in your belly—will help you take in more air when you need it."

She pulls back ever-so-slightly from me. "You don't say."

I nod and scooch closer. "It's also supposed to calm your stress response and help you overcome anxiety."

The quizzical look intensifies and turns into something approaching insult. "Just exactly what anxiety am I overcoming?"

Her negativity is not lost on me. "I mean, nothing right now, but when you find yourself short of breath or when your breathing is labored, that could certainly cause you anxiety, and this will help combat that."

She touches my thigh with her long, thin and well-manicured fingers. "*Mon cygne*, you do realize I'm dying?"

"Of course I do."

"Then don't be trying to cure me, please." She coughed for several moments. "I'm getting that enough from Raymond."

I feared this reaction, expected it, but hoped she would be more receptive to giving it a try. It's clear that she's going to be obstinate.

"Ms. Deborah, believe me. I'm not trying to cure you. I just want to help you be more comfortable in the time you have left, which could be many months from now. Especially if we work on a few exercises and techniques."

She pauses for a moment, and I think maybe I'm getting through to her. She inhales oxygen, then looks at me with sympathy. "Pauline, before you first came rapping on my door, I was in intensive care. They said my only hope was a lung and liver transplant. Told me my odds were little better than a coin flip. Oh, I'd have a hard year of recovery, take all this medication and do all sorts of rehab. If I was lucky, I might live another five or ten years. Without it—" Raise of shoulders and a scowl. "Maybe six months."

I suspect what happened next, but I take the bait. "And?"

Her headshake was adamant. "I told them no. That's why you're here." She moves closer to me and puts both hands on my thighs. "*M'dieu*, I'm seventy-six years old. Don't be chopping me up and piecing me back together with someone else's parts."

I put myself in her position and wonder if I'd make the same decision. Something tells me I might.

"I totally respect that, but listen, I'm not trying to operate on you or dump medications down your throat. I'm only trying to give you simple ways to help you breathe better while you can."

"Let me have what time I've left in peace, not in therapy."

"You've got a lot more story to tell me, and you can't do that without the breath to speak it."

She smiles, squeezes my leg, and I warm to her affection. "I didn't want anyone doting over me, you know. I was ready to boot you out the door soon as you first showed up here."

I laugh. "I know you were."

Sincerity washes over her. "I let you come back because there was something about you, made me think you knew how important it is that someone can still live fully and completely while heading toward the end. Don't disappoint me now. I don't need no nurse. Just need a friend."

I reach out impulsively and carefully envelope her thin, frail frame with my big one. She's hesitant for a moment but then wraps her arms around me.

"I am all that, DeeDee. Don't you worry."

We hold on to each other for a moment, then separate, neither of us quite able to look each other in the eye.

I say, "But, you need to respect that friendship is give and take. As a friend, you have to let me at least try to help you where I can while still respecting your wishes."

She gives me a slow, reluctant nod.

"All I ask is that you try a couple little things that will help to give us more quality time together. We can stop anytime."

She thinks about that for longer than I like but finally shrugs her shoulders. "Fine. Show me this belly breathing of yours."

"Excellent!"

She scowls. "But, don't you dare tell Raymond about this, you hear?"

I smile. "Cross my heart." That's probably a lie, but hopefully God will forgive me that one.

"And maybe I could get out just once more."

She's mentioned this several times. It always hurts me to say no. "Ms. DeeDee, I just don't see how—"

"Just for a night. A few hours." She looks so wistful. It almost appears as if color returns to her cheeks. "Sit and listen to a live band, enjoy a cocktail."

"I know. I know, but—"

She lays a hand over mine. "Pauline. A dying woman's wish..."

She's looking at me so intently, with so much desperation.

"Just think about it, dawlin'. Okay?"

I nod, pat her hand, and think that is the last thing I want to do.

CHAPTER FOURTEEN

Heartbreaker

"When I asked about your time in San Francisco, you told me that it might change my opinion about you. What did you mean by that?"

"Now, now. In time, dawlin'. In time. I have to be careful how I get you there."

"Well, I'll admit, I ache to hear more. Just remember to breathe and to not wear yourself out."

"Don't you worry about me. It's you who may need to remember to breathe. I know what's coming. You don't."

Nervous laugh. "I'm prepared to belly-breathe if I need to."

The first challenge after arriving in San Francisco was simply finding places to stay. Mitsy Blackburn, the local Black Panther Party chapter president, told them that Russell's cousin Joe was in jail following a Panther Patrol that went sour. As for Joe's place, urban renewal—"Or," she said, "what our brother James Baldwin refers to as *Negro removal*"—bulldozed

1860 8th Avenue a couple weeks ago. In the meantime, several Panthers offered up a couch or floor to Alfred, Russell, and Cole. Mitsy herself told DeeDee she could stay with her and her man Trevor until she was able to find a place.

Over the following days, DeeDee fell into survival mode. By necessity, her emotions mostly shut off, and she existed like an alley cat, each day simply a challenge of subsistence and safety. Years later, she would look back and realize she may have been experiencing a form of emotional shell shock or PTSD. Mitsy gave her space during that time, leaving DeeDee to essentially hide within herself. Over several days, though, by both acclimation and necessity, DeeDee came out of her hard cocoon of apprehension and dread to emerge more resilient and determined to survive and thrive.

Certainly, Mitsy and her Black Panthers helped to inspire DeeDee's renewed strength of will. The women Panthers, especially, exuded a different kind of power than their male counterparts, whose fortitude manifested through brawny intimidation as defenders of the people. The Panther Sisterhood meanwhile demonstrated strength through their natural aptitude for organizing, planning, and administration to tackle immediate needs. For the few weeks that DeeDee stayed with Mitsy, she took part in helping support the community initiatives largely developed and maintained by the sisters like free breakfast for school children, the food pantry, free ambulance service, and sickle-cell anemia testing.

She saw little of Alfred and the boys. They were full recruits, taking part in public demonstrations and preparing for when they would be part of the patrols and larger actions to uphold the Ten Point Program of the Black Panther Party. Those points demanded freedom and the power for Blacks to determine their destiny, full employment, restitution and compensation, access to decent housing, teaching the truth, free health care, an end to police brutality, an end to all wars of aggression, and freedom and justice for all imprisoned and oppressed Black and poor people.

"That's unrealistic," DeeDee said to Alfred as they placed food items donated by area stores in paper bags for the free food program.

"It's supposed to be. Those demands are to grab attention, to shake up the oppressive system, to let them know that we're not going back down until real change happens and the Black man can be free."

"And Black woman," DeeDee said, tossing apples into Alfred's bag.

"Right on, right on. It's all about power to the people. Our people. Dig?"

DeeDee understood, and while she certainly believed in the cause, she feared for her brother and was uneasy by what appeared to be a prevalence of weapons and force. In the few weeks she'd been involved with the Panthers, she knew that violence was not what the movement was about, but she also understood that the guns, the black outfits, and the militarized presentations created that perception. Was that suggestion of violence perpetuating more violence? Already, right or wrong, their co-founder, Huey Newton, was serving his third year in jail for voluntary manslaughter in the death of a police officer. Between the Panther's intimidations of the police, and the police's intimidations of the Panthers and the Black community, it seemed to DeeDee that so much of the good being done by the BPP had fallen under the shadowy wingspan of looming violence.

DeeDee rode the bus over the misty span of the Golden Gate Bridge. She'd been taking this same ride to her job at Bayview Diner for weeks now, and she still couldn't get over the feeling that she was sailing through the clouds as the fog obliterated the bay 220 feet down and lopped off the towers of the bridge that rose five hundred feet above.

Just about the time DeeDee had overstayed her welcome with Mitsy and Trevor, she landed a waitress job at the Marin City restaurant snuggled up against the Richardson Bay shoreline. It was a 30-minute ride by bus from the crappy little one-bedroom apartment she and Alfred found on Turk Street on the south side of the Fillmore District. Alfred gave her the bedroom and he slept on the couch—when he came home at all.

The bus travelled past the bridge, down the steep decline of Alexander Avenue and on to Bridgeway Street through the wealthy Sausalito retail district. The bus made a stop and lost most of its White passengers. She watched them join residents and tourists who strolled the collection of shops with bags full of trinkets and clothing and treats. On the other side, the blue expanse of the bay, Angel Island far off to the east, and Alcatraz further away to the south. The quaint, inviting Sausalito retail district brought back memories of her old Claiborne Avenue before it became home to the girth of the six-lane elevated section of I-10.

The bus motored to Marin City and to the end of the line at Gate 6 Road. DeeDee and the few remaining passengers got off as other people climbed on. It was just a little more than a block to the diner where DeeDee started her waitress shift in fifteen minutes.

The pay at the cafe wasn't good, but the tips most days allowed her just enough to help afford the apartment. Alfred still searched for a job in and around the area. She saw little of her brother. When he did come home, it was late every night, after DeeDee had already gone to bed, and he was out the door usually just as DeeDee was waking up.

DeeDee stepped through the front door and to a mostly empty dining area. That was predictable at 10:45 in the morning on a weekday. A man and woman sat quietly in one of the booths lining the exterior wall, the windows overlooking the boats docked at the pier in the bay. Of the dozen or so tables and chairs at the center of the dining room, only one was occupied by four men drinking coffee and chatting. Two men sat apart from one another on stools at the service counter. Dee moved around the counter and poured herself a cup of coffee.

"Hey, Double Dee," Cherise said as she slipped by with a tray of food.

"Morning," DeeDee said. "How was breakfast?"

"Decent, but nothing special." Her long legs and buxom figure maneuvered around the counter. "There's some prep waiting for you." Cherise headed to the table of four men.

"I'll get on it." DeeDee stood and sipped her coffee, trying to ignore the bitter burnt taste from the pot sitting too long on the burner. She stared out the windows looking at the boats on the pier.

"Refill?" The older, heavy-set man closest to her at counter pushed his coffee cup forward.

She wasn't clocked in for another ten minutes, but she grabbed the pot and topped off his cup.

He sipped the coffee and winced. "Gee-zuss. This is burnt to shit. Make another pot, will yeah?"

She gave him a wan smile and held up her cup. "You got that right. I'll get on it in a few when I clock in."

He gave her a stern look. "What are you doing behind the counter if you aren't working yet?"

"Sorry?"

"If you ain't working, get out from behind that counter."

DeeDee lowered her cup and looked at him with annoyance. "Settle down, now. I'll get to it in just a few minutes."

He nodded smugly. "Can't stand someone telling you what to do, eh? I sure do miss the days when you people weren't so uppity and did what you were supposed to."

DeeDee bellowed laughter as her eyes popped. "Are you kidding—"

Cherise came trotting back around the counter. "Hey, Hank. Hold tight, sweetie. Fresh pot coming up."

"See?" Hank said. "Cherise knows how to treat a customer." He leaned over the counter and slapped her ass as she moved past him.

DeeDee moved in, ready to say more, but Cherise stepped in front of her. "Why don't you get your apron on and get ready to clock in, Dee."

DeeDee scowled at the man, then at Cherise, and walked in back to the kitchen area. She stormed past Angelo who was assembling a triple-decker BLT. "Hiya, DeeDee," he said in his thick Filipino accent.

She snatched her apron and hat off her hook, put them on, grabbed her timecard and punched in. At the prep table, she took a butcher knife in hand and hacked away at cabbage for the coleslaw.

After a few minutes, Cherise came back and stood beside the prep table as DeeDee attacked the heads of cabbage.

"Cabbage gonna think twice before ever doing you wrong, girl," she said.

DeeDee swung the knife down. "Why do you put up with that, Cherise?"

Cherise lost her smile and stepped closer. "Because I've got three kids to feed, girl, and it's hard enough for a colored gal to raise her kids without losing her job to boot."

"I'm not going to put up with that. It's not right."

Cherise exhaled and jammed fists into her hips. "Good God, girl. If I made an issue out of every little comment made by a customer, I wouldn't get anything done round here." She gave DeeDee a hard stare. "I know who you've been hanging round with. But you ain't wearing the hat and leather here. Keep disrespecting customers and Darryl will put you on the street so fast that cute little head of yours will be spinning every which way."

Darryl, the owner of the diner, was more likely to slap DeeDee's ass than to defend it.

"I'm not a part of that, Cherise, you know that. Just helping out because they helped me and Alfred out."

"Yeah, well. Be careful you don't help yourself behind bars— or worse. Meantime, Double Dee? You do yourself a favor and suck it up when one of these idiots decide to talk garbage. I've already kind of grown attached to you, you know? And I don't wanna go through the hassle of training someone else."

DeeDee's temper cooled to Cherise's words and she offered a half smile. "Alright, I'll back off. Just to make you happy."

"That's what I like to hear." She squeezed DeeDee's shoulder. "Oh, hey. Reggie's staying home tonight and his mom is over to help look after the kids. Care to join me for a night on the town and some dancing? I thought we'd hit that new club here, Euphoria."

DeeDee smiled. "Been a while since I danced. I think I'm up for that."

"Alright, then. Lady Cherise and Double Dee to set the town on fire tonight!"

The Euphoria was a small dive of a bar that had been around in Marin City for a while but just reopened under its new name with a hipper look and feel. Music blared from the modest venue as people stuffed themselves inside.

It was a three-piece band laying down the heart-pounding funk groove that DeeDee felt against her chest. She and Cherise slowly moved toward the front of the stage and made space for themselves on the dance floor. DeeDee's slinky, alluring motions brought her back to those women at The Dew Drop Inn, and to that nightclub on Bourbon Street, but now, her body was more curvaceous, her dance more sultry, and everyone around her took notice.

Cherise danced alongside her at first, but by the middle of the second song it became apparent that DeeDee was the star of the evening. Cherise backed off and cheered her on as a circle formed around DeeDee. Men and women whooped and hollered as she gyrated to the music. For the first time since arriving in San Franciso, her turbulent emotions of anxiety, nervousness, and fear vaporized. She felt light and as if she were floating across the floor.

DeeDee moved with eyes closed and head in another place, where she could pretend to be whatever she wanted to be. Her dance was almost a witchcraft of desire and need to regain control over her life. She was reveling in this small space within the pulse of the music, taking possession of it and translating it to the audience in a body language uniquely her own. DeeDee opened her eyes, saw her audience encouraging her, and the thrill of it surged through her like electricity.

After the third song ended, she stepped out of the small space the crowd had made for her and found Cherise, who leaned in close among the din of adoring fans. "Girl, you are something else!"

"Let's find a place to sit. I need a drink," DeeDee said.

They slinked through the crowd and found a table. DeeDee relaxed while Cherise stared at her. "Where'd you learn to move like that?"

"I went to dance schools as a kid. It was a big deal in New Orleans."

"They taught you to dance like *that?* Some school!"

"No, dawlin'! That's how we moved at the Dew Drop Inn." She batted eyes, feigned bashfulness. "Well, suppose I may have added just a little of my own sauce."

Cherise laughed and fanned her face. "Well, that was something, honey! You were amazing."

"*Mersi.*"

"What are you having? I'll buy the first round."

"Whatever you're having."

Cherise worked her way through the crowd and toward the bar.

"Hey, beautiful."

DeeDee turned to see a man in his mid-thirties, pale white with thin, blond, piped mustache, small triangular goatee, and wispy swept-back hair gawking at her. His eyes were a bit sunken, his shirt loud. She gave him a nod but no other attention.

He leaned in, voice raised over the music. "I'm sorry, but I just have to know. Are you one of them—what do you call it—mulattos?"

DeeDee rolled her eyes at him. "Get lost, man." She turned to look for Cherise.

He moved in closer. "Hey, sorry. I honestly wasn't asking to offend, but I am curious."

"Well, you failed." She didn't want to give the guy any encouragement, but he also wasn't leaving, despite her cold shoulder. "If you must know, I'm Creole, not that it's any of your business."

The man put his hand to his heart. "I knew it! Oh. God. I love that. New Orleans, right? Jazz and blues and all that culture?"

She tossed her hair back. "Yes sir, that's one way to imagine New Orleans."

He stuffed his hands deep into the pockets of his white bellbottom pants. "You probably hear this all the time, but girl, you are beautiful."

DeeDee hadn't really heard that before. She'd received polite compliments in the past, but the only one who had really paid any attention to her had been Anthony Johnson. DeeDee had just started to realize, however, that in the last year, she'd grown into herself in a much more flattering way.

"Sure," DeeDee said. "Well, thanks."

He reached out and grasped her arm. "I'm not kidding. You're something special."

DeeDee yanked her arm away. "Thanks," she snapped, sharp and insistent.

Cherise returned, giving the man a cold stare as she handed a drink to DeeDee and sat down.

"Hey, listen. I'm not trying to pull anything or harass you." He slid a business card out of his breast pocket. "I run a night-club over on O'Farrell Street. We feature dancers every evening. You've got the moves, babe."

Cherise scoffed. "O'Farrell Street? The Tenderloin District?" Her voice raised. "Get out of town, you jive-ass turkey." She leaned into DeeDee. "It's a strip club, girl. No way you want that."

He handed DeeDee the black business card with gold foil lettering. "Well, if you'd ever want to start making some real money and show off that talent of yours, you give me a call, huh?"

DeeDee looked at the card: Simon DeReznor. Owner, Heartbreakers Gentleman's Club & CEO, Behind Closed Doors Productions. "Whatever."

"I'm not kidding. You could be making almost a hundred dollars a night."

That gave DeeDee a moment of pause. She was making $1.14 an hour plus tips. The idea of making a hundred dollars just from a night of dancing seemed ridiculous.

"I bet. But apparently without any clothes on, right?"

"Not necessarily. Depends on how much you want to earn."

"Right." DeeDee shook her head.

Simon DeReznor moved back into the cluster of friends he was with. "Well, you have my card. If you have any interest, give me a call."

"Whatever," DeeDee slipped the card in her bra and stood

back up. "Come on, Cherise. Time to dance!"

She slipped past Mr. DeReznor, grabbed Cherise by the hand, and pulled her back onto the dance floor. Raising her hands, moving to the rhythm of the music, in no time the night was once again hers.

Three weeks later, DeeDee was bussing her tables at the Bayside Diner when three men stepped in and sat at a table in her section. She vaguely recognized one of them but couldn't place him.

She dropped dirty plates and glasses in the bus tub, walked it to the dishwasher in the back, and headed out front again to the table. She brought three menus with her and handed them to the men. "Hi, fellas. Can I get you some waters to start?"

"Sure," one of the heavy-set guys said.

"You bet," another said.

"Good to see you again," said the third one with the mustache and small goatee.

"Who are you?" DeeDee asked with some annoyance. She was used to forward customers by now and one looked just like another. She did recognize him, but couldn't place him.

"Sorry. I'm Simon DeReznor. Ran into you at the Euphoria. I gave you my card."

Outside the context of dark, frenetic nightclub setting, without the flamboyant shirt, she hadn't made the connection. "Right. I remember."

"And I remember your moves, honey."

DeeDee certainly remembered his smarmy come-ons. "Well, thanks. You need a water?"

"Sure."

She headed back around the counter to pour three waters. Now she remembered. She hadn't entertained his proposal since

Cherise emphatically told her to forget about it the next day at work. And still, to be able to bring home anywhere close to an extra hundred dollars just by dancing? Was he serious? She suspected a huge catch, but supposed the obvious catch was that she'd be doing it naked, which wasn't going to happen. What was the name of the place? Heartbreakers? And then there was that other business of his. Back Door Productions or something like that? Didn't sound like the most legitimate company.

She served their waters. "Are you ready to order? Or do you need more time?"

He looked up to her. "How about you? Are you ready to earn some serious money with those moves of yours?"

She gave a heavy sigh. "Listen. You think I'm stupid? I'm not taking my clothes off for anyone—especially not for a crowd of men."

He nodded. "I'm not asking you to. Like I said, that's up to you. Our opening acts don't strip all the way down."

"Just mostly, right?"

He grinned. "Well, they wear just enough to keep the men guessing. But they also only make a fraction of what the main acts make."

Alfred still hadn't found a steady job, and all of the money she earned at the diner went to last month's rent. They were relying on the Panther's Free Food program, but the fact was, the living was lean. Even an extra twenty-five dollars a night could really make a difference.

"Maybe I'll stop by some time to catch a show."

"You do that. I'm telling you, with your moves and your looks, you could be a top earner."

"Whatever. Now, what can I get you?"

She took their order and, by the end of her shift, convinced herself to stop by the club and check it out. She did not realize just how much that decision would end up changing her life forever.

CHAPTER FIFTEEN

Reconciliation

I t's late in the evening. The Long 9 Lounge is finally settling down after a big surge of patrons came through and ordered just about everything under the sun. Margie, my young energetic accomplice behind the bar, let me take a moment to rest and catch my breath. I fear I'm getting too old to be behind this bar anymore. I tire out more easily, and my back is in considerable pain by the time my shift is over.

At the end of the bar, I sip a glass of seltzer water, and DeeDee's soft voice plays in my head sharing her story with her songful lilt of voice. I had just started to talk about it with Margie before it got busy.

"So, I didn't get to tell you the wildest part about Ms. X."

Margie pours a shot of top-shelf Scotch and hands it to an older gentleman in a suit. She swings back to me. "Oh, that's right! Do tell! Your Ms. X sounds amazing." She drops elbows on the counter, little twenty-something behind stuck out and up under her pleated shirt. I see the older man's eyes linger on

Margie before knocking back his shot.

I return to narrative story mode. "Well, a few days later, she did indeed go to that club—"

"The strip club?"

"Heartbreakers. Yes indeed. She watched a couple of girls dance—"

"You mean strip?" Margie's eyes are almost popping out of her head.

"She didn't hang around for that, but after seeing the first two girls, she went up to that sleezy guy and told him she was in."

Margie's jaw drops. "No. Shit."

I smile and nod. I've had the better part of a day to adjust to that story, but when Ms. Deborah was telling me, I probably looked just like Margie does now. At first, the thought of her dancing in front of a roomful of horny, depraved men in a dark room shocked me, then made me sad to think she had to resort to that. But DeeDee shared the story upright and without shame. Her chest actually puffed out and her shoulders rolled back. That was DeeDee Deneaux surviving by doing what she did best, and she took control of the situation. Sitting here now and retelling the story, I have the deepest admiration for her.

Margie obviously feels the same. "Well, damn! Ain't she the shit? That is so dope!"

"It certainly is. She worked at the diner five and six days a week during the day and danced on Tuesday and Wednesday nights."

Margie's brow arches. "Wow."

"Apparently, she got quite popular, and before long she was a weekend Heartbreaker."

Margie's head slowly shakes as her lips purse, and she stands upright. "Well, respect. I couldn't do it."

My laugh is dry. "No one would *want* me to do it."

Margie's hand goes to her hip as she stares me down. Here comes another lecture. "Just stop that, Pauline. I swear, I'm sick of telling you this. You're beautiful. You don't think so, but you are. Hear me? Say it."

I don't need pep talks from Gen Alpha beauty queens like Margie. She has no concept of growing up in a world where other children call you ape and Sasquatch. A world in which, as an adolescent girl tearing up and filled with dread on your first day in middle school, your mother brushes your hair and consoles by saying, "Make sure you stand up straight and smile, Sweety. Beauty isn't everything."

"Come on, Pauline. Say it. You're beautiful."

I've lived more than five decades. Margie's a sweet girl, but I don't need her Pollyanna attitude. I get up. "*You're* beautiful." I walk around the bar. "And I'm old."

Margie calls after me. "I bet that's not your Ms. X's attitude!"

I tend to three women who come in, looking like they're either celebrating something or otherwise thankful that something is over. I take their order, clear and wipe down the area where that man in the suit had been sitting, look up, and wouldn't you know it? Jack is back.

"Do you mind if I order a drink?" Jack's sad, puppy-dog eyes plead with me to be civil.

"I'm certainly not going to refuse you service. What are you drinking?"

"Can I get a Guiness?"

"Coming right up."

I open the tap on half a pint, then let it sit while I pour a chardonnay and two cabs for the three women. Margie glares at me and motions not so subtly to Jack. Her lips exaggerate the words, *That him?* I nod, come back to his glass and finish the pour.

"Here you go." I set the cascading stout in front of him.

"Thank you."

I nod and step away to check on the few other customers in the bar. As I prepare a Cosmo for a lady from Des Moines and an Old Fashioned for the guy from Michigan, my thoughts start to skip back in time—to twenty years ago and my first engagement with Jack and fifteen years ago with his sudden return. Both times ended in pain and loss for me. I tell myself that, no matter what happens now, I will not be hurt again.

"I'm sorry for being back here."

I give him a nonchalant roll of shoulders. "It's no problem."

"For what it's worth, it's good to see you again."

I give the shaker a rinse of water and start to wipe down my area. "Good to hear," I say.

Silence follows for a bit. I very intentionally avoid any eye contact, but I can sense his eyes follow as I move about the bar to mix drinks and serve others.

Margie has stepped up beside me and leans in to Jack. "Hey, man. Isn't she beautiful?" She hooks a thumb at me, and I want to shout into her clever doll-like face.

Jack's eyes hold to mine like a vice. He wears such a sad smile. "Oh yes. She is beautiful."

"Hah!" Margie whips my arm with a towel. "See? Told you."

If only I could shoot lasers out of my eyes right now. "Isn't it your bedtime?"

Margie steps away. "Good one, Mom!"

I really do love Margie, but she knows how to get under my skin like few others.

I turn back to Jack and his eyes are still locked onto mine. I can't keep hold on that intensity of contact and I look down. His head drops as well.

"Somehow I became the bad guy in all of this, didn't I?" His voice is just above a whisper, "Sorry for that."

Instead of the anger I've held at bay for so many years, I'm just sad now. I respond in a low voice. "Jack, you slept with me when you were engaged." I let that hang in the air in front of him.

Jack shakes his head. "I wish you had understood—I came

back to see if you still had feelings for me. It was the only reason I was holding out on Rachel."

For years, whenever I thought about that night, I'd glow hot like iron in a forge. I would curse Jack and hate myself for allowing it to happen. As much as anything else, AA helped me put it behind me, to put it in the past. Boxed up and put on a shelf, it became separate from me. That box is torn open now, its stony contents crumbled to dusty regret.

"You used me, Jack. You may not have intended to, but you used me to be an excuse to leave her—because you weren't strong enough to do it on your own. I wasn't going to be a means for you to break your commitment and ease your conscience."

He nods, takes a swig of black ale. "I didn't realize that at the time, but I recognize that now. I'm sorry for that."

My arms are crossed in a way that feels overly judgmental, so I lean against the counter and look sideways at him. "You know, the first time, when you left me the way you did? That hurt, but I understood. I didn't blame you for that. It was a terrible mess of a time for both of us. But when I finally got my life back in order, you showed up again and it was like you thought, 'How can I screw her up even more?'" His face falls to that and I try to soften the moment. "It's not that hard to do, you know."

Jack put his head in his hands. "Oh, Christ, I don't even know how to begin to apologize."

I smile. "I'll pretend you're praying for guidance."

There is so much regret and sincerity in his eyes. It's too hard to ignore him, as much as I don't want to hear whatever he says next.

"Why do you think I came back here tonight, Pauline? I realize how much I hurt you, how much I'm the shithead. Knowing that I didn't intend to hurt you means absolutely nothing when my actions did—deeply—hurt you. That's on me. I'm sorry. I can't make up for it, but I just want you to know that I wish more than anything I could go back and approach you honestly. To tell you up front that I was about to marry someone, but that I never stopped thinking about you. When I finally happened upon a way to find you, I felt I had to do it. Back then, I would have risked everything to finally have a chance with you if you felt the same way. But I handled it like a thoughtless idiot. I'm deeply sorry for that." His eyes plead with me—not, it seems, for forgiveness or understanding, but simply to believe him. It's hard not to.

"Well," I say, drying a wine glass and hanging it with the others above me, "you very convincingly make me believe you at least understand my feelings and regret your actions."

"On both counts, I do. Truly."

I look at his face and despite the years, the extra weight, and the facial hair, I see my old Mr. Jack looking at me. "Well, why don't we put all of this behind us?"

"I would like that." He raises his beer glass to me.

"So," I say, "How's life been these last fifteen years?"

Morning sunlight breaks through my bedroom window as I curl into a ball beneath bed covers and wipe at my wet eyes.

I dreamt that Jack and I were married. We were living in a cozy little home somewhere. It was old Jack from many years ago, still slim with his glorious dark blond waves of hair and his clean-shaven face. Kaiya was a beautiful five-year-old with golden curls and an angel's laugh as she rode on Jack's shoulders.

Mother and Father were there in our perfect living room, mother knitting a cap or sweater for Kaiya, while Father called out to Jack about the Bears scoring another touchdown as he munched popcorn.

I brought out a plate of my fanciest Midwest hors d'oeuvres to my parents—crackers stacked with cured meat, cheeses, and veggies. They smiled at me with such pride and happiness for how our lives had turned out. I smiled back at them, then turned to Jack who beamed at me while he held Kaiya's legs around his neck and pranced around, a giddy father.

The dream is hard to shake as I start my day. Is God trying to tell me something by throwing all my regrets and failings into a single dream? That's some tough love there, God.

There's little doubt that the dream was provoked by the time I spent with Jack last night. We had a good talk and I enjoyed our time together. In a way, it was an interesting experience, almost like meeting a new Jack. He is, after all, free of all that nonsense about ending the world, about being obsessed with nothingness. He's the same thoughtful, introspective Jack, but without all that morose nihilistic garbage. He seems genuinely happy, though there were moments when he spoke of his wife that his voice turned somewhat wistful, and I wonder if he isn't completely content in his marriage.

He leaves for home this morning, and I'm glad for that. Happy he is exiting my life once again, but this time on a positive note. It was absurd he ever had that much influence over me. It's time to be over him.

Good bye, Mr. Jack.

CHAPTER SIXTEEN

The Unwanted

My intention is to visit Ms. Deborah at least two times a week. It's been a few days since I stopped by, so I make a special trip on my day off right after Sunday church. On my way over, as I near River Bend senior apartments, I see an ambulance ahead of me, hear its siren blaring and its lights flashing. I pull over to the side as it whizzes past me on the other side of the road, headed in the opposite direction. I can't help but think that someone at River Bend had a medical emergency. It must be a regular stop for ambulance services.

I pull into the parking lot and slip into an empty visitor space. Grab my bag, walk down the hall, and just as I'm about to knock on Ms. Deborah's door, it swings open.

"Oh!" The surprised exclamation from Julienne makes me jump. I laugh out loud.

"Hi!" I say, nervously enthusiastic.

"Pauline!" Jules says.

"Pauline?" I hear Raymond from behind her. He moves into

view behind Jules. "Oh, hello."

They both seem a bit disconcerted, and I'm not sure if it's just my sudden appearance or something else. "Is this a good time?"

Julienne looks up and over at her father, smiles sympathetically at me and slips out of the doorway and against the hallway wall. Raymond steps out after, his countenance somber as he faces me.

"Mother had a rough night."

"Oh no." My heart sinks. The ambulance. It was hers. Oh, my Lord, please look over her. But then rational thought takes over and I realize that she's in hospice, so that wouldn't make sense. There's a recent tendency for me to get too emotional and overreact. I need to calm down. "Is she okay?"

"She's fine. She's resting now. When we came earlier this morning to visit, we found out she had been up all night coughing."

Jules said, "She looked terrible! So tired and pale. She was barely able to talk to us."

"It got so bad she was coughing up a little blood," Raymond says. "We called the doctor, and he had us pick up a heavier prescription of expectorants and a non-invasive ventilator. That seems to have calmed her down enough that she finally fell asleep."

I should have been here yesterday. We could have worked on her diaphragmatic breathing and stretching exercises. Maybe this could have been avoided.

"As soon as she's better, I'll work harder with her on some ways to help her breathing."

Raymond nods, but his lips are pursed tight and jaw clenched. "I wanted to bring her to emergency, but she insists on staying with hospice and not receiving any treatment or care for this. I don't understand it."

Jules rubs her father's back. "I know, Dad. But it's her life. Her wish."

"It's selfish. She's always been selfish."

It's getting a little uncomfortable to hear Raymond refer to Ms. Deborah that way while she's bedridden and suffering. I try to quickly change the subject.

"Well, I'll let her rest for now and stop by later tonight."

"I appreciate that," Raymond says, "But I've secured the services of an on-call nurse. Nancy will be stopping by periodically and will be available as needed. Her number is on the refrigerator. Meanwhile, I'll be back here in a little while to watch over her tonight. But if you could be here tomorrow? That would be a big help."

"Absolutely," I say. "I guess for today I'll just have to find something else to occupy my time." I'm so disappointed that I can't be with Ms. Deborah. Part of me wants to go in there just to be by her side, but the more sensible part of me thinks Raymond needs this time to be the good son and watch over her.

Jules is elbowing her father and mumbling. He looks at her with confusion.

"Ask her," she says just loud enough for me to hear. Raymond shakes his head and Julienne nods back aggressively in retort. In the short time I've known them, I'm getting the impression that Jules holds significant sway over her father.

Poor Raymond looks at me, about as uncomfortable as a person can be. He crosses his arms, only to drop them to his sides. "Pauline? Um, since Mother's unfortunate downturn, um, has caused you a, a vacancy, so to speak, in your schedule today—well, we were wondering, if you didn't have anything better to do, would you be at all interested in joining us for brunch?"

Wow. Tall, imposing Raymond, and he looks ready to break out in beads of sweat on that shaved scalp of his. The poor man really struggled through that. I'm tempted to playfully poke at his awkwardness, but I'm not sure Raymond is one to joke around with—at least not this early in our relationship. I refrain and smile graciously.

"Well, I wouldn't want to intrude—"

Jules steps forward and grabs both my hands. "Oh, please? Please, Pauline? Spend some time with us, would you? Grann won't stop talking about you!"

My smile is so big I can hardly hold it. "Well, if you insist—"

"We do!" Jules says.

"Excellent!" I say. "You can tell me all about your first week at school."

Raymond smiles painfully, and it's unclear if he's upset because he had hoped to spend time alone with his daughter, or if he just doesn't want to spend time with me. Whatever the reason, in some perverse way, his reluctance to invite me makes it that much more enjoyable to join them.

Raymond offers to drive, and we travel a half mile down the boulevard to a family restaurant called The Sunnyside. Jules tells me that they've taken Ms. Deborah here for breakfast many times over the past year. It's still fairly busy at eleven o'clock in the morning, but they're able to get a booth right away. The hostess hands out waters, napkins, and silverware. While we wait for the server, Jules fills me in on the start of her academic career.

"...stupid math and science classes. Ugh. I wish I didn't have to take them. English isn't too bad. But at least I was able to get a couple of my electives signed up. One's a social justice class and I think it's going to be fantastic!"

I vaguely remember my college days, how excited and enthusiastic I was in the beginning, once I got over being completely terrified. Back then, I was on the cusp of my world opening up like a flower bud. I discovered a group of people that not only accepted me, but liked me. I suddenly had dreams and desires I never thought possible before. I was somebody, and I could be almost anything. Of course, the addictions to alcohol and attention, the desperation to be wanted, changed everything. It was an emotional trap door that dropped me down and into a very dark and dismal psychological oubliette.

"Just remember," I say, "those general courses are there for a reason. If you decide to pursue your social work program, you'll need a well-rounded education."

She reluctantly nods and shrugs.

"But it's also important that you don't get lost in all that humanity around you. Just remember—many of your fellow students are experiencing a freedom like they've never had before. Not all of them will be able to moderate it appropriately. Keep your mind on your long-term goals. Don't get lured into the seductive instant gratifications that college can offer."

"Did he pay you to say all that?" Jules says, flicking a thumb at her father. I get the impression she either isn't understanding or doesn't want to hear.

Raymond, whose attention has been on me for my entire diatribe, turns to Jules. "Pauline is right. You may not fully understand it now, but there will be a lot of things on campus that will steer you off-course if you let it. Don't get too wrapped up in your basketball and other extracurriculars and neglect your studies. Be true to yourself, and be focused on your goals, and you'll do great."

Every part of Jule's visage makes it clear she is done with being preached at. She looks with renewed enthusiasm at me. "What did you study in college?"

The waitress appears, and we ask for three coffees.

"I ended up majoring in Library Sciences. I minored in Women's Literature from 19th century to present."

"Huh." Jules doesn't seem very impressed.

"I also wrote risqué poetry and was very popular at the area poetry slams." I give her a devilish grin.

"Awesome," she says. "I figured you had a bit of rebel in you."

That label is a long, taut stretch, but I shamelessly wear it like a badge, even if I can't live up to it.

"So, are you a librarian?" Raymond asks. "I thought Mother mentioned you were a bartender."

I sip my coffee and let the unintended sting of the question subside. "I was. Life took a left turn. I've been tending bar at a downtown convention center for a little over ten years now." I mention Mother's death and moving from St. Louis to be with my father.

"You were close to your parents, then?" Raymond asks.

I'm not sure how prepared I am to share with Raymond any details about my relationship with my parents. I choose words carefully. "Our relationship was…complicated. But I loved them, and they were good parents."

Something about what I said tightens Raymonds face, intensifies his look, but he is quiet.

The pause in conversation lingers until I feel compelled to fill it. "Your mother—grandmother—is an amazing woman. What a story she has to tell!"

Raymond pulls back, nodding only half-heartedly. "She certainly does."

Jules is more enthusiastic. "You probably already know more than I do!"

I start rattling off some of her dramatic life moments like they are favorite scenes from a movie. "Her stories of Claiborne Avenue and the Tremé neighborhood? Her dancing? Her move to San Francisco?"

Jules is almost giddy. "Isn't is all amazing?"

"And there's still so much I don't know."

I see Raymond, and he's swallowing our words like bitter pills.

The waitress returns. We apologize for not looking over the

menu yet but manage to order quickly. Jules gets the breakfast parfait, I order the garden omelet, and Raymond gets two eggs over easy with hashbrowns, sausage and toast.

The three of us eat our brunch. Jules and I continue to talk about Ms. Deborah. Jules refers to one of her grandmother's favorite childhood memories, watching the Black Mardis Gras parade that would run down Claiborne Avenue. It sounds wonderful and I must ask DeeDee about it.

"Excuse me," Jules says. "I'll be right back." She takes off toward the bathrooms.

I sit uncomfortably with Raymond. He is fixated on his food and hasn't said a word since I brought his mother into the conversation. He's clearly unwilling to break our silence, so after a moment I step in with a risky gamble. "The parent-child relationship can certainly be a challenge."

Raymond looks at me with a bit of shock. "Are you referring to my relationship with Jules, with my mother, or some experience of your own?"

"Yes." I hope my smile is more consoling than smug.

He's more sensitive than I expected. His tall stature and broad shoulders, the confident cut of his chin and heavy brow combine to present a stolid demeanor, but Raymond appears to have some insecurities. I need to be careful with him.

"Well," I say, "in all honesty, my father-daughter relationship was challenging to say the least, but I shouldn't assume that compares in any way to your relationship with your mother. I'm sorry if I misread anything."

"We get along fine," he says.

"My father and I did not," I say. "He was uncomfortable with me as a child, nervous around me as a teen, and extremely critical of my young adult years."

"I'm sorry," Raymond says, though he still won't look at me.

"Admittedly, it's not like I didn't deserve it by the time I was a young adult."

I think he tries to chuckle, but it comes out as more of a grunt.

"Well, I didn't have a father," he says, "so I'm equally unable to relate to your situation."

I take a sip of water. "I suppose that was hard? Not having a father in your childhood?"

He connects with my fervent stare. "Why? Your father was so amazing?"

That stops me cold. I'm talking too much. Needling into personal matters I shouldn't be. It wasn't my intention. I'm too nervous around Raymond. I need to keep my mouth closed around him. My finger drags through the water ring my glass leaves, and silence returns to our table.

"Listen," he says finally, sharp enough that I snap my head up. "This gets a little more personal than I'm comfortable with, but that amazing woman you and Julienne are so enamored by was no wonderful mother to me. I was an accident that happened to her, something she was forced to deal with. I was nothing but a regret to her. No father? I never even had a mother. I had a woman who rued the day I was conceived."

I obviously rubbed salt in a much deeper wound than I could have realized. Now I'm regretful but also defensive of Ms. Deneaux. "I'm sorry. I can only imagine how hard it must have been growing up like that. Thinking your mother didn't care about you. I can't believe any of it was intentional on her part."

His head bobs, but every part of his expression is in total disagreement. "You think so, huh? Tell me, do you see any pictures of me in that apartment of hers? Do you see anything to suggest that she cared at all about me? That she likes to reflect fondly on her little boy? Or does she just enjoy reflecting on her oh-so-amazing life as the Amazing Deborah Deneaux?"

It's only as he says it, that I realize the obvious omission of Raymond in that museum of Ms. Deneaux's past. I have come to know her living room well, and I can recall no pictures of Raymond—as baby, child, young adult, or adult. Not even a picture of her granddaughter.

"Uh, huh. I got you, didn't I? Now you can begin to understand. I was an inconvenience to her. An intrusion on her glorious path to success."

I want to say so much. I can't say anything.

He looks and sees Jules returning. "Frankly? I honestly don't know how much I'd have to do with her if not for Julienne. But Jules loves her, and she seems to love Jules. So, I deal with it. But I owe her nothing."

I think I nod, fighting the further urge to say more. My family history is messy enough. Hearing Raymond explain his relationship with Ms. Deborah just makes me more miserable. I can't imagine her being so cold, so apathetic to her son, and yet, Raymond's feelings are sincere, and whether true or not, his pain is real and acute, and it makes me incredibly sad.

James L. Peters

CHAPTER SEVENTEEN

The Request

The following Monday morning, I'm up extra early. I'm anxious to get to Ms. Deborah's apartment and see how she's doing.

Raymond keeps slipping into my thoughts, and it's difficult to parse out my sympathies for him against my admiration for his mother. I suspect—just like my feelings for my parents—more of it lies on him than he may realize. Childhood is a confusing time. Our brains—just starting to build the neuropathways that eventually result in effective reasoning. Our emotions—still raw nerves waiting for the skin of temperance and sensibility to cover over and protect their sensitivities. As children, we are humans in progress. So much of what we perceive and understand at that time tends to carry over into our adulthood. Somehow, by applying rational thought to irrational emotions, we can sometimes misinterpret or worse yet reimagine events that we were too young and foolish to ever understand.

I want to think that's the case with Raymond, because it's hard to believe that DeeDee was negligent and uncaring as a mother.

I look at myself in the bathroom mirror, open my robe to reveal the tattooed Celtic cross that sits just above my navel, Kaiya's name wrapping it in flowing banderole. I was almost a mother. I wasn't ready to be one. I suspect I would have been a horrible one. Maybe Kaiya would have ended up like Raymond and resented me—or worse.

But to the best of my knowledge, DeeDee had never been a drunk. And I don't expect she was ever wayward—not in the way I was. Who knows what path Kaiya would have been led down being raised by a drunken, lost mother.

My stomach aches all the way to my soul. I don't want to think about that anymore.

I rush through my morning preparations, get dressed, and I'm out the door a little after seven in the morning. The sun is just peeking up over the horizon. I don't see the sunrise very often. Working late most nights, I often miss the birth of the day.

Today, before I get into my VW, I stop. I walk over and sit against the tree on the strip of grass between sidewalk and road. I watch as the day miraculously begins again with a melancholy awe.

I approach DeeDee's apartment with a small bouquet of daisies and carnations in my hand. The grocery store on the corner is the only place that sells them this time of day. It's only a little after 7:30 in the morning and I don't want to wake her if she's sleeping, so I knock lightly. After a few moments, the door opens, and Raymond greets me.

"Hi, Pauline. It's good to see you." His voice is just above a whisper, so I assume DeeDee is asleep. His disposition is much more welcoming today. He gives me a little smile.

"Is it a good time?" I ask.

He nods. "Actually, it's a perfect time. I was hoping I could get to work for a morning meeting, but I didn't want to leave her alone."

"Oh, Raymond. Feel free to call me if you ever need me to be here. I'll do whatever I can, whenever I can. You have my number from Hospice, right?"

He waves a hand at me. "Well, I don't want to take advantage of you."

Does he say that sincerely, or is he referencing our earlier conversation in the hallway? That discussion—my soft condemnation of his expectations of me—has played over and over in my head, and I fear I was too harsh. That I wasn't sympathetic enough. However, his intentions now seem genuine, so I refuse to think the worst.

"Don't worry about that. I'll be honest with you about what I am and am not able to do."

He nods. "I believe that."

There's a familiar moment of uncomfortable silence between us.

"Listen," he says. "When we were together last. At the restaurant. I said more than I should have."

"Please. Don't worry about it. Not that I can know in any way what you've experienced, but I certainly have my own issues with my parents."

"Well, I don't want you to think that I'm ungrateful, or that my mother is some kind of horrible person. I— I tend to over-react when she is put on such a high pedestal as Julienne and you do, even though I totally understand why."

I nod. "Duly noted. I can see where that could be frustrating."

He shakes his head. "Perhaps. But it's juvenile. I'm sorry." He looks behind him, to what I assume is DeeDee's bedroom. "I suppose all this has dredged up a lot of feelings I thought I had buried."

Raymond and I have more in common, at least currently,

than I realized. "Raymond, would you be offended if I offered some advice?"

He looks back at me. "I'll do my best not to be." He smiles.

I take a breath. I don't cry often, but my emotions have been all over the place lately. Perimenopause? Likely, but when I think or speak about anything with emotional resonance lately, I tear up and my voice wavers. I don't like it, and I'm hyper-focused on avoiding it now.

"I mentioned that I'm currently clearing out my parent's house for sale. Finding so many objects that recall moments from my past, of their past. It's been an overwhelming experience."

"I bet it has."

I fear I'm looking at him too intensely now, but I'm simply holding back a well of emotion that would otherwise derail me. "Try to talk to your mother about those feelings that have been exhumed from your past. Don't accuse. Don't argue. Just be honest and sincere and loving. Explain to her what you have been confused or hurt about."

He's already deflecting this suggestion by shifting in place and moving his head in resistance. "Oh, I don't think—"

I risk laying a hand on his arm. "Make sure you don't end up like me, where every item I find triggers only pain and regret. There's nothing wrong with feeling angry about things your mother did or didn't do. But if you don't confront her about it, you'll never find out that—maybe—it had nothing to do with you and everything to do with her. Meanwhile, it may be a way to rediscover the good times that may have been buried by the bad."

He at least seems to take in what I've said, though his lack of eye contact tells me he will be processing it for a while.

"I appreciate that. Right now, I'm just trying to do what I need to do for her, and I don't feel like it's been enough."

"Don't be silly. You're doing fine."

He scoffs. "Says the woman who left her career to be

a companion to the father she didn't get along with for a decade. Meanwhile, I'm trying to get to a work meeting. Sure, I'm a real martyr."

"Raymond, you're here. When she needs you. You care. You worry. You are a good son."

That seems to soften the tension on his face. He steps aside and gestures to the living room. "I'm sorry. Please, come in. She's still sleeping, but I'd expect her to wake up any time." He looks at the flowers. "For Mother?"

I nod and offer them to him.

I step inside. My heart beats just a little harder seeing the dark, empty living room instead of having Ms. Deborah on the couch.

"She really has rested well," he says as he finds a vase and fills it with water. "Nancy, the nurse I mentioned, stopped by. She said the ventilator should help at nighttime and during her sleeping. She thought Mother should stay in bed for a few days. She put a wedge pillow under her to keep her upright. She suggested getting a recliner for the living room so she can be more comfortable out of bed."

I nod. "That all sounds good. I'll keep working with her on her breathing."

"Thank you." He puts the flowers in the vase, then looks at his watch. "Listen, I'm so sorry, but if I can make this meeting for work—"

"Go," I say. "Everything is under control. That's what I'm here for."

To this day, I still feel ungainly and oafish at my height. It's nice, however, to not have to look down on someone while they look with gratitude at me. I beam back at him.

He heads for the door. Opening it, he stops and turns around. "You know, she's right about you." Eyes fall, then reconnect. "You are special."

Before I have any chance to respond, he's out the door.

Her bedroom door is open a crack, so I ever-so-gently push against it just enough to peek inside and see if she is awake.

Her bedroom is, if possible, even more a of a time capsule of her past and her family. I feel like I know them enough now to recognize each member of the Deneaux family and the part of history captured in each framed picture hanging on the wall or on top of a dresser or nightstand.

There's Georges and Aurelia Deneaux, her parents, on their wedding day. Here's a photo of George Junior in his military uniform, probably taken when graduating boot camp. A dramatic picture of Alfred, fist raised, while he dons black sunglasses, beret, and leather jacket. There's several of Julienne as a little girl, and one that must be her graduation photo. And yes, despite Raymond's comment the other night, there are pictures that must be him. One picture is of Raymond as a chubby newborn. Another shows DeeDee in graduation gown with a hand resting on the shoulder of a four- or five-year-old Raymond while her other arm drapes around some pretty woman. One picture has Raymond looking to be about seven and holding his mother's hand in front of an elementary school entrance. And then there's Raymond's high school graduation photo.

Joyful baby Raymond. Happy toddler Raymond. By seven, Raymond appears sad and withdrawn. At seventeen, he displays intensity under a large afro and scruffy mustache. Neither frown nor smile in that picture. He seems to be simply pausing for a moment before returning to the angst and frustration of teenage drama.

All these moments draw my attention, but what grabs it and shakes it is the large portrait above her queen poster bed. My cheeks heat up the moment I see it. It's a—what do you call it?—A boudoir oil painting of Deborah Deneaux, at least five feet across. She is reclined on a plush, velvet chaise lounge in a scarlet parlor. She is quite naked, with a poofy, feathery pink boa slinking down and around her body to cover up just enough to hide her private parts. Her expression waxes both seductive and bemused, which somehow makes her all the more alluring. She is beautiful and, in some way I can't begin to explain or understand, powerful.

"Pauline," I hear her whisper, her voice muffled by the ventilator mask.

I didn't realize I had moved so far into the room until this moment. I was too captivated by the surroundings. Now I'm embarrassed.

"I'm sorry," I say softly. "I was just checking on you. Please, rest."

She struggles a bit with the mask and finally pulls it off her face. "I've rested enough. Please. Sit by me. I've missed you."

I take the chair sitting by her bed, move it closer, sit, and take her hand in mine. "How are you feeling, DeeDee?"

"I'm fine, *mon cygne*. Just a bad spell. I'm sorry we missed our time yesterday." She coughs. "They put me back on prednisone and the nurse gave me some steroid injection. It's helping a lot."

"I'm glad to hear it."

Her expression turns very serious. "I did try that silly stomach breathing of yours, you know. Lot of good that did!" She laughs, which immediately turns to more coughing.

I pat her hand. "Now, now. We haven't had nearly enough time with that to get you proficient in the technique. We'll keep working on that as you get better."

A wan smile. "Of course, I won't be getting better."

I try to return the smile while holding back those emotional tears I'm struggling to control. "Yes, but there's so much we can do to help you extend the time you have left." With my other hand, I hold hers close to my heart. "There's so much life in you yet, DeeDee. I plan to squeeze out every ounce. But I'll need your help with that. Okay?"

"You are a dear, you know that?" Weakly lifting her arm, she puts her other hand over mine. We stay like that for some time, each hand covering the other, pale cream over golden brown. Twenty-three years apart, and our experiences a lifetime apart. It's difficult to believe I've only known this woman for little more than a month, but she has had a greater impact on me than almost anyone I have known.

"I'll tell you what," she says. "I'll do your silly exercises and follow the advice of you and that nurse—what's her name?"

"Nancy, I think."

"But you need to do something for me."

I'm not sure I'm going to like where this is going. "Okay…"

She takes a long moment. "Ever since my last time in the hospital, I've been cooped up in this apartment. I know that soon I'm not going to ever be able to leave. Please. Just once, get me out of here. Take me some place with some atmosphere, where a band is playing. I want to enjoy the evening one last time."

"DeeDee, how in the world—"

"Please. Can you do that for me?" Her eyes are moist and pleading as she sputters with more coughing.

I'm flabbergasted. What can I say? She's so frail, needing constant oxygen, and she expects me to take her to some nightclub? That's insane. And where would I even take her? I know nothing about the nightlife in town here. And Raymond. If he found out? He'd go ballistic. On top of that, what would happen if St. John's Hospice found out?

"Oh, DeeDee. I don't know—"

With effort, she shifts her body up higher on the bed to be mostly upright. "It's my last chance, Pauline. I know it. Very soon, my body won't allow it anymore. I need to have this one last time." Her face straining, she leans in closer. "You're not going to refuse the dying wish of an old woman, are you, dawlin'?"

My head is shaking, and I still have no answer for her. The request is unreasonable, but how can I let her down? It's her life, and she wants to live as much of it as she can before she's gone. I'm not going to be the one to deny her that.

"Will you work hard with me on your breathing?"

A dutiful dip of head. "I will."

"And no complaining about your stretching routines?"

"Absolutely not."

"By God, I want your complete cooperation so we can recover your strength and get you breathing better, you understand?"

"I do."

She's looking at me with such exuberant anticipation. It's easy to picture her half a century younger and radiating youthful enthusiasm.

"Okay, then. We'll be two gals out for a good time and on the prowl."

She opens her arms to me. "Oh, thank you, Pauline!"

I accept the embrace, as much as I dread the idea of doing this. I do not want to be responsible for exacerbating her condition, or worse, killing her.

"One condition," I say.

"Anything."

"Keep off the stage and keep your clothes on, okay?"

She laughs, leading to a new spasm of coughs. I pat her back and worry about what I just agreed to.

James L. Peters

CHAPTER EIGHTEEN

Separate Ways

It's been a frantic week. I'm not used to being this busy and pulled in different directions by multiple obligations.

I've been spending extra hours at Ms. DeeDee's place. Raymond has been staying there, only leaving for the office and to shop for her. He's working a few hours remotely so he can be with her longer. Meanwhile, I'm doing my best to fill in the gap during daytime before work. While I'm with her, we play light card games, and I've been reading *The Scarlet Letter* to her. We spend time working on her breathing exercises and stretching routines. The mild stretches primarily help improve flexibility and posture, as well as relax muscles and relieve tension, all of which will help improve breathing.

Gradually, Ms. DeeDee has been able to spend more and more time out of bed without serious bouts of coughing or loss of breath. This has allowed us to do low-level exercises to help build back some of her muscles. All these therapies were things that had been suggested for months, and she had turned her nose up to all of them. Now, it seems the enticement of leaving the apartment has put her into full therapeutic training mode.

She has no idea how terrified I am at the thought of taking her out of this apartment and to some club. Every day, I try to work up the courage to talk her out of it. But seeing the effort she is putting into her therapy, how much it is motivating her and improving her condition, all I can do is support and encourage and hold to my promise.

I'm waking up extra early to spend a few hours at my parent's place doing the final packing. The house is so much closer to being all cleared out—the kitchen, their bedroom, bathrooms, spare room, and den are all empty. A lot was simply thrown out, the rest boxed for auction other than the occasional memento I keep. I took my mother's musical jewelry box. I don't wear jewelry, but as a little girl, I always opened it to hear Tchaikovsky's "Sleeping Beauty" while I closed my eyes and slowly spun around to its melody. When I wound it and once again lifted the lid, it played its tinny tune in the empty room as if the very song rang out from the past.

My mother caught me one time in their bedroom with the jewelry box open and playing. I thought I would be in trouble, but instead she put out her hand and I took it. She held my hand over my head and twirled me around. I turned and turned on my toes like a ballerina.

I try to hold on to such wayward memories, to be warmed by them and cherish them, but inevitably the later moments surface and overtake the tender ones. Me at thirteen and mother scolding me about my appearance and presentation. "Pauline, must you look that way? Have some pride, dear. You have enough going against you as it is. Don't slouch so! And stop scowling. God loves you. Smile!"

She meant well, and perhaps I should have listened more to her advice, but at the time, it only made me more miserable to be reminded I was not beautiful like her, and for her to make that so clear to me.

Dwelling on those negative memories only worsens my mood, and more than anything, I just want to be done with this house and get free from these haunts of my past.

I'm already tired by the time I get to work. There's no energy in me to sustain more than minimal conversations with customers, and I'm slower at mixing cocktails. Margie keeps giving me worried looks as we pass or reach around each other as we work within the confined space behind the bar.

"Hey. You okay?"

"Most certainly." I grab a pint glass from the stack.

"Sure? You don't seem yourself lately."

I pull on an IPA tap and let it run. "I'm fine. Just a busy week." Close the tap, pour off some head, and give it a quick pull again to top it off. "Lot going on." I serve it to a young gentleman chatting it up with a red-headed girl sipping a merlot.

Margie starts mixing a highball beside me. "This have to do with your Ms. X?"

I start on a gin and tonic. "Some of it. A lot of it."

Margie shaves off a lemon peel, gives it a twist, and drapes it over the lip of the Manhattan she serves to an older gentleman. "Can I help?"

I set the gin and tonic in front of a thirty-something who takes it in his manicured hand, looking very metrosexual in soft-collared, patterned shirt and gelled hair combed back with shorn sides. "Well, you could tell me where I can bring a dying seventy-six-year-old woman so she can get her funk on to live music."

Margie freezes in place. Her laugh is incredulous. "'Scuse me? Your Ms. X wants to go clubbing?"

"She wants to get out of that senior apartment while she still can. She wants to experience the joy of live music and a night out on the town—maybe for the last time."

"Aw. That's so sweet! Good for her!"

My hands look for things to do. I put a lid on the limes and put them away. "Sure, it's very sweet...until she keels over."

Margie raises a brow and tilts her head. "That is true."

"I don't have the first clue where to take her."

Fingers snap as Margie's eyes widen. "Oh, I have the perfect place. There's this little cocktail lounge down on South Fifth Street called—um, let me think—The High Ball! They usually have a jazz trio playing every Friday and Saturday night."

"That sounds perfect." Sure, a smaller club means less people. A three-piece jazz group won't be playing anything too loud, but will give DeeDee real live jazz she can sit back and enjoy. I can't imagine doing this alone, however. Taking DeeDee out, having to bring her oxygen with her, and probably a wheelchair. Besides, I'm not a nightlife person. It would be uncomfortable enough for me to be in a nightclub. More than anything, though, I don't want to bear the full responsibility of taking care of DeeDee.

I put pleading eyes on Margie. "How about coming with me?" I'm not begging, but there's desperation keeping my voice taut.

"You know I would, but that's going to be tough. Both of us having off on a Friday or Saturday night?"

True, but with a little juggling of the schedule, Trevor and Julio, our part-time bartenders, could work a Friday or Saturday night, and I could talk with Benny, our manager. He owes me at least one favor, and he could pull away from the restaurant side for one night to cover the bar.

"I think I can make it work," I say, "if you're up to it?"

Little Margie with her young, round face looks up at me with a big smile. "Time to give Ms. X the night of her life!"

"Let's just make sure it's not the last night of her life, okay?"

Margie shrugs. I give her a big hug, hoping this isn't all a huge mistake.

DeeDee's strength and relative health has continued to improve over the following week, and she is back to spending time on her couch for my visits. Her spirit is strong, her mood good, and some color has returned to her cheeks. But, there's no mistaking the toll she paid to her last episode. Her hair continues to thin, the lesions work their way through her hairline, as well as beginning to show on her arms. Her voice, though still with that touch of musicality, now has a faint rasp and her breathing lightly whistles with a wheeze. I remind myself that all of this is minor and exaggerated by my concerns. Plus, she is still regaining more strength and health. I also know, however, that she will never regain all that she has lost. Each episode will take a bit more of her, leave less and less.

After speaking with Benny—maybe pressuring Benny just a bit—he said he'd talk to Trevor and Julio, and if they agreed, he'd give me and Margie the next Friday night off. I can't imagine either of them turning it down. The money they'll make in tips will likely be quadruple what they normally see on a Sunday or Monday. It's just a matter of whether Trevor can juggle his other work schedule, and Julio often has gigs on the weekends with his band.

The biggest adjustment has been acclimating to the amount of time spent with Raymond this past week and a half since DeeDee's relapse. Although he still spends much of the daytime at work, he is staying overnight with his mother, sleeping on her couch, and he is usually here to greet me when I show up around nine in the morning or shortly after. He fills me in on how the evening went and if there's any new developments. Meanwhile,

I share with him her progress with some of the breathing and stretching exercises and light muscle-building we're doing. He thanks me for the extra help I've given in the last few days with dishes and laundry.

Two days ago, he invited me to join him for coffee at Ms. DeeDee's dinette table in the kitchen, and we just talked about incidentals. He asked me about bartending, and I asked about his job. I learned that he's a vice president of marketing in the fast-food industry. He apparently followed in his mother's footsteps to some degree, as I'm fairly certain she did advertising for big fast-food franchises.

At the small kitchen table, casually drinking coffee with him, Raymond can actually be quite charming. He still presents stiffly, as if his every word is being judged and appraised, but there are a few times I'm able to make him smile at something I say, or at something he said that I gently poke fun at.

I get the impression Raymond has had little chance to be anything other than a conflicted but dutiful son, responsible father, and professional executive. Just yesterday, it was on the tip of my tongue to ask him about Jules's mother, but we aren't close enough for that. I am, however, close enough to DeeDee, and I ask her about it now as we play cribbage.

"Ah, Sylvia. Smart woman. Beautiful, and a good mother. She and Raymond were completely wrong for each other."

"Oh, I'm sorry to hear that. Divorced?"

"Yes, a few years ago. But they were actually separated for a while before that."

"That's a shame." How hard that must have been for Jules if the relationship had soured for that many years?

DeeDee sighs, coughs into her hand a few times, and breathes in her oxygen deeply. "They were college sweethearts. Both of them very focused and career-minded. Sylvia got her master's in business management while Raymond got his master's in business communication. Things took off quickly for them after college, and, really, they worked well together when they were busy building their careers. Sylvia told me how they talked and talked for years about having a child but never came to a decision. I guess they left it up to fate because one day Sylvia turns up pregnant. Now they have little Jules to work into their lives. They were good parents, though. Really. Even during the worst of their time together. Sylvia was attentive and always kept Jules busy with games and reading. Raymond was the typical doting father. In some ways, I think Jules more than anyone softened that anger he carried around with him for so long."

My question has come around and hit a personal nerve. I'm feeling a crack in the emotional dam. Kaiya would have been 32 today, 12 years older than Julienne, and about the age I was when I met Jack while trying to get my life back together.

"I sure thought they were the perfect family. I did. But, somehow, they grew more and more distant over the years. They talked less and less and bickered more and more. It broke my heart to see how miserable Raymond became." She shakes her head. "In the end, I really think they were just too much alike, and it drove them apart."

"How was Jules through all of that?"

DeeDee put up a hand. "Oh, Raymond and Sylvia thought they hid it all from her. They finally confronted her when Jules was starting senior year. Told her they were splitting up."

"And she handled it okay?"

She smiles. "Oh, Jules is one smart kid. She knew that her parents had drifted apart well before they told her. I think she knew they needed to separate before they did. When they finally told her, she said, 'It's about time!'" She coughs laughter.

"Where is Sylvia now?"

"She took a huge promotion and moved to Pennsylvania. She's the CEO of a nationwide business advisement company.

She tries to fly here two or three times a year to spend time with Jules, and she wants to have Jules join her for Christmas and summer breaks."

My head is spinning. Here I am, a lowly bartender at a convention center, while Raymond is a VP at a nationwide fast-food franchise and his ex-wife is the CEO of a national business consultation company.

Unable to come up with any other response, I smile, nod, and only manage a "Wow," as I shrink in my seat feeling grossly inadequate.

CHAPTER NINETEEN

Adoration

"So, hold on. Are you telling me you really started to strip? Like totally naked strip?"

Smug nod. "Is that so hard to believe?"

"Yes. Absolutely."

"You have to understand, by that time, it's not like what I had been wearing was very concealing. But the money I was missing out on was huge."

"But—"

"Not only that, the culture of that time was far more open and promiscuous. We really embraced our sexuality."

"But—"

"The hard fact is, I needed money, and there weren't many opportunities for a young Black woman. I came to the realization that I could either struggle and scrape by for the rest of my life, or I could take advantage of an opportunity that could change my life forever."

She was unbearably terrified the first time she stepped out on the Heartbreaker's stage. Her muscles were so clenched in fear and embarrassment, she could barely move. Each piece of clothing removed only managed to reveal another layer of shame. Beyond the humiliation of ending up almost nude, even receiving the comments she did caused her some humiliation, as if she were some vixen or harlot. She made almost no money, and she ran off the stage at the end of her show and into the bathroom, locking herself in a stall. She wept. And, as she heaved her last sob and dried her last tears, she took a breath. She gave herself a vigorous mental shake, committed to owning her decision and the experience. Out of the stall and in front of the mirror, facing down her own hard, brutal stare, she told herself her shame didn't bind to her like skin, but could be peeled away just like another piece of clothing. She would dance it off just like everything else she removed on that stage.

Still, her conscience was plagued by the damning visage of Papa's condemnation and the heartbreak of Maman's disappointment.

Each night, she fought the terror of going out on a tiny stage and stripping down to pasties and a G-string. Her focus slowly began to shift to the rabid attention she received by the men who threw dollars at her and told her how beautiful and sexy she was. Slowly, week after week, she started experiencing the exhilaration and sheer joy of the dancing itself. She had come to Heartbreakers several times before signing up to watch the acts and see what it was all about. So many of the girls—especially the weekday girls, did little more than shake their ass and bounce their breasts as they stripped on stage. Not DeeDee. She would close her eyes and imagine herself back at the Dew Drop Inn, an innocent seductress overcome by the beat and passion of the music. In time, she was choreographing elaborate, elegant routines, flowing like water across the stage, buffeted by erotic winds that seemed to blow the silky fabrics off her body as she undulated and spun.

Over time, the guilt and shame transformed into a much more complicated mixture of control, potency, and dominance. On that stage, she danced before the men, mostly White men, that usually made her feel small and weak at the café and in public, who wanted to keep her and her kind under their heel. Now, they were cheering for her, throwing money at her, reaching out for her, worshipping her.

It took almost six months as an opening dancer at Heartbreakers before DeeDee got tired of seeing what the girls who went on stage after her brought home in tips. Six months of being almost naked and pulling in a fraction of what she could make. She hadn't the humility left in her to deny the lucrative return of removing a few remaining scant pieces of fabric.

In all that time, Simon was surprisingly supportive and applied no pressure on her. Despite the poor first impression he made, he seemed genuinely concerned for her well-being and only wanted what was best for her. He did, of course, gently encourage her to break free of her inhibitions. "Debbie Dee, you have no idea of your potential. If you are ever ready, I could make you a goddess. You just let me know."

Simon regularly bought her flowers, fruit, and candy. She received beautiful dresses and expensive shoes at her apartment. Yet, never once did he lay anything other than an encouraging or sympathetic hand on her.

"There's something special about you, Dee," he said one night after close as they enjoyed sipping a coffee liqueur at the bar. "I don't ever want that to change, do you understand me?"

Dee nodded, smiled and said, "No."

He laughed and stroked the small copse of beard under his lip. "Most of the girls that come through here—hey, they're great gals, okay? But they're damaged. They won't admit that, but they are. I do what I can for them, but they're using sex and drugs to fill a hole in them that is bottomless. But you—I don't know. When I saw you dance that first night, you gave off this impression of being some experienced, sexual machine. I figured you were like these others. You're not, though. There's a purity to you. But there's also a real strength that these other girls could only dream of having." She'd never seen such solemn intensity from him before. "I don't want to be the one responsible for you losing that. Understand?"

DeeDee nodded. Her feelings about the man were complicated. He had been so offensive initially, but what he said, how genuine he sounded, made her begin to think she could trust Simon DeReznor to look out for her.

"What the fuck, DeeDee? Where's all this shit coming from?"

Alfred held a box in his hand as he waved a silky sun dress in front of her.

She snatched at it, but he yanked it away. "That's mine. Don't worry about it."

"You're getting all these gifts, and you suddenly have all this money? Don't tell me it's from the café. What's going on? Do you have a sugar daddy or something?"

DeeDee grabbed for the dress again, got a handful and tried yanking it out of Alfred's hand, but he held on. "Oh my God, I don't have a sugar daddy. What do you take me for?"

Alfred looked angry, but more so, he looked deeply concerned, and DeeDee suddenly had visions of Papa again frowning at and worrying over her recent decisions.

"Listen, I don't dig into what you're doing every night. Keep out of my business." She yanked again and this time got the dress out of his hand as he looked at her with shock.

"Dee, what's going on with you? You've been different.

Coming home late. Sleeping in. You're not at the café as often. And—and you're just acting different."

Poor Alfred. He had rarely had any concern for her as they were growing up, and now, with having brought her here into this new world, it seemed he felt personally responsible for her.

"Alfred. Look at me. Do not worry about me. Everything is fine. Better than fine. I have a little side gig that is going really well. And they really appreciate me."

His eyes widened. "What kind of side gig? Who are *they?*"

"Don't worry about it."

"Christ, of course I worry! When I see this shit going on, I can't help but worry."

DeeDee tried to turn away from him, but he stepped in front of her again.

"Hey! If something happened to you, what would I say to Pop, huh? To Mom?"

"Is that all you're worried about? Having to report to Papa and Maman? Well, remember when you said to me that if I came here with you, I'd have to take care of myself? That's what I'm doing, okay? Not like you're helping out at all with the rent—"

"You know damn well I'm doing what I can—"

"Yeah, well. That's what I'm doing, got it? I'm doing whatever I can."

Alfred sighed. He adjusted his beret and zipped up his jacket. "I have to go. Just—just be *smart*, Dee. Okay?"

"Every day, every way." She gave him a sharp wave and closed the door behind him.

DeeDee sat in the dressing room with two other girls as they got ready for dancing that night. Back when Dee first started dancing, the other girls swooped in with help and support as if she were a wounded bird. They showed her how to dress, enhance her features at the makeup table, and how to handle the crowd. As DeeDee rose in popularity and slowly became the favorite of Simon, the other girls spent less time with her and kept to themselves.

DeeDee sat at the mirror in her station and applied some eye shadow, blushed her cheeks lightly with rouge, and brushed on dark lip stain to fill them out. Gradually, she painted away a bit of that innocence Simon spoke about, as she accented her seductive sensuality. She finished by adding just a dab of glitter to her cheeks and eyelids.

Simon stepped into the dressing room. "Evening, ladies. You all look ravishing. It'll be another marvelous night, I'm sure. Anything you all need? Any issues?"

"We're all good, honey," Gloria, the lead dancer, said, and everyone else sounded their approval.

"Good, good." He moved behind DeeDee and leaned over her, hand gently on her shoulder. "Are you free this Wednesday night?"

DeeDee nodded as she put a styling pick to her hair. She was still getting used to her natural, shorter afro, still excited to see herself in the mirror and how it gave her more mystique and maturity.

"Come with me to a movie debut at the Presidio. There's something I need you to see."

She gave him a dubious look. "Okay." Was this business? A date? Or was it something else entirely? She had become comfortable around Simon as a boss, had grown to trust him, but this was unexpected.

Simon patted her shoulder. "Great." He looked at all the girls. "Make 'em drool tonight, ladies!" He winked at DeeDee and walked out.

DeeDee stood outside the Presidio Theatre waiting for Simon with a twisting stomach of apprehension. It was the marquee glowing above her with its bright, chasing lights that made her uneasy.

In bold letters, it announced tonight's film:

PRESIDIO PREMIER!
Sold Out for Three Weeks at North Beach!
PORNOGRAPHY IN DENMARK:
A NEW APPROACH

An eclectic audience lined up for tickets, considering what the title suggested. Certainly, there was the type of men you would expect at what sounded like a peep show, but there were also a decent number of well-dressed women accompanying men in casual business attire and trendy eveningwear.

DeeDee felt extremely alone standing among the crowd of mostly couples and groups of people who knew each other. Whether true or not, she felt eyes on her.

After standing for ten minutes, and about two minutes before the box office opened, Simon appeared in a white fedora, white bell-bottoms and a flamboyant, big-collared shirt, open to mid-chest. His waxed mustache and goatee were sharply groomed against clean-shaven alabaster skin. He strutted toward her, taking a moment to shake hands with a few people first.

"Well, hi there, beautiful." He gave her a quick peck on the cheek.

DeeDee slapped a hand against his chest and pushed him back. "Simon. What the hell is this all about?"

He smiled and opened his hands to her in complete innocence. "Now, would I ever lead you astray, my sweet Debbie Dee?"

"There's always a first time."

He chuckled. "Calm down. Take a breath. Look up." He gestured at the marquee. "This is the start of a brave new future."

DeeDee had no idea what he was talking about and just gave him a sour expression.

He shrugged. "I'm not going to say anymore. I just want you to watch this documentary with me. And then I want you to think about the future. Okay?"

DeeDee was dubious at best, but Simon had yet to give her a reason why she shouldn't give him the benefit of the doubt.

He put out his arm to her, and DeeDee slipped hers through it. As he guided her into the box office line, much of her discomfort dissipated. On his arm, she found a confidence that lifted her chin and put a strut in her step. Once they got inside the theatre, Simon stopped at the concession stand and bought popcorn and two sodas.

They sat down in the theatre as the clatter of the crowd filled the room with anticipation. Simon tilted the popcorn bag to her. "A while back, I told you that, if you let me, I could turn you into a goddess. This, my dear Debbie Dee, is the opportunity for your deification."

She scoffed. "Whatever, dawlin'." She snatched a kernel of popcorn and settled into her chair, eyes front.

The lights in the theatre went down, the crimson curtains opened, and DeeDee Deneaux was introduced to an entirely new world.

CHAPTER TWENTY

Complicity

When Ms. DeeDee warned me all those weeks ago that I might look at her differently after hearing more about her past, I honestly didn't know what to expect. Learning more of her ever-evolving story, it's true that I'm seeing her in a different light now. It's unclear, however, what exactly that light is revealing.

For many, I suppose her story might be considered tragic, how unfortunate events put her on a stage and forced her to objectify herself in a most degrading way. That reaction is certainly a seed deep down inside me. It sits like a stone in my gut, but it doesn't germinate. Not yet.

My past is replete with the unsavory things I did with more members of the opposite sex than I care to count. Half the time, I was too drunk to even recall them in any way other than faceless, nameless objects of lust and desire that gave a false sense of self-worth but now continues to shame me, no matter how much the attempt is made to reconcile that period in my life. I tell those stories to addicts in the hope of shocking them into sobriety.

Ms. DeeDee shares these parts of her past without shame or remorse. In fact, she expresses a certain pride as she talks about this time in her life. There's even a tinge of nostalgia to her narrative, and I find this to be the greatest mystery to her. It's not that I condemn her past in any way. I hold nothing against her and what she felt she had to do to survive. But, I would have expected a certain amount of embarrassment or even regret, that she had to resort to that life. But there is none.

I'm fascinated by that. I'm envious of her. How does one reconcile and come to embrace the less savory elements of their earlier days, instead of nursing it like a wound?

Is it my upbringing? Am I too much a prude to even look at this aspect of her life and think she should show a certain humility or abashment as she speaks of it? Likely. But it seems to me that, for someone who strips for a living or relies on similar less socially acceptable means to subsist, they might puff their chest in defiant pride because it has become their life and they must embrace it or crumble emotionally. Deborah Deneaux, however, was a hugely successful businesswoman and philanthropist. Normally, this moment of time for her would be a skeleton securely locked away in the steel vault of a closet, never to come out.

I'm confused. I'm intrigued. I'm jealous. Mostly, though, I am just so utterly taken by the courage and strength of her character she wielded then and continues to exhibit today. However, dancing to such a complex and precarious life can lead to stumbles and falls. I can't help but anticipate one coming soon in the story of her past. In the meantime, I pray to God that a stumble and fall does not happen tonight when we take her to evening jazz at The High Ball.

Little Margie is a ball of energy as we approach DeeDee's apartment. I've been sharing so much of Deborah Deneaux's story with her (simply keeping DeeDee's name private), and Margie is as enamored by her as I am. To have the opportunity not only to meet her, but to enjoy a night out with her, has Margie giddy.

I am not giddy. I am full of panic and worry. There are so many things wrong with what is about to happen tonight. First and foremost is DeeDee's health, which although greatly improved, is not in a state that she should physically exert herself in any way. Then, there is Raymond. He returned to sleeping at home almost a week ago as his mother's health stabilized and improved. He complimented me on how much stronger she seems since I have been working with her. He thanked me and told me I've been the best thing to happen to them in a long time. He has no idea about this, and if he finds out I honestly don't know what he will do.

I had a recent meeting with my volunteer coordinator, Bonnie Sygertz, an RN with palliative and hospice care at the hospital. We meet a couple times a month so she can keep track of my progress and be available for any questions. I nonchalantly asked her, "So, what happens if my hospice patient wants to go somewhere or do something that could adversely affect their condition?"

"That's a great question," Bonnie said. "And the answer is easy. Your duty is restricted to where they reside, and what is in their best interest. You provide comfort, consolation, spiritual support, and companionship. Anything else is beyond your purview."

"No exceptions?"

"Absolutely none."

That didn't make me feel any better about what we were about to do. But, I sally forth, trying not to focus on the consequences. I try to summon DeeDee's courage and lead Margie to Ms. DeeDee's apartment door. Margie is dressed to the nines in spiked high heels, black capris, and halter top, and hair styled and moussed so big and dramatic like I've never seen on her. My black flats, jeans and V-neck floral print top, meanwhile, are lacking drama or pizzazz, and, as always, my hair is what it is—a wild pile of mahogany with silver streaks that cascade around my head and neck.

I knock on the apartment door. It's strange to be here in the evening. Everything about this night feels queer and unpredictable.

The door opens and I almost take a step back. I have never seen Ms. DeeDee so ravishing.

She is wearing a wig, something I haven't seen her do but am not surprised by, due to the hair loss. It's elegant and feathers out in blacks and grays that fall across the nape of her neck. I'm relieved that she chose shoes with wide, sturdy heels, but the spaghetti lacing and dramatic burgundy still make for a provocative presentation. Her silken black dress hugs her waist and rounds her hips and chest in just the right way. She's even showing just a hint of cleavage. She has done her makeup subtly but enough to subdue any lesions across her brow and sides.

This is a 76-year-old woman, and she is still overwhelmingly sensual and alluring. As much as her attire and makeup contribute to that, it's her composure and confidence that sells it.

"Wow!" Margie exclaims.

DeeDee smiles. "Oh, dawlin', thank you."

"You look positively ravishing," I say.

She offers a cocky smirk. "I don't feel half-bad, either."

"DeeDee, this is Margie, who I told you about."

Margie thrusts out a hand. "Total thrill, DeeDee!"

DeeDee accepts her hand. "For me as well, Margie. Any friend of Pauline…"

As they shake, I slip into the room. "Where's your oxygen tank and your walker?"

"Oh, dear. We don't need to lug those around, do we?"

I drill my eyes into her. "Yes. Yes we *absolutely* need to. Now where are they?"

DeeDee sighs. "If it will make you happy."

"It will. It really will," I say, and I can't help but notice just how on edge I am. I'm not trying to be. I don't want to be a damper on this evening, but I have to be as responsible as possible.

She points. "Tank beside the couch. Walker around the corner."

I see the oxygen tank that her hose is hooked up to and check it. Only fifteen percent left, so I unscrew the valve from the top and attach it to the tank next to it. Around the corner, I find her walker folded up and against the wall beside her bedroom door. I grab it, open it up and roll it in front of DeeDee. Velcroed to a crossbar is a bag I slip the oxygen tank into. "Okay, let's head out."

'Yes!' Margie says, and I desperately wish I had her enthusiasm as we lead DeeDee out into the hallway and to my car.

Parking is going to be an issue. There's no streetside parking, and the nearest ramp is several blocks away—far too much walking for DeeDee.

"I'm going to pull off to the side and let you two out at the club," I say. "I'll grab a parking spot in a ramp and join you as soon as I can."

"Sounds great," Margie says.

"Do what you need to, dear," DeeDee says.

I slow to a stop in the far-right lane in front of The High Ball and put my hazards on. My eyes bore into Margie's. "Please take care of her."

"Absolutely."

"Don't let her do anything silly, okay?"

"You bet."

"I'll help with her walker if you can grab her oxygen."

"On it, boss."

Margie and I get out of the car, she around back to grab the oxygen tank out of the trunk while I remove the folded walker from the back seat next to her. I open it up and Margie slips the oxygen tank into the bag. She leans into the car. "Time to party, DeeDee!"

"Oh, girl. Like we used to say in the Big Easy, "Let's pass a good time!""

We help DeeDee out of the car and lead her to the walker. She seems stable and strong. Her head turns and takes in the downtown with wide eyes and bright smile. I get back into the driver's seat and watch them as they move down the sidewalk.

"Stick with me, now," Margie says. DeeDee complies and they step toward the establishment, Margie keeping close watch on DeeDee.

Alone in my car, I mumble, "Pauline, what in the hell are you doing?" I almost never talk to myself. It's just not my thing. But that question was deserved, and there's no one else here tonight to ask it. Too bad I don't have a solid answer.

I swing around the block and head back up to the first parking ramp I can find. I stop to grab the ticket, then go round and round until finally finding a spot three floors up. By the time I've got to the stairs and walked down and out of the ramp, it's already been fifteen minutes. It's almost another ten minutes before I can get inside The High Ball and try to find Margie and DeeDee.

It's not a large place. A small bar runs along the side of the room where two bartenders frantically work to serve a cluster of customers. I can certainly sympathize. Tables run down the remaining portion of the room, with a small stage up front. There looks to be about sixty or so people here, which is enough to make the place fairly bustling. All tables but one are full, and the bar is completely occupied with many others standing around it waiting to order or collect drinks.

A three-piece band is just setting up as I walk in looking for Margie and DeeDee. One young musician sets up his keyboard on a stand and plugs it in to a small amplifier. The tall, lanky bass player tunes his upright and a sax player fiddles with her mouthpiece and the microphone.

Ahead of me, DeeDee sits at a small table, chatting with Margie. My eyes immediately lock on to a cocktail in front of DeeDee.

"Hey!" I say above the clamor of the room.

"Greetings, Pauline!" Margie says and raises her cocktail in a toast.

DeeDee radiates pure joy as she sits and looks about the room.

"And what are you drinking, DeeDee?"

Beaming, she holds her drink up into the light. "Whisky sour." She takes a sip.

I scowl at Margie. She looks confused. I look at the drink, at her, and shake my head. Is she that dense that she'd let a woman dying from respiratory failure order a cocktail? Margie just shrugs and moves to the beat of the piped-in music pumping through the speakers.

I lean in to DeeDee. "I want you to take it easy tonight, okay?"

DeeDee isn't even really looking at me, just moving her gaze across the club as she bounces to the beat of background music.

"DeeDee? Do you hear me?"

She gives me a brief look and a nod.

I never should have agreed to bring her out. This is a catastrophe waiting to happen.

While the band sets up, Margie moves closer to DeeDee and starts asking questions.

"Ever marry, Dee?"

She shakes her head. "No. Never felt the need or the desire."

"Are you straight?" Margie asks and I cough at her presumption. A laugh. "As an arrow." She sips her whisky sour.

Margie nods nonchalantly. "Well, I bet you had men waiting in line for you."

DeeDee shrugs, makes a face that seems to say, "I may have, but I'm not saying."

We stay quiet a moment, taking in the room and the atmosphere. DeeDee grins wide, takes dainty sips of her drink. Margie finishes hers in no time and heads back to the bar for another. I'm dry as a bone and ask her to bring me a water.

"Just remember," I say to DeeDee. "The moment you start feeling out of breath, you let me know, okay?"

DeeDee nods and smiles, looking at the band and the open floor in front of the stage.

"Please? For me? Show me you understand."

She really looks at me for the first time tonight, and her expression is full of sympathy. "Thank you, Pauline. For this. It means so much."

I doubt my nod hides my stress.

Despite her empathy, she sits defiantly straight and forthright. "You are a ball of worry, *ma chérie*. I'm so sorry. You must remember, though. Whatever happens, you'll have many years to live past it. I don't. I'm just trying to make the most of what time I got left. You hang tough for me, will you? *C'est la vie.*"

That stings a bit. My worry is all about me, not her. After her appeal, it seems selfish. DeeDee is trying to live the rest of her life to the fullest, and I'm concerned that I might get in trouble for it. Shame on me. I should be reveling in her night, celebrating with her and making the most of it. Well, I will now. Damn any repercussions.

I straighten in my seat and slap the table top. "Ms. Deborah Deneaux…"

"Yes, dawlin'?"

I give the biggest smile I can. "…You just enjoy yourself tonight, is that clear?"

She raises her drink in salute.

The band is supposed to start at 7pm, but it is quarter after before they start to play. It's worth the wait though. The band seems to carry a good groove and I see DeeDee getting into it almost immediately. First in her shoulders as they roll to the beat, then down into her arms and hips that move and sway. No one is dancing as the band plays. It honestly just doesn't seem like that kind of club. The music is intended to be background, to set the mood for drinking and talking.

The second song begins with a running bassline, the musician's fingers stretching and skittering down the fretboard. The keyboardist picks up on it, accenting the offbeats, and when the sax starts wailing, DeeDee stands up, her body grooving to the tune.

"Don't overexert yourself, now," I say.

The smile she gives me and Margie is priceless. Margie laughs out loud and claps her hands as DeeDee rolls her shoulders and pistons her arms to the beat and melody of the tune.

I'm not prepared, however, for her to step forward and take the dance floor.

"DeeDee!" I yell, and reach out for her, although not with any intention of snagging her and yanking her back. She's gone, and my heart skips while my stomach falls.

She takes the floor, moving and grooving to that beat in this minimal motion that still manages to illicit a visceral reaction. Margie sees utter panic on my face and looks back with enthusiastic shock. DeeDee has taken command of the dance floor.

I don't think I'll ever be able to know what it was like to watch her dance when she was young—either those early days at the Dew Drop, or her exotic days at Heartbreakers, but I do get the privilege of watching a seventy-six-year-old woman give a sultry jive and swing to the melody of jazz. She is reserved, her motions contained, but they are fluid and seductive, and it doesn't take long for others to join her. First a couple of women move around her like accent points to her gestures. Then, an older gentleman, maybe in his sixties, steps up and dances next to her in a way that is simply a steady, silent applause to her gentle gyrations. As the song continues, there are more than a half dozen people, several of them young, dancing with her, smiling warmly at her, nodding to her movements and enjoying every moment she communicates through body language.

I keep wiping at my eyes, overwhelmed. I'm watching someone express over seven decades of living, of struggle and resistance and fortitude and endurance, all conveyed in the sway and twirl of dance, and it takes all my strength not to weep at the sight.

Margie jumps up and gets down to the music, hands up in the air, applauding DeeDee's motions. I'm left alone at my table, missing out on something important and transformational. When did I become so reserved, so somber? I hate the part of myself that won't allow me to join them.

DeeDee captivates her crowd until the song ends and she returns with Margie back to the table. Her audience applauds and cheers. Even the band acknowledges her with bows and head nods. She returns to her seat glowing as her breaths heave. "The most fun…I've had…in ages!" Words broken by deep inhales.

I get up, set up her oxygen tank and hand her the hose. She pulls the loop of hose around her head and under her nostrils.

"Take deep breaths, DeeDee," I say. "Remember your belly breathing."

"I'm fine," she gasps and starts coughing, deep sucking breaths between.

"Remember posture. Relax your muscles. Stretch your back. Be calm."

"Really, I—" she starts to say, but coughs and wheezes instead.

I put a glass of water in front of her. "Try this."

She takes it, tries a sip, and barely gets it down before spasmatic coughing sends it back up.

Margie looks at me with concern, and I return that concern to her.

"Should I head for the car so we can take you home?"

DeeDee starts to say, "Yes," but sputters with more coughing and just nods briskly. I get up and walk out of The High Ball and toward the parking ramp.

I trot at a steady pace and get to the car in just a little over ten minutes. I drive back to the club and pull up streetside. Margie is there with DeeDee and they step into the car. DeeDee's coughing is intense. I pass her a tissue and she coughs into it. I see a blotch of red.

Margie's round face drips with worry. I'm on the edge of panic. "Should we head to the emergency room?" I ask.

DeeDee's headshake is adamant. Her look implores through the rearview mirror as she continues to cough. Those burrowing eyes plead with me—does she just want it to end? Is that what she is trying to tell me?

I head in the direction of home, but as we keep driving, I feel less and less confident of the destination. DeeDee just continues to cough and gasps so deeply for air. It's terrifying.

Finally, I turn left instead of right, heading away from River Bend Apartments. "We're going to emergency."

DeeDee's eyes widen and then flare with anger. Her coughing keeps her from saying anything other than hissing a, "No." It is clear that she is furious.

"I'm sorry," I say into the rearview mirror. "I can't just watch you suffer like this."

She has never looked at me in the way she is right now, and I feel I have betrayed her.

In the emergency room, DeeDee's coughing and lack of

oxygen keep her from communicating. As she becomes less and less responsive, they give her Albuterol and Theophylline, but they must respect her enrollment in hospice, so they are unable to do anything more. Within fifteen minutes she is breathing far more normal. However, because of what they had determined as her unresponsive state, they called Raymond, her emergency contact. I did not know they had contacted him until he shows up just past midnight. I am completely unprepared for this.

"Pauline. What is going on?"

"Everything is fine," I say. "Her breathing is under control."

Margie simply smiles and nods and looks completely distressed.

"But why is she here? What happened?"

"They gave her a couple of bronchodilators to open her airways. She's doing fine now."

He is confused, worried, agitated. "Pauline, tell me. Why was she brought here?"

I can't avoid this anymore. But I don't know how to tell him. Everything I had feared is coming true now, and I don't want to face it.

"Raymond, I—"

"What?"

I take a breath. "I took her out."

A moment passes. I can see his expression solidify; his countenance set like concrete. "What?"

"She asked if I could take her to a nightclub, so I did."

"*What?*" The repetition of that word is so much more bitter the second time, so much more incredulous. I just want to run away.

"Raymond—"

"Are you kidding me?" His face is twisting into a bitter rage. "What could you have possibly been thinking?"

Despite the immense regret and guilt I feel, one ember of indignation smolders inside of me and, for good or ill, I stoke the flames. "I was thinking of her, actually. I was respecting her wishes."

"Were you? And what did that get her? The emergency room? How'd that work out for you?"

Frustration grows inside of me. All I wanted to do was take accountability and apologize, but he's not giving me any chance to explain the situation. I didn't just arbitrarily allow her to do something dangerous, but he is obstinate.

"Raymond, please. This was very important to her—"

He's stepping into my space, bullying me with his broad presence. "To *her*? What about *us*? Her family? Don't we get to make any decisions on her welfare?"

"Forget it. I can see you don't want to hear what happened. You've already judged me."

He nods sharply. "Damn right. You took my dying mother out to a nightclub? Are you insane?"

My emotions short circuit. A surge of adrenaline courses through me. I shove my face into his. "Yes! I'm insane! I'm crazy! I want to kill your mother!" I puke out a jagged laugh. "For God's sake, is that what you really think? How could you? How *dare* you?"

"Now just wait a—"

"Your mother is *dying*, Raymond. You keep thinking this is happening to you. It's happening to *her*, and it's up to her how she wants to live it. You don't like that? Then, for all I care, you can go to hell, Mr. Deneaux."

I have to get away as fast as I can before completely falling apart. I race past Margie's wide eyes and gaping mouth.

DeeDee resents me bringing her here, and Raymond thinks I've been reckless and irresponsible. I'm overwhelmed by my own poor judgment and what it's led to.

I dash out of the waiting room just in time as my face crumples up like an apology and I heave sobs in the parking lot.

CHAPTER TWENTY-ONE

Regrets & Resolve

I wake up to the fragments of fitful dreaming—pieces that won't fit together but sit heavy like an anxious ache in my chest. Nestled under the delusion of shelter from conse-quence, there's no impulse to get up. Moments from last night flash and blare like lightning strikes of regret, and I roll over, cover my head, and bob in and out of a rueful consciousness.

Every so often, my eyes open to see the digital clock skip past 9:00am, 9:25am, 9:42am, 9:59am When it shows 10:12am, the dread of having stayed in bed hours past my normal wake time bolts me up and leads me to the bathroom. On the way there, glance at my phone's screen blinking two voice messages and multiple texts. I ignore them and turn the faucet to get a hot shower started.

Peeling off my pajamas and underwear, I stand naked wait-ing for the water temperature to rise and risk a look in the mir-ror. My reflection glares back at me, a miserable, sagging, over-weight woman, soft belly tattooed with regret. I don't want to recognize her, but know her all too well. My gaze jerks away, the jolt of condemnation in those eyes too much to bear.

Memories invade of leaving the hospital in tears, of Margie trying to reassure me from the passenger seat as I drive her home. "You did the right thing. It's what Dee wanted. Don't beat yourself up over this."

I hadn't responded. My damp eyes stayed ahead, a raging smile on my face that felt so much more like a sneer or grimace.

Margie continued to defend and placate all the way to her place. As she got out of the car, she said, "DeeDee is lucky to have you, Pauline."

I nodded, unconvinced, as she shut the passenger door and walked to her upstairs apartment.

In the shower, my mind time travels and undoes every misstep, every wrong decision, and misguided intention. Six weeks' worth of misjudgments rectified and a new, perfect present created where DeeDee is home and fine, Raymond is satisfied with my care of his mother, and there is no risk of losing my hospice volunteer position.

Perhaps that is the reality of another Pauline from an alternate timeline. It's an interesting thought, yet not particularly comforting.

I stand under not quite scalding water for several minutes, as if the spray could melt away the catastrophe of last night and rinse it down the drain. I lethargically shampoo my hair and scrub my body with soap, but as my hands claw at my scalp and rub against my skin, new thoughts begin to spark, events from last evening replay, and frustration builds. I scrub harder, faster, more aggressively. At first, it's all from the rage of allowing what happened to happen. My own accusations against my every action and decision. But then Raymond's enraged face appears in front of mine, and I feel a certain self-righteousness overcome me. Last night, DeeDee was so filled with joy in that bar. She broke free of her illness and debilitation for just a few moments, and transmitted her love of life to those she drew around her on the dance floor.

Raymond's furious words come back, but they are muted and dulled, they reverberate against the rocky walls of my best intentions, and are repelled by DeeDee's heartfelt pleas as a dying woman. Eloquent rebuttals interrupt Raymond's accusations as I defend my reasoning and outcomes, if not my actions themselves.

By the end of my shower, the bathroom is thick with steam, and I pull back the curtain, approach the mirror, drag a hand across it and see a different, defiant Pauline staring back at me.

I give an encouraging smile to a far more sympathetic and understanding reflection.

I finally work up the courage to check my messages. The texts, of course, are all from Margie.

- u ok?
- u did nothing wrong!
- Text or call!
- lmk ur ok.

My thumbs move over the keyboard screen in response.

- I'm fine. No worries.
- See you tonight.
- Thanks for the support. <3

The first voicemail was just spam, but the second, sent this morning at 9:02am, is from Raymond Deneaux.

"Pauline. This is Raymond. Mother is home. She is doing better. Can we talk, please? Call or text me when you are able. Thank you."

The phone goes dark in my hand while I try to decipher his tone, but his delivery was flat, emotionless, and impossible to interpret.

There's anxiety about facing the consequences of my actions and the dread of continuing any in-person dialogue with him. He made his feelings about me pretty clear last night. The only thing I can imagine now is the possible repercussions he is eager to inflict. I consider my words long and hard before I text back:

> **- So glad to hear your mother is home and doing better. Off tomorrow and have availability all day. Let me know when and where.**

I brew coffee, fix a bowl of Corn Flakes, and sit down with the phone by my side. It pings with his response in the middle of my second bite.

> **- Thank you. meet at the Sunnyside? Where we had brunch a few weeks ago. 9am?**

I swallow my corn flakes, sip my coffee, and reply.

Saturday is so busy at the bar that, other than a sympathetic hug, Margie and I hardly have time to reference last night before we focus on mixing cocktails, pouring wine, and tapping beer. Julio is with us from five until nine, which reduces the strain. Bartending is a side-gig for him. He plays keyboards in a band, which is why he isn't normally on weekends, but since he worked last night to cover for us and had no weekend gigs, he decided to put in some Saturday night hours as well. He's one of those odd introverts that interacts well with strangers but not with anyone he knows, making him a quiet but hard-working team member.

He hangs on until quarter after nine, then clears out his till and fades into the night. Margie and I keep going strong until after eleven, then finally find a reprieve as the bar starts to thin out.

"So, you said DeeDee is doing okay?" Margie asks as we do some cleanup around the bar.

"Sounds like it. Raymond told me she's back home, at least, and doing better."

Margie's eyes widen. "Oh. Raymond reached out to you already?"

I nod. "Left a message. Told me she's home and okay."

"Did he apologize?" Said with expectation.

"No. But he was cordial."

She shakes her head. "It was total bullshit how he treated you last night. That was fucked up."

"I think you aren't putting yourself in his shoes. It's his mother. He got a late-night call from the hospital. That had to be a shock."

"He should have shown you more respect. You deserve that."

I don't answer. I'm too confused about everything that happened. I feel sympathy for him, obligation for DeeDee, and responsibility as a volunteer hospice worker. On every level, even though my motives are easily reconciled, there's still a dreadful nagging belief that I've failed each of those duties.

Margie stops drying glasses and looks at me hard. "Pauline, if I'm ever dying, you damn well better listen to me instead of my kids. Promise me?"

I smile. Nod. "Sure. If I live that long. But I hope you realize the position you're putting me in."

Margie shrugs. "Mine, right?"

I pull into the Sunnyside parking lot just a couple minutes past nine and walk inside. At the hostess station, I mention I'm joining someone and point to Raymond when I see him. The hostess waves me forward. Raymond sits, upright and shoulders square, hands folded on the tabletop. I approach as confidently as I can, even though my stomach is turning over.

He stands as I reach the table. "Hello, Pauline."

I smile, pull back the chair. "Good morning." As I take a seat, I struggle to hold eye contact while he locks his brown eyes on mine. His gaze, framed by stern brow under that clean-shaven head, is either confrontational or simply concerned. He returns to his chair, posture stiff and upright. His formality makes me recall being interviewed by Barry at the Long 9 Lounge.

"Thank you for coming."

"Certainly. How is she?"

"Much better. She simply overexerted herself, but with the expectorants they gave her, after a few hours she was fine and ready to go home."

"I'm so very glad to hear that."

He nods. "I want to thank you for all you've done for my mother up to this point." His demeanor seems so rehearsed, or maybe just overly polished. The way he just said that—"up to this point"—gives a vague impression that I may not be as appreciated from this time onward.

I'm overreacting and try to temper my sensitivities. "I've done my absolute best to serve your mother's interests," I say, and I do now look right at him. His eyes fall.

He's slow to speak. "My mother is a...formidable personality."

Uncertain where he's going, I say nothing throughout another pause between his words.

He says, "She is hard to say no to."

He's obviously having difficulty coming to a point. The silence between his sentences do not lure me in. I feel no urge to fill that gap and instead maintain my attention on him.

His eye contact, so direct when I first arrived, becomes more sporadic. He picks at the paper placemat. Shifts in his seat. "Listen, about Friday night…"

I'm fixated on him, and when he finally looks up again, I see genuine remorse.

"… I recognize that I overreacted on Friday night. I'm sorry for that."

The poor man is suffering enough trying to make it through this moment. In an attempt to end his misery, I say, "I understand completely. It was a difficult night."

The tentative cock of his head acknowledges my statement yet doesn't accept it as an excuse. "The fact is, I was transferring most of my frustration at her onto you, and that isn't right."

I place hands flat on the table, take a breath and am very careful choosing my next words. "Raymond, it makes me very sad if the anger you showed me was in any way directed toward your mother."

Some of his stoicism returns. He stiffens and his back straightens. "She wanted to have a good time, and she didn't bother to think about what that would mean for you or for me. I was wrongfully venting my anger onto you, when I know she made you take her out that night."

That uncomfortable smile of mine creeps onto my face. "No one forces me to do anything, Mr. Deneaux. Only I am responsible for my actions."

"But certainly she coerced you—"

My head is shaking. "She asked a favor of me. I did not take that request lightly. I knew exactly what I was doing when I agreed to it. I would, in fact, do it again."

His lower lip squirms as if to find the right words to respond. Instead of saying anything, his mouth clamps shut and his eyes lower again. I've apparently derailed the conversation he expected to have.

My arms want to cross, but I leave my hands on the table-top. "You don't agree with taking her to the club." I'm finding just enough strength to keep eye contact.

Before he can answer, the waitress stops by. I ask for a coffee. He requests a refill. "Coming right up," she says and steps away.

His fingers drum on the Formica tabletop. He inhales deeply. "Yesterday, Mother was very insistent that I apologize."

"Was she," I state, and begin to understand what has precipitated this meeting. "But you feel I was wrong."

He fidgets in his chair. "Well, I'm not happy about what happened, Pauline. I'm sorry, but this is my mother. I had thought we could count on you to look after her well-being."

"The issue, from my vantage point, seems to be that what you believe is best for your mother's well-being may conflict with her wishes."

He moves in, as if I've said something to prove himself. "Yes! That's exactly—"

"But how can you have any interest in her well-being if you have no interest in what her wishes are?"

"I care about what is best for her."

"I fear you care about what makes you feel best in caring for her."

The tension at this table is rising. He's becoming more obstinate. "Oh, I see. So, if my mother asked you to take her hang gliding, or skydiving, or base-jumping, you'd let her do that?"

"Oh, Raymond. Using absurdity as an argument? It's beneath you."

He pushed away from the table, shoulders back with aplomb. "But can't you see? That's exactly my point. That's what I'm trying to explain."

This man can be so exhausting, yet my sympathies for him, for his situation, overwhelm the frustration. Though the implements of our upbringings be different, both have drawn blood, leaving wounds that haven't healed.

I keep to a gentle, soft-spoken voice. "Your mother's request was a far more reasonable one than the extreme ones you are trying to compare it to." I reach out, take hold of his one hand sitting by his coffee cup. "She simply wanted to go out one last time, to experience a nightclub and some live music. Yes, of course, I tried to talk her out of it—and her getting up and dancing certainly wasn't a part of the plan. But then. Oh, Raymond. Then I watched her. I saw how much joy it brought her. The joy she brought to everyone around her. It—it was magical."

His lips are tightly pursed, his head shaking. He's fighting every aspect of this.

"Raymond, have you ever seen your mother dance?"

He pulls his hand away, holding the mug close to him. "No. When in the world would I have?"

I look at my empty hands he drew away from. A terrible sadness overtakes me. When I look back up at him, there is so much hurt and resentment in those eyes.

"Oh, Raymond. I'm so sorry."

"For what? You obviously think you did nothing wrong."

"No. I did do something very wrong." I can't help it as once again my emotions overflow and a tear falls to my cheek. "I should have invited you."

James L. Peters

CHAPTER TWENTY-TWO

Ebony Queen

I leave The Sunnyside restaurant with new regrets I wasn't prepared for and head to DeeDee's apartment with new dreads I don't want to feel. I may be in the middle of a larger family drama than I bargained for.

St. John's Hospice prepared me for a certain amount of family struggles. It's inevitable when a family member, especially a matriarch or patriarch, is dying. So many unresolved regrets and grudges between family members that float to the surface.

When I was being trained, my supervisor, Bonnie Sygertz, told me, "You aren't a counselor, and you aren't there to solve family conflicts. Just be present, be compassionate, and listen. Most likely, they aren't looking for answers, and they don't want your opinion. They want sympathy."

That sounded so easy at the time, but in this moment, it goes against every fiber of my being. I think I'm beginning to understand Raymond more, to know where his resentments come from—or at least a better idea what keeps him and his mother so distant from each other. There's so much I don't know yet, but the pieces are beginning to fit together.

My stomach flutters approaching DeeDee's door. How much resentment does she have for me because I brought her to the emergency room? Perhaps she had just wanted to die and driving her to the ER took that away from her. After talking with Raymond, however, it seems she may have been right when she tried to convince me she didn't need to go the hospital. And she certainly knew exactly what would happen if she was taken there.

So easy to pick away at decisions when already knowing the outcomes. Regardless, I went against her wishes, and expect she is holding a deep grudge about that.

I knock and faintly hear her voice say, "Come in!"

She is laying down on her couch under a purple and fuchsia afghan, pillows propping up her back, oxygen hose under her nose. I approach and she is all smiles, arms out to me. "Oh, *mon cygne*. I'm so glad to see you."

I lean over into her embrace, give a gentle but desperately furtive hug. "I'm glad you're doing better. I'm sorry I didn't stay longer on Friday night."

"Oh, no. I completely understand," she says. I pull away but we keep contact, hands grasping the other's arms. "I shouldn't have put you in that position. I was selfish."

Those sound like Raymond's words. "I wouldn't give that night up for anything. It was wonderful. You owned that night. I will never forget it."

She blushes. "Oh, please. I just wish it hadn't caused you so much worry and trouble." She gives a devilish grin. "It was wonderful, though. Oh, my."

We break away and I take my seat in the chair against the other wall. "Don't you dare worry yourself over me. But, you're doing better?"

"Much. I even did those stretches this morning and some

breathing exercises."

I beam with approval and also from a wave of relief that she doesn't resent me. The pressure of guilt and regret has lifted from my chest. "That's wonderful."

Her expression flattens. "Raymond apologized to you?"

Raymond, in fact, left me not a half-hour ago at the restaurant without any indication that he understood my side of this issue with his mother. In fact, he made himself fairly clear when he snatched the check, stood and said, "You do whatever you feel best. Obviously, I have little say in the matter."

"Raymond and I had a wonderful conversation," I say. "His only concern is your well-being."

She snuffs. "I really don't think that's true."

I'm tempted to pry, to ask her to elaborate. Both of them must have their ideas on why there is so much distance between them, but instead I remind myself of Bonnie's guidance during my orientation.

"Don't you worry yourself over anything. All is well." I give a big smile.

"DeeDee. I can't help but be curious."

"Of course you can't, dawlin'."

"Raymond."

"Yes?"

"I apologize for getting so personal, but…"

"Yes?"

"You mentioned you know who the father is?"

"Of course I do."

"But…"

Raise of eyebrow.

"…He doesn't?"

Long stare.

Somehow, DeeDee managed to find herself with too many men in her life, all either wanting something from her, or wanting her to do and be something else. There were, of course, the ever-growing crowd of men who came every Thursday, Friday, and Saturday night to see her dance. She was smart enough to know that, mostly, they came to see her strip. And yet, other girls before her, girls more voluptuous than her, had never drawn the crowds she now did, so the dancing had to be part of it. At least, it made her feel better to think so.

These men lusted after her, begged for her attention. To simply give them a long, hard look mesmerized them as she danced and peeled away silky layers—and incidentally would turn a dollar into a five, ten, or even a twenty. She quickly learned that eye contact had a tremendous return on investment.

Since Simon took twenty percent of what she brought in through her sultry gaze and sensual sway, he wanted more and more of Double Dee. He put her on posters and in ads promoting Heartbreakers, and he made her hostess to special private events he held as he tried to attract investors to his other business venture that had him so excited, Behind Closed Doors Productions, which Simon was always hounding her to be a part of. DeeDee, however, refused to have any part in it. Dancing on stage a couple nights a week to all the Horny Henrys was one thing. To be part of what he was proposing—

No, she couldn't do it, despite the money he promised she could make. Her dancing had already sent Alfred into a rage when he finally found out what she was doing in the evenings. Imagine what he'd do if she in any way involved herself in his little eight-millimeter skin flicks that ran in the back rooms of seedy little businesses?

Alfred wanted her to go back home to Father and Maman. He said that San Fran was corrupting her, poisoning her, that she was reaching a point of no return.

"Maybe I should tell Pop what you're up to here, huh?" he said one Friday evening when they both arrived home late, her still with painted face.

"Think about that carefully, Alfred," she replied. "You want to hurt Papa any more than he already is?" She set her purse down on the kitchen table and pulled out a thick wad of cash. "You want to say goodbye to the money paying for this place? Money that I'm also sending home to Maman and Papa to help them out?"

Alfred gawked at the money, looked helplessly at DeeDee. "This ain't the way, Sis—"

DeeDee slammed her hand down on the table. "Then you *tell* me the way, Alfred, because I'm not seeing any other way. Not right now. But just maybe, this will let me get somewhere I'm never going to get otherwise, you understand?"

Alfred's face twisted and he turned from her, eyes glistening. "Shoulda never brought you here, damn it."

She grabbed him by the shoulders. "Alfred. Listen to me. You didn't bring me here. I came here with you. Understand?" She stuffed the money back into her purse where she'd hide it later under a floor board in her bedroom along with several thousand more dollars. "You keep fighting the system. I'll keep playing the system. Okay? Maybe, one day, between the two of us, we'll beat this system."

Alfred backed down after that, but DeeDee knew it wasn't from accepting her side hustle as an exotic dancer.

Then there was Darryl at the diner, who was getting less and less tolerant of DeeDee's continual requests for time off so she could attend the fundraising events of Simon's. Cherise warned her that if she kept coming in late and tired, and continued to ask for time off, Darryl would fire her. DeeDee's response was blunt. "Let him."

Because, honestly, the diner had become her side job, even though she put in three times the hours there. And that didn't make sense—working so much harder for so much less money. What was Father's mantra? Survive and thrive? Well, the diner might let her survive, but Heartbreakers was allowing her to thrive.

The Heartbreakers crowd. Simon. Alfred. Darryl. Even Papa. All those men expected something from her or wanted her to be something. They didn't realize that she was the one laying the ground rules and taking from them everything she could.

Nineteen seventy-one came and went like a flash. In that year, all while DeeDee danced, the Native Americans had given up their 19-month occupation of Alcatraz. Charles Manson and his cult had been sentenced for the murders of Sharon Tate and four others. Over 150,000 people gathered in San Francisco's Union Square to hold the largest ever Vietnam protest. And, the City by the Bay welcomed its first McDonalds on Market Street.

The year wrapped up with DeeDee playing main attraction to a special New Year's Eve fundraiser that Friday night for Behind Closed Doors. She danced and stripped away her clothes for a primarily male audience in tuxedos and a few women in fancy gowns while they drank twenty-five-year-old scotch and nibbled on foie gras and caviar. One man insisted on paying for time with DeeDee in a back room and Simon shut him down immediately, likely losing a potential investor.

The next evening, DeeDee arrived at Heartbreakers early. Simon asked to speak with her.

"Hey, Double Dee." He sat at the table where he always did his business. A pencil tapped against his temple as he paged through his ledger.

"What's up, Simon?" She pulled a chair out from the table, swung it around, and straddled it, facing him.

He looked up, the corners of his smile threatening his ears. "Take a guess how much money we've raised in the last three months for BCD Productions."

She looked blankly at him.

"No, seriously. Guess."

"I can't. No idea."

He put his pencil down. "Over twenty thousand. Is that crazy? Twenty *thousand!*"

"Good job." DeeDee settled back in her seat.

He looked at her. "You realize, you raised this with me, right?"

She shrugged.

"This is as much you as it is me."

"So? Write me a check, dawlin'."

He laughed, then crossed his arms and let out a long exhale. "Dee. Listen. These people are investing in the idea that we can make films that will make San Francisco a mecca for erotic cinema. They're buying into what I believe—that this industry is just waiting to explode." He pointed at her, which made DeeDee want to duck. "And they believe it because they think you will be one of the stars of those films."

She shook her head. "I've told you. Count me out. I'm not going to be a part of one of your skin flicks."

He put an intense and focused eye on her. "Dee. Think about it. You're already taking it all off for every guy that comes in here to see your shows. All I'm asking is for you to do the same thing, except in front of a camera instead of an audience."

"You're not listening—"

"Let's just make a few loops, okay? That's all I'm asking. Just a few loops of you doing what you do every Thursday through Saturday on stage. I'll give you a hundred bucks a loop. How does that sound?"

She chewed on his words, tasted them, digested them. The money certainly tempted her. He'd been producing these film loops since before she met him. Little more than risqué matinee for guys to get their jollies off. They were shot on Super 8 film and averaged seven to eight minutes. He distributed them to businesses to run in their seedy back rooms and raked in the dimes from coin-operated sex shops where they ran in perpetual loops. Simon also sold and traded them discreetly to private collectors. It all made her cringe.

Her dancing was a transient moment in time shared with a live and appreciative audience. In a strange way, the experience was personal and intimate. These loops, however, would be played over and over again while people did God-knows-what while they watched. The thought was unsettling.

But, reluctant as she was, she was also loyal to Simon, and she appreciated everything he'd done for her. Beyond that, the pleading and desperate eyes of the Heartbreakers owner was breaking hers.

DeeDee blew out an exasperated breath. "Okay. Fine. Let's try it. But nothing more, okay?"

"Absolutely," he said, and he was all grins.

As with the dancing, there was an acclimation period being part of the loop productions. Her first times dancing on stage were all about getting used to the lusty eyes on her, the men reaching out for her as she bared her body to them and danced. With the loops, it was the sanitary business aspect of it, the cold production as she performed in front of hot halogen lights, a camera man, and accompanying crew. A director shouting out commands. The first few productions were far worse than anything she experienced on stage. There, she was applauded and adored as a performer. Here, she was judged and directed like a marionette.

In the first loop, they played it straightforward and just had her dance on the stage and strip. In the next loop, they had her essentially do the same, but this time in a scarlet bedroom of velvet and satin, tasseled lampshades and poster bed. She had to hold back the cringe she felt all the way in her gut when the director shouted out, "Now touch your tits. Pinch your nipples. Fondle your cunt."

This was not the same. For the first time, she felt dirty. The entire situation felt wrong.

But it was less than an hour of gritted-teeth work, and at the end of it, Simon slapped a hundred dollars in her hand. That, on top of her dancing, on top of the diner, was money like she had never seen before. If she kept this up, within a few years, on top of what she sent home to her parents, she could enroll in the marketing program at City College of San Francisco and cover her entire four-year tuition.

Meanwhile, Simon was already seeing profitability with BCD Productions. Society was opening up to the concept of pornography. The obscenity laws, even if they hadn't changed, were not being enforced as strongly. Essentially, the more it pervaded society, the more of a burden it became on the police and the judicial system. Slaps on the wrist replaced jail time and hefty fines. Simon discovered more and more viable markets for his burgeoning business.

He invested heavily in new equipment: a new 16-millimeter camera, audio board and boom mics, tungsten lighting. He rented out a studio with five sets and hired down-and-out studio hands and film school dropouts on the cheap. He was primed and ready to start producing full-length pornographic films.

"You could be my number-one star, Double Dee. Just think of it. The most well-known and desired porn star of our age.

Not just here. We're already setting up distribution in Canada, France, and Italy. You could be making solid four figures a month in no time."

"I remember back when you told me I was different. That I was somehow pure and you wanted to keep me that way."

Simon smiled. "Sure. Yeah. Absolutely."

"You look me in the eye and tell me you still want that. That you're still looking out for me."

He laid hands on her shoulders and grinned his good-natured, conniving grin. "Baby. Absolutely. With my life, you dig me? You are my number one star. My gold mine."

Friday night at Heartbreakers and DeeDee's normal opener, Annabelle, a young, naïve waif of a girl with big bosoms and tight, dimpled butt who had become popular with the early crowd, was a no-show. Instead, Dolores, a long-time dancer who years ago headlined in the spot DeeDee danced at now, was filling in for her.

"Everything okay with Annie?" DeeDee asked as she looked in the mirror and brushed crimson upon her lips.

Dolores laced her corset and kept eyes off DeeDee. "Simon's got her doing those movies of his now."

"The loops?"

"Nope. Full-length features. She's livin' large as one of his porn stars." Her voice drips envy.

"Really? Annie?"

"Yup." Dolores slipped on a long white glove. "A lot of the girls are moving over to that. More money, no late-night shifts. Tell ya what. I bet you Heartbreakers will fall by the wayside before long."

"Oh, come on." DeeDee rolled stockings up her calves and over her knees. "It's bringing in more money than ever."

"Simon's found a new obsession, and if he's right, it'll make him more money than this place ever could. The girls, too." Dolores pulled on her other glove as she walked past, eyes never falling on DeeDee.

"Break a leg," DeeDee said, but Dolores was gone before she finished her encouragement.

DeeDee lost count on the number of loops she performed in. The outfits and sets changed, but her role was usually the same. She stood and stripped, she sat and stripped, she laid down and stripped. She caressed and fondled herself, stuck a finger here and a thumb there. Over the proceeding months, she found her inhibitions whittled down a bit more with each loop, and she became more painfully aware of each and every notch of dignity that was chipped away. She was losing control, and she wanted it back—with interest.

"Simon," she called out one day between filming. "Let's talk."

He sat down next to her. "Absolutely, beautiful. What's up?"

Despite the negligee she wore, the feather boa around her neck, and the absurd stiletto heels strapped to her feet, she still channeled a power driven by her determination as she stared Simon down. "Pay close attention. I have a proposition for you, and it's non-negotiable. Understand?"

Simon shifted backward slightly. "This sounds serious."

"It's about making you a lot more money. You ready for it?"

He ran thumb and index finger down the pipes of his mustache and stroked his goatee. "Oh, you have me all ears."

She straightened up in her chair, hands flat against the high top. "I'll be a star in your movies—"

"Double Dee!"

Her finger went up. "But—"

"Anything."

"I want producer rights on whatever I'm in. Plus creative control. And forty percent of the returns." She'd been around Simon enough during his fundraisers to have picked up on key aspects of his business, as well as how to take control of a negotiation.

Simon blinked. Blinked again. He expelled a chuckle. "Wow. Okay. Well. Producer rights, creative *input*, and *twenty* percent of returns on any productions that feature you."

"I said non-negotiable."

"And I say get real."

DeeDee leaned back, crossed her arms. "Thirty percent and creative overwrite."

Simon fingered his little triangle of goatee, looking like he had just sucked a lemon. Then, with a wink to her, that sour puss turned into a crooked grin.

"Twenty-five." He threw out a hand. "Deal?"

DeeDee shook it. "Partners, then."

CHAPTER TWENTY-THREE

Road Trip

I didn't realize that this volunteer gig would end up leading me to drive my little Volkswagen further than I've probably driven it yet this year. And I certainly never thought I'd be on the interstate at nine in the morning driving into Chicago.

My knuckles are white on the wheel and I'm perspiring. What did I get myself into?

Stop meddling, Pauline. It'll end up being the death of you one day.

Like today.

But I simply could not pass up the golden opportunity to try and learn more about this fractured relationship between DeeDee and Raymond. So here I am, being passed on the left by every vehicle on the road as I do 65 miles an hour in a 70-mile-an-hour speed zone, heading into the third-largest city in the United States on a Saturday morning to pick up Julienne from the ChicagoU campus so she can spend the weekend with her grandmother and father.

On Thursday, Raymond worked remotely at his mother's place. He's been doing that whenever he's able, as much as two or three times a week. We've spoken little to each other since our last meeting at the Sunnyside Restaurant, but we're cordial and polite. On that morning, he mentioned he had a conflict with work, and he wouldn't be able to pick up Jules on Saturday. Apparently, she was really upset about it.

"I'll pick her up." I blurted that before taking any time to think it over.

Raymond waved off the offer. "I couldn't possibly ask you to do that."

"You aren't asking. I'm simply offering. I would really like to."

Raymond's head shook. "No, that's too much to expect—"

DeeDee cut him off. "Raymond. Hush. Let Pauline decide what is or isn't too much for her."

"Mother—"

"She wants to help. *Pour l'amour de Dieu*, let her!"

Reluctantly, he gave me her cell number and directions on where to go. And if I get there without myself or some other angry driver killing me first, it'll be a miracle.

Traffic slows to a crawl about five miles before my exit at 59th Street. It takes fifteen minutes to get off I-94. I left my house at 6:00am and I'm just hitting the university campus at 9:30. If I'm lucky, we'll get back a little after one o'clock and I'll have an hour and a half to get ready for work.

Mind your own business, Pauline.

I manage to find Julienne's dorm, and I pull into the 15-minute temporary parking at the front of the building.

- I'm parked out front!

It only takes a few moments for her to text back.

- Be right down!

Ten minutes pass, which makes me nervous. A few more minutes and I'll be illegally parked. Of course, no official has been by to mark my time, so I have no idea if I should worry about that. It doesn't matter, though, because here comes Jules with suitcase in hand and backpack over shoulder.

She opens the back door. "Sorry sorry sorry!" She's tossing bag and suitcase inside. "Had some packing to finish, and then *everybody* wanted to say goodbye!"

She closes the back door and hops into the passenger seat with so much youthful energy I expect her body to arc with electricity. "Hi!"

She's all smiles and before I know what's happening, she's reached over to my side and giving me the biggest, warmest hug of my life. "You are so completely awesome to come all this way and pick me up!"

All the stress of the drive that had drawn muscles tight like elastic now release within her fierce embrace, leaving behind the biggest smile.

She settles back in her seat. "I jumped at the opportunity. It's so good to see you again."

She dons a red and white ChicagoU hoodie with a red ChicagoU t-shirt under that. She wears her long box-braided locks of raven hair half up, half down and it falls elegantly in a bundle between her shoulder blades. In the rearview mirror, I see my wild, silver-streaked bushy hair and feel slovenly and old.

"Three hours on the road with the coolest lady I know!" Jules gives a hoot and my cheeks warm.

"You need to get out more," I say.

She giggles, I guffaw, and I put the car into drive.

"So, how's the semester going?"

A groan leaks out of her, tightening to a whine. "It's sooo much work. And it's all stupid general ed courses! Why do all the stupid general courses give us so much make-work?"

That rings a bell from back in my early college days. Of course, I was usually too drunk to care. "Well, those classes are giving you core knowledge, and let's be honest, students don't always exit high school with that foundational education."

Jules looks around her with suspicion. "Is this car bugged? Are you undercover for my advisor?" I startle, and almost cross lanes as she starts patting me down. "You're wired, aren't you?"

"Stop it!" I say, laughing but also wide-eyed. "You'll kill us both, and I definitely don't want to face your father if that happens!"

She barks laughter, and I haven't felt so akin to someone in a long, long time. Jules is flamboyant, outlandish, passionate, and completely fearless. I really am learning to love this girl. She reminds me of the better part of my old self. The one not so staunch and morose. The more exuberant me after going dry— before the Motherhouse. Before Mother's death and all those years with Father. It was a façade, admittedly, one that wasn't sustainable. But for a little while, I had been able to fool even myself and completely indulge in life.

"He'd hunt you down in the afterlife just to tell you how disappointed he is in you!" Jules exclaims.

"Oh, that's bad. That's not nice. We shouldn't talk about him like that."

Jules's face falls. "No, you're right. That's not nice at all."

We're quiet for a moment.

She turns to me. "But doesn't he just ask for it? Seriously?"

My scowl scolds her, but I can't hold the expression. "Oh, *begs* for it. Absolutely."

And we both fill the car with laughter again.

It's her energy that's so contagious. Anything the least bit amusing becomes uproariously funny with her. In the next hour, we talk about her grann, about school, about the books that are blowing her mind, and the music that is swelling her heart. She talks about her social justice course she's taking, and I see in her a passion and drive to change the world. In turn, she wants to know everything about me. I'm skilled at deflecting those questions and turning them back on the person asking. Jules, however, is relentless, and unabashed.

"Did you ever marry?"

I laugh. "Never."

"Why not?"

My entire life story would still only suggest at all the complications of that answer. I'm honestly not even certain I know the why, so simply say, "It just never came to pass."

"Never met the right guy?"

I try to dismiss the question with a shrug. "The right guy never seemed to hang around."

Before she can dig deeper, I ask, "What about you? Is there a special person in your life?"

"There was. A high school romance. Brady Carlisle."

"Sounds like a football star."

"Quarterback. But, not a jock. Know what I mean? Super friendly. Super smart." She shifts abruptly in her seat, drawing a leg up and slipping a foot under her. "Get this. He played the clarinet."

"No."

"Yes! And he was really, *really* good!"

I grin. "Well, that is prime marriage material right there."

She runs her hands slowly down her thighs. "I know. Even my dad loved him."

I shoot her a brief look. "Was that the problem?"

"What? No! I mean, I don't think so?" The last came off distinctly as a question. I may have touched on something she hadn't thought about. "Like, he and my Dad were like father and son, and I really loved that, you know? But also—huh. You know, I guess I never thought about it until now, but—yeah, I suppose

I kind of felt like second string on team Brady and Raymond."

Her confused expression mixes with a spark of realization. In a moment, she shakes her head. "Whatever. I don't know. But I really did like him. He was super sweet, but when the opportunity came to go to University of Chicago, there was no way I could pass that up."

"What about him?"

"Oh, he got an athletic scholarship at Northwestern. We promised each other we'd keep in touch. We've texted a few times, talked about getting together, but it's never happened. I think we've both moved on."

"Good for you," I say. "There's so much world and life for you to experience before you commit to anything. Make the world commit to you first."

She stares at me. "I have no idea what that means, but I *love it*. Wow." She shakes her head. "You know, I can't imagine a more perfect person to be with Grann right now. It's so nuts just how much you two—I don't know—just *click*."

A cozy warmth swells in my chest. "That's so sweet of you. It's been quite an honor, and an amazing experience, getting to know your grandmother."

"She's an incredible woman."

"Indeed." I've held back for well over an hour, but this feels like the perfect conversational fulcrum to pivot upon. "So, do you mind me asking, have your father and grandmother always been at such loggerheads?"

My eyes shift off the road just long enough to watch her face go taut. She draws a hefty breath. "Always and forever."

"But, why?"

A shrug. A headshake. Both a slow, exhaustive surrender. "They just don't get along."

"He's never given a reason?"

"Not really. Just his typical frustrations. She's overbearing.

Selfish. Self-obsessed."

"He's called her all those things to you?"

"Oh, yeah. All the time. Whenever he gets upset or frustrated with her."

I sigh. "That's so sad."

She nods vigorously. "I know! I almost feel guilty anytime I bring her up in conversation! But it's hard *not* to talk about her sometimes, you know?"

"Heh. Most certainly, I know."

I see Jules peering at the dashboard, then at me. "Um, Pauline? You know the speed limit here is seventy, right?"

I glance at my speedometer needle wobbling around sixty-five and see car after car pass me from my periphery. "I sure do."

Jules smiles a confused smile and shakes her head. "Cool."

"Jules," I start, then I pause. Just how dangerously deep do I want to dive? But, as the expression goes, in for a penny, in for a pound. "How much do you know about your grandmother's past?"

Jules gives me a quizzical look. "What do you mean?"

I don't want to share any family secrets, yet DeeDee gave no impression that any of what she's told me is a secret. "I mean, like her time in San Francisco?"

"You mean her porn years?"

I stammer. Jules laughs. "Oh, Pauline. That look of yours is priceless!" She slaps her thigh and belts laughter. "Grann was a porn star! Everyone knows that!"

I expel a light cough. "Well, I've just become privy to that knowledge."

Jules lays a hand on my shoulder. "Oh, no. You aren't put off by that, are you?"

"Well, no, not that. Perhaps a bit of a feministic affront, but really—no. Not at all."

"Good. Different time. Tough decisions. She did what she had to."

Would DeeDee agree with that today? Sure, she isn't ashamed of what she did, and that's good, but she might have been tumbling down a deep, dark rabbit hole, and her story may not have hit bottom yet. All that seems certain is that, somehow, she managed to emerge the better from it.

"And, obviously, your father knows about her past?"

"Jesus, Pauline, of course he does!"

I bristle to that, but let it pass.

"In fact, I had to deal with that most of my life." Her body stiffens, mouth turns rigid, and her voice goes absurdly deep. 'Julienne, I've worked hard so you don't have to resort to the things your grandmother did.' 'Be thankful, Julienne, that you have a mother and father who were responsible and could give you a proper childhood.' 'No matter how difficult life may get, you never have to stoop to the actions your grandmother took.'"

I'm nodding, but only because I'm finally seeing the suggestion of a picture these puzzle pieces are revealing.

"It had to be hard, growing up with such admiration for your grandmother, when your father felt so differently about her."

Part of me regrets bringing any of this up. A quick glance at Jules and I see a different girl—one who is weighed down with conflict and whose emotions are pulled in different directions. It's apparent that this family hasn't worked out some very obvious issues for far too long, or avoided them completely, and now there is little time left to resolve them.

"Actually, for half my life, my mom and dad didn't have a lot to do with Grann. She was still in Chicago at that time, and she'd only visit a few times a year. Dad only had negative things to say about her, and Mom didn't really want anything to do with her. She started visiting more when she retired eight or nine years ago when her health started to get bad. I was around eleven, and that's the first time I really got to know her. Meanwhile, things kept getting worse between Dad and Mom. They thought they were hiding it from me, but, well, it's pretty clear to see when two people don't love each other anymore, you know? Even for a teenaged girl. Well, I guess I wasn't dealing with it too well. At one point, I kind of ran away from home and went to Grann's place. Mom and Dad were furious, mostly at her because she didn't tell them right away. But that's when Grann and I really bonded. It was such a great time. I really got to know her. And, over time, Dad kinda used that as leverage against my Mom."

"What do you mean?"

"Mom played the doting daughter-in-law really well when she was around Grann, but my mom didn't want Grann anywhere near me. It was Dad who let me keep seeing her, even though Mom wasn't keen on it—I think as a way to gain favor with me."

"That's...horrible." My voice is weak. I can't see Raymond being so manipulative.

Jules puts on a wary grin. "Well, don't give my dad too hard of a time. Mom was doing a lot of things at that time to try and tip the scales to her advantage. He was just doing what he could, so he didn't lose me."

"And you recognized all of this? You knew what was going on?"

"Sure. For the most part. I tried to stay as neutral as possible, but like I told them when they finally said they were getting divorced. 'You both tell me you want what's best for me, but you've already crapped all over that, so what's left is just what is least awful for me. I'm taking care of that. This is all about you two, now, not me. Leave me out of it.'"

Imagining those years that Julienne went through, how quickly she matured through it, forces a deep exhale from me. "You are quite an amazing woman, Julienne. You know that?"

She gives me the biggest, brightest, smartest grin. "I sure do!"

And we both laugh.

James L. Peters

CHAPTER TWENTY-FOUR

Atonement

On Monday, I attend an AA meeting. They're held every weekday. Most members choose a day and attend each week. Some long haulers like myself typically attend only once or twice a month, unless we're in crisis. It's a smaller crowd tonight, probably around thirty-five or forty of us. Some nights the head count is over seventy.

We begin as we always do, with the AA Preamble, followed by the Serenity Prayer. Our Chapter Leader, Harold, asks if there is anyone new joining us tonight, but no one raises their hands.

The last meeting I attended had been a "Speaker" meeting. Since I was getting my twenty-year chip, Harold asked if I would like to share my story again. Tonight's meeting is a "Discussion," and we sit in one big circle in the meeting room under the Unitarian Church. Harold wears jeans, brown boots, and a corduroy blazer over a pin-striped button-up shirt. Gray tints his horseshoe ring of sandy hair and has overtaken his closely trimmed beard.

"I thought we'd tackle a topic we haven't discussed for quite some time, and I think it's as important as any. Tonight, I'd like us to talk about forgiveness."

It's hard not to wince at that word, at the thought of spending the next hour talking about something I have great difficulty with. Being a Catholic, I'm much more comfortable with meetings where we read from the *Big Book*, and when we recite the Twelve Steps. I'm more attuned to a liturgical regimen of readings and sermons rather than a group confessional. I like my confessions to be one on one with a priest providing opportunities for contrition. I'll discuss literature and art and anything that brings color and flavor to life with a group of people, but it is painful for me to sit through discussions of demons I haven't exorcised yet.

Harold does pull out the AA *Big Book* and opens it upon his lap. "The Big Book has this to say about forgiveness: 'Forgiveness is a decision, not an emotion, and it must be sincere to get results.' It then emphasizes that, in recovery, it is just as important to forgive ourselves as it is to forgive others." He pauses as his gaze follows along the circle of members.

"So, let me start. As many of you already know, I'm fifteen years recovered. Four years into my marriage, our relationship had begun to slowly drift apart. He claimed my drinking was the problem, but that didn't make sense. To my mind, I was a good husband. I was responsible and had a good job that helped to support us. Alcoholics were not loving and successful husbands. I began to suspect Glen of cheating on me.

"One night, when he was late coming home, I drank my gin and tonics, growing more and more furious as I worked through half a bottle of Beefeater. When he finally came through the door, we had a horrible fight. I lost control. I attacked him. I was throwing things at him, hitting him. I slammed his head against the wall. He had to drive himself to the hospital. And, of course, the cops were called.

"The courts assigned me AA, and I began a path of healing.

One of the hardest things for me to do as I went through the twelve steps was to reconcile what I had done to Glen. I had hurt him. Not just physically, but emotionally. How in the world could I ever forgive myself for such a horrible, dreadful act?

"I obsessed over my overwhelming guilt. It was this huge, heavy weight I was collapsing under. Had I been in my right mind, I would never have done anything like that. The alcohol had done that. In time, as I went through the program, I started to instead focus on reconciling those damaged parts of my character that drove me to drink in the first place—my insecurities and low self-esteem. The abuse I experienced by my father. I realized how the drinking turned my frailties into suspicion and paranoia—and eventually led me to do such a terrible thing. I didn't love myself, and the drinking made me hurt the person I loved more than anything.

"That's when I could face Glen and take responsibility for my actions. I had to stop blaming myself for the past that had traumatized me, that caused me to not like myself. Only then could I forgive myself for almost ruining our marriage. And Glen could forgive me."

He looks around the room. "Anyone else here having troubles with forgiveness? Want to talk about it? There's no judgment here. Maybe we can help you navigate your way toward forgiveness."

I can't look at him. When I even think about sharing that unforgiveable part of my story, no words come. It's too soon. Thirty-two years is too soon.

The meeting is over. I pour coffee into a white Styrofoam cup. AA's logo should be a white Styrofoam cup. I can't look at one without thinking of this group. In fact, just having one in my hand is a kind of comfort and support—a reminder of twenty years of recovery.

Harold's boots clomp against the tiled floor as he approaches. He's looking ministerial, his folded hands resting over his slight paunch. "Can I talk to you for a moment?"

I nod and he pulls me aside to a corner of the room. I anticipate what he's about to say because he says it just about every other meeting, so I start preparing my response.

"That twenty-year chip is quite an accomplishment."

"Thanks, Harold." I sip coffee.

"You know, you're one of our longest and most successful members. For years now, I've really hoped you'd consider being a sponsor."

I begin my pat reply. "I completely appreciate that, Harold. But you know up until a few months ago, I was caring for my father—"

"I know."

"And now, on top of work and settling my parents' estate, I've been volunteering for the hospice program—"

"I know."

"It's all just an issue of availability and—"

Harold cuts me off. "Bullshit, Pauline. Total bullshit. You know as much as anyone that being a sponsor has nothing to do with availability and everything to do with commitment."

"How can I commit when I don't have the time and have so many other obligations?"

He puts up a hand. "Listen, you're not required to be a sponsor for anyone. It's just strongly encouraged. But at least own up to why you refuse being a sponsor. It has nothing to do with time or commitment. I know you too well. There's something else holding you back."

My shoulder blades slap against the wall as I lean into it, cross arms and scowl at the floor. "Harold, I just don't feel I've got it together enough to be a reliable support to someone else."

"Wow. You say that, and yet only twenty percent of alcoholics make it as far as you have. You've done it dealing with a sick and dying father, and now helping a sick and dying woman. Come on. Talk to me, Pauline. Let me help you unload whatever's weighing you down."

Scattered about the room, members are chatting, drinking coffee, puffing e-cigs until they can light up outside.

"Harold, how many of us are married?"

He looks confused. "Huh?"

I nod to everyone else standing around talking about the weather, about the Bear's chances this year, about all things light and topical. "Our group. How many are married? Do you know?"

He's befuddled, but he seems to mull it over. "I don't, exactly, but I can't think of more than a handful off the top of my head. Some divorced, some never married. But there's me, of course. And John is. Theresa, too. Oh, and Will, he's married. Others, too, I'm pretty sure."

Exactly what I expected. "But, more of us aren't married, or never married, right?"

"What are you getting at?"

"We're inherently broken. We're terrible partners with others. Sobriety brought some clarity and focus to our lives, but it hasn't really made us better people, has it? It certainly doesn't absolve us of our actions. It just helps us to better live with them."

"That's why we rely on a higher power, Pauline. You, of all people, should know and appreciate that."

"Don't you ever fear the judgment of that higher power, Harold?"

Harold shifts and squirms against my words. "Pauline, I feel I owe you an apology. I've been your sponsor for, what, seven years now? I've obviously let you down."

"Don't be silly—"

"Let's take some time, maybe revisit the twelve steps again."

"No. Harold. I'm sorry. Let's forget this conversation. I'm being silly." I walk back to the table, put down my cup and start to leave.

"No, Pauline. Hold on—"

"I'll catch you at the next meeting, Harold. Thanks for the talk."

"Pauline—"

Walking up the stairs and out the back door of the church, I'm not able to lock on to what I was trying to say or if there was a point. I just keep thinking about Jack, about my days as a librarian, about my parents, about my fleeting relationships with men from the bar, and of course about Kaiya. I think about DeeDee and how, even when she was compromising herself to make it through difficult times, she had tremendous strength of character and full control of her actions.

At some point early on, I lost control—or it was taken from me—and now I'm not sure how to even begin identifying when and where I first went wrong so I can know what to forgive myself for.

CHAPTER TWENTY-FIVE

The Reckoning

"You seem troubled of late, dawlin'. Something wrong?"

I pick up my crib hand after my dealer's hand only moved my peg six points on the Cribbage board. I manage to find a mere two points more and score it. Yuck. I toss the hand into the discards on the card table next to the couch and look up at her. "What do you mean?"

She coughs. "Oh, I don't know. You're just a bit more quiet than usual."

"Maybe that is because you are quite completely kicking my backside in this game—again."

Ms. DeeDee chuckles and coughs, inhales deep through her nose. "Luck of the draw. But be true to me, now. Something gnawing away at you?"

"Not at all." My smile is tight. "Everything is wonderful."

Ms. DeeDee drops her cards and gives me a stern, dubious glare. "I know that smile. That's not your happy smile. That's your grin-and-bear-it smile."

"What ever would you be referring to?" I point to my mouth. "This, madam, is pure joy."

She scooches herself up a bit, which brings on more coughs. She keeps that intense brow low over her eyes. "Come now, Pauline. You don't share much about yourself. You talk about your books and your job—and all the time, you're asking about me. But what about you?"

This isn't the first time she's tried to dig into the mysteries of Pauline, but I've deflected as much as possible.

"As I've told you, my dear, Miss DeeDee, there's not much to tell."

"I very much doubt that."

I draw all the cards together and start to shuffle the deck for her.

"How is it going with your parent's place?"

I riffle-shuffle and bridge the cards. "Good! I have successfully gathered all the pieces of their lives, salvaging a few relics to cherish, while the bulk of their existence will be auctioned off to the highest bidders."

The scrutiny that hooded her eyes eases to somber reflection. "So fleeting this time of ours on the Earth. I wonder sometimes, how long will any part of me remain until even the memory of me fades, like the last note of a song."

I stop mid-shuffle and gawk at her. "DeeDee. You are a poet."

She lazes a melancholy look to me. "I'm dying, *mon cygne*. We all become poets in the face of death."

I finish shuffling and place the deck of cards before her. "It's your deal."

"Did you mean what you said to Margie at the club that night?"

"What's that?"

"About having no interest in marriage?"

Silence.

"I'm sorry. I didn't mean to ask anything uncomfortable."

"It's fine." Pause. "I certainly grew up thinking I'd meet the right man, have a good, Catholic wedding, and three or four children."

"Was there a particular reason why you didn't?"

"No particular one, but I suppose so many. In the end, though, my priorities simply changed."

Cherise stood, mouth agape, as DeeDee gave her the news.

"I'm sorry," DeeDee said and put her focus back on slicing onions in the back kitchen. Her eyes burned as she sliced and diced, but the tears felt more like the sting of the moment than from the Vadalia. The café was her main connection to Cherise, and she was about to give that up.

"Oh, Dee. Oh, what are you getting yourself into, girl?" Cherise's arms hung limp at her sides.

DeeDee dropped her knife to wipe her eyes. "Cherise, I'm making way more money than I ever could here, and these movies will earn me even more."

Cherise looked devastated, as if DeeDee were dying instead of quitting. "But, sweetie, what you're willing to do for that money—"

"Is exactly what will let me take control of my life and do what I want to do."

Cherise put a gentle hand upon DeeDee's shoulder. "But at what cost, girl?"

DeeDee stood upright, shoulders straight and back. "I'm calling the shots, Cherise. I'm in control."

Cherise nodded, but the tears started to streak her eye liner. "I'm going to miss working with my friend."

"Me, too. But we'll get together all the time, okay?"

Cherise grabbed her by the shoulders and pulled her in for a long, hard hug. "You be careful, you hear me? Be safe."

"I will," DeeDee said into her shoulder.

They pulled away, but Cherise held on tight to her at arm's length. "Don't you disappear on me, you hear? I need to know you're okay."

"I won't." She hoped she and Cherise would stay in contact. She had become DeeDee's closest friend. But DeeDee was moving into a completely different world than the one Cherise existed in. Maybe it was for the best that they didn't cross paths. Cherise didn't understand DeeDee's world, and DeeDee didn't really want her to. Better that Cherise remember DeeDee as her friend and fellow waitress at the café than as Double Dee, star of pornographic films.

Cherise smiled. "I say we go out tonight and dance our asses off."

DeeDee nodded. "I like that idea a lot."

Although DeeDee still danced on many a Friday and Saturday night, the movies, and her role as an executive producer, took up more of her time. As a now-burgeoning star of the movies, she was spending an increasing amount of time in front of the camera and having to learn lines—albeit very few of them. She took her producer role even more seriously than perhaps Simon had expected.

"This dialogue is terrible," she said one day as she paged through the meager script of their latest movie. She cleared her throat. "'I'm here to fix your television.' 'Why don't you fix me, first?'" The script crumbled in her closed fist. "Seriously?"

Simon rolled eyes at her. "Trust me, baby, our audience really doesn't care. Whatever gets them to the good stuff as fast as possible."

DeeDee didn't let it go. "I don't know. I think they do care. This is all fantasy, right? A guy enjoys his fantasy when it seems possible. This dialogue is going to have the same effect as mama coming into his room while he's jacking off."

Simon's eyes popped wide, and he sputtered a laugh. "What?"

DeeDee just nodded.

Simon shook his head and snatched the pages from her. "Wow. Aren't you turning into a little Stanley Kubrick. Fine. Go ahead and tweak it if you'd like. Make it better. But remember, this isn't Tennessee Williams, you dig?"

At the start, they were shooting two or three movies a week, which meant the scripts barely had any story—just a few pages of descriptions with incidental dialogue to set up each scene. The films barely pushed the 70-minute mark. DeeDee did her best to introduce some level of sexual tension as foreplay for the audience. Her input helped their movies become less and less a series of loops and instead offer a thin thread of narrative.

Despite her significant contributions to the scripts that improved the productions, there was little argument that her actions in front of the camera provided a far greater return on investment.

Most of her time on camera as Double-Dee Orlean was alone, doing extended scenes of what all her loops had been. She told Simon she wouldn't perform any actual on-screen intercourse, so she played a secretary who got hot by her boss screwing a client, or she played a nurse assistant who got herself off watching the chief surgeon balling the head nurse. Simon continually confronted DeeDee with his frustration at her refusal to take a lead role and go all the way, but she held her ground.

Annabel was their main star and willingly gave the camera a full show with her co-stars. She was screwing every actor on camera who was under contract with BCD Productions, as well as most of the crew off-camera. She was very open about her sex addiction, especially if cocaine, pills, or alcohol were involved. DeeDee recalled Cherise's concerns, about the cost of what she would be doing, and knew she was witnessing it with this poor girl. DeeDee tried to talk to Annie about it, but so much of the time, she was too out of her head to be rationalized with. DeeDee suspected that her drug and sex addictions were the symptoms of far more complex issues.

After a few months, Simon's pressure on DeeDee intensified. He persistently came at her to step up and get top billing in the movies.

"Double-Dee, listen. Ebony porn is just getting hot right now. We get in early enough and we could corner that market."

DeeDee scowled.

"Listen, I've got a guy all ready to go. His name's Ken. Let's get a good, hot scene between you and him."

"No way."

"He could be a cook, and you could be his waitress."

"Gross."

Simon's look turned serious and penetrating. "Dee. You signed up for this. You agreed to it. As a partner, you have an obligation to do what is best for the business—our business."

The scenes she'd been shooting lately were inching her ever more forward. She was constantly on-screen with other men now, doing just about everything but sucking or fucking. And, top billing meant double the paycheck.

She glared at Simon. "Fine. I'll do one. But I want to be very clear about this. I will not fuck this Ken guy. I won't."

Simon put up his hands. "Fine. We'll simulate it, okay? No penetration. But you need to be all in to sell it. Get me?"

DeeDee shook her head. She really wasn't sure if she could do this.

"Hey, think of it as supporting civil rights, huh? We're out to give the Black man his God-given right and freedom to stiffen his wally to a member of his own race."

"You know, sometimes, you can be a complete pig."

"Hey, all I'm saying—"

"Just shut up before I reconsider this entire business arrangement."

He scrutinized her. "You'll really do it, then?"

"Yes, damn it."

Simon wore his smile like a trophy. "That's my girl."

What DeeDee hadn't expected was how much being touched by an attractive man could turn her on, even in front of a camera with a crew watching and the tungsten bulbs burning.

Her first few scenes had been unbearably squeamish and uncomfortable. She fought him touching her the first few times. The word, "Cut!" came as a tremendous relief. Ken, however, was actually a very nice, sweet guy, and very professional. Slowly, his caresses evoked a stirring in her. The electricity and pleasure of Ken's very experienced and knowledgeable touch began to overwhelm. As time wore on, the director's shout to end the scene became a distant voice lost to the dizziness of an ecstasy that was still so new to her. The ground would fall away, and she would float on air.

She hit the ground hard when the lights shut off and the chatter of the crew took over. She was cold, her body heavy when she stepped off the set. She'd get a few words of encouragement from Ken, "That was nice," or "You were great," and then they'd part ways, and DeeDee would watch him take up a conversation with Tim the key grip as he wrapped a towel around his slim, muscular waist. DeeDee would slip into her robe, wrap it tightly around her, and avoid everyone as much as possible for the next half hour.

Simon stuck to his word. DeeDee did two more movies that week, neither involving any penetration, though the simulated sex was still heated and intense.

As productions continued and the crew and performers improved and fell into a groove, DeeDee started thinking about that absurd comment Simon made about Ebony Porn being a form of civil rights. Such a moronic statement from an ignorant White man, but it made her flash back to a lifetime ago in New Orleans—being seventeen and the one lone Black Bevinetto dancer on the *John Sela Show*. She remembered being separated by a curtain in that Bourbon Street club. She thought again of her childhood hero, little Ruby Bridges, stepping into that all-White school. Suddenly, Simon's ridiculous statement gave her an idea she couldn't get out of her head.

Wrapping up a production called, "Ebony Innocence Lost," she grabbed the robe handed to her by a stagehand and stepped over to Simon who sat in the corner going over the books.

"Hey, Simon. You want to really shake things up?"

Simon looked up with surprise and eagerness. "Oh, yeah. Now you're talking! What's on your mind?"

"Interracial."

Simon's smile froze. He shifted in his seat. "I love how you're thinking, Double Dee, but that could put us in some real trouble."

DeeDee frowned. "How? Why?"

"You haven't heard?"

"Heard what?"

"Mack Trevor. Pussywillow Studios. He was arrested along with three of his actors for indecency while shooting an interracial menage-a-trois."

That shouldn't have surprised her. Less than a decade ago, the owner of the Dew Drop Club was getting arrested simply for having Whites and Blacks together in his establishment. It was hard to think that anything like that could happen here in

San Francisco in the '70s. But, she also knew what Alfred was witnessing and fighting against.

"You sure it wasn't just general public indecency they were being charged with?"

Simon shrugged. "Sure, that's what the cops said. But honey, none of us have had more than a light scolding from the police for over a year now. Don't kid yourself, there are those out there who will fight the idea of interracial mingling to the bitter end."

"That's bullshit."

"That said—" Simon grabbed her by the shoulders, drew her in, and kissed her on the lips. "I fucking love that idea!"

Stunned and a little dizzy by the kiss, DeeDee just blinked and stammered.

"You just name the fellow and we'll pair you up. I'll get to work on the script right now. We'll start filming next week!"

DeeDee pointed out Deke Diamond as her choice. He was growing in popularity with their productions. Their meager female audience fell in love with his chiseled looks and toned body, while their core male audience liked his rugged presentation, low rumble of voice, and swagger. He was kind of the Clint Eastwood of porn instead of either the pretty boy or the mustachioed scuzzy guy, both of which were pervading the industry.

She came up with a storyline—stupidly simple, yet more nuanced than any blue movie out there. Simon went with it, and she sat with him, helping to lay out the script.

It opened in a living room with DeeDee in a fight with Ken, who would play her husband. That will lead to some heated make-up sex, but then he will get violent and she will have to fight him off, throwing an ashtray, lamp, and other items at him.

Enter Deke, playing a police officer, who will arrive to investigate the ruckus. At first, his presence will be threatening as a White cop in a Black woman's apartment. The tension will build as he won't believe her story at first, but will come to sympathize with her and eventually tell her he'll do whatever it takes to keep her safe. Her appreciation will turn to intimacy, which he won't be able to resist, and they'll go all out on the kitchen table. That's when the husband will return.

DeeDee thought it would be exciting to have the police officer fight and subdue the husband and then she would ravish the officer again with thanks. Simon thought the movie was already too situational and dialogue-heavy, so instead, he suggested the husband join in for a threesome. DeeDee said that was the stupidest thing she ever heard. Simon said it was money in the bank.

They started shooting the following week. The dialogue and staging were more complicated than anything they had done before, and the entire first day was just getting through her scenes with Ken. The energy in the studio by the end of that first day was palpable. Even though they were still simply shooting some hot and heavy sex scenes between DeeDee and Ken, this was feeling more like a movie than anything they'd shot up to that point. Steve, their cinematographer, Bobby the sound guy, Sandra on lighting—everybody was getting into it more, and DeeDee loved that. Somehow it made all this feel less dirty, even if the story and dialogue were paper thin. There was still the semblance of a narrative arc, some real emotion expressed, and it felt like she was really, truly acting.

The entire crew jumped into day two's production with eager enthusiasm. Ideas were thrown around about camera angles, different lighting techniques. Shooting began with the introduction of Deke and his imposing presence in his blues. DeeDee went all in on her performance, picking up where yesterday left off. She wept, half-naked, covering herself with torn clothing. Deke picked up on her performance and went in heavy on the initial intimidation. As DeeDee collapsed on the couch, weeping into her hands, Deke turned tender, joining her on the couch and consoling her.

"I'm all alone, and I'm so scared," she sobbed and looked into his eyes with her pleading ones.

"Don't worry, ma'am. I promise, I'll do whatever I can to make sure he won't hurt you again." He placed a reassuring hand on her knee. She dropped her gaze to his hand, placed hers over his, and looked back at him, not just with gratitude, but longing.

He moved in for a gentle kiss. Before long, she was unbuttoning his shirt and undoing his pants, and he was slipping off her torn blouse and pulling down her skirt. He stood, picked her up, and they moved to the kitchen table.

DeeDee was nervous. Everything seemed different this time. She was suddenly feeling outside of the set and existing inside the scene. As silly as the script was, it brought out a more sincere emotion and passion in each of them. And yes, she was also unexpectedly turned on being with a White man—something that she very well knew could have got her lynched not that many years ago in the south. The intercourse was supposed to be simulated as per her insistence, but the moment was overtaking her. Was she really going to allow him—

"Holy shit, cops." It was Tim, their key grip, looking behind him.

Three uniformed officers approached from the back studio door. The first one in the middle, black pompadour over dark, narrow eyes, pointed to the stage. "Good afternoon, everyone! You are all in violation of California penal code section 311a. Shut it down. Now."

The two other officers split up as they moved into the crew. The blond one with beard and mustache yanked out the extension cord powering the lights and the studio went dark.

"Are you serious, man?" Bobby said, pulling his headphones off his ears to hang around his neck. "Why the hassle?"

"You!" The middle officer with the black Elvis hair approached with a swagger, gesturing at Deke. "Get off the lady immediately. No more perversions today."

Deke, naked other than the opened blue police uniform shirt, stumbled off DeeDee, and bent over to grab his pants. The officer stepped up to him, put his boot on Deke's butt, and shoved him over. "Like playing an officer of the law, do you?"

Deke scrambled back up on his feet. He stayed quiet, wide-eyed with fear and embarrassment as he slipped his pants on.

DeeDee, meanwhile, was still on the table, completely nude other than her red pumps, one arm across her chest and her hand covering her crotch.

The officer bent down, grabbed her blouse off the floor, and threw it at her. "Get yourself decent, would you?"

She sat up, held the blouse to her chest, and scowled at him. "You first."

His mouth curled into a sneer, and he took a step toward her.

"Officer, I'm sure we can clear all this up." Simon had moved up from the back of the room and stepped between DeeDee and the cop.

"You're DeReznor, right?"

Simon extended a hand. "Simon DeReznor of Behind Closed Doors Productions. I also run Heartbreakers night club."

The officer looked down at Simon's hand, grinned. "Yeah, we know all about you." He grabbed Simon's hand at the wrist and swung it behind his back. "Mr. DeRenzor, you are under arrest for violating the California obscenity laws."

"No!" DeeDee yelled.

The police officer grabbed his other arm, brought it back and handcuffed Simon's wrists.

Simon was all smiles. "This is ridiculous." He shook his head and winked at DeeDee. She couldn't believe he wasn't taking this seriously. "You don't want to waste your time or the courts with this silliness."

The lead officer pointed to his two fellow policemen. "Handcuff those two as well." He gestured to DeeDee and Deke with one hand as he held Simon's cuffed wrists with the other.

DeeDee's eyes shot wide open. True terror turned her blood cold and shortened her breath.

"No, hold on," Simon said louder and more forceful. The smile was gone now. "That's not necessary. I'm responsible for this production and these people. Leave them be."

The other two officers approached. DeeDee was frozen, sitting on the table, still with only her blouse on. Deke had just finished cinching his belt. He watched the officer approaching him, gave a quick, desperate look at Simon, and bolted barefoot around the false wall of the set, heading for the back door.

"We got a runner," the lead officer called out. Both partners went after Deke.

"Goddamn it, this isn't necessary!" Simon yelled.

"Miss," said the officer. "You just stay put now. Best put some pants on, because you're coming with us."

The two officers had wrestled poor Deke to the ground in the back alley and roughed him up a little. DeeDee later learned he had a warrant out for dealing pot.

Simon and DeeDee got put in a cell overnight, which they shared with a small crowd of drunks, druggies, prostitutes, two Black Panthers, and more than a handful of Black men that, at least by their protestations, had little or no reason to be there other than for their skin color.

Simon tried talking to DeeDee, to reassure her. "Those bastards. Someone ratted us out, I'm sure of it. There's no fucking reason we should be here, but some racist fuckhead decided they didn't like the idea of you and Deke getting it on. I swear to God, if I find out it was one of our crew, I will split their skull."

DeeDee was only hearing his words as if over a chasm, but she wasn't listening. She was huddling deep within her psyche. It wasn't the traumatic shock like she experienced when she first arrived in San Francisco. This was different. She was processing everything—what had just happened, and everything that had led up to that point. She knew they didn't deserve to be in jail right now, and she didn't feel they were doing anything morally wrong. Still, being in that cold, concrete cell with criminals, wayward souls, and those who found themselves in the wrong place at the wrong time, she was realizing that she had strayed from her principles, had fallen too far from where she would feel good about herself. She had slid down a slippery slope, from the relative innocence of the exotic dancing, to objectifying herself as a means to an end. It was time to course-correct.

She finally fell into a fitful sleep on Simon's lap. He apparently stayed up all night. Every time she woke up, he was stroking her hair and reassuring her that everything would be okay. He would make sure of it.

Deke, unfortunately, would stay and face a judge for sentencing, charged with possession of and dealing marijuana. She and Simon, however, were released in the early morning after Simon paid a fine of two hundred dollars. As they grabbed a cab, Simon insisted that the police never intended to press charges; they just wanted to disrupt and punish the entire idea of promoting interracial relations.

"Where to?" The cabbie asked.

"What's your address?" Simon asked.

DeeDee started to answer, then realized how bad it would look to Alfred. He'd just be waking up right now, and for him to see her like this—

"Can we go straight to your place? It's not a good idea for me to head home right now. My brother would flip his lid."

"Yeah, I get that." He gave the cabbie his address in Sausalito, then gently put a reassuring arm around her. She fell onto his shoulder.

The entire ride was in silence. Even the cab driver made no attempt at conversation. At his apartment, Simon paid the driver, then helped DeeDee out of the back. She still felt somewhat out of her body, beside her identity. The sun was just peaking over the eastern horizon, the first birds softly welcoming the morning, and it seemed as if she were moving between the walls of the coming day.

Inside his apartment, he gestured to the couch. "Have a seat. Can I get you a drink? Something to settle your nerves?"

She nodded, looked around. His apartment was clean and respectable, surprisingly sparse. The space conveyed a minimalistic, contemporary aesthetic of white walls and natural wood flooring. She sat on a white leather couch before a fluffy white area rug with a glass coffee table upon it. A large, vibrant canvas pop art of a nude woman hung before her on an otherwise bare wall. Behind her, on a pedestal in the corner of the room was an abstract bronze sculpture of a tall and unnaturally sleek woman either stretching or dancing. The east wall was a huge picture window looking out to Richardson Bay.

He went into the kitchen, and she heard the clink of glasses, the soft pop of a cork. He came back with two tumblers of golden liquid.

"Try this." He handed one glass to her. "It's cognac." He sat next to her.

She'd never had it before and took a sip. It was dry, spicy, and bitter. Not something she would normally enjoy, but today she just needed something to warm her body and fuzz her head.

She took another, longer sip.

"You're welcome to my bed. I can sleep on the couch."

DeeDee shook her head. "No. I'm fine on the couch."

"It's not comfortable. I'll take it."

"That's not necessary."

They sipped cognac, looked out the window as the auburn glow of the new day spread over the bay and blushed the colorless room. She felt the tension of her muscles and nerves loosening.

"I need to apologize to you," he said.

"It was all my idea, Simon. You warned me. Nothing to apologize about."

"No. There is. I told you that I would protect you. That I would keep you pure and innocent."

DeeDee winced and tried to wave away his words. "Please."

She had never seen him look so serious, so sincere. "Well, I don't think I've kept that promise. I'm sorry for that."

She took a final sip of cognac, set her tumbler down with a cold, quiet chink of glass against glass, and turned to him. "You and Alfred. You both seem intent on taking responsibility for my actions. Don't. I've made very conscious decisions and only I am accountable to them."

His smile was so melancholy, wistful. "There is so much strength in you, Dee." He reached out and grazed her cheek with an index finger.

She smiled. "And, since coming here, of all the people currently in my life, you are one of the few I trust and feel safe with."

He smiled warmly. "Thank you."

"Even if you are a sleazebag."

He laughed. "Honest and straightforward as well."

She shrugged and gave a sly grin.

"I've only ever wanted what's best for you. And I think now, what's best for you is to stay the hell away from me."

DeeDee felt a tear drop onto her cheek. "I think you may

be right."

And she moved in and kissed him deeply.

Two months later, she was no longer in front of any camera, no longer dancing on stage. She and Simon had parted ways, and she was working as a sales clerk behind a make-up desk at a department store.

And her period still had not come.

James L. Peters

CHAPTER TWENTY-SIX

Motherhood

At the start of my junior year of college, when I was twenty years old, I got pregnant.

No. Scratch that. It wasn't some affliction, a virus I caught or disease I contracted. It didn't just randomly occur.

Because of actions taken, I became pregnant.

It happened, to the best of my knowledge, on a late September afternoon. All the windows of my crummy apartment were open, and this late summer breeze billowed the sheer white curtains like the haunt of ghosts. Golden afternoon sunlight rippled through the ruffle of muslin like the glimmer of water. The light splashed across a cluttered room of ramshackle furniture while I slowly pulled down the pants of a sophomore gentleman from my creative writing class seated on the couch. He nervously pushed my pants down and I straddled him.

I had enjoyed a few drinks before then but wasn't drunk, simply enamored by this creative and attractive young man I began a rapport with during class. I'm fairly certain he accepted my invitation with little pretense. My pretenses were dripping from my words.

Something about the way he froze with surprise and innocent shock as I started to seduce him, his body screaming yes while he seemed to fight his conscience, aroused me. Most guys were gluttons for any physical attention.

He did not fight my advances and seemed grateful when we finished.

In the days that followed, he was cooly cordial in class but otherwise acted as if nothing had ever happened and wouldn't acknowledge me outside the classroom. That wouldn't have been surprising—in fact, it normally fell within predictable parameters, and was usually appreciated—but our encounter hadn't been the usual fellatio or hand job. It was my first time actually having intercourse. I had honestly been interested in the guy, and it hurt to be cast aside so coldly, but I reminded myself that I had been the aggressor. Regardless, like countless encounters before it, that particular fleeting engagement would be left in the past.

When I missed my period, I took a home test. Those were the longest thirty minutes I ever experienced waiting for the ding of the timer so I could see the results—

—and ultimately confirm my worst fears.

For the next two months, I drank and avoided even thinking about it, unwilling to face the consequences of my actions. But I would have to return home soon for the holidays, have to face my parents, my father, and though I could hide it then, it would be impossible to hide next time.

Instead, while in an almost perpetual drunken fog, I caved to the advice of my friends and simply "got rid of it."

Got rid of her.

Kaiya.

Denial and regret overwhelmed me when I awoke in a clearer state of mind. It was the 90s, and the clinic's procedure at that time was to immediately cremate unless special requests were made beforehand and paperwork filled out. Today, greater sensitivities for the remains appear to be in place at most hospitals and clinics.

The thought of my child's remains incinerated and discarded like trash was too much for me to bear. After I created a terrible fuss at the clinic, I immediately called my father, confessed everything to him, and pleaded for help.

It would be the very last time I would speak with him for twenty-two years. He connected with our local pastor and together they convinced the clinic to have the remains transferred to a mortuary in Skokie. He arranged everything and paid for the burial. We weren't communicating any more by that point, but I assume he chose Skokie instead of Leland Grove because he didn't want an illegitimate child laid to rest eternally in the Swanson family plots.

That decision to terminate my pregnancy has been the one thing I've never been able to forgive myself for, my largest regret in my life.

And it happened because I tried to keep it a secret.

I left DeeDee's apartment quieter than usual. I did my best to hide how disturbing it was to have the identity of Raymond's father shared with me. I'm confused, even angry. Why did she tell me when she has never told Raymond in over five decades?

Honestly, I don't want this in my head. I don't want direct knowledge of Raymond's lineage that he himself doesn't know. And what about Simon? Did he know? Would he care? Was he even still alive?

Human relationships can get so messy. I don't like sloshing through the muck of people's lives. Most of all, I don't want to think ill of DeeDee, but that's getting more difficult now, especially if this is what has further exacerbated the damage to her and Raymond's relationship.

I need to talk with her about this, but her breath was shortening the longer she talked and I told her that we should stop so she could rest.

Today certainly won't offer a better opportunity, as it is Julienne's birthday, it is being celebrated at DeeDee's place, and I've been invited.

The biggest challenge with this birthday was figuring out what to get Jules. I ended up going with a dreamcatcher that has a woven tree at center of the main circle. It seemed like a perfect way to suggest the pursuit of one's dreams while keeping wisdom central to one's decisions. I hope it won't seem trite or, worse, inappropriate.

I don't know if I'm going to step into a room of thirty people or three when I knock on the door. When it opens, I'm received by Raymond. "Hello, Pauline. It's nice of you to come." He gestures me inside.

"It was a pleasure to be invited." I can tell he's still uncomfortable around me. I fear this tension between us may be permanent. I follow his gestured invitation and enter the living room.

It looks to be only Jules, DeeDee, and Raymond at this "party" and that's a relief. I'm not mentally prepared to meet and be appraised by a roomful of strangers. Apparently, Jules is going out later with friends from high school to "officially" celebrate.

DeeDee sits upright at the kitchen table, which is terrific progress considering she has only been in bed or on the couch for so many days. Jules sits across from her. At center of table is a layered cake on a crystal pedestal, sliced strawberries nestled into pink icing, two candles shaped as a '1' and '9' declare her still-young age.

"Hello, Pauline." DeeDee gives me a smile under the twinkle of drooping eyes.

"It's so good to see you up and about," I say.

"I'm good with the 'up.' Don't last too long with the 'about.'"

Jules rushes me and wraps her arms around my waist. "I'm so glad you came, Pauline!"

I hug back. "It's wonderful to be a part of this special day. Happy nineteenth year hitching a ride on this lonely blue ball around the sun."

We separate and I hand over the small, wrapped box and card.

She grabs the present in both eager hands. "Oh, no, you didn't have to!"

"I know." I smile and watch her tear apart the wrapping and open the box. Her eyes widen and her cheeks barely contain her smile. "Oh, Pauline. A dreamcatcher! It's wonderful!" She holds it up for everyone to see.

I take hold of her by the shoulders. "May the pursuit of your dreams be fulfilling rather than fulfilled, and may you never limit yourself to your expectations."

She laughs and hugs me again. "I promise!"

After a brief round of small talk, Jules pulls out a deck of cards in good midwestern tradition and suggests a game of Rummy 500. She's thrilled to learn that I know the game. How could I not? Grandmother Hanzlik taught me and I always begged my mother to play with me. Father never had any interest in games other than poker. He said, "If there's no stakes in the game, there's no reason to play it."

Jules plays with exuberance and energy, slapping down her sets and runs, and eagerly snatching up the piles of discards. DeeDee wears a sly smile and manages her hand with careful, quiet thoughtfulness. Raymond is stoic, telling Jules several times to lower her volume or calm down, with DeeDee quick to roll her eyes at Raymond and tell him to lighten up.

Raymond plays with an interesting strategy, not laying down any of his scoring cards until he is able to empty his hand and end the round. I suspect he does it to keep us from scoring off his cards, but I can't help but wonder if there's another, deeper motivation to hoarding his hand. As the game progresses, it hurts him more than it helps as he is often caught with a full hand of cards when Jules, DeeDee, or I lay down our last meld and discard. He acts shocked each time, and I feel bad for him as he counts up his penalties.

After a few games, Raymond steps away from the table to work on dinner, and I teach Jules and DeeDee how to play Hearts. As we play, I keep glancing over into the kitchen to watch Raymond cook. I never pictured him—this tall, broad-shoul-dered man, always smartly dressed, so often methodical and reserved—doing anything so hands-on and creative. He deftly handles a butcher knife as he dices onions, chops mushrooms, and peels and mashes garlic cloves. It's impressive to watch him as he runs the backside of the knife down the cutting board to scrape the onions and mushrooms into the sauté pan. He gives the pan a few quick jerks and the diced ingredients juggle in the air as flames flare and sizzle. My eyes fall upon his shoulders, usually so square, and his back, usually ironing-board straight. Both now are at ease. Even his movements are looser and flow with comfortable complacency.

"Can I help with anything?" I ask from the table.

"Thank you," Raymond says, "But I have it mostly under control." He smiles, an expression I've seen so rarely on him, yet which finds such a comfortable home upon his face.

And he certainly does have everything under control. His fettucine noodles are boiling. He sets the sautéed onion and mushrooms aside, melts butter in a small sauce pan, and adds the freshly chopped garlic. He shakes in flour, mixes it to a paste, and pours in cream to make a roux. Freshly grated parmesan, oregano leaves, and salt combine to make a creamy alfredo sauce.

"I had no idea you were such a maestro in the kitchen," I say and absently drop a jack of clubs into the center of the table. Jules tosses down a 3 of hearts and rakes in her trick with a laugh.

Raymond pulls out a tray of chicken breasts from the refrigerator. "Oh, by necessity I've learned a few things over time." He rubs seasoning and grinds salt over the meat.

"Dad's an awesome cook," Jules says as she drops a king of hearts on the table from her dwindling hand. "You haven't lived until you've tried his spaghetti."

"My Raymond found his way around the kitchen early on," DeeDee says. "He was cooking up stir-fries and pasta dishes from the time he was fourteen."

"Thirteen, actually." The fry pan hisses and steams as he adds three breasts into the hot oil. "I didn't have much of a choice. It was TV dinners until I was nine, and then nothing but fast food after that."

DeeDee lays an ace of hearts down over Julienne's king.

"Grann!! No!" Jules laughs as she recoils from losing the trick she obviously thought she would win. I'm forced to discard my only trump—a five of hearts.

DeeDee gives her granddaughter a mischievous grin, sputters with a cough, then angles her head toward Raymond. "Your mother was a little busy getting a degree and earning a living, my dawlin' boy."

With tongs, he shifts the breasts in the pan and doesn't look up. "Of course you were," he says, not quite under his breath.

"Excuse me?" Jules declares and points at herself. "Birthday girl here? What did I ask for? No fighting. Both of you."

"You are absolutely right, *ma chérie*," DeeDee says.

Raymond is silent and flips the chicken breasts.

Our game of Hearts ends with DeeDee taking her last trick and scoring twelve points over me. "Beginner's luck," she says and gives me a not quite apologetic smile.

I pat her shoulder lightly. There's so little meat to cover those old bones. "Well played, my fine and beautiful lady."

She starts to rise gingerly. "And now, this master of cards must visit the powder room."

I quickly stand up and guide her to her walker. "Do you need any help?"

"Goodness, no," she says. "But thank you." She heads to the bathroom through her bedroom.

I sit back down and gather the cards into a full deck. Raymond is still in the kitchen, rinsing his fettuccine noodles in a colander. Jules leans over to me from the table.

"I heard you took Grann to a night club?" Her voice is low, just above a whisper. The kitchen is noisy with the static of running water, and I hope Raymond can't hear. Meanwhile, I'm speechless, unable to come up with any words to properly explain all that occurred to lead to that night.

Jules smiles and puts a hand over mine that rests on the table. "That is so freaking awesome, Pauline. Oh my God, I wish I could have been there. She really danced?"

I give a cautious, conservative smile. "She did. I didn't want her to, but she sure did."

She squeezes my hand, and I see her eyes glisten. "What a gift you gave her. That's so cool. Don't you let my dad get to you. He means well, he really, really does. But he just doesn't understand. Too much water, too low and old a bridge, you know?"

I nod and put a hand over hers. "I know. And he has his reasons. Your father is a good man, and we can't fully appreciate what he's experienced and understand how he feels."

Jules nods, but it hurts to see how her eyes and mouth wilt. "It's hard, Pauline. I love those two so much, but it just seems like they have done nothing but cause each other so much pain. I just don't know what to do."

My finger gently collects a tear from her cheek. "I know. I know that. But sometimes, for a parent to do, and be, what they believe the child needs, the unfortunate outcome will always be resentment and regret."

The moment suspends as those words leave my lips. I swallow a bitter aftertaste.

CHAPTER TWENTY-SEVEN

Sins of the Fathers

The dream slithers into my sleep about every other month. It's not an unpleasant dream. In fact, in the dream, there is warmth and comfort inside me. It is peaceful and safe in this dream where I am only eleven years old.

The lighting is dim but cozy in the old rectory and I am working with Father Edward on a Christian Youth Organization project. We sit beside each other on a small couch at a low table.

He smiles at me, which crinkles his kind, blue eyes. His silky black hair, swooped over to the side, partially covers his almost-smooth forehead. As he looks at me, I feel so special. I don't feel like Pauline Swanson at all. And yet, when he says my name, he reminds me that someone can love me for who I am.

"You are a bright and special girl, Pauline," he says, opening his arms to draw me onto his lap. I move over and timidly hop up upon his leg. He gives me a big, long hug, and it is as if Jesus Himself is holding me tight.

Down the front of my pants, I feel his hand slip and squirm

lower to my crotch. His other hand takes mine and moves it over the bulge of his—

I wake up, a sickly guilt rising from my groin all the way up to my throat. For a moment, the dread is exactly as if someone has caught me doing something dirty, something nasty, and I have to get up, head to the bathroom, lean over the sink and splash cold water on my face.

Every time, the dream seems to seduce me—like some devil—and I awake from the dreamlike feelings of intimacy to the conscious crush of shame and disgust.

And every time I awake from this dream, I punish myself with an ice-cold shower.

It has been quite a few months since that dream has haunted me. It's obvious why it returned. The reason still sits on my small kitchen table, spread-eagle open since my breakfast yesterday before work. Wrapped in my bathrobe to beat back my shivering from the piercing cold of the water, armed with coffee cup in hand, I sit at the table and look down at the small news article on page 7A in the regional section of our local paper.

FORMER AREA PRIEST CHARGED WITH 7 COUNTS OF ABUSE

(September 23, Decatur, IL) A priest who served as pastor of St. James Parish in Leland Grove from 1978 to 1987 is facing multiple charges of child molestation and abuse.

A formal accusation has been filed by the Sangamon County State's Attorney's Office and is pressing charges against Father Edward Kilcannon, 86, for seven counts of sexual assault of a minor. Sangamon State's Attorney Randall James, leading the case, says that the investigation has been on-going for the past year, beginning with accusations made by two of his former parishioners who were minors at the time. To date, five additional people have come forward to make official accusations.

In 1987, Father Kilcannon was transferred to St. Luke's Parish in Crisman, where he served for seven years, then to Our Lady of Perpetual Help in Buckhorn for ten additional years, then 15 years teaching at St. Mark's Seminary in Decatur until his retirement in 2018.

Father Kilcannon has made no comment on the allegations other than to say, "I am focusing my strength on my cancer treatments. God's will be done." Father Kilcannon was diagnosed with stage four colon cancer back in July.

Meanwhile, Bishop DeRosa of the Diocese of Springfield says that the Diocese is cooperating fully with the investigation. "We are unaware of any wrongdoing by Father Kilcannon and are certain the truth will prevail."

"The State's Attorney's Office is expediting this case," SA James says, "in order to make certain Father Kilcannon faces justice in lieu of his diagnosis."

Father Kilcannon's arraignment is scheduled for January of next year.

The article includes a small, black and white photo of an old, frail bald man, a pall of death about him and a haunted look in his dripping eyes. Perhaps, like a child who wanders too far from its parent through a busy, sprawling marketplace, Father Edward finally turned around after straying from the hand of God to realize that his Father is nowhere to be seen.

When I first saw the article yesterday, I couldn't even get through it. My heart raced, my breath tightened, and I stumbled up from the table with a surge of anxious energy. A short circuit of emotions sent my nervous system into overdrive and I fled the apartment. Instead of going to DeeDee's, I hopped on the first bus, headed to the park and speedwalked the paved paths, tread the dew-covered grass, trying to outpace and lose some part of myself. I ended up going to work two hours early. Margie wanted to know if something was wrong. I told her everything was wonderful. That entire time at the park walking in circles, and at the bar wiping down clean pint glasses and chopping up too many lemons before my shift, I kept asking myself, "What are you doing? What's wrong with you?"

This morning, especially after the dream, I work hard to fight off that same feeling of imminent danger and flight. That overwhelming sense of looming threat crashes absurdly against the flushed heat of guilt and remorse, of some amount of my culpability and pity for him. Rationally, I discount the reaction, but the pressure on my chest, the churn of my stomach, and warmth in my cheeks will not subside.

I draw my knees up against my beating chest, feet on the seat edge, hug my legs tightly, and rock as I try to catch my breath. I am eleven years old again. I am homely and awkward. I am unclean. I have lost hold of the hand of my God.

"Pauline?"

"I'm in trouble, Harold. I'm really in trouble." My eyes clamp shut against caustic tears.

"You hold on. I'll be right over."

It's little more than a breath. "Hurry."

The door knock comes within twenty-two minutes of my call. From the living room floor, back against the sofa front, I call out, "Come in!" I had unlocked the door as soon as I hung up, then collapsed. My body doesn't want to move. My brain screams for a drink. There's pressure against my chest that a shot of liquor would most certainly release. Just one. That's all. To stop these thoughts, end the raging panic and guilt and disgrace. One drink won't hurt, right?

A different and familiar panic radiates throughout my body and rings in my head, of knowing I could not survive falling off the wagon again—yet knowing how close I am to enthusiastically leaping off the back of it. I am in crisis mode.

Harold bursts in with a similar intensity on his face to what I'm experiencing. Harold isn't used to getting calls from me. I'm the strong one. The stable one.

"What's happened?" he says, rushing over. "You are not alone. We're going to get through this together. I'm not leaving you, and you're not giving up."

My hands tremble and my throat is tight. Anxiety runs like a steady current of electricity through my nerves. Poor Harold looks almost as frazzled. "Calm down, Harold, or you're going to drive yourself to drink."

He crouches next to me, the gravity of concern drawing down his brow. "Do not bottle this in, Pauline. Whatever happened, you need to talk through it. Five minutes or five hours, I'm not leaving your side until you've found something to grab onto again. Understand?"

My smile feels like a kinked and twisted cord.

"So," and he sits down on the floor, giving me just enough space. "Why don't we start wherever you'd like to start, okay?"

I wipe my eyes and try to take a deep breath. "Something resurfaced from my past yesterday. I dodged it for the rest of the day, but it infected my dreams, and this morning, I took it head-on…I tried…I just couldn't…" I sob.

"Take your time. I'm here. I'm not going anywhere." Harold is so good. He doesn't touch me, he doesn't try to comfort me.

He's just present and listening. He knows his stuff, and once I pull myself back together—if I can put myself back together—I'll have to let him know that.

I have no intention of telling Harold about the article, about my dream, about my past with Father Edward. But I need to purge emotionally and open up to him in some way. The acidic bile inside me must be expelled.

"So, something happened to me long ago, when I was young. Something I—I just can't, I can't talk about. Something someone...did to me. But, I should feel good now. I should be happy. Resolution. Closure. That's what anyone would want, right?" I beat my fist against my chest. "But instead, there's this, this, maelstrom of emotions in me that—seriously, Harold, I can't deal with it. All these emotions are colliding, the tectonic plates of my *soul*, and everything is coming down around me like an earthquake." I'm sputtering through heaving sobs again. I'm out of control. Inconsolable. It's as if someone flicked off a switch that powered my gravity, and now I've lost my grounding and am left floating aimlessly, unable to tether myself to anything stable.

"Oh, Pauline. I wish you could share what has happened to you, but I understand. Can you at least tell me why you think you should feel good now?"

It's hard to look at Harold, even though his voice and presence are comforting. "Because. It appears he's finally going to be punished."

His expression softens, head nods with slow and gentle understanding. "And now, crazy as it seems, you are somehow taking on part of the blame for whatever this person has done? You think you should be punished as well?"

Those words bring my head up, my burning, tear-filled eyes snapping to his like magnets. "*Yes.*"

His steady gaze is like a strong and stable support to lean

against. "Can we take a moment to say the serenity prayer?"

I nod.

We speak it together. "God, grant me the serenity to accept the things I cannot change, the courage to change the things I can, and the wisdom to know the difference."

He holds his gaze upon me. "I have no idea if you have any reason to blame yourself. My suspicion is you don't, but regardless, this prayer is recognizing that you should not live within the regrets of those things you could not control, nor stagnate within past decisions you cannot change. You know this. I'm not telling you anything new."

I nod again. It's all I can do.

"So, you need to look me in the eye and tell me right now. Have you really lost all your courage, all your strength? Are you really willing to drown yourself in some past that you may or may not have had any control over? Because that is *not* the Pauline I know."

I reach out, grab his hands. Weep.

"Tell you what. I'm going to call in sick at work today. I need you to do the same. Let's work our way through this day together, okay? But, Pauline. What you're suggesting? What I think you're saying happened to you? I'm no therapist. I'll be here for you—keep that bottle away from you—but it sounds like there's something you've buried deep down inside, and it's eating away at you. I think you need to see someone about that. Someone who knows more than me about that kind of thing. You know?"

I acknowledge with a wan smile, but without conviction.

For the first time in my ten years as a bartender, I fear going to work. Once the demon has stirred from its slumber, any disruption, any temptation, can awaken it.

Yesterday, after several hours, Harold managed to get me off the floor and to the DayBreak Café coffee house where we occasionally meet to touch base—sponsor to sponsee. For many years now, our meetups have been more like close co-workers out for the occasional drink. Yesterday felt more like my first six months in AA. Me, the raw and broken twelve-stepper needing a hand to pull me up each rung of the sobriety ladder—Harold the patient, understanding sponsor reaching down with encouragement and strength of faith in his arm to bear my weight.

We spent almost five hours in the coffee shop, loading up with enough caffeine to, as Harold put it, "Give a hibernating bear insomnia." He listened until I stopped talking, then spoke just enough to get me talking again. Twice, we took a moment to pray together—once when the creep of despair threatened to cast me to the wind like a fallen leaf, and once toward the end, when I was able to anchor myself to the ground. Five hours of babbling about everything and nothing—on the floor of my living room and from the chair of the café.

I spoke about my father more than I intended. His lack of affection to a young Pauline desperate to receive it. The forgiveness he refused to offer the adult Pauline. The years of my life I sacrificed to his companionship and care so wounds could be mended. How instead those wounds still fester.

Yet somehow, without coming to any epiphanies, life-changing insights, or acknowledgements, by the end of that day, I was emotionally cleansed.

Today, with cup of coffee poured, I head to the table where that newspaper still sits open, daring me to once again confront this ghost from my past. Instead, coffee sloshes to the sharp clink of cup to counter when I set it down, snatch the paper up, and throw it in my recycling bin under the sink. Even that makes my heart beat faster.

I could call in sick again today. I *should* call in sick again today. Maybe I will. Wednesdays aren't typically busy this time of year anyway.

Before making a decision, I drink half my coffee, then head to the bathroom to get ready. Time to crawl out of the sinkhole of these last two days that dropped me into a raging river of the past and almost swept me away. I have obligations, and one of them is DeeDee.

Some changes have taken place at DeeDee's. Her black sofa is gone. In its place, a large black recliner with a control panel. DeeDee hasn't looked this excited about something since taking her out to the bar.

"It reclines all the way back. Watch." She holds the button and the chair flattens out. "You see?" She holds another button and in moments she's sitting upright again. "And watch this." She presses a button, and the chair rises up and tilts forward until she is standing in front of me. "Isn't that just something?"

"It is. That's wonderful."

She lets the chair guide her back to an upright sitting position. "And, it has all these different massage settings. I tell you, it's like having my own private masseuse." She coughs lightly, which more and more is the only way she can laugh.

"Well, you deserve it."

She draws her blanket up, slips her oxygen tube under her nose, and nestles into the chair. "And just where've you been, dawlin'? Haven't seen you since Jules's birthday."

"I know. I'm sorry."

"Everything okay?"

"Of course."

She side-eyes me with dubious scrutiny. "You don't look

okay. What's wrong, dear?"

I force the biggest, most sincere false smile I can manage. "Nothing some time spent with my favorite lady won't cure."

Her expression makes no indication that she's convinced, but it at least seems to derail the topic.

I ask how her last few days have been as I head to the kitchen around the corner to get the small collection of dirty dishes in the sink. She offers little detail but talks more about Raymond buying her the chair and having it delivered.

"How have your meals been?" In the sink, only a teacup and glass, a few spoons and forks, three bowls and two small, mostly clean plates. DeeDee isn't cooking anymore. It's too exhausting for her to stand for more than a few minutes.

"There's a Cajun place I've been ordering from lately. Use a delivery service and they bring it over. Not bad."

I start filling the sink, squirt in a bit of dish detergent. "Appetite holding?" At the garbage can, I step on the pedal and the lid flips up with a waft of cayenne pepper, oregano, garlic, and chicken. Piled over discarded carry-out boxes is a lot of discarded food—rice and beans, half a chicken-fried steak, a mostly untouched fried catfish.

"Never better," she says, unable to see me looking down at the garbage. I let the lid close.

"Glad to hear it. Careful with that spicy food, though."

"Bah. What they serve round here? Nothing like it was back home."

I shut off the water, step around the corner. "Funny you say that, considering how many homes you've had."

A wistful pride and acceptance shines within those still-clear and vibrant brown eyes peeking under the drooping lids of age and regret. "May have left it long ago, but New Orleans never leaves you, *mon chanson du cygne*."

Back at the sink, I start washing the dishes. I take advantage of the silence and having my back to her so I can ask her something I don't think I could do looking her in the eye. "Why have you never told Raymond who his father is?"

My sudsy hands hold the rag in one hand, a glass in the other, frozen over the water as I wait for a response. It's quiet just long enough that I fear I've offended.

"Sorry if I—"

"He refuses to let me."

I abandon the glass and rag, grab a towel, and walk back around the corner to face her, drying my hands. "What?"

Her gaze is to her hands, ever more wrinkled and bony. I remember only two months ago when I had admired those slim, well-manicured hands. She tries to take in a breath and coughs out a gurgly exhale.

"I tried telling him a few times—oh my, thirty years ago or more. But he wouldn't let me. In fact, he told me that if I ever told him anything about his father, he would never talk to me again."

I move over to the Queen Anne chair, sit down across from her and lean in, elbows to knees. "I don't understand."

I've only witnessed what seemed at first to be a mother driven to frustration by Raymond—her exhausting love a typical development between mother and son. More recently, I suspected it was more of a callousness toward him I was seeing.

Now, it's beyond question—the woman looking at me now is a despairing mother.

"He's ashamed of me. Always has been. The first time I tried tell him who his father was, he got so angry at me. He told me to shut up. 'Don't you dare!' he shouted. He said he'd never speak to me again if I ever told him."

My thoughts stall, unable to process what she says.

DeeDee raises two thin nubs of shoulders and forces a meek smile. "He was fifteen at the time. Just an angry, angry boy.

I was very worried for him—the direction he was going. Leaving for college years later here in Springfield—getting some distance from me—was probably the best thing for him."

"I'm so sorry, DeeDee. I—I can't imagine."

She waves it off. "It smoothed over a bit between us when he got married. I know I wasn't the most welcome person in his or Sylvia's life, but at least there was enough to our relationship that he felt an obligation."

I draw in a breath and hold it, not sure if I should ask my next question.

"Question, dawlin'? Don't be shy now." DeeDee smiles.

"Did you ever tell Simon?"

She seems to have anticipated the question. "No. We went our separate ways. He was right, God bless him. He wasn't any good for me, even though he was always, always good *to* me. He was a decent man doing some bad things. He knew where he was heading, and he wasn't going to take me with him. I certainly wasn't going to complicate his life."

"Is he—?"

"Cirrhosis. Back in ninety-five. Man was only in his early sixties. Sad."

I lean back. There is nothing to add, but so much pain and sadness to feel, for both DeeDee and Raymond. It brings Jules's despairing words back from memory: "They have done nothing but cause each other so much pain. I just don't know what to do."

Neither do I, Jules. But I have to try.

CHAPTER TWENTY-EIGHT

The Winds of Change

"I have to admit, I'm having trouble picturing Raymond as a child."
"Oh, but he was such a cute little boy. So happy and full of energy."
"I can't imagine raising him all alone, especially back then."
"Well, I certainly had help."

DeeDee never went behind the camera again, but she did continue to dance at Heartbreakers for a month until she found a job behind the make-up counter of the Emporium department store in Union Square. It only paid a few cents over minimum wage, but over the course of two years dancing, being in over a hundred loops, and a score of movies, she sat on almost twenty thousand dollars.

That, even after sending $50 a month back home to Maman and Papa. She had wanted to send more, but she knew they would be suspicious.

Wrapped around the money each month was a short letter

to them, saying she and Alfred were doing fine. Lying was difficult for her, so she avoided specifics and instead spoke about places she'd seen and general things happening.

Letters back from her mother were regular at first but became fewer and fewer as time passed. Papa took a job as a sales clerk at a men's clothing store while Maman started cleaning houses. Many of their neighbors, the few not immediately displaced, saw their homes foreclosed from ballooning mortgages and left the Seventh Ward. Maman said they would hold on as long as they could, as they had nowhere else to go. Meanwhile, the Tremé neighborhood they once knew was all but gone.

The letter she found herself writing to them after quitting Heartbreakers and BCD Productions proved to be the hardest yet, as it would find itself with far less presidential company within the envelope.

Dearest Papa and Maman,

I'm so happy to hear of Papa's promotion and salary increase. I know it isn't much, but it's good to know his hard work and his skills are being acknowledged. I'm also glad to hear the housekeeping business continues to grow. I just hope you don't wear yourself out, Maman. Please do not take on more than you can handle!

I am so sorry I can't send more than a few dollars home to you. Unfortunately, my situation has changed and money will be much tighter for a while. Please do not worry, though! All is well, and all will be well. I just needed to change direction. It will be hard for a while—I have some challenges I must face—but you both made me strong enough to overcome them.

My love to you both,

DeeDee

She folded the note around a ten-dollar bill, slipped it in the addressed envelope, and put it in in the mailbox to travel the twenty-two hundred miles home.

"You're *what?*" Alfred's hands balled into tight, white-knuckled fists.

"Settle down," DeeDee said.

"Who the fuck did it to you, huh?" He shifted in place, from leg to leg, a slight roll to his shoulders—in the boxing ring of some match in his head against a nameless, faceless figure.

"Alfred, cool it. My God."

"Cool it? Are you serious? You get knocked up and you want me to cool it? Christ, girl, this is some heavy shit."

Arms crossed, DeeDee glared at him. "And what does this have to do with you anyway?"

He dropped to the couch of their small, sparse living room, against the cracked plaster wall. His demeanor switched from hot and furious to brow-stitched worry, his big, dark eyes looking up at her. "Is this dude still around? Does he know?"

DeeDee sat down next to Alfred. "No. And no. He doesn't need to know."

His eyes fell to his lap, hands flopping helplessly, until he locked eyes with her again with intent. "So you're going to take care of it, then?"

"'Course I will."

"Do—Do you need money? Do you know who'll do it?"

"What do you mean?"

"For the operation. You know."

DeeDee drew back with a noisy, high-pitched exhale. "What?

287

No!" She smacked him on the shoulder. "I'm having it, you jerk."

Alfred was silent, mouth open.

DeeDee, eyebrows arched with insistence, nodded her head sharply.

"Oh, Sis—"

"Don't 'Oh, Sis' me. I didn't make this decision overnight. I've had over a month to think about it—"

"Not long enough, apparently—"

"—and, I think I want this. I think I'm ready for it."

"You ain't half-ready for this. You got no husband, no man to look after you—"

"Maybe I don't want one."

"Don't talk foolish. You can't do this alone."

DeeDee's initial defensiveness softened as she saw how distressed Alfred appeared. She, on the other hand, felt more strongly about her decision with each argument she made. Perhaps some of it simply stemmed from her defiance, and some from the fear of having a back-alley abortion. There was something else, though, some innate urge or drive, triggered by her condition. She felt protective of the little sprout of life gestating inside of her. Had she been in a more difficult situation, perhaps her decision would be different, but despite the challenges she knew she'd face, she felt not only more prepared and eager to overcome them than any challenge she'd faced so far, but the thought of becoming a mother and raising a child also felt purifying—cleansing. A way to move past these last two sordid years.

"I can do this alone. I want to do this alone. I'm not ready for a man to be in my life." She'd been surrounded by ogling men for years now, watched them lust over her, desire her like an object to have or get off on. She had craved that attention, but when the lights came on and the cameras rolled, the illusion shattered and she realized what she had become—exactly what the men wanted her to be, not who she wanted to be.

Heartbreakers and the movies were a means to an end. She would not fall into regret, but she had to make sure the end made those means worth it.

"You're nuts, Dee. I don't think you know what you're doing."

"Maybe not. We'll see. And what about you, Alfred?"

"What about me?"

"How long before you get yourself arrested. Or worse?"

He stood up, adjusted his beret cocked sideways on his cropped afro. "Don't be worrying about me."

"You mean like I shouldn't worry about what happened to Cole?" DeeDee's unblinking eyes did not waver from his. After a few seconds, Alfred turned away to pace the small room.

"Man, Cole is a chump, alright? He didn't follow the plan and didn't keep his cool. And he got nabbed. Fucker cried the whole time he was running from them." Alfred's eyes squinted, lips stretched, as if feeling pain. "Got nothing to say about dumb-ass Cole."

Poor Cole. She'd barely seen him since their adventurous road trip to San Francisco from New Orleans, but she had the impression, even then, that he was far too nervous for donning the black of a Panther uniform.

DeeDee shook her head. "And what about Russell's cousin? What about Joe?"

His face wrung tighter. "Enough, Dee—"

She stood up, cut off his pacing, and held him by his arms. "I don't want some Panther party member I don't know coming to my door telling me my brother was shivved in his cell."

Alfred yanked away from her grasp, the pained look turning to rage. "This ain't some game. I've been putting myself on the line *every night* for our people while you've been slutting it up at that bar and doing God-knows what else—"

The slap happened before she consciously thought to do it. A primitive, instinctive reaction. It turned Alfred's face slightly askew, but otherwise he bore no reaction to it.

"Truth hurts a bit, don't it, Dee?"

"No," she said, a minimal shake of head as she tried to rein in her own anger. "What hurts is my brother insulting my virtue when he's been living off my vice for two years now."

Alfred just nodded at her, jaw clenched.

"I'm serious, Alfred. And I've been hearing things. About bad apples in the movement. About things starting to fall apart."

His reaction was swift, intensely defensive, as he darted at her and grabbed her shoulders. "Who? Who's talking shit like that?"

"Mitsy, Alfred. Your president."

"Bullshit."

"She's hearing things. She's seeing things. She's worried."

He let go and turned away from her. "Fucking woman. Too many goddamn women leaders in the Panthers, that's what's wrong with it. Change ain't going to happen playing happy-clappy with kiddie breakfasts and Goddamn community outreach. Not while our boys are being yanked off the streets by the fucking pigs and rotting away in their prisons. Not while we're only given the shittiest jobs, redlined from loans, and losing our homes to urban renewal."

"Settle down—"

"There's a fucking *war* going on out there, and *we* didn't start it. But by God, we'll fight until the last of us is standing."

In the spring of 1973, DeeDee was rushed to the hospital by Alfred after her water broke. Her labor pains were eight minutes apart.

The birth was long—over eighteen hours—and she experienced pain unlike anything before. Alfred paced and worried in the waiting room. Finally, utterly exhausted, DeeDee gave birth to an eight-pound, five-ounce baby boy. She named him Raymond George Deneaux after her brother George, who's middle name was Raymond. Raymond had been their gran papa, who had died when she was only seven.

She didn't know what to expect, with his father being a White man, but Raymond was as beautifully brown-skinned as any New Orleans Deneaux, not that it would have mattered to her.

Caring for a newborn was far beyond what DeeDee had expected. The department store had forced her out by the time she was nearing nine months, cutting her hours so drastically that she was virtually unemployed. She was able to claim unemployment, but that only offered minimal support. Meanwhile, the hospital bill came and drained her coffers of almost one thousand dollars.

But little Raymond was worth it. He hardly cried or fussed at all for his first six months, and he slept so well. His appetite was tremendous, and her nipples were painfully sore from his aggressive suckling. By four months, Raymond was sitting upright, neck supporting that big, round, mostly bald head, and she switched him over to pureed baby food, which he gobbled up by the jarful.

Cherise was such a tremendous help. She was visiting DeeDee as soon as she came back from the hospital. A mother of three, she was a repository of knowledge, guiding DeeDee on how to change diapers, warm baby bottles, burp him, and swaddle him when he cried. She brought over old baby toys and a playpen, and minded Raymond so DeeDee could break away and run errands.

DeeDee returned to Bayside Café part time. Darryl was happy to hire her back, as one of his other waitresses had just not shown up one day and was never seen again. She was working mostly opposite Cherise now, as DeeDee's shift covered

Cherise's days off. On the two days they worked together, Cherise's shift covered breakfast through lunch, and DeeDee handled lunch and supper. The plus side of this was Cherise being more than happy to watch over Raymond during many of the hours DeeDee worked, keeping the daycare to a minimum.

"Mama, Mama, Mama Mama."

DeeDee reached down and scooped up her sixteen-month-old Raymond and put him in her lap at the kitchen table. His two chubby legs were awkward perpetual motion machines that he wobbled around on throughout the apartment, getting him into everything. His wet little hand clung to her hair pick that he must have nabbed from her bedroom end table. She added it to the lipstick, wooden spoon, and the crumpled and chewed June 29th TV Guide with Esther Rolle and John Amos from *Good Times* on the cover.

"Thank you, Ray-Ray. It's lovely, yes. I'll cherish it." She looked across the table at Cherise, wrapped her bathrobe more tightly around her with one hand as the other kept pulling Raymond's hands away from her coffee cup. "You sure you're okay taking him this morning? I always hate imposing."

"It's no trouble, honey. You do what you've got to do. This is important."

DeeDee looked about her, then lowered her voice and leaned in closer to Cherise. "I'm so angry at Alfred. I almost never ask a thing of him. He said I could count on him, and now suddenly he can't do it."

"How's that warehouse job of his?"

DeeDee brushed Raymond's hand away from her face and hair. "Like every other job he's had since we first got here—over. That one lasted four months. One before that, on the dock?

Three weeks. Raymond, stop that." She pulled her face away from him as his finger worked its way up her nose. He grunted and mumbled and started to bounce.

"That man just don't want to be told what to do."

DeeDee nodded, reaching over to grab Raymond's stuffed bunny. "That's it. You know it. Mr. High and Mighty Black Panther won't be bossed around by anyone." She pushed the bunny into Raymond's chest and he wrapped arms around it, one floppy ear going into his mouth.

Cherise reached across the table to touch DeeDee's elbow resting on the table edge. "You look tired, hon. How you holding up?"

"I'm fine. Long night at the Café, and this here little Ray-Ray of sunshine is always up by five a.m., aren't you?" She kissed his cheek loudly, then blew hard to make her kiss a sloppy fart. Raymond giggled and squirmed and slipped down between her legs to trot off, abandoning his bun-bun to the floor.

Alfred's bedroom door opened, and he stepped into the hall. Raymond squealed and ran up to him. "A-fed! A-fed!"

"Hey, there, little man." He rubbed the wild, frizzy hair sprouting from the top of Raymond's head. "No feds here, brother, that's for damn sure." He picked Raymond up and slung the toddler over his shoulder like a sack. Raymond cackled laughter.

"Hey, Cherise. How's things?"

Cherise gave Alfred the judgmental glare she usually did. It was a look that implied a petulant, "Hmph!" over crossed arms. But she smiled graciously, if somewhat indignantly. "I'm just fine, Alfred."

"Can you at least drop off the rent check like you promised?" DeeDee said. "Murray's been calling me about July rent for three days now."

Alfred took Raymond by the ankles, swung him around, and held him upside down in front of him. Raymond's chuckles were guttural gasps as his arms reached out aimlessly. "Sure, sis. Got the check right here in my back pocket."

He gently set Raymond on the ground, and Raymond snatched at Alfred's pant legs to hoist himself up and peer eagerly at his uncle. "Again!"

"No, little man. Your uncle's got important things to do. Freeing our people from the man!" He crouched down to Raymond's level. "You know what we think of the man, right?"

"Down wif the man," Raymond said.

Alfred put his hand out. "Truth, my brother. Gimme five."

Raymond put his whole body into the hand slap and Alfred raised his fist. "Right on."

"Oh, could you pick up some eggs and milk on your way home?" DeeDee said to his back as Alfred was heading out the door.

His shoulders slumped. "Dee, I don't even know if I'm coming home tonight, okay? I've got no time for that."

She shook her head. "Yeah, you don't have time for much of anything."

He turned around, eyes intense as he pointed a finger at her. "It was your decision to do this, Dee. In fact, didn't you tell me that I had nothing to do with it? Well—" he threw out both hands with a shrug. "Here you are."

DeeDee could say nothing.

He sighed. "Listen, if I can break away for a bit this afternoon, I'll see what I can do."

"Whatever."

"Good luck today, Sis."

"Yeah."

He went out the door, and DeeDee could only wonder and fret about what he would be doing.

"I do worry about that man," Cherise said and whistled. "Say, you better get ready. You don't have much time and you need to make it cross town and back."

DeeDee took a sip of coffee, sighed, and steeled herself for the day. "You're right."

"Oh! Just hold on, girl. I brought you something!" Cherise stood and moved over to the counter where she grabbed a white box and brought it over to DeeDee. "Here. See what you think."

"What did you do?" DeeDee smiled and looked at the white, thin cardboard box.

"Now, I didn't do anything. Just something I found in my closet and thought it might be appropriate. Open it."

"Oh my, what in the world—" DeeDee lifted the lid off the box to reveal a stiff-collared eggshell-white blouse and gray, pin-striped cotton A-line skirt. "What—?"

"Listen, I bought it a long time ago—certainly a lot of pounds ago! Back when I was applying for office work. I just couldn't part with it, even though I'll never fit in it again. Not sure if it'll fit you, but maybe?"

"Oh, dawlin'! Very sharp! So professional."

"Well, it never got me a job, but maybe it'll bring you some luck."

"I love it, Cherise. But, I'm not exactly going for a job interview."

"It never hurts to make a strong impression and present yourself proper-like."

DeeDee set the box down and gave Cherise a hug. "Thank you. It's wonderful. I can't wait to try it on."

Cherise kept DeeDee at arm's length, locking her gaze. "I'm just so glad you got out of that crazy business and are heading in a better direction. I've got high hopes for you, you know."

"Mama, Mama." Raymond tugged on DeeDee's robe. "Eat, Mama. Fute and wedgies!"

"I can take care of him, Dee. You go on. Get ready."

DeeDee picked up Raymond and bounced him in her arms. "Such a healthy child, you are! You'll get your fruits and veggies. Aunt Cherise will take care of you. You have to let your Maman get ready. She needs to apply for college. What do you think about that? Isn't that exciting?"

Raymond smiled, laughed, and spit up on her shoulder.

"Pauline?"

"I'm sorry."

"Oh dear, are you okay?"

Rising from the chair.

"Mon cygne? What did I say?"

"I'm not feeling well. I'm so sorry." Rush to the door.

"Please, is it something I—"

CHAPTER TWENTY-NINE

Avoidance & Denial

Thursday, and my third day in a row calling in sick. I can tell that Benny is getting upset. Margie has also sent several texts asking me if I'm all right.

I'm not.

Something is happening to me and I don't know what. First there's my meltdown seeing the article about Father Edward, and now I'm short-circuiting over listening to DeeDee yesterday. I ran out of her apartment in tears. Inconsolable.

I recognize why the article and DeeDee talking about raising Raymond would be sensitive to me, but I shouldn't be falling apart because of them. It's all ancient history, for goodness' sake. This could very well be menopause, but I fear there's more to it than that.

I'm tired of dwelling in my past, and every time I do, it becomes a pathetic, self-indulgent exercise that only manages to glorify the tragedy of my life as if I were Jane Eyre or Hester Prynne.

The simple truth is, DeeDee's story hit too close to home. It opened a portal to an alternate timeline that revealed the hint of what could have been. She reminded me how my life still pivots upon one choice from the past that sent it in a very different direction. What if I had been strong enough? Brave enough? Sober enough? Here I am, fifty-three years old and still unable to put this behind me.

I spend the day walking around town, hitting comfortable haunts. The coffee shop, where I sip lattes in an overstuffed chair by the fireplace and read Walt Whitman while folk guitar plays behind the soft chatter of patrons. I walk the aisles of the library, soaking in the spines of fiction, the pages of historical lives and times, and the tomes of reference material. The towering shelves laden with literature are almost like coming home after being away for a very long time. The silence, the musty, pulpy smells, transport me back to times when I still had hope, when I felt the promise of a meaningful life still awaiting me.

It's late afternoon when I return to my apartment. I turn on classical music on public radio. I boil water for tea, steep it, and walk into my small living room. I grab my Bible to do some reading from the Gospel of Luke. As I take a seat in my rocker, I notice my phone—something I rarely take anywhere with me—flashing a voicemail message as it sits on the end table.

"This is a message for Ms. Pauline Swanson. My name is Erica Simmons, assistant state's attorney for Sangamon County. I'm contacting you because our records show you were part of a Christian Youth Group at St. James Parish between the years of 1985 and 1987 while under the direction of one Father Edward Kilcannon. I was hoping to speak with you about your time with Father Kilcannon. It is very important that you return my call at 312-678-5400. Again, my name is Erica Simmons with the Sangamon County State's Attorney's Office. 312-678-5400."

My body is rigid. The automated voice tells me I have no

more new messages and that, to delete this message, I should press "7". I can only stare at the phone.

It tells me again that I should press "7" if I want to delete the message.

I force myself to have a sip of tea. After that, I take a very intentional, thoughtful breath.

And I press "7."

Friday morning. The weight of obligations hold me down in bed like a lead blanket.

Three days absent from work. I simply cannot abandon my team on a Friday night. Meanwhile, what could DeeDee be thinking after I left her so abruptly and emotionally two days ago?

I must follow through on both responsibilities, and yet I'm too fragile to face either.

Despite the weakness webbing through my persona like cracks in concrete, I force myself out of bed and into the shower. Teeth brushed, deodorant applied, clothes selected and donned, I say to my reflection the few words of advice or encouragement my father ever gave me in my childhood: "Buck up."

I drive to DeeDee's apartment, take my lumbering steps to her door and give it a few gentle raps. I'm momentarily confused when it opens to reveal a Raymond that I don't immediately recognize. He's wearing jeans and a stained Northwestern sweatshirt that hangs loosely on his tall frame.

"Raymond?" My voice is pitched high and sharp looking at his sunken, dark eyes and gaunt cheeks. "What's wrong?"

"Bad night last night. Come in." He guides me to the dimly lit living room.

I sit down in my usual chair, and he rests his backside on the very edge of DeeDee's new recliner, as if he doesn't feel worthy to sit in it comfortably and completely. "Mother's had another...episode."

"Oh, no."

Raymond nods, then puts up a hand. "She's okay now. She's resting. But I think it's taken a lot out of her. From this point on, I suppose every episode will."

I simply nod as my heart beats faster.

"She woke up a little after one a.m. coughing and apparently couldn't catch her breath. She managed to call me, and I raced over. Even with the respirator, she just couldn't get enough oxygen. And the coughing—it was bad. Just choking on fluid. A decent amount of blood came up. I wanted to take her to the ER, but she refused, so I called our nurse, Nancy. When she got here, she gave mother some relaxants and expectorants. That helped a little and after a few hours she was able to sleep."

"You should have called. I could have been here to help."

"I'm sorry. I thought of calling you, but I didn't know how serious it was. Once our nurse got here, she assured me that things would subside with the medicine."

"Did she give any other prognosis on her condition?"

He runs a hand down his bristly cheek and goateed chin. "She was hesitant to say anything definitively, but she suspects this could be the start of the last phase."

I stare and try to take that in. My eyes burn and I hold back tears that threaten. My mouth starts to open but I keep it clamped shut.

Raymond's shrug is sad and resigned. "We all knew these days were coming. Now they're here."

My head bobs mechanically and without acceptance.

He leans back, hands on knees, and inhales deep. "Well, I'll be staying here indefinitely, working remotely. Nancy will be stopping by regularly now for palliative care."

"Have you been in contact with Julienne about all this?"

"Not yet. I thought I'd let her wrap up her week of classes first."

That seems sensible. This will be hard on her, especially being hours away and managing her schooling while worried about her grann.

Raymond is looking at me quizzically. "You're smiling. What are you thinking?"

I wasn't even aware. Emotionally, I'm breaking. I'm not ready for this. I've been in denial since first meeting DeeDee, perhaps about the whole idea of being strong enough to be a hospice volunteer.

"I'm sorry," I say. "It's a reflex of mine. When I'm nervous or anxious or over-wrought. I'm—" I raise my head up, breathe deep, and hold back this sudden ongoing sorrow corroding my emotional plumbing.

I feel a light, tentative hand on my knee. "Hey, it's okay. I—I know she means a lot to you."

Through blurry eyes, I connect with his sympathetic gaze. "I don't think I'm ready to face this."

His mouth opens, but words don't come immediately as he pulls his hand away. "You know, I thought your job was to comfort the family, not the other way around." His grin is playful and innocent, but the words hang on the air of truth.

"I'm not sure I'm really cut out to be a hospice volunteer. I'm sorry."

Raymond flushes and eyes pinch. "No, no. I didn't mean—"

"Oh, I know you didn't. Please don't feel bad. But I'm realizing how, in so many ways, I haven't done a good job providing support—to DeeDee, or to you and Jules."

I have to lower my eyes because Raymond's gaze is too penetrating. Irrational fear warns that he will bore too deep and find secrets I don't want him to know. The parts of me that bear heavy regret, that fill me with shame.

"Nonsense," he says, leaning closer. "From the beginning, you've been exactly what we've needed. You've been an audience, support, and friend to my mother, a reassurance and encouragement to my daughter, and you've certainly challenged me—"

I chuckle to that. "You mean your patience?"

"Well…" He grins. "But seriously, I realize I don't tend to listen to my daughter. I certainly don't listen to my mother. But for some reason, I find I listen to you."

"Eventually."

Shoulders shrug. "Eventually. The fact is, you encourage a moment of pause. I'm sorry I've often been reluctant to take it."

My turn to flush—I'm sure my cheeks are glowing. "Well. Thank you, Raymond. That means a lot to me. You all have come to mean a lot to me."

Silence overtakes in the still-early morning gloom of the living room, but Raymond doesn't look away and my eyes linger on his. There's a fluttering in my stomach that I haven't experienced for a very long time.

"Well," he says with a slap of knees as he springs up, giving me a start. "Do you plan to stay for a bit? I was hoping to make a stop at work to grab my laptop and some files to bring back here. I'll only be gone for an hour, if that's okay?"

My head is still floating upon the previous moment and what he says only starts to make sense after a couple seconds. "What? Oh, um, of course. I'm more than happy to stay."

He peers down at me. "You're sure?"

I stand and wave him off. "Go. Do what you need to."

He smiles again, and it's that rare smile of his that is free of heavy thoughts, unchained from the burdens of responsibility. For just the flicker of a moment, I can believe he could have been a happy, carefree toddler.

He nods and waves, opens the door and steps out. Before the door closes, he leans his head in. "Thanks again, Pauline."

I give a big, devilish smile as the door almost shuts. "You're most welcome—Ray-Ray."

His head peeks back through the door, his expression shifting between confusion, shock, and annoyance. With a headshake, he shuts the door with a thump. I can't help but laugh.

I check in on DeeDee while she rests in her room. I make sure not to disturb her, but I step as close as I can to the bed. Although she sleeps deeply, there's a slight distress to her face and a labored breathing under the ventilation mask that is concerning. I look up at that almost life-size oil painting above her bed, of a young DeeDee in her prime—beautiful, bold, uninhibited, and what I see now under the covers in her bed is the smoldering wick of a flame that had once burned so bright.

In the living room, I sit down on her recliner and pull out *The Scarlet Letter* I was reading to her as she recovered from her last episode. Perhaps she'll be awake enough so we can return to it. Dimmesdale was just stepping up the weathered stairs of the scaffolding.

Reading ahead, I just reach the end of the chapter when Raymond returns, laptop bag and suitcase in each hand as he fumbles through the door.

"Welcome back," I say, jumping up to try and help him as he manages the door despite two full hands.

"Thanks," he says as I grab hold of the door for him. He works his way through, past the entryway, and to the kitchen table where he sets both bags down. "This will be a challenge, but I'll make it work."

"Of course you will."

He starts to unpack his laptop. "Any troubles with Mother?"

"None at all. She's still sleeping."

"Good." He pulls out his laptop and cord, as well as a small secondary monitor. He plugs into the wall, into his system, and connects the second monitor that folds out and sets upright. From his briefcase, he pulls a hefty stack of files.

"That's an impressive mobile office," I say.

He starts hitting keys. "I don't know what I would've done ten years ago. Fortunately, remote work is pretty standard now."

I return to my seat in the recliner. "I can't even imagine."

He starts moving and clicking his mouse.

"Well, don't let me bother you," I say and break open my book again.

He peers around his screen at me. "You know, you could take off if you'd like. I'll be here all day and night. I can give you a call if anything develops." Keys resume clacking and mouse continues to click.

"Oh. Well," I look at him, my book. "I'm happy to stay if you'd like me to."

His eyes don't leave the monitor. "There's just no reason. Go on, I'm sure you have better things to do. I'll hold down the fort."

I hesitate a moment, look behind me through the wall to DeeDee's bedroom, then close my book. "Well, if you don't need me, then—"

"Not at all. Go and enjoy the day."

Book stuffed into my bag, I stand up, linger a moment, looking about the room, then to Raymond. "Okay, then. I guess I'll head out for the day."

He waves, eyes still upon his screens. "Appreciate you, Pauline. Thanks for all your help."

"Sure," I say and head slowly to the door. "See you tomorrow, then?"

He nods and waves, attention focused on his work, and I walk out the door, somehow feeling summarily dismissed.

CHAPTER THIRTY

Framing the Past

Saturday morning, I'm at St. James the Greater for confession at 8:30am. There is only one other woman in the church—there are rarely more than a person or two ahead of me, if any. We are a select few who still participate in the ritual. Personally, I depend upon it.

Confession is offered every Wednesday and Saturday morning. For me, it is more than just a way to perform contrition for my sins. It keeps me closer to my pastor and personalizes him.

When it is my turn, I do not enter the dark closet of the confessional. I prefer face to face, which is still offered at St. James. I enter a door adjacent to the confessionals and into a warmly-lit room behind them. This is where Father Tom gets access to the confessional booths. I sit down and the younger priest steps out from the confessional and takes a seat across from me.

I make the sign of the cross. "Bless me father, for I have sinned. My last confession was six months ago."

"It is good to see you, Pauline," Father Tom says with a kind and gentle smile. His balding head, catching a glint of light from above, is ringed by a closely trimmed horseshoe of hair. "May the Lord bless you." With hands folded, he bows to me in his green stole draped over white robes from which his priestly collar just peeks out. "Tell me what sins you wish to confess today."

"Since my last confession, I am ashamed and regretful about feeling relief for my father's death. I have lusted after several gentlemen bar patrons. I've recently been tempted by alcohol. I have been selfish and lacking in my duties as a hospice volunteer."

The younger priest—late thirties or early forties at most—leans back and relaxes in his chair. "Do you mind if I take these one by one, Pauline?"

"That is your prerogative, Father. They are already offered to God."

He smiles at me. "And I am certain He receives them with mercy and forgiveness. But, if you will indulge me, perhaps I may act as intermediary."

"As you wish."

His smile doesn't falter as he lays hands upon his thighs and scrutinizes me from his chair. He does this often during my confessions. He impresses me as one who would run an AA meeting exceptionally well. "My condolences for your father. He was a good man. I know he resides with God."

"Thank you, Father."

"How are you managing his passing?"

"I am okay, Father. Thank you for asking."

He nods. "You gave up a fair amount of your life to be with him after your mother died, correct?"

"I came here to support him, yes."

"And several years caring for him when he fell ill, is that right?"
I nod.

"Pauline, I *myself* feel relief for you that your father has passed. That is not a reflection on your father, but rather for your sake alone. You have been a good daughter and sacrificed many years for your father's well-being. Do not feel guilty that God has relieved you of your duty."

I smile and nod. Father Tom is a good, gentle soul. He tries hard to focus on the positive. It is touching and I tolerate this tendency of his. I do not, however, come to confession to be consoled.

Father Tom continues. "I won't touch upon this lust for patrons. You will know better than I if your feelings go beyond what is natural for an unmarried woman to feel toward a man. I will simply ask that you do not confuse lust for mere loneliness and a natural desire for companionship. You do, after all, deserve that."

I squirm in my seat. This is, again, very nice of him to try and minimize my confession, thus diverting my penance, but I'm here for a reason. I don't need his patronizing.

"Let's see. You also mentioned your drinking. Did you succumb to that temptation?"

"I did not, Father."

"And you sought help through your support group?"

"I did."

He gives me that dubious look, shrugs his shoulders and puts his hands up as if everything I've said is nonsense.

"Finally. You're volunteering as a hospice nurse? Really? How is that going?"

I roll my shoulders, eyes skimming off his gaze. "Fine, father. Except, I—" I can't find the words to express how inferior I feel.

He leans in quizzically and patiently.

"I just don't feel I'm really helping at all. I'm just—there."

"What exactly do you think you should be doing that you aren't doing?"

I falter a bit to gather my thoughts. "I'm not sure. Perhaps that's the problem. I find myself too busy enjoying my time with DeeDee—she has sarcoidosis and her condition is terminal—but not offering any spiritual or carnal guidance for her. Meanwhile, I don't think I've been the support her son and granddaughter need. There is a lot of pain and regret between mother and son, and it is hurting the entire family. All I am doing is being witness to it. I worry that, instead of being a valuable resource to them, I am just someone in the way."

Father Tom nods and leans back in his chair, quiet and ponderous. The moment hangs on silence until finally, he speaks.

"Have they given any indication of this?"

"No. To the contrary, actually."

He stares at me with a smile that is too smug for a priest to wear.

I sigh. "You don't understand. There is a very real, painful conflict between the mother and the son, and I am not helping that at all. I don't know what to do, and I fear I don't have much time left."

Father Tom leans forward again, hands folded as his expression pleads with me. "Pauline. You are a good person, but you are perpetually living in penance. Catholicism, despite popular belief, is *not* focused on guilt. A key aspect of our faith is forgiveness, about being able to ask for and *accept* forgiveness, and living in a way to atone for our sins. Sooner or later, you simply have no choice but to accept God's forgiveness and move on with your life."

I hear the echo of Sister Iphegenia from a lifetime ago. "So you've said."

"And one day, maybe you'll actually listen to me."

He means well, and my nod is out of respect, not in agreement. "Until then, perhaps you'll suffer me once more and give me penance."

His expression wavers, and he concedes with a nod.

I bow my head. "For these and all my sins, I am truly sorry."

"Speak now the Act of Contrition."

"O my God, I am heartily sorry for having offended Thee, and I detest all my sins because of thy just punishments, but most of all because they offend Thee, my God, who art all good and deserving of all my love. I firmly resolve with the help of Thy grace to sin no more and to avoid the near occasion of sin. Amen."

"Amen. For the next week, I'd like you to take time each day to sit without distraction and contemplate God's love for you."

I stare at him. There is silence between us for many seconds.

Finally, almost dismissively, "And say three Hail Marys and an Our Father."

"Thank you, Father."

"Now go in peace, child of God."

I stand, and he stands with me.

"Pauline, you are one of the very few left who even partake in the sacrament of reconciliation. You are also the youngest of anyone who still does. You've been coming to me now since my arrival six years ago. And I'm sure you were coming to Father Christian before me. Is there, perhaps, a confession yet unspoken that drives you here two to three times a year?"

I face him, smiling my big, taut smile. "Oh yes, father. There most certainly is." I hold the smile for a moment. "Good day, Father." I turn and reach for the door handle.

"Pauline," he calls out and I pause. "As long as you are the best you can be, you are all that family needs. I hope you can understand that."

I turn the handle. "Until Sunday, Father."

I head to DeeDee's place after confession. It's only nine-thirty. I'm not sure if she will be up yet or feeling well enough to see anyone, but I gamble that Raymond is around and awake.

He greets me at the door, looking much better than yesterday, dressed in a collared, navy blue button-up shirt tucked into a pair of khaki chinos.

"How's she doing today?" I ask as I step in.

"She's better, for sure. But she's still very weak and tired. Not the same person you've come to know, for certain."

"I was hoping that, somehow—"

"I know. But I think it's time for us to face the inevitable." He sits down at the end of the kitchen table, still facing me. "I thought we'd check on her in a few minutes and see if she's up for coming out here for a while today."

I sit down on the chair in my normal place against the wall. "I would very much look forward to that."

He reaches for a mug on the table. "Oh, would you like some coffee?"

"Sounds wonderful. Thank you."

He rises, grabs another mug from the cupboard, and pours a cup. "Jules should be arriving in an hour or so as well."

"Oh! Is she getting a ride?"

He hands me the cup, and I thank him.

"No, she's driving. Finally got her license last week."

"Really!"

He nods, but his eyebrows knit together with worry as he sits back down. "Yeah, it was past time. She found this little used Toyota Yaris for cheap. I helped her pay for it. I just don't want her driving around Chicago."

Imagining her navigating Chicago intersections makes my muscles want to twitch and shudder. "I certainly hope she would stick with public transit in the city."

"My exact advice to her as well. I hope she heeds it." He takes a sip of coffee and eases back in his chair. No words are spoken for a few moments and the silence swells to a buzz in my ears. I don't know where to put my eyes, so I look at my coffee as I wait for it to cool. When I look back up, Raymond is gazing out the window, shoulders relaxed. This is a Raymond I've yet to encounter—casual and at ease. Comfortably calm. It lowers my defenses, settles my nerves around him in a way I haven't experienced with Raymond before.

I take a sip of coffee. Medium roast. Rich and bold. I'm a fan. "How has your remote work been going?" The silence had to be broken, and although small talk is detestable, it is a safe tactic with Raymond.

"Fine. Much of our team meets virtually anyway. And, I suppose I'm kind of enjoying the lack of interruptions office life can sometimes create."

"I bet. I would have to think, though, that in a more creative element like yours, ideas and inspirations generate and transmit differently across a digital landscape."

"Honestly? At my age—absolutely. I feed off the energy of other people, and that energy dissipates quickly with distance. Virtual communication has just enough lag time and lack of spatial awareness that it hinders dialogue, action, and reaction. We respond not only to each other's words, but facial expressions and gestures. We process all that in nanoseconds. Add a quarter-second of lag, and we're talking over each other, bumping into each other's thoughts and ideas and misreading the room."

"That rings so true. I've never thought about it that way before."

"But, I suspect the younger generations are doing fine. They've probably developed completely different ways of processing the virtual situation. Their reactions trigger off alternate cues that those of us at our age don't identify. It's the personal interactions I think they're having more and more trouble with."

This is a different Raymond talking to me at the table. Not the take-charge son who has expectations of me. The stern, stoic marketing executive who can sometimes intimidate with calm reason and attack with measured logic. Now, at this kitchen table, I see what Raymond can be like when the tension in his muscles release and his demeanor relaxes. His body reclines slightly in the chair, his eyes invite instead of compel.

I quietly agree and enjoy a sip of coffee. "I just feel fortunate that I'm still able to have direct interaction with real live people—co-workers and public. I don't think I'd ever do well in a cubicle or an office, let alone having to work via computer interface."

Above the slightest of smiles, his eyes brighten. "No, I'd hate the idea of you working remotely. I think it would be a crime to keep you away from other people."

Heat flushes my cheeks as bashfulness tugs at the corners of my lips and I look back at my coffee.

"Well, would you like to see if Mother is ready to come out for a while? I can get her chair set up and ready for her."

I set down my coffee and stand. "Wonderful. Yes."

At DeeDee's bedroom door, I give a few soft raps and a polite moment, then open it a crack. "DeeDee?" Just a whisper. "Are you awake?"

"Come in, dear," The words are thin and gravelly. "I'm up." Her voice has aged a decade.

I approach her bed as she uprights herself against the foam pillow wedge with some effort. So much of her scalp is visible now through the wisps of that beautiful silvery hair. Eyes are dark and set in, cheeks sunken. Her very skin seems to hold more tightly around her skull.

"How are you doing?" My hand rests upon hers, skin like tissue paper.

Her breathing is forced and labored. "Don't you be fooled, dawlin'. Plenty of life left in me yet. I plan to stick around for a while."

I give her a watery wink. "Never any doubt of that. In fact, I think I must insist upon it. I'm depending too much on you to be here for a long time."

She pats my hand with her other one. "Well, *mon cygne*, soon enough you'll need to rely on your own strengths. I have no doubt you'll do just fine."

I look away, not at all ready to lose her in my life. I cannot rely on my emotional fortitude to withstand the storm brewing inside and around me. Instead, I look up again at that big, beautiful oil painting.

"Now, Ms. DeeDee, you simply must tell me what the story of that painting is."

"That silly old thing? You like that, huh?"

"I do. I have a deep affection for the subject matter."

"Oh, now. You are a sweetheart."

"Was that when you were still…performing?"

She coughs for a spell. "Yes. And also no. I acquired the portrait a lifetime later."

That confuses me. "So, when did you pose for it? You still look so young."

She smiles. "I didn't. Not for it. It's a reproduction based off promotional material for an early movie of mine, *The Nymph of New Orleans*."

"Did Simon have it done for you?"

She coughs again. "Not exactly."

I cross my arms and scowl in mock frustration. "Yes, I get it. A mysterious token of your past. You've built up sufficient intrigue."

Her laugh is more a cackle from her raspy breath. "Simon commissioned some artist to paint it. I never knew anything about it. Must have had it done after we went our separate ways. Cherise got hold of me in ninety-five when Simon died and his estate went up for auction. Randy, my old boss from the café, knew him—Simon was a semi-regular at the café—and went to the auction. Won it for $1,500. Couldn't wait to show Cherise. I told her to tell Randy to name his price. I couldn't talk him down lower than $3,000. Of course, by that time, I was making so much money, and the poor idiot had no idea I would have paid a lot more." She put a hand on my arm. "Help me up, dear."

I keep my arm out to her as she shimmies and swings her legs over the side of the bed.

"Do you want the wheelchair?"

"Absolutely not," she says. "I'll need it soon enough. Let me walk out—show Raymond I'm not a total invalid yet."

"Use me however much you need me."

"Already have been, dawlin'."

Gingerly, we make steps toward the door. I bear a decent amount of her weight, but more as precaution. I'm fairly certain she could still make the short trip on her own.

"So, you bought the painting…?"

"Just to keep it out of other's hands. I kept it boxed up in my basement." She stops and we stand by the door as she cranes her head up to meet my eyes. "After I was diagnosed, I hung it up. It reminds me how that young woman is still part of me. No good shedding the skin of my youth or feeling regret. I embrace it, keep her flame burning inside me." She takes a breath. "And, it reminds me of Simon." She winks. "I like that young, impetuous girl up there. Wouldn't be here without her."

"Me, too," I say. "And I like the woman she's become even more."

CHAPTER THIRTY-ONE

Transitions

"It still amazes me how you managed both college and raising a toddler."

"Lots of support. Lots of sacrifice."

Raymond's stiffness returns.

"And you got your masters, right?"

"I did."

"So, Raymond, you must have been around, what, one or two when she started?"

Stone-faced. "Something like that."

$\mathcal{D}$eeDee's first semester at San Francisco State University overwhelmed her. All alone, she struggled initially with the logistics as a nontraditional, off-campus student—getting to SF State by bus, finding her way around the campus grounds, locating her classes, and getting her textbooks. Then there was the culture. Her only academic experience was St. Mary's Catholic School back in New Orleans.

The students were Black, and from grades 8-12, her classmates were all girls her age.

Now, she was in an almost entirely White school of co-ed students up to five years younger than her. Despite being generally treated well by the student body—and there being an active Black Union—the isolation she felt at times threatened to crush her spirit.

Only a few years prior, SF State started the Associated Students Lilliput Childcare Center. Without that option, DeeDee didn't know how she could have managed her academic life. Every morning at 5:30am, she rustled a sluggish and whiny Raymond out of bed, got him cleaned up, dressed and fed, then did the same for herself while he watched *Sesame Street*. She scooped him up by quarter to seven and raced to catch the bus to campus, where she'd drop off a bawling Raymond at childcare so she could get to her eight o'clock English comp class just in time.

She picked up little Ray-Ray by 3:15 to either be dropped off with Cherise on her days off or looked after by Lindsey Flores, a teenager who lived down the street and babysat two or three nights a week for a buck an hour. Thursday through Sunday, DeeDee headed off to Bayside Café to wait tables in the evening, often taking advantage of breaks to go over reading and homework assignments.

Alfred, meanwhile, started getting serious with Tabitha, the younger sister of Mitsy Carmichael, president of the San Franciso Chapter of Black Panthers. Their courtship began casually enough, mostly surrounding Black Panther events and demonstrations. Tabitha wore the attire, but her involvement was minimal and mostly for display. She graduated in 1973 from SFSU in their Black studies program, which developed after the 1968 student strike on campus. Tabitha worked at Black Women Organized for Political Action (BWOPA) and was constantly trying to pull Alfred further away from the Black Panther Party. Alfred, however, was rising in the ranks, and by the end of 1974, he could usually be found beside Mitsy or leading one of her initiatives. Despite his operational proximity to Mitsy, however, his ideology was polar opposite of hers.

"She's too afraid to confront the man head-to-head," he complained to DeeDee one day as he dressed in preparation for a date with Tabitha. "She's too focused on public image—not enough on social revolution. Meanwhile, our people keep getting beat and jailed by the cops."

DeeDee finished chopping up a hot dog, put it on a plate with a small stick of cheese and some peas, and set it on the tray of Raymond's highchair while he fussed. Raymond had almost outgrown the chair at 18 months.

"Is that what Tabby thinks?" She sat down and huddled around Ray-Ray's chair to supervise his dinner.

Alfred's face contorted in distaste. "Tabitha is all bullshit academics—non-aggression, social change and a lot of textbook crap. She doesn't understand being on the line, get me?"

Raymond pinched a piece of hot dog between chubby thumb and forefinger and brought it to his eager mouth. "No, Alfred. I'm sorry. It's not that I don't understand what you're trying to do, or your reaction to it, but all the aggression and suspicious activity are hurting what had been a really good thing." She wiped a drip of drool off Raymond's lower lip with a rag. He squirmed away from her and fisted a stick of cheese.

Alfred glared as he finished tying his red tie, flipped down the collar of his black shirt, and leaned against the counter with crossed arms. "And this is why women shouldn't lead."

A forceful huff as she turned and gaped at him. "I'm sorry?"

Raymond grabbed a handful of peas and unsuccessfully tried to get all them all into his mouth.

Alfred put up his hands in surrender. "I'm not going to argue this with you again."

Shaking her head, she turned back to Raymond's mess and

picked up mushed peas from his shirt and lap. "What about that missing accountant? Any news on her?"

Alfred's expression shifted. It wasn't concern so much as worry. "Who knows? That's Oakland business. That new chick CEO, Brown? She brought that White woman in. Who knows why she'd want her doing the Panther books. No surprise she didn't jive with the organization. See what I'm saying about women leading?"

"Come on, Alfred. She's been missing for almost a week now. And that doesn't worry you? The police are involved. You really haven't heard anything?"

"Why should I?"

"Because you're right up there with leadership."

"And why should they know anything?"

DeeDee could only shrug her shoulders. Alfred had most certainly heard something. How could he not when even DeeDee was hearing things?

As she understood it, after their esteemed leader, Huey Newton, fled to Cuba to avoid conviction of his alleged murder of a 17-year-old prostitute, Elaine Brown took over the organization. She brought in Betty Van Patter early in the year to do all the accounting for the party. When Patter disappeared back on December 13th, the rumors spread quickly that she was about to come forward to accuse leadership of embezzlement and racketeering. There were those—Mitsy among them—who were dubious of the Oakland leadership and Huey's continued influence of it while his drug use and violent tendencies increased.

"Face it, Dee. You'll never have any trust in, or appreciation for, what the Panthers are trying to do for our people. What hurts me the most, though, is that you have no respect for what I've accomplished. What I've given to and sacrificed for our people."

The fire and intensity drained from that militant face, leaving behind the deflated pride and pain of her brother. He wore the bravado of the defiant, rebellious warrior so often, it gave her pause when the insecurities and desperate need of approval bled through his stony, angry veneer.

DeeDee stood, stepped over to Alfred, and wrapped her arms around him. "Hey. You are a good man. Papa would be proud. I'm proud. You're fighting for something important. Not just for us, but for Raymond's future. You got my respect."

His arms squeezed tight around her waist. "Thanks, sis. 'preciate it."

She pulled away from him, though still grasping his arms. "But sooner or later, you need to stop seeing that black jacket and hat as what you want them to be and start seeing them for what they've become."

His shoulders swung away from her, the rebellious disgust in his eyes and mouth returning.

She gave him a shake. "Hey. Just promise me you'll look out for yourself while you're looking out for our people. Okay? Keep your eyes and ears open."

His expression softened and he gave her unspoken agreement.

A knock on the door distracted them.

DeeDee smiled at him. "I think that's your lady."

DeeDee wrapped up her first semester as 1974 drew to a close. Diving into the new year and her second semester at San Francisco State University, Betty Van Patter's body was discovered on a beach, severely beaten, and raped. As the investigation progressed, no suspects were identified. No convictions made.

DeeDee fretted all the more for Alfred and what he was becoming ever-more-deeply involved in.

DeeDee clipped the bow tie around Raymond's neck in the living room of the apartment. "There." She stood upright and looked down at the dapper three-year-old in his black suit. "Look at my little man. Mmm-mm."

Raymond tugged at the bow-tie, fidgeted in the suit, and his face crumpled.

DeeDee batted lightly at Raymond's hand. "Stop that, now. You want to look your best for your uncle's wedding, don't you?"

"No." A whiny mutter.

She hunkered down again, straightened his bow tie and suit coat. "Of course you do. You're a ring-bearer, Ray-Ray. That's an important job. The most important job. Uncle Alfred is depending on you."

He pulled at the tie strap again. "Want it off."

"Stop your fussing, now. Don't be that way. You can take it off after the service."

Raymond's lip curled to a pout and he mumbled and moaned.

DeeDee grabbed his chin and lifted his face close to hers. "Now listen to me, Raymond George Deneaux. No more whining and crying. You be my strong little man, okay? I want you to be on your absolute best behavior for your Grann and Granpapa. Understood?"

Raymond nodded and sniffed, eyes red.

She stood straight, returned the drooping shoulder strap of her black dress onto her right shoulder and gave a downward tug around her hips. She grabbed her small purse, slung it over her shoulder and put her hand out to little Raymond.

"Hey there, handsome. Will you be my date for the wedding?"

Raymond wiped his snotty nose, giggled and smiled, then took his mother's hand.

DeeDee could not hold back her joy and excitement as she shouted out, "Maman! Papa!"

She weaved through a dozen people, crossing the vestibule with Raymond trotting awkwardly behind her, and met her parents as they came through the front doors. The three of them embraced, DeeDee squeezing tight, as if to hold back time itself from moving forward.

"Oh, my baby girl," Aurelia Deneaux sobbed as she held DeeDee.

Georges Deneaux's firm and steady grasp, almost desperate, was louder than words.

They held to the three-way embrace for a long time until finally, DeeDee felt the firm pat-pat-pat of Papa's hand on her back. They pulled away and the wheel of time turned once again.

"Lord in Heaven, girl, but you've grown into a beautiful woman," Papa said.

DeeDee's smile froze as she saw how much her parents had aged in the past five years. Papa's hair had gone mostly gray and receded from his forehead. He was heavier in frame, yet more gaunt in appearance. Droopy eyes over sullen cheeks and weeping jowls. Maman, though also heavily streaked by silver, still carried upon her façade an ageless elegance and beauty, but it was fatigued by a crinkling under the eyes and creased skin below her lips. Both of them looked worn and tired.

"I have missed you so much," DeeDee said.

"The house has been so empty without you and Alfred," Maman said, reaching out to run her hand down DeeDee's shoulder and arm, as if to reaffirm DeeDee's physical presence. "I started to worry we'd never see either of you again."

DeeDee looked to where Raymond hid behind her leg, clinging to it, and she grasped his hand. "I want you to meet someone very important to me." She drew him forward and he pressed tight against her legs, bashful and staring downward.

"This is your grandson. Raymond." She smiled. "Ray-Ray."

Raymond's existence wasn't a surprise to them. She had announced in her letters that she would be a mother, had kept them up to date on his first word, his first step. She could tell, however, that they were still struggling with the idea of their unwed daughter having a child. Whatever waivered across their faces, however, dissipated quickly.

Aurelia hunkered down and laid hands on bashful Raymond's arms. "Why look at you! What a handsome young man! Do you know who I am?"

DeeDee knew Raymond did, even if his head shook slightly and slowly. "Of course you do, Ray-Ray. I told you you'd meet your Grann. This is her!"

Aurelia drew Raymond close to her and hugged his limp, resistant body. She pulled back, smiled wide at him and stood back up.

Georges Deneaux put out his meaty hand to the little boy. "Hello there, *gason*."

Raymond retreated to his mother's dress, clutching it while his wide eyes gawked at his Grannpapa.

"Ray-Ray!" DeeDee said, nudging Raymond toward his grandfather. "That's your Grannpapa. Shake his hand!"

Raymond put out a timid little hand for Papa to grasp, then yanked it away and fell back into the safety of DeeDee's legs.

"Sorry, Papa. He's a bit shy."

"Oh, it's fine." Georges reached out and rubbed Raymond's full head of hair. "We're strangers." He hunkered down to Raymond's level. "But, strange as we may be, we're family." He smiled at Raymond who buried his face into his mother's thigh.

"Have you seen Alfred yet?" DeeDee asked.

"No," Maman replied. "We've only just arrived late last night. We had hoped to get here earlier, but it didn't work out."

"I still wish you would have stayed with us. We could have figured something out."

"Nonsense," Papa said. "We know you don't have much room, and we're fine at the hotel." He looked around the vestibule at the small group of guests and through the entryway to the church. "Expecting a lot of people?"

A few more guests entered, but there was still no one DeeDee recognized. She couldn't help but peg a small group of men dressed in black slacks and ties as Panthers, but no one she knew.

"I think Alfred said there'd be around forty or so? Mostly the Williams side—Tabby's family."

"It's a shame more of our family couldn't be part of this," Maman said, and DeeDee assumed she was still upset about her and Alfred leaving. Papa just gave a weak nod as he smiled under the sad eyes of resignation.

Cherise strolled into the foyer in a glittery scarlet dress, her hand around her husband Reggie, who she often called her big teddy bear. A black suitcoat draped over his large rotund frame, big peach collar flapped over the coat. Although his eyes darted about the room nervously, his expression was congenial as usual below that big hair and his close-trimmed, horseshoe mustache.

DeeDee waved her arm wide and high. "Cherise!" she called out on tiptoe. After a few waves, Cherise locked onto DeeDee and towed Reggie along by his arm through a few guests.

"You look absolutely beautiful!" DeeDee said as she gave Cherise a big hug and a kiss on the cheek.

"Not as fine as you, girl!" Cherise exclaimed and whistled.

DeeDee motioned to Maman and Papa. "Cherise, these are my parents, Georges and Aurelia. Maman, Papa, this is Cherise and her husband, Reggie."

Reggie threw out a quick hand to them and received each with a "How you do?"

Cherise extended a polite hand first to Aurelia. "All the way from New Orleans. So glad you could make it."

Maman took Cherise's hand and held it with both of hers.

"We've heard so much about you. Thank you for being such a wonderful support to our daughter and her boy. I can't tell you how much it's meant to us."

Georges accepted her hand and Cherise gave a big smile. "You've got a terrific daughter here, Mr. and Mrs. Deneaux. Love her like a little sister. Feel I'm meeting the rest of my family for the first time." Cherise let out her sharp, fast laugh.

"Thank you for helping to look out for our grandson, Cherise," Papa said. "I can't imagine our DeeDee having to manage that on her own."

Hearing those words stung DeeDee, but she tried to take them as an innocent expression of gratitude. There was, however, an implied meaning—that her father didn't approve of her single motherhood, and felt her incapable of raising her son properly without a man to lead and support.

Cherise put a hand around DeeDee's neck and over her shoulder. "I've learned not to doubt what DeeDee is capable of, Mr. Deneaux."

Alfred, short in stature but broad and tall with pride in his black tuxedo, stepped out into the vestibule to greet everyone before the ceremony began. DeeDee marveled at her brother displaying such warmth and satisfaction as he smoothly spoke with guests, shook hands, gave hugs, and looked so much more hopeful and happier in the black uniform he wore now rather than his other, more intimidating all-black uniform. When he first laid eyes upon Papa and Maman, DeeDee doubted her vision—she had never seen her brother cry. But, she watched him hitch his breath twice while his mouth spasmed. He rubbed his forearm across his glistening eyes once, ran to them, and hugged them desperately.

A family reunited again, DeeDee cherished the moments in the vestibule where they could be together. The talk was inconsequential, but those few minutes together again reapplied and intensified a bond severely loosened by the wiggle and shake of adversity. Now, an almost magnetic force held them together.

The deep resonance of the organ worked its way between them and the ushers began to seat the thirty-plus guests. DeeDee took her place with the bridal party, standing next to a young groomsman and brother to Tabitha. At the front of the procession, Mitsy, Tabby's sister and maid of honor, had her arm hooked around best man Russell. DeeDee remembered how intense Russell had been during their journey to San Francisco, his aggression to the police officers that night when they arrived. He had become even more severe and intimidating once he joined the Panthers. Despite being Alfred's best friend, DeeDee didn't see him often, and she was thankful for that. She was uneasy around him.

Toward the back of the procession, Cherise stood beside Raymond as he held the pillow with the rings before him as if handling dynamite. At the back, the bride stood with arm around her father, and just in front of them, the groom had his arm around the mother he had not seen for half a decade.

When the bridal party began their steps down the center aisle as organ churned out the processional, a roomful of weeping followed—those in the bridal party, and those in the pews. It was loud and cathartic. DeeDee reached the steps of the altar with the three other bridesmaids, all donning elegant black dresses. Standing in that big sacred space of the chapel, she felt she had turned the page of some fairytale. A bundle of emotion backed up inside of her, pushed against her eyes that threatened to water, yet she stood quiet and still. It made her feel oddly isolated and alone to maintain her composure among and before a room of people enjoying the loud release of their emotions. She could only smile and wipe at eyes that did not give up their tears.

Papa and Maman stayed for two more days and DeeDee, along with Alfred and Tabitha, gave them a tour of San Francisco. They wandered Chinatown, the winding road of Lombard Street, and the docks on the coast. They visited the Muir Woods and traipsed Golden Gate Park.

Their visit kept DeeDee in a peculiar mood that carried over from the wedding. When she had last seen her parents, she had been a child living in their home, cared for and protected by them. After what she had experienced in the last five years—some of which she hoped her parents would never know—she realized how much she had changed. She felt it on that altar as well—wore it as she wore the dress. And, had anything caused a metamorphosis of her person and identity, it was certainly being a mother for the last three years.

None of that transformation distanced herself from her parents, however; it drew her closer to them as much as it moved her further away from that long-ago childish DeeDee. As a young girl, any difficult situation her parents faced bore little or no significance to her but was rather a natural and expected part of them being the mysterious entities referred to as adults. Even when she was a teenager and her father was losing the business, her juvenile brain hadn't fully processed what that meant to them, only vaguely what it would mean for her. Now, as an adult and a mother struggling through the adversities and challenges of life, she could relate to them emotionally, and her heart ached for what they had gone though and were now experiencing when they should be enjoying their later years.

During her, Alfred, and Tabby's time with them, Maman and Papa asked many questions about their lives in San Francisco. Many of DeeDee's answers were so generalized she feared they would lead to suspicion, but much of her parent's curiosity was directed at Alfred and his involvement in the Black Panthers.

"Son, just what do you hope to accomplish with all of this?" Papa asked one day while they sat outdoors at a café on Haight Street.

Alfred showed exasperation almost immediately, as it was the third time coming up in conversation. "What don't you understand, Pop? Just look what happened to the Seventh Ward. Same thing is happening here and all over America. Their 'urban renewal' is systematically pushing our people out of our homes, our neighborhoods. Meanwhile their so-called law enforcement is *relocating* us directly into their prison systems!"

Papa showed no anger or frustration, simply exhaustion. "But, son. Guns? Intimidation? Thuggery? You think that's going to change anything?"

"Boys," Maman said. "Please. Let's keep this civil. We came all this way."

"What else, Pop?" Alfred said. "Huh? Peaceful protest like King did? You see where that got him! But where'd it get us?"

"Look where violence got Malcolm X," Papa said.

Alfred's hands sliced through the air. "No no no. It was his backpedaling that got him killed."

Papa sighed and put forward a calming hand. "I realize the deck is stacked, son. But there are still rules to the game."

Alfred belted a short, sharp laugh. "Are you kidding me? Pop, please—"

"That's about enough," Maman said.

Tabby put a hand on Alfred's shoulder. "Baby, calm down. This is my first chance to get to know your parents. Not this way, okay?" Her smile snuffed out his lit fuse.

Alfred stewed in silence for a while, but he eventually mellowed so that the remaining visit went well. Their parents doted and fawned over Raymond as loving grandparents, and little Raymond quickly warmed to them. Most of all, their parents seemed to be comforted by what they saw as their children doing okay—if not thriving, more than surviving.

In the quicksilver spill of time, Papa and Maman were back in their car and returning home to New Orleans before any of them were ready to say goodbye. Their absence left a much larger hole than DeeDee had been prepared for.

It was early morning two days later that, during the sleepy hours before dawn, a neighborhood just south of the Tenderloin District and west of the Oakland Bay Bridge awoke to an explosion that blew out all the windows at the corner of the Market Street McDonalds.

CHAPTER THIRTY-TWO

Another Piece

"Whoa. Grann. What's this about an explosion at a McDonalds?"

DeeDee is coughing a lot. We've been talking for a half hour with her sharing stories about her early college days and Alfred's wedding. Even a few weeks ago, this wouldn't have been much trouble for her at all, but now her tight breaths and persistent coughing is evident.

"I think that'll have to wait until another time, Jules," Raymond says as he steps over to his mother and puts a hand on her back. "You need to rest."

DeeDee, still coughing that gurgling, phlegmy cough, nods.

I step up to her and take her hand. "I'm so sorry, DeeDee," I say. "But we can catch up again after you rest and get on your ventilator."

Some of DeeDee's pills are in the kitchen. It's a half-hour early, but that won't do any real harm to get some more expectorants into her. I shake out two pills, fill a glass with water and bring them to her. "Here. Close enough to time."

She nods, still sputtering, and takes the pills along with a sip of water. "Thank you, dear."

"Should we get you back into your bed?" I ask.

DeeDee shakes her head. "I like my chair." She coughs more. "Could you—could you bring my ventilator to me, please?"

"Absolutely." After unplugging and curling the hose, it's a simple thing to grab the handle of the large, gray machine and wheel it into the living room. While I set it up next to her chair, Julienne comes to her grann and gives her a hug. "Oh, Grann. I so love getting this time with you. You rest up so we can have some fun later on, okay?"

DeeDee pats Julienne's arm and then turns to let me put the respirator around her face and adjust the strap behind her head. Machine on, she takes some deep breaths, reclines her chair, and closes her eyes.

I obsess over the rise and fall of her chest. I'm doing irrational math in my head, subtracting DeeDee's current age from some average life expectancy, and mourning the over decade of life she will be losing out on. It's a terribly inappropriate and useless exercise. I know better. You cherish the life; mourn the death. Celebrate every rise and fall of that chest. Be thankful for having some small role in her amazing life.

"Dad. What about that McDonalds?"

"Shhh. Your grandmother is trying to sleep."

Julienne lowers her voice. "But, is this about your Uncle Alfred?"

I move in on what has become a middle-of-the-room huddle and whisper, "I'll admit, I'm awfully curious myself."

Raymond gives DeeDee a darting glance, then shakes his head. "I don't want to disturb her. We can talk about it later."

"I'm starving," Julienne says. "Let's grab something to eat and you can tell us there."

Raymond looks uncomfortable. "I don't like the idea of leaving her."

I nod. "I'm not sure I'm too crazy about that, either, Jules. Maybe it's best to order in?"

DeeDee's muffled voice interrupts them. "Go."

"Mother—"

"Go!" She waves a floppy hand at us.

"What if you need us?"

DeeDee reaches for the phone on the end table next to her and holds it up for a moment, then sets it back down.

Raymond looks at me. "What do you think?"

I honestly don't know what to think. Part of me realizes that, whether we're here or not, when her body finally decides to give up, we will merely be witnesses. There will be no ambulance, no ER. No resuscitation. Her wishes. Another part of me, however, panics from the thought of her dying without anyone here. More than anything, that's my role. I'm to ensure she doesn't die alone.

I also know that she knows her body better than we do. In actuality, she is by no means at death's door yet. We all know that, I suspect, but we're too shaken by her worsening condition to think sensibly.

I give Raymond a reassuring look. "She'll be fine. We won't be gone long."

Raymond processes that, his expression shows resistance, then acceptance. He leans in a bit toward his mother. "Okay, then. We'll be back in about an hour. You rest up."

DeeDee lifts her hand and gives a thumbs up with eyes still closed.

I look at Julienne, and she is softly clapping and looking so eager, as if we were going on some exciting trip. She seems to treat every moment in life as part of a wondrous journey.

I remember when I used to be that way.

Raymond drives us to a bar and grill about three miles away. It's only a little past eleven, so the lunch rush hasn't hit yet, and the breakfast crowd has mostly left. The place is low-lit, and the dining room is wide open with two TVs on each wall. I detest the distraction of televisions in a restaurant. I don't even own a television, and to be lured like a mindless zombie to a screen filled with sitcom people or athletes without any idea what is happening only serves to remind me how little we are present in the moment and so distracted from what is important.

Today, however, I have excellent company, and I fully expect that they will win over any temptation to gawk at meaningless movement on a digital screen.

We take a seat, and the waitress comes by with three waters for us. Julienne orders an iced tea and Raymond orders a Stella Artois, pronouncing it too authentically for the waitress to at first understand. I stick to my water.

"Pauline," Raymond says. "Lunch is on me. Go ahead and order a drink."

"No, water's fine," I say, nod to the waitress and she walks off.

"Are you sure? I feel we owe you."

In the Midwest, this comes up far too often for me to even be phased by it, although what I tend to say next causes more reaction than I like.

"Yes. I'm actually a recovering alcoholic."

Those brown cheeks blanche almost to gray. "Oh, I'm sorry. I didn't know."

"Nothing to be sorry for. It's no problem at all."

I give them both a reassuring smile. The inevitable, awkward silence follows. I look between them, then laugh abruptly, startling Raymond and throwing Julienne's eyes wide.

"Amazing how quickly sobriety can silence a crowd! Are we

okay? Can we move past this?"

Jules turns to me. "Awesome." She bubbles up with giggles.

Raymond raises his glass of water. "Well, congratulations."

I take my glass and clink his. "Thank you."

Jules turns serious. "Okay, father. Spill it. What do you know about this whole bomb thing? Grann wouldn't have mentioned it if it didn't have something to do with her or Alfred."

Raymond splays hands upon the table and exhales. "Well, I'm a little sketchy on details. It's been a long time since I've heard this talked about. Your Grann has hardly ever mentioned it, and I was too young to remember anything."

"But I'm right, right? This is about Uncle Alfred?"

Raymond nods. "Okay, much of this is speculation, so keep that in mind. From what I understand, the food programs being run by the Black Panthers were largely supported by area grocers and restaurants. In many cases, this was done willingly. However, some say that the Panthers put pressure on a few restaurants that weren't supporting their cause. The McDonalds your Grann mentioned was a newer location. The owner had been holding out on support of the pantry and breakfast program. Then, one day…"

My raised eyebrows prod.

"One day…boom. Fortunately, no one was hurt. It just blew out windows and messed up their dining area. However, apparently, within a week, they were fully supporting the Panther programs with food and money."

Julienne's eyes widen. "Wow."

Raymond shrugs his shoulders. "Anyway, the police held an investigation and, well, it eventually led them to Alfred."

"Oh my God," Julienne gasps. "Did he do it?"

Raymond nods. "Apparently. He told your Grann that the assignment came directly from the Oakland office, and that he and Russell were specifically requested to carry out the job."

Jules said, "Wait, so that Russell guy was arrested as well?"

Raymond shook his head. "Nope."

I scrutinize Raymond with a sideways glance. "That sounds like a set-up."

The bob of Raymond's head agrees. "Alfred believed Russell ratted him out. To this day, Mother claims that—"

The waitress returns with Julienne's tea and Raymond's beer. "Are you folks ready to order?"

"I'm sorry," Raymond says. "We haven't even looked at the menu yet. Could you give us a few minutes?"

"Absolutely," she says and saunters away.

Raymond continues. "You see, after that accountant woman's body was found, that's when Alfred finally decided to pull away from the Party. And Mother suspects that he knew more about it than he was willing to share with her, but apparently the head office knew all too well. When he started to pull away from them, they had Russell recruit him for the job of bombing the McDonalds—to make sure he'd go through with it—and then they turned over evidence to the police."

"And Alfred never told the police about Russell?" I ask.

Raymond shrugs. "Maybe he did, maybe he didn't. They didn't really care. They had all the evidence to hang someone for the crime without the trouble of an investigation."

Poor Alfred. Only married for a brief time, trying to start a new life, and then to be facing prison. "What happened?"

Raymond turned somber and his voice fell. "Within four months, he was tried, convicted, and sent to prison."

I ask, "For how long?"

"Not long, unfortunately. I don't remember what the sentence was, but it doesn't matter. He was murdered inside within a month."

I gasp. A glance over to Julienne, who looks devastated.

"Wait…" Julienne cries. *"That's* how Alfred died? Are you *serious?"*

Raymond puts his hand out to Julienne to lower her volume.

"Yes. And your Grann believes it was orchestrated by the Panthers."

Julienne's face is shifting between shock, confusion and anger. "Why has Grann never mentioned this?"

"I think she didn't want to tarnish her brother's reputation. She wanted to keep his memory on a pedestal as some noble freedom fighter. I suppose I can understand that."

"Oh my God." Julienne isn't looking at anyone. She's processing what I can only assume to be a mix of emotions all tangling together into knots. Mostly, I'm sure she's mourning a family tragedy she's just learned about. She's more emotional than I would usually expect learning about a long-passed relative, yet it's obvious she is a sensitive, empathetic young woman.

"That's just so—horrible," Jules says, and she's close to tears. "I'm so sorry you had to lose your uncle that way."

Raymond gives her a sympathetic look. "It's okay. It's a long time ago. And I really was too young to have much memory of my Uncle Alfred at all."

What had DeeDee gone through during that entire time? Her only remaining sibling dead. The second of two brothers gone so young. From that point on, she was removed from her remaining family. Suddenly, she's all alone struggling to make a life for herself and her three-year-old son.

This may just be another piece to the puzzle, but I'm still too ignorant to figure out where exactly it fits.

James L. Peters

CHAPTER THIRTY-THREE

Blame

A chapter of my life is one step closer to being over. I want to simply be happy. Grateful. But, of course, in life, that's rarely the option. Instead? Melancholy.

Sitting in my little Volkswagen, I see the Century 21 Realty sign in the front yard of my parent's house. My childhood home. My father's place of mourning, illness, and dying. My purgatory for almost ten years.

I have a vision of watching it burn to the ground while that 'For-Sale' sign stands before the flames, and I feel terrible at how satisfying that vision is. Then my guilt takes over, my sadness that I wasn't the daughter my parents had hoped for, but how much my parents still tried to love me and be the best parents they could.

Oddly, I don't remember being so bitter about them when they were alive. So much of that manifested itself in these last four or so months since Father died. The truth of the matter is, up until his death, I didn't feel as much bitterness as I did unworthiness and remorse.

Once home, pour coffee, and relax in my favorite rocking chair. My thoughts refocus on what happens when it sells. Of course, that just leads to even more confusing thoughts. I will suddenly have a significant amount of money. Do I attempt to secure my retirement and roll it all into my 401K? Do I quit the bartending job and go on the global adventure I've always wanted?

As an unmarried fifty-three-year-old, my feelings spill and pool at the extremes. I sit in my little living room sipping coffee and listening to classical music on the radio, look out my second-story apartment window at the beginnings of life filling the streets and sidewalk, and I'm not sure I need the stress and anxiety of travel and foreign lands.

However, there is still the remnant of a youthful zest for life and adventure that remains in me. It screams, "For the love of all that is good and right, get yourself out of here and see the world while you still can!"

My passion, of course, has always been to visit Italy—to walk the streets of Rome, tour the Vatican. Somehow, I can't help but think my soul could be replenished with a trip like that. A spiritual rejuvenation. I've needed it for a while. It's not so much the Church itself that attracts my attention, but rather the history, of being able to see the manifestations of passion and inspiration that resulted on the canvas, in the stone and marble of creative genius. I need to be inspired by the purest forms of the human condition.

Perhaps that's what I'll do. It would only require a relatively small amount of that money to travel for a month or so while the rest gets put away for retirement. Maybe the bar will let me off for that long. If not, I just quit and find a new job when I get back. Yes, that's probably the most sensible thing to do.

My phone rings and I swipe up and answer. "Hello?"

"Pauline Swanson?"

Why did I answer this blindly? Stupid of me. I was too deep in daydreams. See what money and greed gets you?

"Who is this?"

"This is Erica Simmons, first assistant to the Sangamon County State's Attorney's office. I've left you several messages."

"Oh, yes. Well, I'm sorry that I can't—"

Desperation. "Please. Ms. Swanson. If you'll just give me thirty seconds."

"But I don't have—"

"Just thirty seconds. Please."

I could hang up. Right now. Why don't I? Am I so socially conditioned that I need this stranger's permission to end this call? It's absurd.

"Fine."

A pause. "I currently have six women and one man who have found the courage to step forward and testify against Father Edward Kilcannon for what he has done to them."

"Wonderful. Sounds like you have a solid case."

"Not in the least. Ms. Swanson. We need as many more as we can get. We see you were in the Christian Youth Group during Father Edward's time of supervision. So now I ask you—if Father Edward in any way acted inappropriately with you, would you consider testifying in court?"

"I have nothing to share. Nothing to say, so thank you, but—"

"Just tell me one thing, Ms. Swanson, and I'll leave you alone."

My exasperation is quickly reaching its limit. "Fine. What."

"Could you look one of his victims in the eye and tell them that Father Edward is a good man and never did you any harm?"

My denial sits on my tongue, just behind my parted lips. I want to say yes. It seems so easy. So painless. Yes, Erica. He did nothing to me during my years with him. I am unaware of him doing anything wrong. He was a Godly man of the cloth, the epitome of decency and appropriateness.

Say it. Say any of those things. Say it, damn it! Get rid of this person—this past—forever! Just be fucking done with it for God's sake! Cut it, excise it, rip it from the skin of your life! Bleed it out! Jesus, Lord, help me!

"Ms. Swanson. Ms. Swanson? Are you alright?"

I'm weeping uncontrollably. I've lost all ability to keep myself together. The phone drops to the table.

"You are not to blame, Ms. Swanson. And you are not alone."

I'm rocking in place, my sobs like a humming mantra. Her voice buzzes thinly from the phone's earhole.

"Ms. Swanson. Please. It's time to heal. You deserve that. And he deserves to face justice."

The hitch of breath as I inhale. I focus myself, slow my heart rate, calm my breathing. Phone returns to my hand. From somewhere, almost outside of myself, I hear my voice say. "Call me Pauline."

Coffee with Harold in our usual café on Sunday morning settles my nerves and calms my emotions.

"I hope I didn't mess up any plans with Glen," I say.

"Not at all," Harold says. "Glen has been through the ropes with me. I was a drunkard when we first met, a blathering alcoholic when we married, and he stuck with me through each of the twelve steps. He understands. That's why I love him."

I smile. "He's a good guy."

Harold winks. "And an even better husband."

"You deserve no less."

"And you deserve so much more."

I wave a hand. "I'm perfectly fine."

Harold raises an eyebrow. "Really? Why are we here, then?"

"Ha."

Harold sips his coffee and gives me a penetrating stare. "What's going on, Pauline? You've pulled the rip cord twice in, what, two weeks? And never a time before that. I'm worried about you."

"Don't be."

"But I am. I've seen this before. Something happens in an alcoholic's life—often times it's a ghost of something come back to haunt them. And it drives them off the wagon and into the grave. That's what I see when I look at you now. You are haunted."

"That's very melodramatic."

"Thank you."

Over the café speakers, an acoustic guitar plays and a female voice wrenches her heart out. It helps to hear the strength of a woman pushing through the pain of experience. Her soft intensity resonates, like a tremor in the soul, seismic. Close my eyes, let the vocal desperation envelope me, ride out the moment to the end of the measure. Harold, as ever, is obscenely patient.

I take one very long, very deep breath. "Between the ages of eleven and thirteen, I was sexually assaulted by my priest." I speak the words like I am tearing out a rotten tooth from my mouth.

Harold is unphased. He doesn't break eye contact, but he does lean back slightly, folding his hands in front of him, holding a white-knuckled prayer. "Have you shared this with anyone else?"

I shake my head. "Never."

His face is so passive—calm but sad. "And why is that?"

"I don't know."

One eyebrow squints in a dubious manner. "Are you sure?"

I take a big swallow of coffee. "Of course I am."

"I'm...dubious."

"Why?"

"Because." He sips coffee, sets the cup down gently. "You're

Pauline Swanson. You always know exactly what you do and why you do it."

I feel my head nodding before I can even emotionally or rationally agree with him. "Perhaps, I've never told anyone because I'm ashamed."

Harold's head cocks with sympathetic scrutiny. "A natural response. But, can I ask, why are you ashamed about what someone else did to you?"

This is so uncomfortable. Maybe even more so because this is a close, dear friend. I'd rather be spilling the guts of this story to a stranger and being judged by them rather than face down the scrutiny of someone I love and respect.

"I don't know. Embarrassment?"

He doesn't buy that. I don't buy that. I try again.

"Regret?"

That brings the scrunch of disgust to his face. "Please," he says, as if he could taste the sourness of my words.

I sit there, hopelessly flap my hands on the table, even though I feel the squirm of the real answer crouching deep down inside me. It's ready to pounce. It has tasted blood, and it wants to feed. If it comes out, it will quite possibly devour me.

I'm breathing heavy now. I'm perspiring.

"What are you ashamed of, Pauline? Tell me."

My thoughts are a blizzard of flakes in a shaken snow globe. They swirl and fall, one by one settling upon the floor of my conscious mind. The nights with Father Edward, with him so tender and gentle as he touched my thigh and rubbed my back. The recurring dreams where I remember him making me feel euphoric, causing sensations I've never felt before. Him always telling me how special I was, and how much he loved me.

"Pauline. What. Tell my why you are ashamed."

I slam my fist down on the table and my voice shatters the mellow mood of the coffee room. "Because! I never did or said anything! Every week I went back to him. Willingly. I looked forward to seeing him. I *liked* it, damn it. I *craved* it! Alright? Do you understand?" I bury my face in my hands. These are words I wasn't prepared to hear myself say, let alone confess to someone else. For all this time, as long as I left it unspoken, it would not be true.

A cautious hand gently lays on my forearm. "Oh, Pauline. Don't you see? You've punished yourself all these years for having a natural, normal response to someone doing something very wrong and abnormal to you. Can you understand that?"

I'm beyond understanding anything. I'm in a very deep, dark hole. I don't know how to feel anymore. Yet, old emotions are surfacing. They come to me powerfully, as potent as an olfactory trigger. It's almost mental time travel. The essence of my eleven-year-old self is clawing her way to the surface.

That very first night with Father Edward is suddenly right there, playing out in my head. I didn't realize it was gone until now. I had forgotten it. Or erased it. But now it's running full-color 3D. I remember that first afternoon, when he drew me close, his hands suddenly moving all around my little body, unbuttoning things, slipping into areas, touching me where I had never been touched, where it was bad to be touched. I was scared. Confused. And, yes, I feel it now as that little girl. I was ashamed. I didn't know what was happening, what I should do, how to process it. But my body was responding, and I had no control. That night, I was sick in the bathroom. In my bedroom, I laid there, terrified someone would find out. I begged God to help me, to save me, to forgive me.

And then, somehow, I woke up and that scared little girl was gone. So much was gone. I'm just now realizing how much was lost. And I went back to him. Again and again.

Harold withdraws his hand, but I sense him leaning in closer to me over the table. "I'm not equipped to deal with this, Pauline. I'm sorry. I wish I was. I want to help you. But you need someone with the skills and knowledge to address this level of trauma. All I can tell you is that you are not to blame. Okay? If there is only one thing you hear in this entire meeting, you really need to hear and understand this. *You are not to blame.*"

Regret. Remorse. Ruefulness. I've lived with all those my entire life. I've worn them like a skin, flexed them like muscle. In all this time, has blame been the bone and sinew that has given my regret and remorse its form and structure? I've always taken responsibility for my actions, but I thought I had deflected that blame onto my unattractiveness, my social awkwardness, my parents, my drinking. I always believed I was accountable, if not responsible. There was always only one thing I truly blamed myself for, and that was Kaiya.

Now, I don't know anymore. I truly don't know anything. It is as if my life has been a lie, that I've been intentionally deceived, only now to find that I myself may have been behind the deception.

Have I been carrying the burden of Father Edward's sin all along?

CHAPTER THIRTY-FOUR

Chrysalis

I t's not quite noon when I return to my apartment from my meeting with Harold. I don't turn anything on. I don't have any thought or plan. Lost in the middle of my living room, I stand and wait for some impulse to nudge me in a direction.

I don't know exactly who I am anymore. Or, more to the point, I don't know where I am anymore. Some part of me has been sneaking away, crawling down into a hidden recess of my mind. All that remains of me is this avatar that interacts and goes where expected and does what is needed.

I want to cocoon in my apartment for a couple days during my time off from work, to pull away from everything and withdraw completely down into that hiding place inside me. Let myself melt into a goo of loss, pain and penitence. Let it stew and form into something else, so I can emerge as something more beautiful, something that could take flight. It's a fantasy, but the thought comforts me.

My obligation to those I care about, however, keeps me from sheltering in place. I have commitments to honor. There are those who depend on me. I muster up the strength of spirit to move forward, to hold on. Still, it takes effort to open my door and command this flesh to step back out into the world.

When I arrive at DeeDee's apartment, she and Raymond are just saying farewell to Julienne, who's about to head back to Chicago and school.

"Pauline!" Jules exclaims. "Just in time to say good bye!" She runs up and hugs me. "Oh, I'm going to miss you!"

I hug her back, still feeling disjointed and not myself. Or too much myself. I really don't know. "I'll miss you, too, my future world-changer. You take care of yourself."

We pull apart, and she gives me her warm, wonderful smile under that amazing artwork of braided hair. "Oh! You have to come to my show!"

That totally confuses me. "What show?"

With head cocked up, she beams at me. "*A Raisin in the Sun*!"

I saw the movie. Sidney Pointier. Loved it. "Oh, wow! You're in a play?"

"Yes! It's just a bit part, but I'd love it if you could come." Her eyes plead so intensely.

"Well, when?"

"Next weekend. I would have told you sooner, but I was the understudy. The original girl sprained her ankle in volleyball, so I'm in! Dad's coming next Saturday night."

I look at Raymond, who gives an uncomfortable nod as his eyes dart from me to Julienne to where his mother sits in her recliner.

"Oh, I'm so sorry, Jules. I work that night."

She looks crestfallen. "Maybe you could get the night off?"

Raymond chastises her. "Jules. Don't. Try to be more understanding."

I've already taken off so much work, there's no way I can

get out of a Saturday night. "I really wish I could, Jules…"

"It's okay." I can tell she's disappointed.

Raymond looks at me. "Pauline, don't you worry about it. You have work. Honestly, I wish you could come, too. I hate going to these things alone."

Raymond seems sincere about wanting me there, which compels me all the more. "Well, I can't promise anything, but I'll check and see if there's any wiggle room with the schedule."

Julienne is giddy, hopping in place and clapping hands. "Yay! That's all I ask!"

"Raymond," DeeDee says from her chair. "Make sure to get me a video!"

"I will, Mother, don't you worry."

Now I'm invested in this show. I want to make it happen. Of course I want to be there for Jules, but I also saw in Raymond a sincere wish that I could join him, and it has been the first time today I've felt like I could catch the tail of myself as I run in circles.

Julienne leaves and I spend the afternoon with DeeDee and Raymond. It's a casual, easy day. None of us seem to feel the urge to plug the silence. We dip into light chit-chat about weather, local news, and incidentals in our lives. I give DeeDee her pills when its time, and Raymond joins me when I start working on the light dishes in the kitchen sink.

It has taken several months, but I am truly comfortable around Raymond now, and I feel he is equally comfortable around me. We joke lightly with each other and neither of us are bothered by a misspoken word or fumbled action. We work together in our care of his mother, and we relax together in the comfort of our company. I'm realizing just how much the Deneauxs are beginning to feel like an extended family to me. As the day draws to an end and I take my leave, I start to feel like myself again—

—Well, at least that delusional part of myself that seemed to be perfectly fine until recently.

And that gets me wondering. For the better part of twenty-five years, ever since leaving the Motherhouse, my life has been stable. From my time in St. Louis working at the library, to the last ten years taking care of my father and working at the Long 9 Lounge. Always, life has been manageable, predictable, grounded in the present. Now, the past is surging upon me like a flood, and I'm suddenly treading the turgid waters of an emotional crisis. I'm losing control.

Do I really want to put myself through the torturous introspection this trial will become? I'm a recovered alcoholic with a job I enjoy, and I'm volunteering for a family I've come to cherish. Why would I want to sully my life with the flotsam and jetsam of a ruined past?

I do an excellent job of almost convincing myself to rebury the past, let it alone forever, and cancel my meeting with Ms. Simmons.

Almost.

CHAPTER THIRTY-FIVE

The Scales of Themis

I'm still second-guessing this. I want to turn around, go back to my apartment, call her and tell her something came up and I can't meet. Sorry your time has been wasted.

But I don't. I agreed to meet with this woman from the state's attorney's office, and I'll hold to my promise. But this is not doing me any good.

Despite what Harold suggests, digging into this past is only tearing open an old wound. Maybe it scarred over poorly, perhaps there was nerve damage, but at least it wasn't bleeding. If I see a therapist about it, that wound will open right up. And, if I do what this woman wants me to do, by the end, it will be hemorrhaging.

I chose to meet at the Daybreak Café because it's a safe place for me. Where Harold and I meet. It's a sanctuary, where I can find peace and center myself. Let's hope it does the job this morning as I step inside.

Despite being a regular here, I have no real rapport with

the baristas. I've been coming here regularly for almost a decade now, and have probably seen around twenty young college-age staff members come and go. Each time I start to get on a first-name basis with one of them, they're gone within the month. I miss the old days, in Skokie, stepping into Capos and Cantos, having Jazz or the owner, Byron, call out to me as soon as I'd step through the door.

But, now that I'm older, there's also something to be said for being able to walk in discreetly, order directly, and sit quietly and alone. Maybe all the years in the bar, constantly interacting with customers, has made me crave my solitude more.

The café is somewhat busy—a spattering of young professionals perhaps needing a little something extra to work off the weekend mixed with what look like liberal arts college students either skipping their morning classes or just starting late. I may be thirty years past that time, but I can still recognize my own.

Standing apart from this crowd is the woman in a gray, pin-striped dress suit with matching low-heel shoes, black-framed glasses and brown hair drawn tight and cleanly tied back. She clacks keys on her small laptop, oblivious to everything around her. I could still turn around and walk out right now. She'd never even notice me.

"Ms. Simmons?"

She looks up, cranes her neck to make eye contact with me. "Pauline?"

I nod.

She puts out her hand. I accept it. "Please, call me Erica."

I sit down across from her in the two-seater table against the wall under a picture of the Springfield downtown from a hundred years ago.

Erica closes her laptop and quickly stuffs it away in a soft, black leather briefcase. From the same bag, she pulls out a manila file, a legal notepad and a pen.

"It's a pleasure to meet you in person, Pauline. I truly appreciate you coming here. I know this must be very difficult. It says a lot about you that you showed up."

I can only give a slight nod and wincing grin.

"I'll be honest, considering the nature of our meeting, I had hoped to meet you in a more private location."

"I'm more comfortable here."

She opens up the manilla file and starts diving into the pages. "Then I'm more than happy to accommodate you."

I feel stone cold, even though trying to be receptive and understanding. There's no denying the fact, however, that I do not want to be here.

"Pauline, if you don't mind, let me back up so you can understand how all this started. Several months ago, we were contacted by two individuals who made accusations against Father Kilcannon." Her voice is low. She speaks above a whisper, but softly enough as to not be heard by others several tables away. "In the course of investigating those allegations, we discovered five more individuals willing to testify that Father Edward Kilcannon sexually assaulted them as minors. Our records show that, during the time he was supervising the St. Mary's Christian Youth Group, you were a member of that group."

I'm listening, but no part of me wants to react. I sit there, very aware of how rigid I am.

"Is that true? Were you a part of the Youth Group being supervised by Father Kilcannon?"

"I was."

She makes a note on her pad. "Do you recall the years?"

"'85 to '87."

Erica has kept herself fairly professional up to this point, but now her fine-lined dark eyebrows and thin lips relax with a certain sympathy. "Take your time in answering this. I realize it may be difficult. Can you tell me if, at any time, Father Edward

Kilcannon made inappropriate contact with you?"

"What if I said, 'Yes'? What would happen next?"

She's still riffling through pages, as if she were juggling a caseload of facts in the air. Her eyes flit up toward me as she looks through them. "I would ask for you to come down to our office to record your statement. After that, you'd receive a subpoena as an official summons to testify at your deposition. We'd likely meet one last time to prepare you for the trial in January."

Months of dealing with this, of reliving it. For what purpose?

"What are the chances he's found guilty?"

She holds her eyes on me, pages frozen in her grasp. "At the moment? Maybe fifty percent if we're lucky? Only three of the seven are willing to testify, and those three weren't with the Youth Group for long. Their stories have holes. You, on the other hand, were there for two years. We've been told by several of these people that you worked very closely with Father Kilcannon. If he was inappropriate in any way with you, and if you testified to that effect, it could make all the difference in finding him guilty."

I drill my gaze into her, as if staring down an opponent, offensively, trying to psych her out. I'm not sure why. It's reflexive, involuntary. I'm impressed how much she is unperturbed by my cold, steely glare. She holds her eyes on mine, and I'm the one to finally back down and look away.

"Listen," I say. "What good does any of this do anyone? The man is almost dead from what I understand. What can you possibly hope to accomplish?"

For the first time, Erica lets go of her files, hands come away from the papers before her, and she peers intently at me. "This man did horrible things. I know it may sound cliché, but justice needs to be served."

"Very soon, he will be judged by God. That's enough for me."

Erica gives a sad shake of her head. "But it isn't enough for us here on Earth."

"That really doesn't matter to me." Those words leave me like a cough from the tickle at the back of my throat. I have no confidence that I really mean them.

Erica moves in with intensity in her eyes. I can tell she is passionate about her job, perhaps even believes she is doing the right thing. "It should, Pauline. It must. You see, no one ever completes the sentence. 'Justice must be served.' What never follows is that it must be served for the sake of society. Justice isn't being served to the one who has committed the crime or to the victims of the crime. That's the law, and that's different. The law is fallible. The law is malleable. The law can be manipulated. But justice. True justice is the lynch pin on which the entire framework of society rests upon. People need to know that the truly wicked are punished. They need to believe that there is order in this world. They have to see that someone like Father Edward cannot escape justice in life. So often, I question when the law convolutes justice. But I'm telling you right now, Pauline. It's for cases like these that I do this job—when true and pure justice can and must prevail. When there is no question. When it is righteous. Do you understand?"

Suddenly, the woman in front of me—still young by my standards—is no longer an adversary, an antagonist. It's clear that she isn't here to add a prosecutorial notch to her belt. This isn't a job for her. This is her calling. She is a crusader, and that lights a spark in me. But I'm also cautious. Crusaders tend to ignore the damage they do in pursuit of their mission—the collateral damage for the sake of the cause. I do not want me, or the other victims, to be that collateral damage.

"Yes," I say, and hold my rigid stare on her. "Just remember, there is no justice when it is at the expense of the innocent."

Her expression is curious, confused.

"You need to respect just how deep the wounds are that you're about to open up in order to seek your justice."

Erica offers a solemn nod. "I understand."

I take a deep breath, and I begin to share the details of a story I've never told anyone.

I leave the café a little after ten o'clock. Next Monday, I'm to arrive at the State's Attorney's office downtown to give my official statement and prepare for my deposition, which will mean potential cross-examination by Father Edward's defense attorney. The thought of that sits in my throat like a lump. Erica tells me that, based on what I shared with her, I will likely be their key witness, and that sends waves through my stomach.

I expected to be emotionally drained after an hour and a half with Erica. I planned to call Raymond and let him know I wouldn't be stopping by today. Oddly, though, I feel okay.

What a stupid word. Okay. I'm not okay and I don't feel okay. That's not it at all. It's more appropriate to say I don't feel much of anything right now. A part of me is shut off. Perhaps it's like an emotional circuit breaker. I'm really not sure, and although I try to lock down what I'm experiencing, it's like a little itch under numb skin.

So, I head to DeeDee's place because lately that's the best place to find myself, to feel normal and regulated. Balanced. I was smart enough to bring my handbag with me, so I'm prepared to keep myself occupied while Raymond works and DeeDee sleeps. And, for when she's awake, we can try some cribbage, or I can read more from *The Scarlet Letter*. Walking the hallway toward her door, I start to worry. Should I say anything about what's happening? Is this something I need to divulge to them?

No. Of course not. Somehow, though, whereas my past could be easily locked away without concern, now it has changed into this large, unwieldy object, something that can be covered, concealed, but not hidden. It's a massive thing under a sheet out in the open that everyone can see and wonder what it is.

I am beginning to realize that what hides under that sheet is me.

My knock at the door is answered. Tall, sturdy Raymond smiles and lets me in, to where strong, resolute DeeDee sits in her chair, still defying the killer inside of her.

CHAPTER THIRTY-SIX

Getting Schooled

"So horrible to hear about what happened to Alfred."
Nod. "Not a good time. I got cold. Didn't want to feel anything anymore."
"But you got through school. Got your Masters?"
Raymond's flat expression. "She was top of her class."
"You must have been seven when she finished?"
"Yes."
"I get the impression it was a difficult time for both of you."
Eyes of mother and son meet. Hold. Fall away.

Alfred's funeral somehow managed to make his death seem even more meaningless. No one from the Black Panthers attended other than Mitsy and her husband. DeeDee, little three-year-old Raymond, Tabitha, Cherise and Reggie were the only other attendees to the small ceremony. Seven people, to honor the life of someone who did what he could to fight for the rights and freedom of his people. Who believed in a mission that was ultimately tainted by its leadership and that eventually led to his death. Now, buried as a criminal and an outcast.

The cool, hazy San Franciso morning simply made the memorial service in the chapel at Mission San Francisco de Asis Cemetery all that much more dreary. Of course, the ceremony was a courtesy for those few who attended. His body would be flown back to New Orleans for his proper funeral and burial in the family plot at St. Roch Cemetery so her parents and extended family could say their final goodbyes. DeeDee withdrew money from her savings to pay for most of it, though Mitsy discretely shifted some dollars from the SF Panther coffers to help out.

Tabitha wept. Cherise cried. Even Mitsy, who was always at odds with him, teared up for her brother-in-law and companion-in-arms. DeeDee simply smoldered with anger and resentment. She wanted to cry, but somehow her emotions had cauterized, holding back any potential purifying tears. Lately, DeeDee wasn't sure she would ever cry again. Life had simply been adding lesson after lesson to the education it was giving her.

To think, things were better when she was morally at her lowest at Heartbreakers and with Behind Closed Doors Productions. Back then, she was valued and rewarded. She felt special—even adored. She had power, control of her life, and the future had promise.

Her brother George, on the other hand, had taken all the right turns in his short life, did good in school, worked hard for the family, became a respected member of the neighborhood, and he was sent to his death in a war he didn't start by a country that didn't even recognize his equal rights. Alfred had stood upright against adversity and injustice and, whether or not misguided, had sacrificed so much to try and give others a little taste of justice. For that, he was almost definitely murdered by his own people.

In the weeks that followed, DeeDee wallowed in a hopelessness that threatened to consume her. Raymond craved her constant attention, but all she could do was attend to his needs and hand him over to Cherise, to the university childcare during her summer classes, or to Lindsey the babysitter. Raymond became easily upset, irritable, prone to fits. He developed a tendency for destruction—throwing, hitting, or smashing any object he could get his little hands on. In response, DeeDee switched between easily triggered irritability to apathy.

"You need to snap out of it right now, girl," Cherise said when she'd had enough, confronting DeeDee on one of the few times they worked together at the Bayside Café.

"I'm fine," DeeDee said, unable to make eye contact as she prepped vegetables for lunch.

"Nah-uh. You aren't close to fine, and it's been over a month since Alfred's funeral. School's starting up for you again. And you have that baby boy who's aching for his mama to come back to him."

The butcher knife chopped away at green peppers. "It's all good, Cherise. Stop fussing." Eyes still to the cutting board.

Cherise grabbed DeeDee by the shoulders. "No it's not, and stop acting like it is. I'm serious. You've got a responsibility to that little boy and to your future. Don't fuck it all up now. Don't let them win."

She'd never heard Cherise talk that way before, to reference 'them.' DeeDee didn't even realize that Cherise had ever identified a 'them.'

She dropped the knife and slapped her hands down on the table. "Just who is 'them,' Cherise? Because I'll tell you, I really don't know anymore. Their faces keep changing. All I do know is that they seem to be everywhere, and that I'm sure not one of them."

Cherise let go of DeeDee and crossed her arms over her chest. "Oh, I see. The whole world's out to get you, is it? That how it feels, girl?"

"It ain't getting any easier."

"Just how would Alfred feel about you giving up like this?"

That statement, as obvious as it seemed, drilled deep down into DeeDee's pride. A few stupid words, but now all she could see was Alfred shaking his head and looking disappointed by DeeDee's surrender. Because that's what she was doing, right? Giving up? Not just on her. But on Raymond and on any future their family might have. She was buckling under.

DeeDee finally made eye contact with Cherise. "I'm all alone now."

Cherise winced. "You're—what?"

"I'm alone now. Alfred was the only family I had here."

The punch to her shoulder wasn't hard, but the shock of it coming so unexpected and so fast made DeeDee cry out.

"How dare you say that to me." Her scowl was searing. "How *dare* you."

DeeDee couldn't look Cherise in the eyes, but Cherise reached out and forced DeeDee's chin up. "No, you look at me. I've been a friend to you for five years now. I've taken care of Raymond for you, I got you your job back here, I've been by your side. You've been like family to me. But you stand there and tell me you're all alone."

"I didn't mean—"

Cherise pulled her hand back, held it out obstinately in front of DeeDee's face "Nuh-uh. You've said enough. You let me know when you come back to your senses. I've had about enough of this shitty, self-absorbed version of you." She headed for the swinging doors leading to the dining room. "You really want to know what it's like to be alone? Keep it up."

The doors flung open as Cherise burst through, leaving DeeDee with her regret.

The next three years were an anomalous passing of time where every hour of class, study, waitressing, and homework slowly ground forward, while every day and every week rapidly advanced in a frantic jumble of single motherhood, school, and job.

Cherise's words that one day in the café never left her mind. In certain ways, it calcified her bitterness, while redirecting her self-pity to an almost vengeful ambition. From that moment on, DeeDee was determined to build up a defiance to every road-block that individuals and society would put up against her. She would put all her energy into being top of her class, to make it impossible for her to be ignored. She would do everything she could to force herself into a society that didn't want her, and experience as much success and appreciation in academia and professional career as she did as a dancer and a porn star.

And she'd be damn sure she raised a son who would do the same thing—who would in fact be impervious to the injustices of society.

By the end of her second year, she was on the dean's list.

Halfway through her third year, she was on honor roll.

As she approached graduation with a Bachelor's of Science degree in Marketing, she earned her Summa Cum Laude honor and was top of her class.

"To my fellow graduates—

"Today, I'm working to beat the odds. I stand here now, a black woman graduating with honors in a time and a society uncomfortable by minority's insistence to receive the same opportunities as their White neighbors, and for women to be accepted as equals to their male counterparts.

"In the sixties, I watched my thriving Tremé Neighborhood

in New Orlean's Seventh Ward be decimated by urban renewal. I saw my father's business ruined and my parents' life squeezed by the financial institutions' intent on revitalization through minority removal. When I arrived in San Francisco in the beginning of the seventies, I saw the same thing happening to the Fillmore district and its once-vibrant Black community.

"But I'm not here today to pound my fist upon my Creole heart and puff my chest at my achievements. I do hope, however, it can stand as an example to others here today who are themselves not part of the majority and who will, as my father once told me when I was a child, 'have to work three times as hard to earn half as much.'

"No, today, I want to celebrate adversity, because in our histories, whether White, Black, Native American, Indian, Middle-Eastern or Asian—whether Christian, Jew, Muslim, Hindu or Buddhist—our moral, spiritual, and social leaders were born of adversity. Many whom we admire and have inspired us were mostly everyday people who helped shape our society and often did so through tremendous sacrifice. They chose to be leaders, they led by example, and they were judged and respected by how they faced adversity.

"The very best of our humanity tends to evolve from the very worst of what we humans are capable of. It would be nice to believe that goodness begets goodness, that peace and understanding generates more peace and understanding. That empathy and compassion and caring for one another is contagious and will spread like a virus.

"It does not.

"In fact, here in America, we too often perceive these concepts as symptoms to be overcome by economics. To be redefined by capitalism. To be manipulated by the institutions of religion. Altruism is not self-perpetuating, it cannot be sown by government or business and is not harvested by Wall Street. Nor is it sustainable.

"I do not speak to those in our graduating body who simply look to succeed and be profitable. To you, I can only say I wish you all the very best.

"No. Today, I speak to those of you who wish to be world-shapers and social-changers. To you, I tell you now—seek out adversity, lunge at it, pounce upon it like a cat upon its prey—for that is where you will make a difference. It is complacency and apathy that are symptoms, and hopelessness is the true virus. Only with hope can one believe in the possibility of a better world where people follow the Golden Rule. Without hope, it becomes every person for themselves. From there, greed and hatred germinate.

"We, my dear graduates, are in a unique position to combat adversity in our world. We are privileged to have the opportunity to wrestle with adversities we will come across within our chosen professions. For those of us facing it directly, we can either buckle under and accept the consolation prize of being a minority in this society, or we can stand up against it, work three times as hard NOT to make half as much, but instead to set an example and make twice the difference.

"For those of you today who are of the majority, congratulations. You won the genetic lottery. Now, you can simply continue to work hard, take advantage of the privileges granted you, raise your family and be a good person and a good citizen. No one will fault you for that.

"But, to do that, I promise you, you will have to continually turn the other way when you see adversity in the workplace, or in the community you live, or on the TV news you watch. You will need to convince yourself you are okay with that. In time, you will create reasons why he or she or they actually deserve it. You will conform to an ethos of justification so you can live contentedly in your convenient life.

"You will have been infected by a very contagious and comfortable virus.

"Or you too can step forward as a leader by confronting adversity. You can be an agent of change. Become immune to the sickness that has continually infected the human race since the moment we stood upright and declared with club in hand that something was 'ours' instead of 'theirs.'

"Martin Luther King, Jr. said, 'The ultimate measure of a man is not where he stands in moments of comfort and convenience, but where he stands at times of challenge and controversy.'

"Adversity, my fellow graduates, is not something to run from, or to fear. It is an opportunity for us to be better human beings and to make our society better. Seek it out, and let's all make this world better for us, for our children, and our children's children.

"Thank you."

Cherise and Reggie were waiting for DeeDee outside Jack Adams Hall. They had five-year-old Raymond with them. Erika, sixteen and their oldest, was home watching their two younger children, Curtis and Delilah.

DeeDee saw them as she stepped out the front doors and into the crowd of family and friends already hugging and taking polaroids of their graduates. She ran over to them, her purple gown and gold honor cord flapping behind her, holding her diploma in one hand and her mortarboard in the other. She hugged Cherise hard and long.

"Congratulations, girl. You did it!" Cherise said.

"I couldn't have done it without you," DeeDee said. "Thank you. For everything."

They finally split apart and DeeDee turned to Reggie and

hugged him. "You too, you big ol' bear. Thank you for everything."

"Nothing but a thing, Dee. You worked hard for it."

DeeDee bent down and looked Raymond in the eye. "So, kid? How'd your ol' Maman do?"

Raymond squirmed and moved back into Cherise's legs.

"Raymond," Cherise said. "Give your Mom a big hug. She just graduated the top of her class!" Cherise nudged him forward.

DeeDee put out her arms. "Come on, little man. I need a hug from my Ray-Ray. My little Ray of Sunshine. Give it up."

Raymond smiled, moved in, and gave her a quick hug. "Will you be home now, Mommy?"

DeeDee kept a hand on his shoulder. "I'm home, baby. But I still have some schooling to do. Your maman is going to get her masters. How do you like that?"

Raymond stared at her, fidgeted, and fell back into Cherise.

Cherise looked down at him, hands rested on his shoulders, and she gave DeeDee an apologetic look. "Hey, DeeDee. Your speech was amazing. The room went crazy over it. You were so good."

"I was so nervous about it. I'm thinking I ruffled some feathers with that one."

Cherise gave a big smile. "I know. And I loved it." She cuffed Reggie on the shoulder. "Hey! You gotta take our picture!"

Reggie nodded and grabbed the camera. "Get over there, on the grass. We'll get the backdrop of the auditorium."

"Come on, Ray-Ray," DeeDee said, beckoning him. "Let's get a picture together."

"Go on, Raymond," Cherise said and gave him a gentle push. Raymond stepped over to his mother.

DeeDee put her graduation cap back on. She and Cherise stood together, arms around each other as DeeDee rested a hand on Raymond's shoulder, who stood in front of them and looked uncomfortable. With the click and whir of the camera, the moment in time was captured.

Reggie gave Cherise a look. "Hon, we should probably get going. Erika's got that party she wants to get to."

"Right," Cherise said. "I'm so sorry, DeeDee. I wish we could spend more time to celebrate with you, but we got to get back or Erika will never forgive us."

"Oh, goodness. I totally understand. I'm just so glad you could make it."

"We wouldn't have missed it." She gave DeeDee another big, tight hug. "I'm so proud of you."

DeeDee hugged back while Raymond stood beside them. "And I'm so thankful for you. I love you so much."

"I love you, too, girl." She pulled away from DeeDee. "The world is yours for the taking."

DeeDee smiled and waved as Cherise and Reggie headed to the parking lot.

Crouching down again to Raymond, DeeDee said, "So, little man. How about some ice cream to celebrate?"

Raymond grinned and nodded.

"Then we can go home and play a little bit, maybe watch some TV."

"Can we watch Spider-Man?"

"Spider-Man, huh? You like Spider-Man?"

He nodded. "Reg and me watch it."

"Reg and I, Ray-Ray. Reg and I."

He nodded and looked down.

"Say it."

"Reggie and I." Timid and quiet.

She rubbed the top of his head. "That's my boy."

Raymond gave a small, proud smile.

"Okay, then," she said and lifted his chin with a finger. "Spider-Man it is." DeeDee hugged him tight. "And, one day, you'll grow up to be a superhero, won't you? Smart and strong and not letting anyone hold you back." She held him at arm's length and winked at him. "Isn't that right, little man?"

Raymond stared and nodded slowly.

Raymond was halfway through first grade as DeeDee studied and worked her way to the end of the first quarter of her master's program. His schooling made it easier in one way, as there was less dependence on daycare but also challenging because Raymond was supposedly exhibiting some anxieties and social issues that the teacher was concerned about. Raymond's teacher asked DeeDee to see her after school, which only managed to make her more self-conscious and nervous.

"I want to assure you that Raymond is a great little boy," Miss Young explained to DeeDee one afternoon. "So smart! We just wanted to alert you to a couple things in the hopes that it can make Raymond's early academic career even stronger."

"I appreciate that."

Miss Young's name was a perfect descriptor. She had to be no older than DeeDee herself, maybe even a year or two younger. She had big, sensitive eyes set in a thin face with dark skin and hair tight to her scalp. "Raymond is a very curious, inquisitive boy who loves to read and draw pictures and build things. A reason for concern is his aversion to social interaction. He doesn't really play with others, and when the other children are playing together, Raymond has exhibited some stress that is concerning."

"Is there a particular reason for the concern?" DeeDee said, crossing her legs and arms. "I mean, he's a shy and reserved boy to be sure, but there's nothing necessarily wrong with that, is there?"

Miss Young shook her head. "Absolutely not. However, a few days ago, on the playground, Raymond said something odd. He told several other children that he didn't have any parents. He insisted on it and got into a fight with another student over it."

DeeDee couldn't immediately find a way to respond to this and stared at the teacher.

"When I confronted him about it, he said that his uncle was killed, and he lived with an aunt and different uncle. After questioning him several times about having a mother, he finally said that he sometimes lived with her, too."

DeeDee stammered for words. "Is—Should I be concerned?"

"Not necessarily, but certainly something to be aware of. Can you tell me a little bit about his home life?"

DeeDee drew back in her seat, not sure how to take the question. She felt defensive, even a little offended, but tried to keep calm. "Sure. Listen. I'm a single mother working toward my Masters while also working thirty hours a week, so I'm not with him as much as I'd like. I also just started an internship at a marketing firm here in town and do ten to fifteen hours a week there. So yes, I do depend on my friend Cherise or a babysitter to watch him. But I'm still home with him as much as possible. Plus, we have the weekends to spend a lot of the day together, as long as I don't have too much homework, of course. But I try to not let that get in the way."

Miss Young nods aggressively. "Oh, of course. I totally understand."

"I mean, I realize I'm not there for him as much as I'd like to be, but I'm sacrificing a lot so we can have a good life, and he can have an excellent opportunity to succeed. You know what I mean? It isn't always easy for us."

Miss Young put up a hand. "Please, I get it, and there's no accusations here. I'm just trying to sort out in what ways we might be able to bring Raymond out of his shell a bit, and make sure there are no larger issues."

DeeDee stiffened in her chair. It didn't make any sense what the teacher was saying. It's not that DeeDee wasn't in Raymond's life at all. In fact, she took extra pains to be in it as much as possible. She made him breakfast every morning, brought him to McDonalds for his McNuggets two or three times a week, read to him almost every night, took him to the park on Sundays. And for all her efforts, he cried. He complained. He moped. More than once, he'd told her he wanted to be with Cherise and Reg. Did she get impatient with him? Angry? No. But it hurt. It hurt every time he made it clear he'd prefer to be doing anything else but be with her.

He was best when he just kept himself busy while she studied. He seemed happiest then. And he never complained. He seemed to like playing on his own, and she would always check on him and let him know that the building he made out of blocks or the drawing he colored was so good. The television was another saving grace. He never seemed to mind when she plopped him in front of that little screen so he could watch his Amazing Spider-Man, The Incredible Hulk, and Battlestar Galactica while she did her homework.

"The fact is, Miss Young, I either choose to be the best mother I can now and raise my boy in poverty and expect the same for him, or I work my ass off now so he can have the best possible opportunities in life as he grows up."

Miss Young waved her hand. "Oh, I don't want you to think—"

"But I do appreciate you notifying me of this. I'm sure he was just being a silly boy and making up a story. In fact, he's really into the Spider-Man TV show, and that character was raised by his aunt and uncle. Could be what he's talking about."

Miss Young stood and put out her hand. "That makes perfect sense, Ms. Deneaux. You are a wonderful mother, and I appreciate your understanding and patience with me."

DeeDee stood as well, accepted the teacher's hand as she stared her down hard. "Of course. Thank you. Have a nice night."

James L. Peters

CHAPTER THIRTY-SEVEN

Pivot

"You have not been yourself, lately. What's going on with you?"

Tuesday night and the bar is slow as we move into fall. The conventions start to slow down and won't pick up again until after the holidays. We'll still see traffic from the occasional conference, but not like the spring and summer months. Margie and I are alone behind the bar with one older gentleman sitting at a table drinking a Manhattan while two primped and preened silver-haired ladies sit at the end of the bar sipping chardonnays. Through the overhead speakers, light jazz wafts across the quiet, dimly lit room, mixing with the din of conversations and clatter of China from the adjacent dining room.

"What do you mean?" I say, not looking at Margie and knowing exactly what she means.

She's slumped over the counter, a distant stare in the direction of the lounge, but her gaze extends out far beyond it. I'm stuffing the drink menus with our new fall seasonal lineup.

"Well, I don't know. You seem to have a lot on your mind. You aren't talking as much, and you missed all those days this week. Are you still sick?"

I slip the narrow cardstock sheets into the corners of the menu pages. "I'm fine."

"How's Dee doing, huh? You know, you never filled me in on what happened after she stopped making the, um, you know—" She raised her head toward mine and whispered, "Adult films."

I step away to grab a glass and shoot it full of water. "I'm sorry. I'll be honest, what she's been sharing just started to get really—personal. Really hard to share."

"Aw, really? You mean even more personal than what you've already told me?"

I take a sip of water, curse my brain for insisting to me that I want it to be something else. That's been happening too often lately. But I won't cave in. The thought of falling off the wagon is terrifying. It would most certainly be the end of me. That doesn't keep my brain from its irrational, nagging craving, however.

I get back to the bar and start stuffing menus again. "Fine. But keep this to yourself, okay?"

"Promise."

"So, quick synopsis. I told you she left Simon, right? But not, it seems, before she got pregnant."

Margie's jaw drops. "No shit?"

I can only nod.

"So Raymond's dad is…"

My head keeps bobbing.

"Wow. But he doesn't know?"

"He doesn't want to know," I say. "He refuses to let her tell him."

"Huh."

"So then she has Raymond, starts college, her brother gets married, tries to get out of the Panthers, and that's when he gets killed."

"What?" Margie's face freezes.

"It's confusing. Essentially, he blew up a McDonalds, but it was all a setup by the Black Panthers to get him arrested and sent to prison, where they had him killed."

It's giving me a bad taste in my mouth to summarize DeeDee's story like this, as if I'm talking about what happened yesterday on a TV soap opera.

Margie looks dumbfounded. "You've got to be kidding me!"

I stop stuffing menus. "This is why I stopped talking about it. To tell the story is almost like sensationalizing it. But it's all so horrible. And then I wonder if any of this has to do with the issues between DeeDee and Raymond."

Margie stands upright, which only brings her head to my chest. Yet, she somehow always seems taller. She's giving me a very dubious, challenging look, so I brace myself. "Hold on. Back up the bus. What's this got to you with what's been bothering you?"

"Why do you think it doesn't? Now you're some kind of psychiatrist?"

"No, but I *am* a psychology major. Come on, Pauline. Something is bothering you—something personal. Spill it."

I hesitate, needing to look away from her penetrating stare. I absolutely will not talk about Father Edward and meeting with the State's Attorney's Office. But I know Margie. She won't back down once she's sniffed the scent of drama, so I quickly think of a way to deflect her intense curiosity.

"The house is finally up for sale. Sooner or later, I'm going to come into a lot of money, and I'm not sure what to do."

Margie's eyes just about bulge out from their sockets. "*That's* your problem? Holy shit, I *wish* I had that problem!"

"I didn't say it was a problem, but it is a serious question that I haven't come to any decisions yet."

"What, exactly, is the question? Because I already have an

answer." Margie throws up her hands. "Par-tay!"

I can't help smiling, but only while shaking my head. "Exactly what a twenty-three-year-old would answer."

"Twenty-four."

"Did I miss your birthday?"

"Yeah. Last week."

"Shoot. Happy birthday."

"Thanks."

"But, no, the real question is, do I put it all away so I can actually retire in fifteen years? Or do I live in the now and use the money to go on an adventure to see the world?"

Margie quickly shifts through several emotions, but she lands enthusiastically on a final expression of excitement and joy. "Good God, see the world! If you have that opportunity, how can you pass it up? I'd do it in a heartbeat!"

"So says the twenty-four-year-old who isn't even thinking about retirement and old age."

She frowns as she looks up at me. "Excuse me? Have I read you wrong all this time? Since when do you focus on how to end your life instead of how to live your life?"

Margie is such an interesting young woman. In some ways, she reminds me of Jazz from my long-ago days at Capos and Cantos Café. She has all the energy and carefree enthusiasm of a teenager but also the pathos and empathy to share in someone's sorrow and rejoice in their happiness. Her wisdom transcends her years and that's why she's a good friend despite being more than half my age. She's an old soul with a young heart, and I love her for that.

"You're right." My quiet words are more for me than for her. "You are so very right."

Margie smiles at me and puts out her hands matter-of-factly. "Of course." She smiles.

I give her a big hug.

While we embrace, she says, "But you'll bring me with you, right?"

For the rest of the week, I spend mornings and early afternoons at DeeDee's place while Raymond works. DeeDee is finding less and less energy to talk or play games. I continue reading *The Scarlet Letter* to her and she seems to enjoy it, though she continually nods off.

She and Raymond are at a disturbing juncture in their relationship. I'm uncomfortable with it. DeeDee has refrained from her jabs and her little criticisms of him. Raymond, in turn, is simply attentive to her without any actual interaction with her. Both of them seem to be going through robotic motions with each other. I start to worry that I have uncovered elements of their past that were better off buried in the sands of time.

That last Monday with them, when they had talked about DeeDee' graduation, I could sense the tension in the air. Raymond's continual interjections, sharing what he could remember of his five-year-old self. DeeDee's defensiveness when she mentioned being interrogated by that teacher.

But not just defensiveness. I could tell DeeDee experienced some pain in remembering those days. Was it the pain of remembering Raymond's lack of attachment to her as a child? Or was it a regret that she wasn't there more for Raymond as a mother?

So often, I wonder what I've gotten myself into, but then immediately look at the two of them, at this shared wound between them that just won't seem to close, and all I know is that I must help them, and I'm running out of time.

I managed to get that following Saturday night off, though

not without a lecture from Benny about how much of a strain I'm putting on everyone and how I need to rein in the vacation requests. Part of me sympathizes with him and totally understands his concern. Another part can't help but think, "So, fire me. As soon as that house sells, I'm Italy-bound."

Tonight, though, I'm far more excited to see Jules in her stage debut. I'm also anxious—in both a good and a nervous way—to spend almost three hours in a car with Raymond and sit through an entire play with him.

I'm outside my apartment and standing at the curb ten minutes before his expected arrival. The late afternoon is cool but refreshing. Autumn teases my nose and colors my vision with the yellows, oranges, and reds of changing leaves. Even on the outskirts of the suburban downtown of Leland Grove, there's enough arboreal presence to showcase the season. I throw my face into it and let the air, the smells, and the sounds overtake me.

A few minutes go by, and the loud purr of an engine draws close and next to me. My eyes open to see Raymond in his fancy metallic-gold sportscar, leaning across the passenger seat to open the passenger door. I don't know what kind of car it is. I don't know cars. But I don't need that knowledge to know the car is expensive.

"Hello." I hunker down and fumble my way inside the low overhead and fall back into the plush leather seat.

"I hope you weren't waiting too long," he says. He's in a merlot-colored, crew-neck cashmere sweater and cream dress pants.

"Not at all," I say. "Oh, I like your cap." It's a cream-colored flat cap that fits snug over his bald pate. It somehow manages to smooth over his sharper edges. On some it might add a touch of pretention, but it fits him well.

He dedicates his attention on me, maybe for the first time. "You look very nice tonight," he says, and it sounds sincere, almost surprised. I don't necessarily feel like I look good. I simply have no savvy with presentation. Tonight was extra challenging, because I didn't want to overdress or underdress, but wasn't certain where the appropriate middle ground was, so I went with a long black pleated skirt and a thin, loose charcoal sweater. There's no taming my hair other than to restrain it, so I tied it back with a silk, burgundy scrunchy. I was going to wear an old pair of gold hoop earrings, but it's been too long since I've worn earrings so my piercings have completely closed. I slipped on my double-looped gold box link chain necklace, put on my nicest pair of black flats, and now, here I am.

"Thank you," I say and smile.

Conversation starts lightly and easily enough as he gets us on the interstate heading north to Chicago. We touch on the most recent developments with DeeDee—how her appetite continues to falter, but how she seems to do well enough with a soft-boiled egg for breakfast, a small bowl of soup or some canned fruit for lunch, and beans and rice with a small piece of either a pork or chicken for dinner.

"You're doing so good with her, Raymond," I say, and I mean it. He's with her all the time now, preparing most of her meals and carrying out so much of the household maintenance and her general care. I just wish he could be as present emotionally.

"I'm doing what has to be done." Eyes sternly on the road ahead.

The distance he's keeping from his mother is so intentional, so forced. He refuses to acknowledge any love for her, but I have to believe it's there.

"I don't think you're giving yourself the appropriate credit. Not many sons or daughters would be putting career and life second to their mother's well-being. Not to the extent you are."

Raymond doesn't respond for longer than is comfortable, and I fear I've killed the conversation. After a very long moment, however, he briefly makes eye contact. "You did the same for your father, didn't you? Even more so?"

The last thing I want is to have this conversation become about me, especially with that subject. "I suppose so. Like you, I did what I had to." My intentions have sent me down a back alley of this conversation and led me into a wall.

Raymond nods. "So, you understand. You appreciate the importance of obligation over and above sentimentality."

I wince to that cold, hard statement. "Oh, Raymond. I can't help but feel you're intentionally trying to bury any genuine concern you have for your mother."

Me, going too far, saying too much. Inwardly, I'm cowering at what I expect to be an aggressively defensive response.

"Let me ask you something," he says, and I'm completely unprepared for the junction he's switching on the rails of our conversation.

"Okay," I say with caution.

"Tell me if I'm wrong, but it wasn't simply obligation that made you sacrifice what you did for your father, was it?" He sneaks another look at me from off the road before putting his attention fixedly back on it.

How did I lose control of this conversation so quickly? "No. It wasn't."

"So, what was it, then?"

I try to think of a way to answer, but take too long.

"Really," he insists. "Why did you do it for so long?"

I'm still hesitant to answer but feel the pressure to. "I guess I also did it in the hope that I would get some closure to our relationship."

"Closure?"

I nod, even though his attention isn't on me but the interstate ahead of him. "We hadn't spoken for over twenty years. Something I did that had severed our relationship. I was hoping to put that behind us. I—I was hoping for him to somehow acknowledge that it was behind us, and we were okay. That he was okay with me. That he still loved me."

Raymond's face was softer as he looked briefly at me again. "Did that happen?"

I shake my head. "No. It didn't."

Raymond nods slowly. "Perhaps, in some small way, you more than anyone can understand my situation."

I nod, and I do. I realize that. Have I realized it for a while? I don't know. But it feels like it has been lurking under the surface for some time. I lay a sympathetic hand on this thigh, and he places his hand over mine. We stay like that for several miles and say nothing, and I'm very comfortable in that silence.

The remainder of the drive, over two hours, is nonstop talking. A lot of the conversation revolves around Julienne—from her continued drive to move into social justice and the nonprofit world, to her early days as a precocious child obsessed with gymnastics and basketball. How she had always been close to her mother until her teenage years when things started to get tense between Raymond and Sylvia. How Raymond and she grew closer during that time as Sylvia became more distant to both of them.

"I don't mean to pry, but was there something in particular that drove the wedge between you and your wife?" Raymond's expression by this point is so casual and comfortable that I have no trepidation with what I say or ask.

"Oh, I don't know. I wish I could say it was the result of something dramatic—one of us having an affair, or either of us being abusive. Sadly, I think we just fell out of love with each other. We were both heavily invested in our careers, but she much more so than I." He paused, head shifted in thought. "In some ways, I suppose she really *did* cheat on me—with her career." He gave me a brief look. "She's a bigwig CEO now, you know."

"Wow."

Raymond nods. "Yeah, wow. Unfortunately, that doesn't leave her much time to be a mother to Jules. I think that really bothers her. Jules, I mean. Her mother's absence in her life is prevalent, you know what I mean?"

"I'm so sorry to hear that."

He smiles, and I really like to see that smile when it makes an appearance. "She sure has taken to you, though."

Now I can't help but smile. "And I to her. She's really something special. And I'm not being prosaic. I truly mean that she is uniquely amazing. You should be extremely proud."

"I am."

"Then tell her that."

It comes out before any thought registers in my brain. I want to take it back. Damn me and my impetuousness.

"What?"

I look at him, worried, and I see that he is ready to aggressively defend himself. His lips have sealed shut tight, his brow has furrowed.

"Listen, I didn't mean—"

"Stop."

I'm certain I've just poisoned the entire night by one reflexive comment. "I'm so sorry—"

"Pauline, *stop*." The intensity and aggressiveness strikes me mute. I just stare at him. But his face gradually wilts. "You're right, Goddamn it. I'm just like my fucking mother, aren't I?"

"Raymond, no—"

"Yes. And I knew it. I'm not an idiot. Some part of me knew what I was doing. Despite how resentful I am about my mother, there's this subconscious part of me that recognizes how it made me resilient. Strong. When Sylvia left us, I somehow fell into that same role, thinking that was what Jules needed to keep her going."

I stop talking and just listen. There's nothing for me to say in this moment.

"Unbelievable. I never made the connection. Never really stepped back to know what I was doing and why. But it's so obvious now."

After a moment, I put a hand on his shoulder. "Whatever you've done, she's becoming a magnificent woman, and that is thanks to you."

He acknowledges that, but I can see he is facing a turning point in his relationship with his daughter.

If only it could also be a pivot in the relationship with his mother.

The show is incredible. It's the first time I've seen *A Raisin in the Sun* live as a play, and it's poignant and emotional. Jules plays Mrs. Johnson, the irritating neighbor of the Youngers. I eat up every moment she grabs attention while on that stage. Whenever I look at Raymond, I see a proud father, perhaps even a pleasantly shocked one.

We join the rest of the audience to give a standing ovation to the cast, then wait in the lobby for Jules to join up with us. When she finally breaks free of the cast and all the attention of patrons, she runs up to us with her arms out.

"Hey!" she cries and dives into Raymond and me, drawing us together into a group hug. "I'm so glad you could both be here."

"We wouldn't have missed it for anything," I say.

She pulls back from us. "So? What did you think?"

"You were amazing, honey," Raymond says. "I hardly recognized you."

Jules beams. "I did okay?"

Raymond draws her in and hugs her again. "You were amazing. You nailed it."

I have a moment, standing there, looking at Raymond and Julienne together celebrating her night, where I wonder what I'm doing here. I'm intruding on an important father-daughter moment. I'm an interloper.

But then, Julienne lunges into me with the biggest hug. "I can't tell you how much it means to me that you came. Thank you!"

I hug her back, hard and fierce. "I can't tell you how much it means to me to be here now."

The three of us hug each other amid a swarming crowd of people, but for me, it is just us. The three of us. Here and now. I don't want to ever let go.

We take Julienne out for a late dinner celebration. The entire time is an enthusiastic monologue from her about every possible aspect of the production—gossip about the director, the starring cast, about the costumes, the set design and the make-up. Raymond and I interject when we can, but Jules is so fully charged with the energy of the performance that we can barely get a word in.

We drop her off at her dorm so she can get some rest before her matinee performance tomorrow, and we head home.

We talk a bit about the play—the symbolism of the mother's plant and Beneatha's hair—but we spend a lot of the drive in comfortable silence. I nod off a couple of times in the passenger seat. The rest of the time, I just watch the headlights pass us by and the lines on the road tick along.

Raymond pulls over to the curb at my apartment and puts his car in park.

"Let me walk you up," he says, pushing the button to turn off the car.

"Oh, you don't have to do that," I say.

"My pleasure," he says.

We step out into the night, walk to the front door, and I key in the code to enter. Up the stairs, we get to my door.

"Well, thank you," I say. "I can't express enough how much I enjoyed myself."

Raymond gives me a smile. "Thank you for being such enjoyable company."

"Well, you and Jules make that very easy for me."

We stand there, neither speaking for a moment, just looking at each other.

"Your family means a great deal to me," I say.

"You mean a great deal to us."

I smile.

"To me."

His stare is deep and long. Mine doesn't falter, even as he leans in to me. My eyes close and heart thrums as our lips share so many unspoken words.

This moment of intimacy, this kiss, exists upon the point of a moment, a fulcrum I teeter upon. I am in motion.

"Good night." Softly spoken inches from me, my eyes still shut. His large hand slowly slides off my cheek like a caress as he pulls away and leaves me in sway.

I nod. Words cannot escape my smile as I watch him walk away.

James L. Peters

CHAPTER THIRTY-EIGHT

Adjustments

Sunday is not a good day for DeeDee. I've come directly from early Sunday morning Mass at St. James. Knocking on her door, I can hear her bronchial, continuous coughing.

A harried Raymond lets me in, shoulders slumped, eyes tired but intense, and I follow him into DeeDee's bedroom where she is upright and hunched over, a handkerchief to her mouth as she gurgles and gasps between coughs. Raymond goes to his mother's side, hand to her back. I go to the other side of the bed and pull out the saline nebulizer Nancy had dropped off a few days ago. I do what she showed me and use the syringe to draw in a dose of saline and hydrogen peroxide. I inject it into the nebulizer cup, turn the machine on and hold out the mask to DeeDee.

"DeeDee, cover your nose and mouth with this."

She nods, pulls the handkerchief away from her face, a large splotch of blood at its center.

When the mask is against her face, I draw the rubber strap

around the back of her head.

"Try to breathe deep, DeeDee. This will help."

Between coughs, she takes short, sharp breaths.

I look at Raymond, whose intense eyes implore. "I'll be right back," I say. "I'm going to get her a dose of mucolytics and another dose of expectorants."

He nods and I dash to the kitchen where all her medications are. I grab 600 milligrams of mucolytic and 400 milligrams of Guaifenesin, pour a glass of water, and rush back to the bedroom.

Already, her coughing has lessened, and she's able to take slightly deeper breaths.

"Do you feel able to take these?" I hold out the pills and the glass. She nods and pulls down the mask. A pop of the pills and she chases them down with the water. Another fit of coughing follows, but she gets the mask back on and the heaviest coughing subsides.

She looks at me, and I almost fall apart. It's such a look of desperation, of exhaustion, of surrender. When I trained for hospice, I was told to watch for a look like this from the patient. A stare that lets you know that, mentally, they have transitioned. They are no longer fighting to live, they are preparing to die.

Somehow, I manage to fight back my tears. I give her a big, stupid smile and shake my head. "You hang in there, beautiful. We're here with you."

She nods, breathes.

I hold her hand from my side of the bed, and I notice a large, brown hand reach out to hold DeeDee's other one. I look up at Raymond, and he shows me the faintest curl of sad smile.

DeeDee eventually falls back against the big, wedged foam pillow that helps to keep her from drowning in the fluid building up in her lungs. Raymond and I withdraw to the kitchen table where we sit next to each other. I reach out my hand to him and he takes it.

I stare into those tired brown eyes of his. "How are you doing?"

He nods, gives me a wan smile. "How are *you* doing?"

I sputter a sharp, high laugh. "Not so good, really." I stare down at the table, at our hands entwined. "Not so good." It leaves my lips as a sigh, an exhale. He squeezes my hand and I squeeze back. "But better here with you."

"You came just in time. I didn't know what to do. She woke up that way a half-hour ago and it just wouldn't stop."

"I'll show you how to set up that nebulizer. It should help with episodes like this."

DeeDee's condition is deteriorating faster than I expected. A seed of hope still germinates in me that she will be with us for many more months yet, but today is a weed that chokes that growth out.

"I had a wonderful time last night," he says, and that smile is back, the one that makes me want to do whatever I can to keep it there. It's vanity on my part, but I like to think that smile is just for me, that it's mine. I wasn't sure I'd ever fall hard for a man again, but I am with this guy—at thirty-two feet per second.

"I didn't want it to end." I'm just above a whisper, partly to not bother DeeDee, but mostly because the thrill of being here with Raymond, having physical contact with him, is drawing the breath right out of me.

He strokes my hand and his eyes widen coyly. "Then let's not let it end. Can I take you to dinner tonight?"

My other hand covers his as we draw closer to each other over the table. "I would simply adore that."

We kiss for the second time. A short, soft, lingering kiss, as if whispering unspoken affection to each other. His gentleness and timid approach suggest a cautious advancement in what can now comfortably be called a burgeoning relationship, and

I like that. In fact, it brings an electricity between my legs that I haven't felt for so long. My occasional one-night stands from the bar were fun but fleeting, physically satisfying but lacking much anticipation and exhilaration within the suspense of the moment. No personal connection, just raw arousal. My heart is pumping a youthful, oxygenated blood that is going right to my head.

"I'm sorry I left so quickly last night," he says as we part but keep close. "Nancy was on overtime to be here while we were at the play."

"I wasn't bothered by it at all." I pat his hand and ease back. "Your mom did okay last night, though? No troubles?"

Raymond settles back in his chair. "Nancy said she was great all night. She was talkative and they even played a game of cards together."

"Maybe she just overexerted herself?"

"Maybe." Raymond pushed out from the table and stands. "I really need some coffee. Do you want some?"

"That sounds wonderful."

Raymond starts preparing to brew some fresh coffee and I watch him, enjoying his casual domesticity in the kitchen.

"So, when did DeeDee first get diagnosed with Sarcoidosis? I don't know that part of her story. How old were you?"

He holds in place a moment in the middle of scooping coffee grounds. "Oh, geez. Well, that would have been shortly after my wedding, if I remember right. Around 2003 or 2004? She was in her early fifties."

That surprises me. "That late, huh? It normally develops a lot sooner."

"Well, that's just it. Her symptoms developed way before then. She was just continually misdiagnosed. In fact, a big part of my memories of my mother were with that cough of hers."

"Really?"

He pours the carafe of water into the coffee maker and hits the button to start it brewing. "Oh, yeah. I was probably thirteen or fourteen when it really started to develop. She would have been—boy—mid-thirties?"

That upsets me. To think this could have been diagnosed so much earlier. It's usually treatable, but so often overlooked by doctors, particularly when among Black women, even today.

Raymond sits back down at the table. "By the time they did diagnose it, it had already done so much damage to her lungs and liver. They put her on a variety of treatments, but they weren't as successful as they had hoped."

I'm hesitant to ask the next question, but I also want to learn more about DeeDee's story. Although it is completely irrational, I'm desperate to know all I can about her before she's gone, as if somehow the story itself can keep her alive. And I have someone I'm even more interested in now, who is a living part of that story.

The look I give Raymond is cautious—almost apologetic. "So, what happened to her after college? What happened to you? I'd love to hear more if you're willing to share."

I watch Raymond's face drop, and I fear that, not only will I not hear the story, I've somehow abused our burgeoning relationship.

"Ah, yes. The epic narrative of Deborah Deneaux." He gives a succinct nod. "Sure, what do you want to know?"

James L. Peters

CHAPTER THIRTY-NINE

Social Franchising

"If you don't want to talk about her—"

"It's fine."

"You'll have to forgive me, but I do have a deeper interest in this story now, you realize."

"You do, huh?" A smile.

"I'm not trying to pry, and I'm not trying to make anyone do anything."

"Oh, yeah?" Still grinning. "Just what are you trying to do?"

"To understand two very special people better."

He sat outside the principal's office at Lakeside Middle School. Again. Two girls walked past him, quickly looked away and giggled. Stu Phillips, a real jerk from his class, approached and pointed as he passed by, laughed and said, "Smooth move, Ex-Lax" under his breath.

It was the second time that semester he found himself on that bench outside the administrative offices. His mother would show up any moment, and she most definitely wouldn't be coming to defend him.

The first time he was dragged to the principal's office, he had been foolish to think she'd take his side and defend him. An older White kid had called him a bastard. "You know what that is, kid? It means you don't got a Dad. It means your mom is a skank." The punch he delivered to the kid's jaw certainly seemed justified and well worth the black eye and sore ribs he got from the beating he took.

When she wasn't spewing her mantra about working harder than everyone else, being the best you can be, his mother was incessant with her speeches about standing up for himself, about not being disrespected. Well, he was getting good grades. He was excelling at sports. And he didn't take shit from that kid disrespecting him and her. Why wouldn't she come here and take his side for defending himself, or at least give him the benefit of the doubt?

Because, he was never good enough. No matter what he did, it was always wrong.

His mother, of course, was becoming a top marketing figure in her industry. Thirty-three years old and already an ad executive with Burrell Communications Group. She helped create McDonalds campaigns to secure a foothold in the Black American market. In fact, that's partly why he sat there now on the bench in front of the principal's office.

Two White boys railed at him on the playground, said he was just a poor Black boy who was only at the school to meet some quota—so said their parents. He didn't know what a quota was, but he certainly got the gist of what they were saying. Raymond balled his fists and replied that he didn't need any damn quota because his mom worked on McDonald's ads and was a super-important person. They laughed and called bullshit on him, called her names he wouldn't stand for. His rebuttal was his fist flying into their faces.

So now he sat, waiting for his mother—the person he stood up for against their insults—to arrive and seal his doom.

Why did she have to bring them to this shithole anyway? They were happy in San Francisco. He was certainly happy there. If they were to move, why not to New Orleans and get back with Grann and Grannpapa and the rest of their family?

But Chicago? He had nothing in common with these Black kids, let alone the Hispanics and Whites. Everything here was about your color, your background. You were preassigned to your group by birth, and you were forced to keep to that group like some kind of gang. It was bullshit.

And don't get him started on the winters. Holy hell, what a goddamn frozen nightmare.

He hated it here. That was the plain truth. And he hated her for bringing him here.

The clack of heels echoed down the hallway, heading toward him. Fast and deliberate. He knew that sound, that pace. Something about the way his mother walked, how those legs of hers drove her toward him, that made his gut wrench. He sat like a lump as her approach got louder and louder.

"What did you do now, kid?" All five-foot-six feet of her loomed over him, her gray tweed jacket broadening her shoulders over her straight, gray mid-length skirt. "Did you overthrow some ruthless teacher? Protest some unlawful rule stripping you of your rights? What's your noble cause this time, huh?" Burgundy lips twisted with sarcasm under her straight and feathered hair.

He looked up at her, stone-faced. "I hate this Goddamn place, and I want to go home? Is that cause enough for you?"

Stepping fast and heavy from Principal Harrington's office and through the administration door, his mother turned to stare

Raymond down. "You got off easy. Get yourself home and right to your room. We'll talk when I get there."

And she was off, click-clacking down the hall and back to her work so she could come up with new television and print campaigns to sell Black America on burgers, fries and shakes. Raymond trudged out of the school and started his long walk home to their apartment in South Shore.

Being a key member of the PTA and a major donor to the school likely helped to lighten Raymond's punishment. Yay for Mom. But she just didn't understand what it was like to not be one of them—a neighborhood kid. They didn't like outsiders. Even the non-White kids didn't completely accept him. It had been over a year since they moved here and it's barely gotten any better.

His mother just kept telling him to work harder—in school, on the football field, and in track. Don't give them any other choice but to like you. Respect is earned.

Well, that's a two-way street, and not too many kids at his school had earned his respect, and they only resented how hard he worked. He tried to explain that to his mother, but she would just come back at him with, "Don't ever think life is fair. It isn't. It doesn't owe you anything, and things won't magically be okay. Life can be hard. But it'll also make you strong if you don't let it beat you down."

He was so tired of those pep talks.

Ahead, he saw a bus stop shelter. On its one side, a McDonalds poster showing a young Black boy about Raymond's age, holding a football and grinning as he looked up at an older man smiling down at him while he held a McDonald's bag and paper cup. At the bottom, the golden arches of the fast-food logo and the words, "Sure is good to have around."

He recognized the ad because a framed picture of it hung on their apartment wall. It was one of his mother's. He saw it every single day as he walked from his bedroom and down the short hall to the bathroom. She won some kind of award for it.

He hated that ad. He hated everything about it.

He gave the sign at the side of the bus stop a karate kick and a spiderweb of cracks spread through the torso of the man in the ad. He threw a quick look around to make sure no one saw him, then kept walking.

He'd asked about his father a couple of times—who he was, where was he—but his mother danced around his questions. "Someone who was very good to me, who I cared a lot about, but who isn't a part of my life anymore," was one answer. "He lives in the past I left behind," was another answer. Each time, she would conclude by putting a hand on Raymond's shoulder and saying, "We're doing just fine on our own, little man."

In whose eye? It had been Uncle Reg who had taught him how to throw a football and a punch. It was Aunt Cherise who had shown him how to knot his shoes and a necktie. It was his babysitter Lindsey who introduced him to Blackjack and to Curtis Mayfield and Smoky Robinson. Fine on our own? When had he and his mother ever been on their own?

And now Reg, Cherise, and Lindsey were two thousand miles away. He missed them terribly.

He fantasized about this mysterious father figure sometimes, daydreamed about running away and finding him, discovering he was some ex-athlete or some other successful man that would take him in. They'd toss the ball around, work on car engines, or build things out of wood. At some point, he'd put his arm around Raymond and say, "Proud of you, Son."

And then his dad would pass him some McDonald's fries, and they'd laugh and everything would be right with the world.

It was spring of '86 and Raymond just stepped out of the bathroom after showering and brushing teeth. He dressed quickly, grabbed his book bag and jacket and headed to the door to leave for school.

"Where're you going?" his mother called out from the kitchen table as she sipped coffee.

"Wha'dya mean?"

"*What do you* mean.'"

He rolled his eyes, exaggerated his enunciation. "What. Do. You. Mean?"

She set her coffee down. "Do you *want* to go to school today?"

He gaped at her, cocked his head. "I *have* to go to school today."

"No, you don't."

He could only look with confusion. Her face, meanwhile, was enjoying some little game of hers that he had no idea what the rules were. All it did was make him more testy and annoyed.

"What are you talking about, Mother?"

She took on a cocky, self-assured pose with crossed arms. "I don't know. I thought you might want to come with me to work today."

That sounded like the most awful thing in the world. "What? Why?"

An exaggeration of hurt across her face. "You don't have any interest in what I do?"

His muscles let go in exhaustive frustration, shoulders dropping, arms hanging at his side. "Mother—"

"And I suppose you have no interest in the Chicago Bears?"

He froze, any words inside him clogging his throat like a backed-up pipe.

She smiled wide. "Mm-hmm. I had a feeling. We're shooting a commercial with the offensive front line today. I've already called the school and excused you if you want to come."

His heart still belonged to the San Francisco Forty-Niners. It always would. But just in the last year, he'd really started to follow the Bears and their dominance on the field. It was inevitable that they would get to the Super Bowl, and as a running back himself for his middle-school team, he was obsessed with Walter Payton.

"Really?"

His mother gave him a big smile. "You bet, Kiddo. I've been dying to surprise you with this. Is that cool or what?"

He ran over to her and gave her a big hug. "Oh my God, that's so awesome! I can't believe it!"

He felt her arms tight around him. When they finally pulled away, she looked at him. "Coolest Mom ever?"

He looked back at her, hesitated, then smiled. "Today? For sure."

He watched his mother's expression shift, her face fall with disappointment or hurt. Then, finally, a weak smile. "Well, I guess I'll take what I can."

At fourteen years old, Raymond was too young to understand, or even know, everything happening with his mother's career at that time. He only learned about and understood it many years later when she would talk about it with him—especially as he started to enter the marketing world himself.

The fact was, Thomas Burrell, the founder and CEO of Burrell Communications Group, was her idol and mentor. She loved working for him. Most of what she learned was from him and that agency. His achievements as an innovator in marketing and advertising, of targeting the Black audience directly as an important and viable market, were unprecedented in the industry. The fact that he, too, came from modest origins and didn't get interested in marketing until his college years made him all that much more relatable.

But in the three-plus years she worked on the McDonalds and Marlboro campaigns, she slowly became jaded. It was exciting and invigorating at first to help emphasize the importance of the Black community as a significant representation of society and an important market share. She truly believed that by representing and valuing minority audiences through advertising, she could also represent that audience in a way that broke stereotypes. Her double-dutch campaigns, showing young athletic inner-city girls doing amazing feats with jump ropes and celebrating their achievements, was a highlight of her early career—and certainly propelled her to senior partner at the agency.

As time went on, however, the idea of Black Capitalism and its promise of fueling and liberating the Black population rang false. As McDonald's franchises continued to open up in urban communities, the jobs did not propel the population, and Black franchisees continued to struggle against the biases of financial institutions. They were also being denied more profitable locations by McDonald's corporate headquarters and stuck with the urban locations White franchise owners didn't want because those areas were rife with crime and poverty. Meanwhile, instead of avoiding stereotypes, so much of their advertising only advanced them. What at first felt like a way to raise up Black capital and the position of the Black community started to feel more like perpetuating the machine that kept them down with low-wage jobs and cheap, unhealthy food.

A fourteen-year-old Raymond didn't understand all of this, but he definitely saw that his mother was frustrated, more short-tempered, and unhappy with her work. One day, a particularly frazzled, worried, but intensely determined DeeDee sat Raymond down.

"Raymond. I have some news. Your mother is about to take a big leap. It's a risky one, but I have to do it. But that means you're just as involved. I wish I could explain it to you more, but the fact is, it'll be rough for us at first, but it could also be a huge opportunity. I've established myself enough that I really think I can do my own thing, do it well, and do good while doing it. Do you understand?"

Raymond nodded, even though he really wasn't certain what she was talking about.

"I'm going to start my own ad agency. I'm going to support Black businesses while trying to support our community, you get me?"

He nodded again, no less sure of her meaning.

"But there'll be lean times for us for a while. I just want you to be prepared. Okay?"

He nodded.

"Do you believe in your mother?"

He bobbed his head.

She drew him to her, arms wrapped around him. "I love you, my little man. I'll do everything I can to make this work. But there's going to be sacrifices for a while. Have patience with me, okay?"

He nodded as she withdrew and cupped a hand over her mouth as she started to cough.

James L. Peters

CHAPTER FORTY

Repudiation

My alarm wakes me up at 6:00am on Monday morning and dread sits on my chest like a stone.

I fell asleep Sunday night aloft on the gentle currents of remembrance dining with Raymond. I think about each time our hands reached over the table for each other—once for comfort, twice with affection. Each contact pumped my blood more fiercely.

He had wanted a finer dining option, but there were none open on a Sunday night, so our ambiance became nostalgic eighties pop softly playing while we sat across from each other at a big booth in the darkened corner of a kitschy chain restaurant.

Even though we spent three hours alone together in a car only a couple nights ago, and are together almost every day as he works and I watch over DeeDee, the dinner felt different. It was our first actual date, creating an added tension between us. But that didn't last much beyond first being seated.

We politely rummaged through topics, poking about the

piles of our interests with curiosity, looking for a subject that glinted with promise.

Raymond mentioned a recent visit with Julienne to the Field Museum in Chicago—I raved about the Native American and Egyptian exhibits. He recalled his trip to Morocco and tour of the Atlas Mountains. I told him how much I dreamed of visiting Rome and Venice. Our conversation enthusiastically ricocheted off each topic.

Inevitably, past relationships snuck into our conversation, but neither of us obsessed. He referenced the divorce two years ago, how the house was sold, Sylvia took the job out east, and Jules moved in with him at his condo to finish out high school. For my part, there was little need to bring up Jack, other than to reference him as a significant turning point in my life.

It was a wonderful night, strategically laying down our personal interests and philosophies like cards in a trick-taking game, with neither of us wanting to throw down any trump card of too heavy a topic. I think back all those years ago, falling head over heels for Jack, and how different that was to this burgeoning relationship with Raymond. When I met Jack, I had still been so emotionally fragile. Psychologically fractured. He had been mysterious and alluring—an enigma to be solved, a lost soul to be found. Raymond is sturdy and rooted—what one holds on to in a storm, who leads you out of the maze.

We ended the evening back at my place, where I invited him in for tea. We sat on my couch, talked more, then explored simple physical pleasures in much the same way we explored our intellectual desires. Raymond seemed content with our slow pace, maybe even tantalized by our leisurely progress, just as I have. We're partaking in high-level, extended foreplay.

He didn't stay long, but he never left my thoughts until I awoke this morning.

Lying in bed now, I dread where I need to go and what I

have to do. I continue to second guess what I agreed to, and by the time I get up and ready for the day, I convince myself that this is a very bad idea.

Erica Simmons removes her round, black-rimmed glasses as if they somehow distorted what I just told her. "I'm very sorry to hear that, Pauline."

Her small yet still somewhat spacious office predominantly showcases richly stained walnut furniture. The bookshelves behind her are stacked with antiquated law books, the bindings stamped with gold-foil dates. She sits behind an old, heavy desk that her laptop rests on along with a pile of papers off to the side and a laser printer behind her.

"Please. Have a seat." She motions to the wooden armchair in front of her desk that beckons like a baited trap.

"No, I should really get going." My eyes drift to the window at my right, to the parking lot and bustling street beyond.

She implores with cool, stern eyes. "Please?" Her hand still directs toward the chair. "A moment is all I ask."

Every second of hesitation intensifies my doubt about backing out of my testimony. Worse, it seems more and more wrong to not do it.

I broke my middle finger in my first year of college. It was a Friday afternoon taking a one-credit PE volleyball course. The physical fitness instructor, Mrs. Thiesen, taped my finger to a tongue depressor and then wrapped it to my index finger. I didn't get to a doctor until that Monday, and they had to rebreak it to set it properly. It was excruciating.

I can't go through it again. I can't relive those years with Father Edward. I can't be broken again.

"Ms. Simmons—"

"Erica, please."

"My life is going really well right now. I'm happy. I have things to look forward to."

Erica slips her glasses back on. For some reason, I find her more intimidating framed by those round spectacles. "I'm glad to hear that, Pauline. But not everyone who was victimized by Father Edward has been so lucky."

"I understand that, but—"

She pulls out the photo of a woman. It's an older photo, slightly faded. I don't recognize her. "This woman also won't be testifying."

Confused, I can only shake my head at the picture of the smiling woman who looks to be in her late thirties. Very pretty with red hair and fawning hazel eyes.

"Mary Ellen Thompson. A husband and two young children. She killed herself fourteen years ago. Twenty-five years after being under Father Kilcannon's supervision in the St. James Parish Christian Youth Group."

I stutter weakly. "I'm sorry, but I—"

"One witness has given a statement to being in the same room with Mary Ellen and Father Edward several times." I wince to Erica's finger jamming down on the picture. "Out of over 180 kids who were in that youth group during Father Edward's time at St. Mary's, I have seven people willing to testify. None can claim more than a few instances of inappropriate behavior, and two of them can only offer second-hand accounts."

She leans forward over the desk, folding her hands in front of her, and her stare presses against the back of my head. "I have spoken to two drug addicts, four alcoholics, a convict, and over half a dozen people in therapy—all who came out of that youth group between '78 and '87. They won't come forward. No one else will. Your story is the best chance of making this man face his crimes."

My legs won't hold me up anymore. I sit down heavily and exhale as I keep my eyes on my lap. "You don't understand. I escaped that burning house of my past. It took a lot of years, but the burns have healed. I have scars, but the pain is now a memory." I Look up, all my desperation crashing against her defiant, insistent glare. "Don't ask me to run back into that fire. Please. I won't survive it." Tears blur my vision.

Erica puts her hands up. "Hey. Pauline." Her expression softens. "I can't imagine what it must be like for you. For all of his victims. My job is simply to do whatever I can to bring his crimes to light, and hope that it will be a little harder for anyone to do this to others in the future. I can't force you to give a statement today, or to testify. I can tell you that, sometimes, testifying against an assailant can actually help the healing process. Knowing they played a part in their abuser's conviction can help victims move on and find some peace."

I need to say something to wrap up this meeting without completely dismissing what she's saying. It's not that I don't want to help, but there simply isn't the strength in me to testify. I try to find words, but they are lost to me.

"Listen," she says, and she stands up. "Forget about today, okay? Take a couple days. Think about it. Talk to someone." She pulls open a drawer, scavenges for something, and hands me a business card. "If it would help, this is a therapist in the area who specializes in early childhood trauma. Maybe give her a call."

I take the card, put it in my pocket without looking at it. "Thank you."

"I'll give you a call in a few days if I don't hear from you, okay?"

My eyes keep to the floor. "I'm sorry. I thought I could, but I just—"

"Let's see how you feel in a few days." She puts out her hand. "Okay?"

I take it limply. "Okay."

I leave her office, exit the building, and have no intention of speaking to her again.

In the bus, I escape from the Sangamon County Complex and any responsibility I have to Erica's idea of justice. I wield a machete of excuses and chop through the dense growth of condemnation obscuring my path. Father Edward can't hurt anyone anymore. He will never even survive the trial. There must be others better than me to testify. I hack away at my guilt and self-loathing but am unable to force my way down any path of justification.

The question that bothers me most, the one that leaps from the bushes to crouch and growl before me on the trail, is a simple one:

Why?

And that question leaves my mouth dry. I think back to my conversation with Harold. My admission. The rational part of me vehemently denies the guilt and shame I feel, yet I'm still struck mute by those emotions. There is also something about speaking the details out loud, retelling each moment, that would be like stepping into a time machine—not one to send me back as I am now and face Father Edward, but rather one that would put me back into that little girl's head as she experiences every moment.

A shudder runs through me, and I shake my head to get the thought out of me.

No, I cannot go back. I must go forward.

Ironic, really. In my early days of recovery, I couldn't abide my present. It was a sickness, and I could only look back or forward. I so despised my present that I did everything I could to step around or over it. I obsessed over elements of my past and daydreamed about the future. Somehow, age and complacency has inverted that. I'm discovering just how much I avoid making plans for the future, and how much I now flee from my past. And is that so surprising? My damaged childhood, my failures and mistakes all lie in the past, DeeDee's death and my indecision about the house sale is my future. My present embraces me—it is Raymond, it is Julienne, it is the bar and working with Margie. It is dear, sweet Deborah Deneaux, still hanging on to a life of so much more substance and courage than mine.

Midmorning and back at my apartment building. I am stuck at the curb, fighting irrational compulsions. There's a part of me that simply wants to run away. To get out of this town, away from my past and from the future where there is no more DeeDee. And, without DeeDee, will there be no more Raymond and Julienne as well?

Time to get real, Pauline. Raymond is completely out of your league. Attractive, successful, worldly. It's not hard to believe that family members might experience a heightened emotional bond to the caretaker of their dying loved one. Once DeeDee is gone, will the delicate thread that ties Raymond and Jules to me break as they return to their busy, successful lives?

Stop it. Flee the past and avoid the future. It's worked for most of the last decade. Keep to it. Climb under the covers of this moment, draw it tight to the chin and snuggle in.

I grab the keys out of my pocket, head to my car, and drive to DeeDee's.

Seeing DeeDee alert and in her chair helps to lift me out of my funk. She greets with a raised hand, and I give her a gentle hug.

"Pauline." More mouthed than said. So little voice left to her.

"Hello, beautiful. I'm so glad to see you doing better."

Those frail shoulders shrug as she rocks a raised hand back

and forth in a so-so gesture.

Raymond's hand lays against my shoulder as he steps up beside me. "She had a good night's rest." He nods to her. "You even enjoyed a scrambled egg and piece of toast for breakfast, didn't you?"

She nods and a smile shows through the fog of oxygen mask. Her eyes stick for a moment to Raymond's hand on my shoulder. Her smile widens and she winks at me. My cheeks warm and I step back, go around Raymond and head toward the kitchen.

I glance at the pill organizer on the counter. "It looks like you took your pills this morning?"

"She did. I gave them to her an hour ago."

"Good. I'll just take care of these few dishes here." I run the tap and look for the dish detergent under the sink. "Any laundry that needs to be done?"

"We should be good until Wednesday," Raymond says. "I can take care of that."

I let the sink fill, tossing in the few cups, plate and bowl into the soapy water along with silverware. Raymond comes up behind me, hands resting on my hips. His voice is low as he leans in over my shoulder. "Is everything alright?"

"Of course." I start to scrub the plate.

"You seem a little…tense." He starts to rub my shoulders, and it feels wonderful, but my muscles resist with taut rigidity.

"Challenging morning. Nothing to worry about."

His hands slowly make their way down my arms. "Are you sure?"

Rag dropped, hands wet and sudsy, I turn and give him a slow, soft kiss. "Now I'm fine." A half-smile for a half-truth.

The concern straining his eyes releases. "Good. Was hoping for dinner again tonight?"

"There's nothing I'd like more."

"Great," he says. "I need to get back to work. But let's plan on heading out at five?"

He gives a quick kiss. I turn back to the sink and take care of the remaining dishes, relishing the present.

DeeDee and I play Cribbage on a TV stand at her recliner while Raymond stays engrossed in his work at the kitchen table, ear buds in as he sits through a virtual conference. I'm preoccupied for more than half the game because there is so much I want to say to her but don't know if and how I should. As I shuffle the next round, the compulsion to speak becomes too strong to ignore.

"You know, when I was taking care of my father, we never really talked. Even when he got quite sick, we never said much to each other. I kept wanting to say things to him, but I was too afraid to. And my father—well, he wasn't the type of man to talk about his feelings or to discuss his condition. He certainly didn't want to discuss the inevitable."

I look up at DeeDee and her eyes are locked onto me.

"When he passed, I just felt like there was a lot left unsaid between us. That was hard for me. It still is hard. There were things I needed him to say to me, so that I could say things to him. But it didn't happen. It still haunts me. I think it always will, really."

I start dealing. DeeDee is silent, staring at the cards piling up in front of her.

"It's your crib hand," I say as I pick up my cards.

DeeDee just continues to stare at hers. She slides the mask down from her face. "What are you trying to say, dawlin'?" A hoarse whisper.

I group my face cards and number cards together. "Maybe I'm suggesting that there's something you aren't saying that perhaps you should consider saying."

DeeDee chuckle-coughs through raspy breaths. "You looking for my last confession, *Mon Cynge?*"

"At the moment, I'm just trying to not seed your crib hand." I pull two cards from my hand and set them face down in front of her. "But I'm also trying to be a friend. I don't want there to be any regrets with you, or about you, like I had with my father."

DeeDee scrutinizes her hand, pulls out two cards and adds them to her crib hand. "You should know me well enough. I don't have regrets." She coughs, moves the mask up to take in a couple deep breaths, and cuts the deck. I turn up a seven of hearts.

I decide on my first card to play. "I'm sure that's what my father thought as well." I play a jack of hearts. "Nobs for one."

"I once knew a Pauline Swanson who wasn't afraid to speak directly." DeeDee plays a five of spades. "Fifteen for two."

"Okay, then." I glance over at Raymond. He's still plugged in to his video conference and oblivious to us. I lean in closer to DeeDee. "I think Raymond is waiting to hear something from you. I think there'll be a hole in the rest of his life if he doesn't." I play a five of diamonds from my hand. "Twenty for two."

I've only received that smoldering glare by DeeDee once before—looking into the rearview mirror when I went against her wishes and took her to the ER that night. I can't hold eye contact and instead put my attention on the two remaining cards in my hand.

"If Raymond has unfinished business with me," she says in a hiss of forced breath, "he's welcome to come forward with it."

Culled, I keep my head down with a stammering nod.

"No offense, my dear, but Raymond and I know exactly where we stand with each other." She lays down a five of clubs. "Twenty-five for six."

"Go," I say with surrender, and she takes another point.

That evening, DeeDee is doing well enough that Raymond and I slip out for a quick dinner at a family restaurant down the street. Standard midwestern American fair. Back in Skokie, I loved trying new things, diving into the strange and exotic. It was titillating to experience unique textures and foreign flavors as if pretending to travel distant lands for a few savory bites.

By the time I was cooking for my father, my taste buds slowly atrophied. I acclimated to meat and potatoes, to casseroles and noodle salads. Rarely do I revel in my food anymore. It's no longer an experience I immerse myself in, but instead simply mindless chewing, the satisfaction more like a scratched itch than a sensual stimulation.

I continue to realize how much of me was lost in all those years looking after my father.

From behind the large, laminated menu, I say, "I must insist we find a night to have a true dining experience."

Raymond chuckles, and it only now dawns on me that I have never heard him laugh until this moment. His is guttural and loose, from the belly, yet properly restrained.

"You, *dawlin'*, speak truth."

Said with exaggerated buoyancy, but I hold on to that endearment like a warm embrace.

"What is your preferred cuisine?" he asks. "I haven't had a chance to find out."

I sneak around the side of my menu with a grin. "Anything I have never tried before."

Even his eyes smile back. "Ah, a woman after my heart. Or, should I say, appetite."

"Well, there's a wonderful Vietnamese restaurant I haven't been to in ages that I would take great pleasure bringing you to."

"I'm sold."

The waitress comes by with waters, and we order drinks.

Silence carries for a few moments while we look over our dinner options.

From behind his menu, Raymond asks, "What looks good to you?"

"Oh, I don't know. The Vietnamese blood pudding looks good but perhaps I'll just go with Prawn Ceviche. You?"

After a suspended moment, Raymond bursts out laughing. It's deep and rich and contagious and I start to giggle with him.

"Oh, well, my eye was on the Moroccan B'stilla pigeon-meat pie, but then I saw the Japanese Fugu fish and I'm thinking, 'what the hell'?"

We're both laughing now in fits that neither of us can stop.

When the waitress returns, we are just regaining our control, wiping tear-filled eyes and sighing out the exhaustion of hilarity.

"What can I get you both?"

"Turkey club with coleslaw," I say.

"Cheeseburger and fries," Raymond says.

She jots the order down on her pad. "Coming right up."

I can only imagine what she's thinking as she walks away from our bursts of laughter.

Our talk is casual as we eat. It's hard for any conversation to be very thoughtful or intimate when trying to fit large sandwiches into one's mouth.

"Do you think," I ask as I toss a small potato chip in my mouth, "the reason we American's tend to avoid deep discussions at restaurants is because the architecture of our meals exceeds the capacity of our mouths?"

Raymond coughs out a chuckle through a large bite of hamburger. He puts a hand over his mouthful. "What?"

I point. "See? This is exactly what I'm talking about. Everything is so big here. I'm eating a triple-decker turkey club as tall as my face, and your burger just about requires you to unhinge your jaw. Our mouths are kept too full to reach any suppertime epiphanies."

Raymond takes extra effort to swallow his bite of burger with a slight wince. "Well, you may have just uncovered a deep conspiracy. Perhaps portion size is the new opiate of the people?"

"It's very possible." I begin disassembling the remaining two wedges of my sandwich, nibbling at the deli slices of turkey, the piece of tomato. I'm self-aware that I've become fairly silent. Over our dinner, my mind went to places, to questions and curiosities that haven't left my head yet.

"Is there a particular revelation you'd like to share?"

I cast aside another piece of bread and peel off pieces of sandwich to nibble on. "I'm sorry. I'm just still thinking about your mother. And you."

His arched brow might be quizzical or exasperated.

As nonchalant as possible, I say, "I just know there's still a lot I don't know. And it has me curious."

He drags a fry through a splotch of ketchup. "Oh? And just what are you curious about?"

"Well, from what you shared before, I definitely got the impression your mother could be hard and demanding at times."

"Yes, she could."

"But at the same time, it seemed like she could still be loving and caring."

The fry went into his mouth. "Mm-hmm."

"So, what makes me curious is, what happened to put you at such odds with each other?"

There's tension in his cheek muscles and severity narrows his eyes. The serious, intimidating Raymond has returned, and I hate myself for ruining such a perfect evening.

He shifts in his seat. "Just what do you hope to achieve

dumpster-diving into our entire family history?"

I reach my hand out, fold it around his. "For your mother to die in peace, and for you to live without regret."

CHAPTER FORTY-ONE

Confession
& Recrimination

"You mentioned your mother ended up starting her own agency?"

"Yes. It was a difficult time for her. She was hugely successful with the marketing campaigns she was creating with Burrell Communications, but she ended up being forced out."

"Oh, no. Really?"

"It was for the best, at least for her. She had been getting frustrated there, tired of profiteering off the Black audience without them benefiting from it. The NAACP was protesting McDonalds blocking Black franchise owners from more profitable locations. And she felt she was perpetuating stereotypes instead of breaking them. So, being pushed out ended up allowing her to focus more on what would benefit minority populations."

"How old were you when that happened?"

"Fifteen."

"Why did they make her leave?"

A small, sour smile.

Raymond stared down at his spicy chicken sandwich. "I don't like this place."

They sat at a small table in a little dining area. The décor committed itself to blazing reds and whites, from the menu board to the white tables and red chairs.

DeeDee took a chicken tender in hand, tore it apart to get as small a piece as she was able and brought it to her mouth. "Come on, we've only been here a few times."

Raymond removed the top bun to look at the spicy fillet of chicken drenched in a Cajun sauce. "I'd rather have a McDonalds burger and fries." With a fork, he poked at the side dish of collard greens.

DeeDee dropped the piece of chicken and gave Raymond a hard stare. "Listen, Chicken George is my biggest client, do you understand that?" She hesitated, put both hands over her mouth, and had one of her coughing fits. She had these bouts sometimes two or three times a day. She'd been to the doctor a few times and they first told her it was a sinus infection. Now they said it was bronchitis, but that was becoming more doubtful since she'd had the cough for over a year.

She dug in her purse for the bottle of cough syrup she always carried with her and took a swig. Catching her breath, she continued. "I need to immerse myself in the Chicken George experience regularly if I'm going to sell it to the public, you understand? Plus, I'm supporting a client that's supporting me." She ate the piece of chicken. "Besides, you have to admit, it's really good chicken."

She had already given him the whole story, not that he cared. How Ted Holmes was a Black east coast businessman trying to bring an authentic Black experience and cuisine to the American people while also providing a viable business opportunity for other Black entrepreneurs. To Raymond, though, it was just another crappy fast-food place, but without burgers and shakes.

The place was packed, though, even with some White folks, so people seemed to like it a lot.

The occasional dinner like this constituted the few instances he spent any extended time with his mother. She flew to Chicken George headquarters in Maryland almost every other week, or was on the road for business trips to pander to her other clients. It didn't bother him anymore. In fact, more often he dreaded the times he did have to spend with her. She was all business. Being a mother was her business. He just felt like a product for her to develop and make more marketable. Ever since leaving Burrell's agency, she had become ever more intense, and imbedded in her work.

He still didn't understand why she left Burrell. She was doing really well there, and their life had turned around from those lean times in the Fillmore district of San Franciso. Now, she worked more than ever as head of her own little agency. Riding off the notoriety of her McDonald's campaigns got her Chicken George, and she had a small list of other clients that followed her over from Burrell, but it just didn't seem worth it.

He took a bite of sandwich. Half-way through chewing he asked, "Why'd you have to leave your other job?"

Her face strained, a confused hesitation lowering her brow. "What do you mean? Why ask about that now?"

He took another bite, answered through a mouthful of seasoned poultry. "Things were better then."

Her body shifted into her cocky defensive stance that told him he should be careful what he said next. "Better how? And don't talk with your mouth full."

He swallowed. "I don't know. Better. You weren't gone so much. You didn't complain about money so much."

"I wouldn't complain about money at all if you didn't eat enough to feed three people and keep growing out of your clothes."

He poked at his collard greens with a fork. "It just seemed

like a better time for us, okay?" And it was. Middle school right after the move had been rough, but things smoothed over after that between him and his mother. He got in less trouble, started to focus more on sports and grades. It wasn't often, but they would occasionally go to the Navy Pier and ride the rides, watch the jugglers and magicians, and listen to the bands. They'd catch a matinee at the movie house, play Skee-Ball and pinball at the bowling alley. In the last year, all that stopped.

His eyes kept to his plate and his voice stayed as low as his breath. "I don't get why you had to ruin it."

He expected a viper-strike response and for her to lay into him about how ungrateful he was, but when he finally looked up after a few seconds of silence, she was just staring at him, mouth slightly agape.

"Forget it." Quickly said as he forked salty greens into his mouth.

"No," she said evenly. "I won't forget it. It bothers me that you would say something like that, like I've done something on purpose to hurt you."

"I didn't mean that—"

"Yes, you did. You did. But, I forgive you. I've kept some things from you. You were still too young to understand. But you're fifteen now, close enough to being a man that I suppose it's time for you to know. Everything."

How she said that—*everything*—made him nervously curious. He set his fork down, sat up and focused his attention on her.

"I didn't quit Burrell. Well, not willingly. They forced me out."

That widened his eyes. "You were fired?"

"*No.* I was strongly encouraged to resign."

"Why?"

Her fingers tapped on the table as she scrutinized him. "I don't want there to be secrets between us, Raymond. We should never be afraid of telling each other anything, okay? Do you agree with that?"

He nodded, even though every fiber of his being was thinking the opposite.

"They discovered something about my past and they feared it could tarnish the reputation of the company."

That made no sense. He couldn't even imagine what it would be about his mother that could hurt the reputation of anything. "What, you cheat on your taxes or something?"

"No, Raymond." A pause, a dropped gaze, then a very determined raise of head and piercing look. "For a couple years before you came and blessed my life, I was a dancer."

He almost laughed. "You? A dancer? Really? That's kinda cool! Were you in musicals or something?"

She shook her head, eyes glued to his. "No. Not that. I danced in a club. I was an exotic dancer."

He knew the word, but he wasn't completely sure what she meant. "You mean, like, belly-dancing or something?"

"Stripping, Raymond. I was a stripper."

"You're joking."

"I most certainly am not."

His cheeks got hot. Could his eyes go any wider? Unwelcome images spilled into his imagination, and he immediately pushed them away. His mouth was going dry and all he could muster out from his lips was, "Why?"

She sighed and tugged at a piece of chicken. "It was hard times for me and Alfred when we first got to San Francisco. I waitressed, but that was barely clearing the rent. Your Uncle Alfred wasn't landing any steady work. I turned down the offer when it first came to me, but—I don't know. I danced for many years when I was younger—up until about your age. I loved it more than anything. Dancing at Heartbreakers gave me a chance to do it again. And, I made a lot of money doing something I loved."

"While you took your clothes off in front of men?" Raymond didn't like hearing about any of this. A mother didn't do that kind of thing. His stomach churned with every unwanted image that seeped into his thoughts. To even imagine her naked—in public—made him almost gag.

"Keep your voice down, Raymond." She kept her stare locked on him. "Not at first, not completely. But yes, over time, I took all my clothes off."

This was a nightmare. He wished he had never learned this. No wonder they fired her. "Wait. I don't get it. That was in San Francisco? Then how did anyone at your job find out about it?"

His mother nibbled on a piece of chicken and as she drew back slightly, a deepening concern weighed down her gaze. "Maybe this isn't such a good idea to talk about right now. I can see you're upset."

"No. It doesn't make sense. Did one of them see you dance however many years ago and just recognize you now? What the hell?"

She put a hand out to him. "Settle down, Raymond. Take a breath." She pushed the remainder of her food away from her. "Someone at the office turned in a VHS tape to Thomas Burrell."

"What? Mother, that makes no sense. Someone filmed you dancing?"

She shook her head. "It was a movie I starred in."

The nausea pressed against the back of his throat. There was only one kind of movie she could star in that would make her boss want to get rid of her.

"Jesus Christ, Mother!"

She reached over and threw a hand up in front of his face. "Calm down. And watch your language."

Hot disgust rose up in waves of heat in his cheeks. His hands clenched into tight fists. "How could you?"

He watched his mother go cold, stolid. Her shoulders

straightened. "I feel no shame about what I did. You have no idea how hard it was to exist in that place in that time with everything going on. There were no legitimate opportunities. What I did made me enough money to go to school, to build a better life—for me *and* for you. I will not apologize, nor will I feel less about what I did."

"Why? Why tell me this?"

"Better you hear it from me than find out some other way."

A realization bombarded his thoughts, rocked his entire world. Everything he thought he knew, who he thought he was, shifted under his feet. He glared at his mother. "Oh my God. Oh my God. That's why you had me. That's how you got pregnant. Oh, Jesus." He rubbed at his arms, as if they were grimy. He felt filthy all over.

Her bold, forthright exterior wilted in front of him and became shock and apologetic sympathy. "Oh, God, no, Raymond. No. It's not what you're thinking. That's not true."

"Bullshit."

"No, really. Listen, your father—"

"Stop! Don't you dare. Don't you dare try to tell me who that sleazeball is. I don't want to know. I don't want to hear it."

"Just let me—"

He stood up and glared down at her. "I swear to God, you tell me who my father is and I will never speak to you again. You hear me?"

"Raymond—"

"Just leave me alone. I feel sick. " He stepped away from the table.

"Raymond, damn it. Get back here."

"You make me sick." He walked across the dining room and out the door.

Antagonism pumped his heart and anger boiled his blood. All of that converted to a steam of aggression he released on the football field. It drove his legs like pistons through defensive lines and across the goal line. The grid iron became his focus, his driving passion. A growth spurt between his sophomore and junior year only added fuel to his athleticism, and his six-foot-three, broad-shouldered stature became virtually unstoppable, fired by his angst and rage.

His academic life also improved significantly. Before, he had maintained decent grades so he could stay in athletics. His new motivation ignited a far more intense determination—he would be better than her, in every way. He would cleanse the corruption of some unknown degenerate from his genes.

His mother, of course, told him how proud she was of him, though she only attended one of his games. It didn't matter to Ray. Her approval no longer had any worth or meaning to him.

As time passed, their relationship returned to a stiff, uncomfortable normalcy—she immersed herself in her work, building up her client list, winning awards, and by the end of his junior year, she exceeded her success at Burrell. The topic of her past did not come up again, and their family life subsisted through his high school days.

He began dating Susan Jackson, the star forward on the girls' basketball team. Being the MVP running back for the Evanston Township Wildkits, in addition to his stature, had earned him all the respect he hadn't received in middle school as the newcomer and outcast. There were still moments when he felt out of place, even carrying some resentment against these privileged kids coming from upper-middle-class families, only to realize he was now one of them. But the struggles and lean living of their early life in San Francisco and those first couple of years in Chicago still clung to him faintly like the musty odor of that old

Fillmore apartment. Plus, he now had a much more embarrassing skeleton in the family closet.

He and Susan lasted half-way through senior year. Their relationship was buffeted by the typical gusts of teen drama, but in truth, over time they simply became bored of each other. The passion fizzled while they focused more on making the most of their final year in high school and prepared for college. He had some casual hook-ups after that, but he laser-focused his efforts on earning a football scholarship to the University of Illinois Springfield, a prestigious school, and one that that would get him away from his mother.

His mother, from the little he could tell, only seemed interested in casual hookups. At least, he assumed that was the case. He was never introduced to any men, but throughout high school, she would occasionally mention a Bill or a Kevin or an Andrew she was heading out to meet. None of these names kept within their limited conversations for long. Whenever she did actually go out to meet one on a Friday or Saturday night, he'd simply say, "Have fun," or, "See you later," as if sending off a casual roommate.

Because that's what they had become. It was the only way he could mitigate the prickly pokes of betrayal and shame brought on whenever he thought about her as Mother.

Her cough, meanwhile, kept bringing her back to doctors. After changing their diagnosis to a chronic bronchitis, now they were suggesting it was a fungal pneumonia, possibly acquired from that old apartment. They put her on different drugs, and she forced him to go in and get a lung screening as well, just in case.

As far as Raymond was concerned, that cough began when she started working seventy or eighty hours a week. She didn't eat well and didn't get much physical activity. Her coughing fits usually came in the evenings when he could see she was exhausted. It was useless to talk to her, though. She hadn't listened to him when she first started the Deneaux Agency. She would probably work herself to death, and if that was what she wanted, fine. He had given up on her ever choosing motherhood over career long ago.

The letter came in the mail a month before graduation. He held on to it, staring at the return address: University of Illinois Springfield.

"Don't just stare at it, Raymond. Open it." His mother stood next to him, an expectant smirk on her face. She kept telling him that he was a shoo-in to get the scholarship. He did not have that level of confidence; however, he did believe he earned it and deserved it. She didn't understand how important it was for him to get the scholarship. How desperate he had become to earn it. The last thing he wanted was to have his mother pay for any of his schooling. He didn't want to owe her anything. He needed to do this on his own.

"For goodness' sake," she said, reaching for it. "If you won't open it, I will."

He yanked it away from her. "Quit it! Would you just let me do it myself?"

"But you aren't doing it, Raymond."

"Mother, *please*." He glared down at her, as if his anger and frustration would have any effect. As usual, it had the opposite result and she just returned his stabbing look with steel resolve.

"It's not going to open itself," she prodded, eyes darting between letter and Raymond.

He expelled an exasperated breath and tore open the envelope. With letter unfolded, he scanned through each serifed line of type.

"Well?"

He carefully refolded the letter and slipped it back into the envelope.

She smacked him on the arm. "Tell me!"

"I got it." He couldn't help the slightest smile, even though he didn't want to reveal anything to his mother. Inside, he was screaming and jumping.

Her eyes widened. "Full scholarship?"

He nodded.

"Oh, Raymond!" She moved in and hugged him. "*Felicitation!*" Unprepared, he stumbled back a step as his arms went up and forward awkwardly, looking for a place to land. To return her embrace seemed odd, foreign, almost inappropriate. He finally wrapped one arm timidly around her back as the other fell limp.

They separated, but she kept hold of him by his arms. "Everything is coming together, now. Don't take this opportunity for granted, you hear me?"

"Yeah." An eye-roll and sigh.

She gave him a shake. "I'm serious, now. I was there not that long ago myself. College life can be a breeding ground for poor decisions at a critical point in your life. You stay focused, you hear me?"

"Yes." More hiss than word.

"I realize your football is important to you, but don't let it overtake your academic career. You need to focus on a solid major. Don't expect to be drafted by the Forty-Niners."

He pulled away from her, that anger increasing the pressure in his veins, raising the temperature of his blood. "Mother, would you just back off?"

It was hard to read her expression—a hurtful downturn of eyes and an angry curl of lips. "I'm sorry. I'm just trying to help you. I'm your mother, and I care what happens to you. I don't want you to have to struggle like I did."

"I'd never resort to anything like you've done, don't worry."

Her smile was taut and tight, her eyes narrow. "I don't know. You'd make a hell of a Chippendale, dawlin'."

"That's so gross." That was his mother. She had to ruin everything. She so enjoyed making him squirm.

"Settle down. You blow everything out of proportion. I just want to help."

"I've done just fine without your help or support up until now. I'll do just as fine a hundred miles away from you."

Her stare was long and hard as iron. A noxious silence hung between them. Finally, she said, "So that's how it's going to be between us, is it, Raymond? This is what you want?"

He gave her the coldest look back he could. "Never been anything else."

Her nods were slow, minimal. "Fine. It's your life. I did all I could for you." She turned away, walked to her bedroom and her door very slowly, very quietly shut.

His eyes stuck to that closed door. Under his breath, eighteen-year-old Raymond said, "It was never enough."

CHAPTER FORTY-TWO

Selah

I've been starting many days in my trusty rocking chair enjoying a morning cup of medium roast coffee in the dawn of silence as I read from the Bible. Usually just for a half hour or so. I finished the Book of Psalms yesterday. They offered a certain emotional shelter that comforted like the protective arms of a loving parent.

The word *selah* appears throughout Psalms beside the text of certain verses. It's a Hebrew word that means to pause and reflect. I've not practiced this for a long time, but it is essentially the penance Father Tom assigned me. Now, when life seems to be balancing upon the edge of some keen blade of pertinence, it seems crucial.

That's what these quiet moments at the sunrise of the day have become for me. The imploration in the margins of my life to stop, be quiet and still, and allow the eyes and ears of the soul to open and receive.

Selah.

Raymond's voice from last night's dinner echoes from memory. Resentment turned a vise upon his words as he related his teen years, his recollections burdened by cumbersome bitterness over the perception of his mother's neglect, and by the embarrassment of her past.

In the stillness, listening again with quiet mind, I detect something else beneath that surface-level animosity. An undertone of personal regret and remorse. I remember watching the remnants of his teenage self twist his features as he relived those moments, but here in the dusky dawn, my soulful eye opens and recalls a moment when the adult Raymond resurfaced with a wince of regret.

And now I wonder—was he simply sharing his past, or offering up a confession?

I had asked him if he was sorry for anything he had done or said back then. He bristled to my question and seemed to sort through his words carefully. "I do not blame my younger self for much of what was said or done back then. She chose her career over her fatherless, only child. To this day, instead of understanding the pain and hurt that could cause, she instead only feels unappreciated and misjudged."

I reached out for his hand. "I'm sorry if I caused you additional pain by having you share any of this."

"I'm fine. It's all in the past."

"If only that were true," I said, and he withdrew his hand and his gaze, putting an end to that topic.

Our night ended pleasantly enough, but now, in the morning as I pause from reading the first chapters of Proverbs and its call for, and adoration of, wisdom, I think about DeeDee and Raymond and how these two might forgive each other and find peace. If they do not, regret will sit upon her last thoughts and be a residue that clouds any memory Raymond will have of her.

My phone vibrates on the stand next to my chair. I glance at it, knowing even before I look that it is Erica from the State's Attorney's office. The caller ID on the screen flashes like an accusation. I do not answer. The angry insistence of the buzzing phone pulls me out of my spiritual depths and back to convincing myself why testifying is a terrible idea for me.

I have a new and potent reason for not testifying. Raymond. If I agree, I will have to tell Raymond about my past, and I fear that will end us. There are enough strikes against me already in the genesis of this relationship. If he learns how damaged I am, how tainted, I may never see him again.

I turn back to the Bible, to Proverbs and its almost stream-of-consciousness list of do's and don'ts, its platitudes and observations. Words and meanings begin to blur and I'm about to set the Book down for the day and get ready to head over to DeeDee's place. Before I close it, my eyes fall upon the fifteenth verse of chapter 21:

> "When justice is done, it is a joy to the righteous
> but dismay to evildoers."

Selah.

I didn't cry. I didn't really feel any emotion at all. I answered every question, shared my every experience with Father Edward into the microphone, including details I had not exhumed from memory for forty years. I think Pauline went away, crawled under some blanket of subconsciousness to hide from the monster in the closet. Out of some dark, faraway place, I listened to my cold, dispassionate voice share the fuel of four decades of nightmares.

Erica brought in a man from her staff to cross-examine

me. Hard questions. About my alcoholism. I answered honestly, directly, and succinctly, as directed. When my statement was given, and all of Erica's questions were answered, she thanked me and told me how strong and brave I was, what an important thing I am doing. She explained that I would be receiving a subpoena and had me sign a document so it could be emailed to me. She said it would include the day and time I would be required to appear for the deposition. At one point, she stopped, her expression concerned. "Pauline, are you okay? Are you going to be alright?" I nodded, feeling my mouth stretch taut into my widest smile.

Here in my car, facing the dun-colored bricks of the Sangamon County Complex that rise before me as an edifice of law, order, and civil management, I fall apart with heaving sobs. I wretch and suck in air. I shake and shudder. It is as if a beast writhes and claws inside of me, working its way out. Inhaling with a sucking wheeze, I wail, almost a scream. It escapes from me like some demon has pried my mouth open to fly out.

I gasp and take deep breaths. My racing heart slows. I wipe my eyes, close them, rest my head against the headrest, and I simply attend to my breathing, still my body, quiet my thoughts.

Selah.

It is just after noon by the time I get back to my apartment. I call Raymond and apologize for not being there, that something unexpected came up.

"Is everything alright?" That question again. It's stalking me.

"Yes," I say, slowly. Cautiously. "Just something I've needed to take care of that could no longer be avoided."

"You have me worried, Pauline. What's going on?"

"Don't be worried. Everything is fine. I'll see you tomorrow?"

"Yes. But, something's come up…" His voice trails.

"Something with DeeDee?" Now I'm concerned.

"No, no. She's doing okay. I got a call from Sylvia this morning. She's flying in this week to visit."

"Oh." The news is too immediate to express any clear emotion. In all honestly, I'm simply confused.

Raymond sighs. "She knows Mother doesn't have a lot of time left and wants to see her before…"

"Of course." I was under the impression that Sylvia didn't care for DeeDee, but perhaps that relationship, like Raymond's, is more complicated than I was aware of.

"I think she mainly wants to be here for Jules, since she knows how much Mother means to her."

"Well, that's wonderful. I'm glad she can make it. When is she arriving?"

"Thursday. She plans to stay through Sunday."

"Well then, I'll see you tomorrow at least."

"You still plan on stopping by the other days, don't you?"

"That doesn't seem appropriate, Raymond."

"Please, I don't want this to keep you away."

I wish we weren't on the phone discussing this. It's difficult to discern if he is simply being polite but preferring I stay away, or if he truly wants me there while his ex-wife visits.

"It would be very uncomfortable for me."

"I know that, and I'm sorry. But listen, you won't need to worry about Thursday. She'll be arriving shortly before you usually leave for work. For Friday, she said she wants to take time visiting old friends. And Saturday, I'm sure she'll be carting Julienne around various stores buying her daughter's affections."

Every fiber of my being does not want to meet her. "Raymond—"

"Please." Even over the phone, his request seems sincere and heartfelt. It's as difficult to say no as it is to say yes.

"We'll talk more tomorrow," I say. "Okay?"

"That sounds good. Thank you. And Pauline? I missed you today."

I smile. "I missed you, too. See you tomorrow."

I hang up, sit back and close my eyes as the din of thoughts and buzz of emotions crowd my mind and darken my spirit.

CHAPTER FORTY-THREE

Memories & Mortality

e're together at the table, the three of us, playing cards. I'm excited to have Raymond with us, playing a game with his mother, both of them enjoying—rather than simply tolerating—each other's company. I have several moments of giddiness that break out in embarrassing laughter as Raymond plays a card or DeeDee swipes up several of them from the face-up pile as we play Rummy 500. I can't stop looking between them, feeling in this moment the warmth and love of family. It's something I haven't experienced for a long time and rarely felt as a child, other than my earliest memories with my mother before I grew into the ugly duckling she slowly withdrew from.

My feelings for Mother will likely never be resolved. My father's aloofness, armored within the cool steel of his Christianity, was always easy to suss out. I knew I was a disappointment, that I could never climb the summits of his expectations, and that his love was obligatory and dutiful. My quiet, demur mother, on the other hand, could be quite tender and loving, and the unsullied little girl inside of me still remembers being within her embrace, under her affectionate eyes, and an accompaniment to her songs of praise. She would tell me what a beautiful little girl I was as she put me in dresses and tied bows in my hair.

By the time I was eleven or twelve, she had difficulty seeing through my adolescent awkwardness, the slouch of my posture, the slump of my shoulders, my wild mane of hair and the chubbiness that rounded my cheeks and peared my body. For a time, she tried so hard to turn me into a beautiful young woman, but I was unwieldly, unmalleable. By the time I was fifteen, I was hostile to her withering intentions. It was only after I hit bottom after college and Mother tried to put my broken pieces back together through love and faith that we became close again for that all-too-brief time before her heart betrayed her.

Reliving my childhood horrors with Father Edward, there is a correlation I never made until just recently. I don't know how much merit there is to it, but I suspect it may be an important piece to my broken self that I didn't know was missing.

Although my sudden accelerated growth in adolescence certainly contributed to my cloddish and ungainly appearance, it is curious just how much it coincided with when Father Edward first began to steal my childhood from me.

Outside DeeDee's kitchen window, a chill wind blows. It's a dark and dreary November second, but we're cozy inside. Miles Davis's trumpet softly soothes our mood as she and I sit in the living room. Raymond is in his 'office' at the kitchen table, tapping away at his laptop.

DeeDee continues to slightly improve from her last major

episode, and I relish this moment with her, savor it, for I fear how long before her next health crisis comes, and how much, if any, of her it will leave behind.

"What are your fondest childhood memories, DeeDee?" I ask. "What warms your heart just to think about them?"

She's in her chair, and for the moment, only the oxygen tube under her nose. "Oh, my. Let me think." Her voice is thin and hoarse as a haunt, but her eyes are bright and alive. "Most certainly, one of my fondest memories is being on Papa's shoulders during the Mardi Gras parade that would run down Claiborne Avenue before that highway ruined it. Oh, Lord, what a sight that was. The Mardi Gras Indians in their colorful feathers, the brass bands, the Baby Dolls in their teal and white dresses and painted faces, twirling those fancy parasols. And oh, how scared I was of the Bone Man with his skull face! Papa would hold me so tight as he passed!"

"That sounds positively enchanting," I say.

"It was." She coughs for a bit, takes slow breaths. "I remember one year. Papa's store sponsored the Lions Club Krewe and my brother George was in the float. He looked so mature and handsome up there representing Papa's haberdashery in his fancy gray suit, top hat, and white gloves. We were so proud of him." Her smile thins as her eyes grow more distant. "It was only a little while after that George got picked at the Custom House draft and went off to war."

We sit in silence a moment. Miles's horn seems to cry a little for George and his fate, and for memories lost to a world that keeps moving forward, slow and steady as a bulldozer.

"But, there were so many good memories, dear. My first dance revue at Municipal Auditorium. Canal Street at Christmas time. Oh, the lights and the decorations in every storefront." She leans forward, her look intense. "But, in all honestly, there's one moment that keeps coming to my mind. I still dream about it every so often. Every time, I wake up feeling the magic of it."

She settles back in her chair, closes her eyes and struggles to draw a deep breath. "It was New Year's Eve of 1963. I still remember it clearly. I was twelve. We were at home. Maman made a special sausage gumbo and baked a pecan pie. We played dominoes and Bourré that night. At midnight, we hooted and hollered. Papa took Maman in his arms and they kissed and danced to the phonograph spinning Count Basie. George grabbed my hands and spun me around in a circle, and Alfred threw cards in the air over us, laughing. Then, a miracle happened."

She coughs again, but lies still, eyes closed, a smile surviving through the small fit. I say nothing, unwilling to break this spell that has fallen over the room. I look over at Raymond, and he has abandoned his laptop. He is hunched forward, elbows on knees, focused on his mother. His gaze has followed hers, slipping back through the decades as if he were travelling back in time with her to that New Years' night of '63.

"Maman suddenly called out, 'Oh my Lord, would you look at that!' We turned to the living room window that faced the dark thoroughfare. There, you could see, in the glow the street lamps, something I had never witnessed before. Falling snow."

Her voice is getting softer, raspier. All this talking is too much for her. I should tell her to stop, but I honestly wouldn't, couldn't stop her even if these were her final breaths. This is important. This is necessary.

"I ran outside. Maman called out to put my coat on, but I didn't listen. I stepped out into our wonderfully still Tremé neighborhood. Stood below a street lamp. It was so quiet, so peaceful. I swear, I could almost hear the falling snow, like the softest hum. I turned my head up to catch a snowflake on my tongue. And then, I danced. I twirled and spun under that puddle of light and the sparkle of flakes as they caught the glow of the lamp. It was like I was in a snow globe." Her head is back, arms slightly extended, having captured a moment of bliss in her chair as her mind takes her back to that moment.

When her arms finally drop, her eyes open and she looks at me with melancholy eyes. "I think it was one of the last times I truly felt safe and secure, when the world seemed wondrous and mine."

I smile wide, and reach out to lay a hand on her knee. In my periphery, I catch Raymond absently wipe at his eye.

It's close to one o'clock. DeeDee's coughing had increased and her breathing shallowed, so we did five minutes with the nebulizer, followed by a dose of medication. I put the respirator on her and read a little more to her from *The Scarlet Letter* until she started to nod off. She naps peacefully now in her chair. For the last minute, I've simply listened to her forced, regulated breaths while Raymond works.

I need to get back to the apartment and get ready for work. I go over incidentals with Raymond—reminding him of when doses are due, how to set up the nebulizer, and make sure her oxygen supply is good.

"You're going over all this with me as if I'm not going to see you for a while."

We're standing in the entryway as I slip on my coat. The plan was to discuss the next few days, but I decided to change those plans and just try to avoid the conversation. It had worked well up to this point.

"Raymond, I hope you can understand. It would just be too uncomfortable for me."

"Hey." His big hands rest on my arms. "I don't want to put you in any situation that would make you uncomfortable, but I also don't want to miss out on seeing you this weekend."

"I know, but—"

"And Jules would be particularly disappointed if she

couldn't see you."

I hate the thought of not seeing Jules this weekend. But I loathe the idea of being put beside Raymond's ex and Jules's mother even more.

"And what if something were to happen to Mother when you could have been here?"

It's bad enough worrying about that happening while I'm at work or home in my apartment. If something happened when I could have been here, it would devastate me.

My exhale is heavy and exaggerated. "Fine, Raymond. Fine." I hold up my arm. "This limb is a pretzel after all your arm-twisting. Are you happy?"

He gives me a ridiculous smile and hugs me. "Very much so."

With a good squeeze returned to him, I pull away for a quick kiss. "I really don't understand why this is so important to you, though."

There's sincerity and feeling in the look he gives. It radiates all through me. "Because. If we continue in the direction we're heading, this will have to happen sooner or later. The longer we put it off, the more dread it will cause. Better to face it now and get it over with, put it behind us, so we can move on. I don't want this to get in the way of our relationship. Does that make sense?"

It does, and his words land heavily upon my heart and my mind. They put in focus something else that needs to be brought out into the open so it can be put behind us.

"Raymond." The words are there, rolling about my tongue, sticky and thick as molasses.

His expectant look, his anticipation for me to say something, clamps my vocal cords tight and I swallow hard. Instead of what I mean to say, I tell him, "Thank you. It means a lot that you want me here."

"You mean a lot to me."

But oh, Raymond, you don't realize just how broken I am.

I invest more effort into getting ready the next morning. After my shower, I take extra time brushing my hair and spray on a conditioning agent to try and tame it. I apply eye liner. I put on my favorite pair of black jeans that are slimming and seem to accentuate the right curves. I follow that up with a push-up bra I haven't pulled from its drawer in five years—not since the fleeting relationship I had with an accountant who was attending a week-long conference at the hotel. I finish with my dark blue cowl neck sweater that hugs my waistline while hiding my fat rolls and the extra weight around the sides of my chest.

Standing in front of the full-length mirror on my bedroom door, I smile, tell myself I look okay, and for just a moment, I almost believe it. I wasn't this worried about my appearance when going to see Julienne's play with Raymond. Still looking into the mirror, I laugh loud at that poor, insecure middle-aged woman, and shrink a little before her mockery of me.

"Wow. You look fantastic." Raymond gives me a kiss at the door, eyes linger and scroll over me, then he steps aside.

"This old thing? Why, I only wear it when I don't care how I look." I laugh and step in. "That's a movie quote, by the way."

I wave to DeeDee. She has her respirator strapped on and her body hitches as she tries to hold back a light bout of coughs.

"Good morning, beautiful woman," I say.

"Morning, dawlin'." Weak and through a sputter of coughs.

Raymond looks confused. "I'm not familiar, but I'd certainly love to see what happens when you do care. What movie?"

I sit in my usual chair. "Three hints. First clue: Christmas movie."

"Die Hard?" Raymond grins.

"No, smart aleck. Second clue: Frank Capra."

DeeDee puts up her hand. "I know it."

I look at DeeDee, finger to my lips. "This is a desperately important quiz for Mr. Raymond. Much hangs upon his ability to answer correctly."

"Is it the Bing Crosby one…White Christmas?"

I shake my head. "Oh, dear. It isn't looking good for our handsome gentleman contestant. Last chance. Third clue: James Stewart."

Perplexity scrunches Raymond's face, then his eyes flash and mouth makes an 'O'. "Of course! White Heat!" He sticks out index fingers, cocks his thumbs while putting on a terrible gangster accent. "You dirty rat…"

"Oh, Raymond!" DeeDee laughs and coughs, fogging up her respiratory mask.

I gape at him. "You have *got* to be kidding. Not James Cagney, for goodness' sake. Jimmy Stewart!"

He laughs and holsters his finger pistols. "Of course I'm kidding. *It's a Wonderful life.*"

I relax and cross my legs. "Yes, it is, but it almost wasn't for you, my dear sir."

He heads to the kitchen and grabs the coffee pot. "The movie's that important, is it?"

"Indeed. To all human beings. It demonstrates the relevance each of us have to each other, what true wealth is, and where real happiness lies."

Coffee poured, Raymond sits at the kitchen table and opens up his laptop. "Well. Perhaps I should watch it again."

"You should." I grin. "With me."

"It's a date."

I look over to DeeDee and she is smiling broadly, giving me her knowing wink. It's almost as much a thrill to receive DeeDee's unspoken blessing as it is Raymond's affection. In a wistful, fleeting moment, I regret that there won't be any years ahead of enjoying these moments with both of them. Just as quickly, I crumple up that thought and throw it away, condemn the idea of mourning DeeDee's death when she is here and alive now. That is the absolute worst thing I can do for her, for me, for us.

"I need to get back to work," Raymond says, pressing a few keys. "But how does getting lunch delivered sound?"

"Absolutely splendid," I say. I turn to DeeDee. "Meanwhile, I am all yours for the morning, my lady. What is your bidding?"

"I would love to hear more about you, dear."

"Oh, there's just nothing very special about me, DeeDee."

She pulls her mask down, eyes penetrating. "About that you are very, very wrong, *mon cygne*."

As I share what I can of my life, DeeDee a rapt audience and Raymond very consciously within ear shot, there's a sense of navigating through a mine field. To honor my father and mother, I must avoid much of my childhood. Thanks to Father Edward, there's nothing but volatility between the ages of eleven and thirteen. To avoid condemnation, I do not mention my lurid college days, nor anything about Kaiya. I certainly won't speak about Jack with Raymond listening. From this vantage point, so much of my life seems to lie just under the surface, live munitions with pressure plates.

I stick to my year of travel after leaving the Motherhouse, talk about my time spent in so many midwestern towns, the people I met and things I saw. Six months working as a dishwasher at an upscale restaurant in Indianapolis. Seeing that awesome war monument raising three hundred feet into the air in the center of downtown. Nine months in Cleveland cleaning offices in the evenings while working part time in the day answering phones at a small concrete company. My walks along the Lake Eerie shoreline, past the Rock and Roll Hall of Fame and the science museum. I toured the Cod, an old World War Two naval submarine. I strolled the small International Women's Air & Space Museum tucked inside Burke Lakefront Airport and learned about all the amazing women who helped to conquer air and space, going all the way back to the French woman, Raymonde de Laroche, who got her pilot's license in 1910 and flew further than anyone at that time. A short stint in Louisville and quick stops in little towns all along the way.

But it was the eight years in that tired, run-down, beautiful St. Louis I loved the most, enjoying my last stint working at the magnificent Central Library in downtown. Those wonderful women I worked with, some as old and storied as those books on the shelf. My ride to the top of the Gateway Arch. My regular visits to the Cathedral Basilica of St. Louis, one of the most wondrous places I have ever been. Completed in 1914, it was consecrated as a basilica by Pope John Paul II in 1997, and its interior displays the most expansive mosaic tile work in the world. I attended several holiday services there. One of the hardest things I ever did was leave that old city, my old friends and those old, wonderful books in the library to return to Springfield after Mother died, but I knew my father would simply languish and fade if left alone.

All that history seemed silly to share with someone who had experienced so much, done so many things, endured so many challenges. But DeeDee listened, reacted, asked questions, and made me feel as if there was some value to my past other than a means to get me from there to here.

When the sandwiches and soups arrive, we set up a tray for DeeDee at her recliner while Raymond and I have our lunch at the kitchen table.

"So, when did they finally diagnose you with sarcoidosis?" I ask DeeDee as I pry the lid off my chicken and wild rice soup.

"I was around fifty-five."

Raymond unwraps his sandwich. "After they said it was fungal pneumonia, they then said it was pneumoconiosis—"

My spoon freezes over my soup. "Wait. Isn't that black lung disease?"

He nods. "Yes. Essentially, they gave her a death sentence. Blamed it on asbestos."

"They gave me an inhaler and said good luck," DeeDee says and coughs out a little laugh. She samples a spoonful of black bean soup.

Raymond says, "Her sarcoidosis essentially went untreated for another five or six years. It was when she went in for a routine visit and saw a Black doctor that she was finally, correctly diagnosed. He realized how absurd the diagnosis was, and how sarcoidosis is so commonly misdiagnosed in our population."

"I've been on corticosteroids and TNF inhibitors ever since, but they've only managed to slow it down." Coughing interrupted her.

Raymond wipes his mouth with a napkin. "Too much damage had already been done to her lungs."

DeeDee finishes chewing a small bite of her sandwich. "And to be put on a list now for new lungs? At my age? Let someone younger have their shot. I've lived well and long enough."

I nod to let her know I understand, but her words linger. It's a curious thing, to believe you've lived long enough. How exactly does one come to that conclusion? Is it even possible, or do we all at some point simply manage to fool ourselves into believing it? Do we live long enough once we have achieved all the goals we have aimed for? Is it when we simply become too weary pursuing the goals we failed to obtain? Is it when we have achieved some form of inner peace and contentment from righting the wrongs in our lives? Or must we shed all earthly concerns before we can accept and embrace our end?

I have spent my life surrendering myself to the will of my God. Now, over three-quarters of the way through my life on this earth and watching someone twenty-three years my senior facing her final days, I'm not sure I would simply surrender. I do have wrongs to right. I still have goals to pursue. Most of all, I want a chance to have peace and contentment, perhaps find that while sharing my life with someone else.

More than anything, I'm afraid to die alone.

We are just finishing our lunch. I am content within the moment of silence in this place that has become almost as comfortable as home. Just the soft, sweet jazz in the background to help smooth out my mood.

Until one o'clock sharp, when quick knocks on the door break the silence.

CHAPTER FORTY-FOUR

Competition & Comparison

"How are you, Ray?"

"Fine, Sylvie. You?"

They give each other polite, sanitary air kisses beside cheeks, then she leans sideways to look around Raymond. Gliding past him across the room, her long, tan cashmere coat billows behind her. I stay in my seat at the kitchen table and try to remain invisible for as long as possible during this family reunion.

"Oh, Dee. It's so good to see you. I've missed you." She bends down and gives DeeDee the most delicate hug.

"Hello, dear," DeeDee says, "It's been too long."

Sylvia draws away, her red-lipped smile accenting her high, rosy cheekbones. Wisps of burgundy highlight her black satin hair that swoops across her forehead and falls around her face.

"It was Jule's graduation back in June."

DeeDee nods and slips her oxygen tube back under her

nose. "Yes. Such a wonderful day."

Sylvia's smile and eyes drop with concern. "How are you managing? Are you comfortable?"

DeeDee waves her concern away. "Fine, dear. I'm doing as well as can be expected."

Sylvia gives her a sympathetic smile. She then turns her head to me and my stomach twists.

"You must be Pauline?" A perfectly manicured hand with elegant, clear-glossed fingernails extends toward me.

I stand, a full head taller than her, but dwarfed by her sophisticated air, and accept her hand. "I was never given another option." Am I squeezing too hard against her gentle grip?

She's generous with her reply, offering me a light, short laugh. "I've heard so much about you from Ray and Jules. It's wonderful of you to volunteer like this to help Dee."

"It's been my pleasure. Good of you to make it here for her."

"I wanted to come sooner, but I've had several crises at the firm these last few months which required my full attention."

Raymond chuckles as he steps into the living room. "Too many businesses needing to be downsized?"

"Very funny, Ray. It just so happens that corporate growth often leads to inefficiency, duplication, and waste."

He smiles at her smugly, then gives me a wink. "Hey, businesses like yours do me a favor anyway since you tend to annihilate in-house marketing departments first."

She sighs and slips off her jacket, revealing tan slacks and olive-green blouse that make her look straight out of a fashion catalog. "Whatever you say, Ray." At the closet, she hangs up the coat. Back in the living room, she sits in the Queen Anne chair across from DeeDee where I usually sit. Raymond takes a seat beside me at the kitchen table where his laptop remains closed.

"So," he says, "How is the City of Brotherly Love treating you?"

"I've acclimated," she says. "East coast business culture is very different from the Midwest. Extremely fast-paced, very results-driven. It took me a while just to get used to how direct people from there are with each other."

"Sounds like you fit right in," Raymond says.

DeeDee coughs. "Raymond. Stop it, now."

Sylvia crosses her legs and arms, smiling. "It's fine, Dee. It's all in fun, right, Ray?"

"Most certainly."

I look between the two of them, already more uncomfortable than I want to be.

"How's your middle-of-the-road agency doing promoting those mid-market clients?" Her grin is as sharp as her tongue.

"Really good. We took home the district American Advertising Award and are up for the national AAF award for our Jimmy Johns campaign. We're on our third year in a row with revenue growth of over twenty percent with 26 current active clients—one global and four national. Sorry to disappoint, but we're not in need of any services from Harris Young Advisors at this time."

I reach over and slap his arm. "Behave."

She gives me a curious look that I can't help but notice and pull myself back to my seat.

With a coy smile, she says, "It's just a little game we play." Back to Raymond, the grin turns devilish. "Mostly innocent, right, dear?"

"Mostly."

DeeDee shakes her head. "It never changes with you two. I had to play referee half the time."

"And usually took her side," Raymond says.

Sylvia's mouth gapes with shock. "Absolutely untrue!" She puts hands to hips. "Actually, I don't remember her taking sides."

"Only side I ever took, dawlin', was Jules."

I watch Sylvia's face set like cement. She breaks eye contact with DeeDee.

It may be fun for them and how they are used to acting with each other, but my comfort level has dropped below my threshold of tolerance. "How did you two meet?" I ask, or actually more blurt out, and almost as quickly regret it. "Sorry. That's probably very inappropriate to ask."

Sylvia, still looking flustered, attempts a gracious smile. "Not at all. It's fine. Let's see, that was, what, thirty-five years ago now?"

Raymond shrugs. "Something like that."

"UIS campus. We had a business communications class together. I was in the hall outside the classroom, waiting for the previous one to let out. Here comes this big brute of a guy with an adorable baby face hobbling up on crutches."

"Sophomore year. Blew my knee out in football. I was done for the season. Ended up being done permanently."

"He dropped his backpack—"

"No, I dropped my crutch when my backpack slid off my shoulder."

"Whatever. I watched as he fumbled with that backpack, teetering on one crutch, and knew he was ready to go down like a felled tree. So I leapt up to his rescue—"

"—just in time to give me something soft to land on."

She cracks an embarrassed smile. "We both went crashing to the floor. I sprained my ankle and had one heck of a bruise on my elbow and hip." She gives him a time-travelling smile of youthful desire from over thirty years ago that makes me deflate. "The next day, he brought flowers to class for me."

"I picked them from the landscaping behind the School of Business."

Sylvia scoffs at that. "That's terrible. I forgot about that. Shame on you."

"Well, I was a poor college student, and it worked, didn't it?"

"Yeah, well, he gave me the flowers and said—"

"I've never fallen so hard so quickly for anyone before." He doesn't look at her when he says it, but I can see he has followed her smile back to that moment in time.

"We dated on and off throughout college," Sylvia Says. "During our senior year, he proposed."

Raymond slapped a hand down on the table. "Oh, come on, you're not going to say how?"

Sylvia's eyes roll. I'm deeply regretting asking the question, preferring the jabs they were taking at each other. Despite being divorced, they are far too comfortable with each other and have vastly more history together than I could ever hope to have with Raymond.

"He dragged me to the homecoming game. During halftime, he had the guys in the booth announce his proposal over the loud speakers."

"Cost me a hundred bucks and a special favor to get them to do that." I try to smile when he says that to me, but I honestly don't know if I succeed. At this point, I'm just looking for the right place to cut in and say I have to go.

"Yes," Sylvia says. "How romantic to have a public proposal preceded by a thanks to Ploski's Meat Emporium."

Raymond throws out his hands and smirks in a, 'Hey, it's the thought that counts' gesture. DeeDee chuckles in coughing spurts and Sylvia shakes her head in bemusement. I take advantage of the break in story to stand.

"Well, I need to head off and get ready for work."

"Oh, I'm sorry you need to go so soon," Sylvia says. "We'll see you more this weekend, though, right? Jules is really looking forward to seeing you again."

"Sure, I'll be back," I say, even though I'm really thinking twice about that promise.

I move to the closet next to the front door and grab my jacket. My motions are quick, abrupt. I'm tense and agitated. My insecurities have swelled to a bursting blister seeping out my confidence.

Raymond walks up to me. Quietly, he asks, "Is everything okay?"

Again with that question. I want to flail arms and scream my response, but instead stretch out a tight smile and simply say. "Good night."

I slip out the door as fast as possible.

"They have a story, Margie."

Another Thursday night at the Long Nine Lounge in the Crown Plaza Conference Center. November is a quieter month, but still with enough people to keep us at a steady pace. I've been focused on serving, and on cleaning and prepping when there's no one to serve. Margie has done all the talking tonight, and when it finally thins out to just a few patrons, she cracks and asks me what's wrong.

"What are you talking about? Who has a story? What story?"

The paring knife in my hand slaps down on the cutting board next to the orange I'm slicing. "Raymond and his ex-wife."

It takes a moment, Margie just stares blankly, then realization sets in. She grabs my shoulders and turns me to her. "Holy shit. You and Raymond? Seriously?"

My expression is sheepish. I shrug. Nod.

"How long has this been going on? Why didn't you tell me?"

"Just recently. Only for about a week. It seemed too soon to mention."

"You have got to be fucking kidding me. Pauline. This is huge!"

"Stop it."

"No! Seriously! This is awesome!"

I pull away, her enthusiasm somehow making my crisis feel worse. "You don't understand. His ex-wife is here."

"So?"

"So? She's gorgeous—"

"And totally divorced from him!"

"—and they have a story about how they got together."

Her look is incredulous. "Everyone has a story about how they got together."

"Not like they do. He was on crutches, fell on her and sprained her ankle. Brought her flowers. Proposed through a homecoming game announcement."

Margie looks impressed. "Wow. That—that is a story, all right."

"See?"

She shakes her head, looking up at me with confused sympathy. "No. I don't." She takes hold of my wrists. "They're divorced, Pauline. Their relationship failed. How is this woman a threat to you?"

"She's so beautiful."

"So are you."

"Stop it!" The false flattery is unwanted. It only magnifies my insecurities. "I'm going to be weighed and measured against Sylvia and their fairytale courtship. She's a damn beauty queen and corporate CEO. I'm just a frumpy bartender at a hotel."

I don't want to be this way. It's embarrassing to be so melodramatic, as if I'm still in high school, but controlling these emotions has been like trying to calm a feral animal in a cage. There are too many situations I'm being forced to deal with that threaten to overwhelm me. I'm trapped by them.

Margie tugs at my arms, pulls me down closer to her eye level. "Listen to me. I am your friend, and I am being completely honest with you. You're right You're no beauty queen. Who wants to be that, anyway? You're real. You're unique."

I try to interrupt her, but she doesn't give me a chance.

"I know you don't realize this, but who you are shines so brightly. I see it every night we work together. I may get the occasional meaningless pass from some drunk I serve, but you?

They want to know you. They engage with you. You have real conversations with them. Don't you understand? When I say you are beautiful, I am talking about the whole you. You are truly beautiful, Pauline. That's why we're friends. And I absolutely know that's why Raymond has fallen for you."

Those tears I can't seem to control any more well up. I smile and grab Margie, hold her close. Such a wise soul and compassionate heart in such a young person.

"You, friend, are so sweet. You cannot possibly know how much I needed to hear that tonight."

I feel her arms return my embrace. "Hey, I'm just glad to have you in my life, and I can't be the only one to feel that way."

The next morning, I am much less interested in impressing my audience than in simply being respectful of who I am. I brush my teeth. I bathe. I put on deodorant. I do not, however, put on airs. I don't do anything I would not otherwise do. I will go as normal, typical Pauline, and not worry about any judgement of my presentation. I do choose some of my favorite outfits—but I do that for Raymond, not to compete against Sylvia.

I head out feeling better about myself. It is, after all, the me that has voluntarily helped to care for Deborah Deneaux for the better part of four months, who has given a significant amount of her free time—in fact, for the last three weeks, most of it— to watching over her and taking care of her. It is also me who has been a companion to Raymond and a support to Julienne. Come what may, I have been the best I can be, and that is all I can be. I need no resumé to submit to Sylvia or anyone else to validate my worth.

Of course, thinking that and believing it are two very different things.

There's nothing to worry about when I arrive, however. Sylvia is spending the day visiting friends and family. I'll be at work by the time she returns here for Julienne's arrival.

It ends up being a very quiet morning. Raymond has a string of meetings that keeps him plugged into earphones and locked onto the screen. With DeeDee doing a little better now, he's feeling pressure to get back into the office at least for a few mornings next week, and I told him that would be fine. This has become my life now, one I've embraced without thought. I barely remember those first few months stopping by here two or three times a week for a couple hours. Back then, I was merely a hospice volunteer providing a little extra support and companionship to a dying older woman. That is not the case anymore. Now, I am spending as much time as God will grant with a dear friend. I am gathering the flowers and pricked by the thorns of DeeDee's life so the blossoms may be dried and pressed into memory.

It's clear DeeDee wore herself out with Sylvia's visit yesterday. It didn't take long for her to nod off.

As she naps and Raymond works, I walk around the room, looking again at the pictures and memorabilia that are so much more personal to me now than when I first encountered them. The picture of her family in front of her father's haberdashery on Claiborne Avenue. An image that charmed from ignorance now haunts with knowledge. The store, shuttered only a few years later due to urban renewal. Tall, lanky George, smart and headed for a bright future, but soon to become a casualty of war. Short, stout Alfred, proud and angry and about to take his first steps toward rebellion and eventual ruin. And little DeeDee, so young and innocent, years away from falling into the exotic, risqué world of sexual proclivity only to emerge as a Mastered business woman of marketing and communications—all while a sword a Damocles hangs above her in the form of an auto-immune disease that would topple her at her career high.

I come to the wide picture of the large group of dancers and the plaque tacked to the lower frame that states, "To Deborah Deneaux, In Recognition of 12 years of support and service—The American Dance Theatre of Chicago." I lean in, look closer at the forty or fifty faces looking up at the camera from the stage, holding a banner declaring, "We Love You, DeeDee!"

"I do miss my Chicago dance family." DeeDee's voice is little more than a whisper. I turn, see her respiratory mask pulled down. Her drowsy open eyes droop.

"That's the nonprofit you were involved with?"

She nods. "After I saw one of their performances. So wonderful. Getting disadvantaged inner-city children and young adults off the streets and onto the stage. To express their emotions through dance. Brought me back to my early days in dance school."

I take my seat across from her. "Did you dance with them?"

She coughs out a chuckle. "Heavens no. But I donated marketing services to them. That would have been around 2004. The Deneaux Agency sponsored a lot of their advertising. By that time, though, I was getting sicker. Able to work less and less."

"This would have been about the time you were finally diagnosed, right?"

She coughs. Nods. Brings the mask briefly over her mouth and nose to take a deep breath. "Having learned about this lovely condition, I sold majority rights of the agency to a competitor. That was 2006."

"It must have been hard."

"With my health, and the changing world of marketing, it felt like time. I was fifty-five. That's when I started volunteering for the dance company."

"You sat on the board, didn't you?"

"I started out on some ad hoc committees, then sat on an advisory council, finally on the board. I was chair from 2012-2018. Then my health started to get really bad. I started to pull away from the organization, spent more time with Raymond and his family. Eventually, I moved here to be closer to Raymond, Sylvia, and Jules a few years ago."

What must that have been like, to move back into Raymond's life after almost three decades of distance and animosity between them? The son, bitter over a mother's absence and overbearance, and embarrassed by her past. The mother, wounded by a son's underappreciation and indignant of his condemnation. Based on all that I have seen between them, the last two years of close proximity amid her failing health did no more for their relationship than it did for mine with my father.

"Did you and Raymond see each other a lot before you moved back?"

"Occasionally." Bubbly, phlegmy coughs. "Some holidays. His wedding, of course. That was the last time I ever saw my father. He died a year later. Maman had passed years before." She becomes wistful. "Raymond was so handsome. Sylvia…just ravishing. They really looked like a fairytale couple." She leans forward with more coughing. "I tried to visit more often after Jules was born."

"I'm sorry. I shouldn't be having you talk so much. You rest yourself."

She smiles, agrees with a head bob and slips the mask back over her face. I stand, thinking I'll grab a cup of coffee. Before I can take a step, DeeDee pulls her mask down again.

"Pauline."

I turn and step in close to her.

She is slow to speak, as if the words are clogged in her

throat. "Your father. Do you feel— Have you found—" The strain of her eyes, twist of lips. I fear she is in distress. Her thin, desperate inhale wavers. "Do you still resent your father?"

The question disturbs me. I've spoken generally to her about caring for my father and how that led me to volunteer for St. John's Hospice. I may have mentioned our estranged relationship, but I don't remember giving any indication that I resented him. I don't think I ever resented him, only the relationship between us, and that it could never be resolved. Or is that distinction too thin to even be differentiated?

I sit back down, absorb the question. Process it. "I am sad he couldn't see in me the daughter he wanted me to be, and I feel sorry for him that he couldn't be the father I needed him to be. Most of all, though, I wish he would have left me the words I had hoped to hear, instead of haunting me with his silence."

Those words come raw and unplanned. They have never been spoken, never fully realized in that specific way until now. There's a queer comfort in saying them, as if some part of my past is closing like a book.

DeeDee turns her face from me as a tear kisses her cheek.

I get ready to leave at noon. It's always a good idea to get to the bar early on Fridays to get condiments fully stocked, check the tap lines and tend to all the other preparations that can help to make a busy night go smoothly. DeeDee is napping so I don't disturb her. I step in front of Raymond behind his computer and give a wave. He looks up, taps a key, and pulls out his earbuds.

"Leaving already? I was hoping we could have lunch."

"I'm sorry. I need to head in to work early."

He stands. "Sorry I was so plugged in to work today. Just a very busy time."

"I completely understand."

'Let me walk you out."

I grab my coat, and we walk out the door and down the hall together.

"I want to apologize about yesterday," he says.

"What do you mean?"

"I could tell you were upset."

"No, I was fine—"

He puts a hand on my arm and stops me. "I didn't fully appreciate how uncomfortable it might be for you. I'm sorry about that."

My smile is forgiving. "I appreciate you caring enough to say it. And I promise to be less sensitive."

The hug that follows sends warm ripples down to my toes. It's hard to let go.

"See you tomorrow?" he says as we break away.

"Most definitely."

It's a strange sensation as I step outside into the chill, gray November day and climb into my car. I'm not sure how much it has to do with the changing of season and the slow approach of the new year, but I feel suspended in time. These moments hang in the air like the final, fading notes of a cherished melody. A cold, silent pause looms, and I'm filled with a sudden dread.

James L. Peters

CHAPTER FORTY-FIVE

Reconciliation

Somehow, mail has lost its relevance for me over time. As a young child, I would always trot home from school eager to check the mailbox for a letter from my German pen pal, Gretchen. Later, I looked forward to my parents' magazines to arrive—*Reader's Digest*, *National Geographic* and *Catholic Digest* among them. Leading up to Christmas, it was the *JC Penney Catalog*. In college, it was the anticipation of my quarterly grades.

Now, physical mail is only relevant a few times a year. In January, three birthday cards—one from my friend Jasmine back in Skokie; one from Carol Lymen, a coworker and friend from the St. Louis Library; and one from my insurance agent, Bob. In late January, it's my W2. April sees my small tax refund. In June, my invitation to the St. James Parish Summer Cookout I no longer attend since Father's death. My lease renewal comes in July, and in December, there are two Christmas cards—one from Jazz and one from Carol. Perhaps Bob is Jewish.

The remaining physical mail, usually addressed to "Current Resident" is routed directly to the trash, unopened.

I remember when email had its brief time of significance. Email renewed my relationship with my mother, kept me in contact with a few friends and even the occasional distant relative. Email resulted in my brief but life-changing relationship with Jack Cross. Then social media came, smart phones took over, and the way we communicated and stayed connected with others forever changed. We text and private message the brevity of whims instead of any sincerity of thought or sentiment. Email went the way of letters and printed correspondence to become a digital trash heap of spam and scams.

Except on this Saturday morning. In my hand, I hold an official-looking envelope with a return address in blue identifying it as coming from the Sangamon County State's Attorney's office. My name is printed in black serif font across the front. It arrived yesterday, but I always check my mail the following morning after a late night at work.

It's a letter from Erica on official letterhead notifying me that I will receive a subpoena by email and to acknowledge receipt no later than Wednesday. She summarizes the subpoena in her letter, that my deposition will be two weeks from Monday in the conference room of the state's attorney's office. That the defending attorney will be present as well as a court reporter. That I am bound by law to attend.

When I check my email, I find it in my inbox amid fifteen other emails trying to clickbait me with recipes, fake invoices, and misleading headlines.

I trudge through the legalese, confirm the date and time of the deposition and add it to my calendar, reply to confirm I've received it, then try as hard as possible not to think any more about it. I finish my coffee and head over to DeeDee's apartment.

"Pauline!"

Julienne dashes up to me as soon as Raymond lets me in, and her arms wrap around my waist. I can't help but give out a guffaw as I'm squeezed and pushed back a step from her enthusiastic force. It feels wonderfully natural to hug her back.

"Oof! Grip life just as tight and the world will be yours."

She pulls away, bright eyes as wide as her smile. "It's so good to see you."

"Hello, my shiny Jule."

Sylvia scoffs from her seat in the living room. "Well, I certainly didn't get such a warm greeting as that." Her arms cross dramatically and it's clear she's joking, yet there's a tinge of sincerity underneath her exaggerated reaction.

"Oh, Mother. Of course you did!" Jules trots over to Sylvia, leans down and gives her a flamboyant hug. "So sensitive!" A wet smack of a kiss on her mother's cheek. Raymond grins and shakes his head, stepping from the entryway and past me into the living room. DeeDee giggles from her chair. I'm glad to see just the oxygen tube under her nose.

"Stop that, now!" Sylvia lets out a flustered laugh, waves off her daughter and shakes her head. "You are such a silly girl."

Jules drives her fists into her hips and huffs. "And you," she mocks in low, stern voice, "are a very serious Mother."

Sylvia turns her head away with a *tsk*. "Girl, I sure hope you take your schooling more serious than you do the rest of your life."

"Oh, Sylvia," DeeDee says through a cough. "Don't be crushing her spirit, now."

Jules gives me a crumpled smile and eye roll. I return a wink and nod.

Raymond says, "If you wanted to see a very serious Jules, you should have been at her play last month."

"She was absolutely wonderful," I add, still hanging back just ahead of the entryway.

Sylvia's face falls. "Oh, Jules, honey. I did so want to see you. But Ray sent me some videos of it, and you really were amazing."

Jules takes a dramatic bow. "Well, thank you very much."

Their conversations continue and I keep behind, standing at the edge of the living room. I watch as the four of them interact, playing off each other's beats and measures, keeping time with one another.

These last few days have been confusing to me. I'm really not certain what my role is supposed to be. Am I here as hospice volunteer? As companion to DeeDee? Or as Raymond's significant other? My hospice supervisor Bonnie certainly never prepared me for this scenario.

I'm not even sure if Raymond has mentioned our relationship to Sylvia, and the whole situation has been too awkward for me to ask him about it. Yesterday, however, when I had playfully slapped his arm, she gave us a particular look that made me think she didn't know about us but is now perhaps suspicious.

There's also an elephant in this room that I have tried to ignore. It should not be here, and I'm not happy with myself for summoning it. Unfortunately, however, it has me unnecessarily uncomfortable and nervous.

Until meeting Sylvia, my Whiteness has never been a factor. I felt perfectly comfortable and welcome with DeeDee, and my only discomfort with Raymond had nothing to do with his race and everything to do with his stature and stoic presence. Why then do I now feel like an intruder among this Black family? Why am I so nervous about Sylvia learning about Raymond and me? Shouldn't my intimidation of her success and her beauty be enough? Now I have to also feel racially out of place?

As Sylvia, Jules, and Raymond's banter plays spectacle to DeeDee's whimsy, I try to calm down, to remember Margie's words to me the other night. I remind myself how good DeeDee, Raymond, and Jules make me feel. My insecurities will not get the best of me.

"It's true!" Jules exclaims in the middle of something she's telling her mother that I wasn't paying attention to. "Pauline! What was the name of that club where you brought Grann to dance?"

I look over to them, see all of them looking at me. "It was the High Ball," I say, and I walk over and join them in conversation.

We're sitting together in the living room, Sylvia in the Queen Anne chair against the wall, Raymond, Jules, and I in chairs we brought from the kitchen. They reminisce about past holidays, birthday dinners, picnics in the park, and other times they've shared together. My interjections are few, and I mainly enjoy their banter and reminiscing. A picture begins to form as to what the last ten years were like having DeeDee back in Raymond's life. Some of their passive aggression even begins to resurface as certain events are recalled—Raymond's displeasure with DeeDee giving Jules a make-up kit for her twelfth birthday. DeeDee chastising Raymond for punishing a fourteen-year-old Jules who punched a boy for making fun of her then wild, curly afro. Sylvia, meanwhile, seems to have played peacekeeper at the time, but it's hard to ignore my impression that, at least back then, she saw DeeDee as somewhat of an intrusion upon their family and their parenting.

All this history is shared with good-natured ribbing and laughing, but with Raymond and Sylvia, the tension between them and DeeDee is, at least to me, subtle but detectable.

Sylvia brings up the time DeeDee bought Julienne a Victoria's Secret gift certificate for her thirteenth birthday, and they all laugh, Sylvia shaking her head and Raymond blushing and rolling eyes.

DeeDee smiles indignantly. "They happen to make very good bras, and my grandchild was becoming a young lady."

"You two," Julienne says, directed at her parents. "You always thought Grann was going to corrupt me somehow."

"Oh, that's not true," Sylvia says with the wave of a hand.

"She just had the benefit of being a grandparent," Raymond says, "whereas we had the dirty job of being the parents."

DeeDee coughs lightly. "The child does speak some truth."

"Mother, please," Raymond says, still chuckling as he strokes his graying goatee. It's a nervous tick I've noticed in him when he is getting uncomfortable with a topic of conversation.

"No, no, now," DeeDee says, the lightness fading from her expression and voice. "Maybe time to let any cats out of the family bag." She coughs again. "You weren't comfortable having me around Jules."

"Dee, that is positively ridiculous," Sylvia says, not looking her in the eyes, trying to hold on to her withering smile.

"Mother, really." Raymond is tugging at those whiskers hard enough to pluck them.

"I had wanted to take her to Victoria's Secret, get her properly measured and sized, but I knew—That wasn't going to happen. So many times, I wanted to take her places. Downtown shopping. Out for lunch." DeeDee shakes her head, lips pursed. "Mmm-mmm."

"You took her out plenty of times," Raymond says, but his eyes narrow and concede.

"Hardly at all!" Jules says. "The first real time I feel I got to know Grann was when I ran away."

I can almost hear the loud drag of a needle across a record. The mood of the room immediately changes.

Sylvia stiffens in her seat. "Now, let's not go bringing all that mess up."

"Why not?" DeeDee says with provocative brow.

"Because, Mother Dee," Sylvia says in pointed syllables, "Why ruin a nice time revisiting old grievances?"

"Grann didn't do anything wrong," Jules says.

Raymond stands, goes behind his chair and leans against it. "Well, she took an entire day to call us and let us know where you were."

"I called you that evening," DeeDee says evenly.

"We were worried sick," Sylvia says.

"I waited until the child was asleep."

Jules is becoming more animated. "I *told* you. She didn't know. I told her you knew I was coming for a visit."

DeeDee is looking between them all, the slightest curl of lip that I can't decipher. Maybe a defensive smirk? A resilient grin? Or is she pleased, maybe relieved, that this family is actually confronting something instead of talking around it? The few hours I've been with them this morning, on top of all I have learned about DeeDee and Raymond, suggest that it has been a pattern with all of them.

Raymond uprights himself, squares his shoulders and folds arms. "A fifteen-year-old arrives alone, two hundred miles from home, unexpected, and there's nothing to be suspicious about? Meanwhile, we're calling everyone we know and talking to the police."

"But you didn't call me, did you?" DeeDee glares at her son as she pulls down her oxygen tube, reaches for her respirator mask and takes a deep breath. A long exhale as she pulls the mask away and gives Raymond and Sylvia a piercing look.

"You want the truth? I was upset with you both. I—I regret it now, but at the time, I suppose I wanted to punish you just a little bit. You kept me at such a distance—"

Sylvia balks. "Dee, I did no such—"

"Sure you did," DeeDee says. She points a severe finger at Raymond. "Because *he* did."

"Mother—"

She stifles him with one hand, coughs into the other. "Do not even pretend otherwise, Raymond." She takes another breath into the respirator. Her voice muffles through it. "You shut me out long ago."

Raymond recoils, his body attempting to deny, but his silence, his pursed lips, clearly say otherwise.

I've been uncomfortably quiet and still for a while. This is not the place for me right now. "Perhaps I should go—"

"No, dear," DeeDee gasps. "Stay."

I look to Raymond. His troubled face relaxes slightly when our eyes meet, and he gives me a reassuring nod.

She sets the respirator down. "I hated that you couldn't see what you were doing to Jules." Her words squeeze through each tight inhale as she coughs through her exhale.

"We were not *doing* anything to her, Dee," Sylvia says. "You know we were having troubles—"

Julienne stands, a defiant lean into the group. "That was always the problem with both of you! You thought that, by pretending everything was just fine around me, your problems would be invisible. They weren't! You think I didn't notice how I was stuck in a tug of war between the two of you? Seriously? Every single day I felt I had to make a choice between the two of you, and I didn't want to!"

"Jules—" Sylvia reaches out for her but Jules steps back.

"And then you—" She glares at Sylvia. "You just up and leave as soon as you can."

Raymond steps forward. "Now, Julienne, that's not fair—"

"No, it's not fair. Not at all," Jules says, and now I see tears in her eyes. Before thinking, I reach a hand up to her and she takes it, squeezes it.

Sylvia's eyes hang on Jules's hand in mine as she stands and approaches her daughter. "I'm sorry, Darling. But you need to realize that our troubles weren't just happening to you. My marriage was failing. My life was fracturing. When an opportunity came that could put my life back on track, I couldn't turn it down."

"You ran away," Jules says.

Sylvia lays a hand on Jule's shoulder. "Baby girl, I did run away, but not from you. It killed me to put so much distance between us, but I honestly didn't know it would hurt you this much. You were seventeen. It was your senior year and soon you'd be on your way to college. I didn't think you'd even have time to miss me."

Jules wipes her eyes. "Well, you were wrong."

"Oh, sweetheart." Sylvia draws a sobbing Julienne in, wraps arms around her and rubs her back. "I'm so, so sorry, baby."

Poor Raymond looks lost as he stands there, strained eyes falling between sobbing daughter, teary-eyed ex-wife, and resentful, dying mother. This certainly wasn't what he must have planned. The tension in the room slumps his shoulders and crimps his mouth. It must seem to him like everything has turned sour. I ache for him, desperately want to console him and hold him.

He faces DeeDee, head low and voice soft. "I suppose I did keep Jules away from you. I think—I don't know. It bothered me. Seeing you with her. Fawning over her. Trying to be something you never were for me."

DeeDee doesn't respond, she just keeps her eyes on a son who won't look at her, holding the respirator mask against her face. Jules and Sylvia part but keep arms around each other.

I cannot remain seated. I move beside him and gently touch his shoulder. "I know you feel that way, Raymond, but you must realize that your mother really loved you. She just wanted a better life for you."

His head shakes. "You're so enamored by her story. You and Jules both. You don't really understand that a story just sifts through the best or most interesting parts. I lived through all the rest of it."

DeeDee is coughing more. She pulls the mask away and it's taking so much effort for her to get words out. "You were the one who cast me aside. Remember?" She struggles with her breath. "Everything I did was for you—"

"No, Mother, everything you did was for your career. For you."

"For *us!*" Her breathy shout sends her into a coughing fit.

I snatch several tissues from the box next to her and she covers her mouth. "Shh. DeeDee. Please. Try not to overexcite yourself." I rub her back, give Raymond a desperate look.

Raymond winces and responds with agitation. "Of course. I'm the bad guy. It's all me. Christ."

"Dad—"

"Ray, calm down."

"Raymond." I place the respirator back over DeeDee's mouth, stand and face him, my temperament calm and passive. "Shut up."

His mouth drops. There's a fire in his eyes, and I know I'm crossing emotional territory I may not be welcome in, but God help me, I'm not turning back.

"I would like you to listen to me very closely, Mr. Raymond. Not the teenage boy still squirming inside of you all full of angst. I need the ears of the charming, sensitive, mature Raymond I've grown so fond of."

I grab his big hands that momentarily resist with stiff arms. I am flush and intense while his gaze slips and slides around me. In this moment, I realize that I might be falling in love with him, but my emotions are too frayed and scattered to be certain of anything.

"It's time to let it go."

He's confused, starts to say something, but I interrupt.

"Stop bearing the shame of your mother's past."

I hear DeeDee take in a sharp breath. Sylvia's eyes widen at me. Jules is frozen in mid-sob.

"What are you talking about?" His sharp tone is either

anger or shock. Perhaps both. But I have to believe it's also a reluctant awareness.

"You have no right to it, Raymond. Nor do you have the right to expect her to claim that burden for herself."

"Pauline, you really don't know what—"

My finger goes to his lips. I keep my voice flat and calm. "None of those things that bother you so much from her past ever hurt you or anyone else. It's time you stopped thinking you need to carry shame in her stead."

Everything about him is protesting, but I won't allow him to rebut my words.

"And, you need to forgive her for trying to be the absolute best mother she could, and not always succeeding."

A scowl rolls across his face, then ebbs, leaving behind the tired countenance of surrender.

I take my hand away, look between him and DeeDee. "I care for you both very much, and it's been so hard for me to see the two of you poking away at the embers of a fire that should have burned out long ago."

I focus on DeeDee, her watery eyes sharp, and bend over to hold her hand. "And you, my dear, magnificent woman, need to forgive that teenage boy and console him. It's not too late. He's been in there all this time, waiting for his Mother."

Everyone in the room is motionless. Their silence is blaring. Was anything I've said right or appropriate? My heart dictated and my body simply responded. Now my cheeks and forehead flare up, and face feels puffy. I've made a spectacle of myself, like some obnoxious blatherer trying to be the center of attention. I take steps back, feel the squeeze of my hand by Julienne, and am momentarily reassured.

DeeDee slowly drops the mask, red eyes blinking back tears as her attention falls on Raymond. "I do wish I could have been there more for you, my boy. It's my deepest regret. I was just trying to give you the best world possible."

Raymond moves beside her chair and gets down on a knee. "You gave me that, Mother. You did. I'm sorry I wasn't able to appreciate it more. I always felt like I wasn't good enough, like I was just getting in the way of your life."

"Goodness, no. No, no, no. You weren't in the way. You were the light to guide my way." She reaches out and touches his cheek. Her voice nothing but a whisper. "My little Ray of sunshine. Do you remember?"

Raymond sniffs, wipes at his eyes. "I do. I do remember." He leans in, buries his head into her chest. "Love you, Mom."

She pats his head, rests her cheek against his. "And I adore you, my boy."

Julienne is sobbing all over again. She runs to them and hugs Father and Grandmother. "Oh, I love you both so much!"

I don't know what to do at this point. I am the intruder again, the interloper on this most tender scene between a mending family. I turn, my eyes briefly connecting with Sylvia's. With a nod and bow of head, I slip quietly away, grab my coat, and leave them. I'll apologize tomorrow, but they'll certainly understand—maybe even appreciate the privacy I'm giving them.

Two steps down the hall, the door opens behind me and Sylvia follows me out.

"Pauline. Wait a moment. Please."

My gut lurches. I had hoped to avoid this and dread whatever she is about to say.

I turn but keep my two paces of distance. "Sorry for leaving like that. I'm late for work."

It's impossible to read her. She shifts in place, words seeming to sit upon her lips but unable to form. Finally, with a hand to her hip, she shakes her head and says, "You ruined my Friday night with my daughter, you know. I had to suffer through her gushing over you. It was quite annoying."

All my fears coming true right here in this hallway. She resents me and my relationship with Jules. I stammer the start of an apology but she waves me off.

"Truth is, I was predisposed to dislike you. No offense."

How do I even respond to that? I raise an eyebrow as the muscles in my legs twitch with desperation to get as far away from her as possible.

"But I suppose I understand now. It's not hard to see what Jules—and Ray—see in you."

There's nothing I can say. I'm still waiting to hear why she's out in this hallway speaking to me.

She lets out a terse laugh. "You're certainly unique, I'll give you that."

"Oh…kay."

She's studying me with such scrutiny, as if she's trying to take me apart and figure out what makes me tick. I'm having trouble returning her stare.

"I think you'll be good for him."

My eyeballs feel half out of their sockets. I blink hard. "Wh—What's that?"

"Raymond. You're good for him."

Cautiously. "You…know? About us?"

She laughs. "Of course I do. Believe it or not, we still talk with each other. Our separation has been fairly pleasant. It was our marriage that wasn't."

"When did you…"

"He told me about you two last week. I didn't know what to think then, but now I can see that you're just what he needs."

I'm not sure how to take that. "What do you mean?"

"Ray and I competed against each other too much. Always trying to one-up the other, get the upper hand—whether it was our careers or Julienne. But with you, it's different. You aren't competition to him."

So, there it is. She knew right where to hurt me. This is exactly what I have expected all along. She knows I can't compare to her beauty, her success, and she certainly doesn't want Raymond to be happy, so she belittles me in order to hurt me and denigrate him. "So, you're saying that I'm inferior. That he has no reason to be threatened by me."

"What?" She looks shocked, then she laughs softly. "No, honey. No. That's not it at all. What I'm saying is that, sometimes, despite two people being on the same team, instead of working together, they antagonize each other. That's how it was with us. We were too similar. We measured our worth against each other. You, on the other hand, are uniquely you. He can admire you without being intimidated by you. You can call him out, stand up to him, and still be on his team. He respects you for it. The way you handled him in there? I could have never done that."

I'm staggered. The last thing I expected was to get Sylvia's blessing, let alone a compliment. I'm at a loss for words, which makes the soft, weak words I do say seem so pathetically inadequate.

"Thank you. Truly."

She closes the distance between us. "No, thank you. You really are a blessing to this family. And, I do envy you. Raymond is a good man. But I think you'll make him a better one."

She extends her hand to me, and I take it gratefully.

CHAPTER FORTY-SIX

Absolution

Something is happening to me, and I'm not sure what it is. An awareness of change or of things changing. Difficult to define, this complexity of emotions and thoughts. A synergy of sentiment and sensation. Every aspect of it has the suggestion of being a paradigm shift, but lacking definition or substance.

Classical music on the radio, soft as down, a whiff of Tchaikovsky, and the warm spark of childhood memory. Three or four years old. Spinning around on our back patio on a sunny summer day in my little white, feathery tutu while my mother's music box plays and the poplar cotton gently falls like snow. Little Pauline Swanson with her cares as light and fresh as the August breeze. Mother scooping me up and spinning me round, telling me to fly, fly my pretty little fledging.

It's a wisp of memory, the scent of muslin, and lilt of song, that comes not as vision but shaped by pure emotion. That little girl is lost now to time and tragedies, but like a butterfly carefully caught between cupped hands, the kiss of this moment's ephemeral wings brush against my very soul, and I know that I can forgive myself. That I can be happy.

I mistook my own shame and regret for sin.

I sinned so that I could deserve the shame and regret I bore.

For thirty years, I've served penance for the sins I created because of the sins inflicted upon me.

I hear Sister Iphegenia's hard accent and soft words, and I am finally ready to heed them. Like hands parting, I open my heart to forgiveness, release what has been captured in darkness for so long. Let it fly.

I am ready to be loved. To love myself. I am ready.

Over the course of the next two weeks, I watch over DeeDee and give Raymond a chance to get back into his office in the mornings. He returns each day between noon and one to relieve me and finish his work day at the apartment. His spirit has lightened ever so much, but his demeanor is slumped by his work. He returns to the apartment with the rumpled brow of stress and pressure, which I know is being exacerbated by his mother's declining condition.

She spends much of her time in bed, now. The respirator has become a constant necessity other than regular sessions with her nebulizer. Nancy, the home health nurse, has increased her medication doses, but it's clear her lungs are failing her. I've also noticed her swollen feet. Nancy tells me that the swelling, along with her waning appetite and more time sleeping, indicates her kidneys are also giving up on her. I, however, am not ready to.

Raymond has been sleeping at DeeDee's apartment every night, hardly spending any time at his place. He brought an air mattress and tried a few nights on that but found it too uncomfortable and now just sleeps in the chair. I know he knows that there isn't much time left. That knowledge, too, sits heavy under his eyes and bows his frame.

DeeDee tells Raymond, Jules, and me that she wants to make it to Thanksgiving. I rebuke her and tell her I expect to spend Christmas with her. How wonderful if that could be. I take a moment fantasizing about what it would have been like to spend a Christmas with DeeDee, Raymond, and Julienne. How magical it would have been. How different from the solemnity of my last ten years of Christmas sharing space with my father and the loneliness of so many other Christmases before that.

She is able to get out of bed and into her chair for a few hours a day. She doesn't have the energy to play a game and her speech is limited, but I do continue to read to her. It's been slow progress through *The Scarlet Letter*. She usually falls asleep after a page or two. As I near the end of Hawthorne's novel, a passage resonates with me:

> Never afterwards did it quit her bosom. But, in the lapse of the toilsome, thoughtful, and self-devoted years that made up Hester's life, the scarlet letter ceased to be a stigma which attracted the world's scorn and bitterness, and became a type of something to be sorrowed over, and looked upon with awe, yet with reverence too.

My vision blurs as I read the last words aloud. I look up to see a certain peacefulness wash over DeeDee's face and closed eyes. I touch my stomach, my heart, then reach out and lay my hand over hers. A sudden wave of serenity washes over me, and beyond my love for her, there is also kinship.

I go to early mass on the Sunday before Thanksgiving. I am less burdened now being present before my Lord, yet also, strangely, less reliant or dependent upon Him and my faith. Less penitent, more filled with wonder. My head is higher, my song more joyful.

On this particular Sunday, however, I am in need of strength. Tomorrow is my deposition. I have yet to share this with Raymond or the reason for having it. Although the most sensible part of me says he will be caring and supportive, there is still no scenario in my head that has me successfully expelling that dark, terrible part of my history. Any words I think to say are sharp as the shards of a broken mirror.

After mass, I go to DeeDee's place. I no longer wait to be let in but simply knock and open the door. I have the whole day to spend with her and Raymond. Julienne didn't come down this weekend. She has two papers to finish and exams to study for before the Thanksgiving holiday. She'll be here Wednesday evening and all through Thanksgiving weekend. I managed to get that Friday and Saturday off. It will be wonderful—four days with the closest thing to a family I've known for a very long time.

DeeDee is much the same, which is neither discouraging nor a blessing. To see this once radiant, strong, vibrant woman reduced to a frail, wheezing shadow of her former self is heartbreaking. Even her coughing has become a lifeless, out-of-breath huffing that drains her of all energy.

Despite that, though, she still manages a smile and raises a weak hand when she sees me arrive.

Raymond greets me with a hug and a light kiss, and we sit at the table. We have plans for dinner tonight. He has been able to secure Nancy to work a few hours while we're gone. I dream about a day when we will be able to go out on a Friday or Saturday night, to someplace nice, instead of the only places open on a Sunday or Monday—family restaurants, bar and grills, and homogenized chains.

There have been three offers on my parent's home. My realtor is telling me to hold off and let them fight it out, but I'm getting antsy to just accept the highest one and be done with it. I think I've decided that I will quit the bar. Perhaps I'll return to school, update my library science degree and be a librarian again.

Or maybe I'll do something else completely. I'm not sure of anything, but for the first time since my year on walkabout across the Midwest all those years ago, I'm excited about the unknown.

But first I need to face this last demon blocking my path.

"Listen, I still plan to be here tomorrow night, but I apologize, I won't be able to come in the morning."

Raymond does not hide his disappointment. "Oh, no."

"I hope that doesn't put you out."

"Well, I had intended to lead a morning meeting at the office tomorrow. What's come up?"

Every word that comes to mind is barbed and buried deep. "I have an … appointment … at the State's Attorney's office."

Concern and confusion puckers his mouth with unspoken questions.

"For my deposition."

Head cocked sideways, his hand runs along the back of his smooth, bald head and comes around to tug at his whiskers. "Pauline, what in the world—"

I feel that numbness coming over me, like when I was last in the attorney's office with Erica. The peeling away of my consciousness from the nervous system that reflexively commands the body to act and react. "When I was young, I was in a Christian Youth Group at my church. During that time, the priest who ran the group and supervised the children molested many of them."

I hear DeeDee gasp through her mask. Raymond sucks in breath. "Oh. My God."

"For two of those years, I was one of those children." I'm moving further away from myself, trying to reach minimum safe distance.

"Oh, Jesus. Pauline. Oh my God."

I am not present in the moment. The husk of Pauline sitting rigid before him is cold and emotionless, while I, insubstantial as vapor, cower from afar behind a boulder of shame and embarrassment.

"Oh, *mon cygne*." So faint as to be a passing breeze.

The fear of everything unraveling around me, of losing all that has become hopeful and promising, is a tremor through my very soul.

Raymond rises from his seat, steps behind me. Those big arms engulf me, hold me tight, hold my broken pieces together. Into my ear, his whisper travels a vast psychological distance to me. "You are so strong. I'm so, so sorry."

My big, beautiful man. He is a tether. He draws me back from the edge of the abyss.

"What do you need me to do?" he asks.

I clasp his arms. "Just hold me tight. Hold me tight. Please. Don't let go."

"I'm not going anywhere."

And that, more than anything, is what I needed to hear.

CHAPTER FORTY-SEVEN

Endings & Beginnings

For four hours and twenty-two minutes, inside a chill sanitary government conference room, the spirit of a young Midwestern Catholic girl was dragged from her grave to relive her abuse by a man of God, all while interrogated by a stranger and measured by the click-clack of a stenograph.

I tried to escape mentally, to be removed from the scene as I have before, but those events are no longer amputated from my being like a severed limb. This trauma exists in every cell of my body. It has become part of my DNA. It defines me.

But it no longer controls me. It pervades me much like my alcohol addiction. It is ever a part of me, but no longer the negative force manipulating my desires and demanding to be fed the poison it craves.

In the early morning hours before the deposition, I tried to center myself. I opened my Bible, returned once again to Psalms in an attempt to find peace and strength. When I reached chapter 51, I had to go back and read four verses aloud:

> ¹⁰Create a pure heart for me, O God; renew a
> steadfast spirit within me.
> ¹¹Do not cast me away from your presence;
> take not your holy spirit from me.
> ¹²Restore in me the joy of your salvation;
> sustain in me a willing spirit.
> ¹³I will teach transgressors your ways, that
> sinners may return to you.

Throughout those four-plus hours, within the darkness of my answers to sharp, direct questions, I kept thinking of those verses, and I didn't feel alone.

Raymond greets me when I arrive at the apartment. With a hug, he gently asks how I am doing, and I tell him I'm fine. That is true, too. I am fine. Surprisingly fine. Tired, physically and emotionally—my past picked up like a soiled rug and beat against my psyche—but fine. And I know now that I will be fine when it comes time for the trial. Not only did Erica tell me I did a good job—keeping to the truth and not reacting to the defense attorney's intimidations—but, after being forced to share those events a second time, I'm confident I have steeled myself for the trial ahead.

DeeDee opens her arms to me from her chair when I step inside, and we hold each other until her breath runs out. She struggles to speak. "I wish...you had...told me...sooner." Every other word follows a struggle for air.

"My dear, sweet woman. If only you knew how much you have helped me. I could not have come this far without you."

She looks at me skeptically, huffing through a cough. "Don't know…what I've…done…"

I take her hands in mine, recognizing how much more human contact I've had in the last four months than I can remember having in the last fifteen years. "You let me in that door so many months ago. You shared your story with me. You shared your *strength* with me. For as long as I live, you will be a part of me, my dear Ms. Deborah Deneaux."

Raymond boils rice, peels shrimp, chops onions, and slices andouille sausage for Jambalaya. He goes light on the spices for DeeDee's sake. He serves her at her chair while we eat at the kitchen table. The talk is light and casual, and as I enjoy Raymond's cooking and the company of them both, I realize that I will be going into St. John's Hospice on Monday morning to resign as a volunteer. For one, I haven't been one for over a month. Not really. I've shirked those duties in favor of friendship and intimacy. Which takes me to the second point: I'm not cut out for this. I get too emotionally attached. Although volunteering led to the absolute best thing that could ever happen to me by being introduced to DeeDee and Raymond and Jules, I don't have the emotional fortitude to become this close to the next person, the next family. And I'm not supposed to. The fact is, as a hospice volunteer, I am a failure, and I'm perfectly fine with that. Apparently, there were other reasons why fate sent me to the hospice program, and based on that outcome, I certainly have no regrets.

Thanksgiving is spent in the community room of the senior living facility. Raymond had booked it two weeks ago, and fortunately it was still available. It has a larger kitchen, and Raymond really wants to pull out all the stops with this dinner. Jules arrived Wednesday night as planned. Since Raymond is sleeping at DeeDee's place, I offer her the couch at my apartment. "It'll be a girl's sleepover," I said, and she was giddy with the idea. We picked up snacks and loaded up a movie to stream that we never ended up watching because we talked all night long—about her classes, and about a boy she's interested in. I even shared a little bit about my first real love, Jack, and how Raymond has become everything Jack couldn't be for me. We giggled, we held each other, we even cried together. It was magic, and we stayed up far longer than we should have.

Sylvia had originally planned to come for Thanksgiving—Raymond extended the invitation to her months ago—but when DeeDee's health started to decline so quickly, she moved up her visit. Her Thanksgiving is being spent with the family of a gentleman she is seeing.

Jules and I both help where we can with Thanksgiving dinner, but the turkey is all Raymond. He's making a traditional Creole turkey. Into butter he mixes garlic, Worcestershire sauce, sage, thyme, allspice and pepper, rubbing that under and over the skin of the turkey. He stuffs it with mixed vegetables sauteed in white wine along with chopped heart, liver, and gizzards. He also makes a rice dressing, and Jules and I stumble through making a sweet potato pie while DeeDee directs us.

DeeDee exhibits just a little more life in her, having finally come out of that apartment after so many months cooped up in there. Just getting down the hall and into the community room is a thrill for her. I would swear she's breathing a little easier. She's in her wheelchair, her respirator with her. She even finds enough breath to playfully rib Raymond a few times as he finalizes the meal.

At the dinner table, Raymond carves the bird. We all give thanks, celebrate, and cherish this moment, pass the plates and enjoy this special meal, knowing it is a singular moment that cannot be repeated. It is a gift, a blessing.

As we enjoy the slightly overbaked pie, I mention to Raymond and Jules the imminent sale of my parents' home and my plans to quit the Long 9 Lounge. "With the windfall I have coming to me, this summer, I want to take a trip. I've always wanted to visit Rome, and I would love for both of you to join me. My treat."

Julienne squeals. "Oh, Pauline. Rome! That sounds absolutely fabulous!"

Raymond balks. "We of course would love to go, but you don't need to pay for us."

"Please. Let me have the pleasure of being able to share my good fortune with two very important people in my life."

He smiles. "Well, fine. We have plenty of time to discuss. But, I think it's a date."

Dinner ends with satisfied bellies and full hearts. We take a tired DeeDee back to her room and put her to bed. Raymond, Jules, and I play games into the night, and Jules returns with me to my apartment where we retire for the evening. Nestled into my bed, I close my eyes, relish the embers of a perfect day that still glow warm in my heart and head.

I dream of Rome.

They spoke of it in my training. I was told to be alert, to look for signs of it in my patient so I would be prepared. I already had some idea from witnessing a little bit of it in my father in his final days. Raymond and Jules do not know about it, and I will not ruin this day for them by mentioning it. Today is a good day, come what may tomorrow. But it is a bittersweet day for me.

It's called terminal lucidity, and it can happen with patients at the end-stage of a terminal illness. They suddenly rebound, seem much improved, regain mental clarity and even some physical strength.

It is the body's last flame of life, when it exhausts its remaining fuel, and it marks the end of their journey. I see this today in DeeDee.

I have not seen her look at me with such bright, attentive eyes for many weeks now. She's doing well with just the oxygen hose under her nose as long as she doesn't talk too much.

And her voice. There's just the hint of that mellifluous lilt coming through the rasp. She sits erect and alert. She smiles. She puts herself to jovial coughing as Raymond recalls her missteps in the kitchen.

"No," she squeaks with bright smile. "Was never much...of a cook. But...I tried!"

Raymond sits directly beside his mother, often laying a hand over hers, leaning his head against her shoulder. He's taking in has much of her as he can. Jules is close by on the other side of her. I sit in my normal chair, scootched forward just a bit, but comfortably, reassuringly where I have always been. Today is for Raymond and Jules, and I need to give them space. This chair is also the only way to anchor my emotions.

Raymond and Jules must sense something, for there is a different quality about the day—more personal, more intimate. It is a day of remembrance, of honoring this magnificent, bold, flawed, wonderful woman. The mood of the room forces a comparison it hurts for me to make, but today feels like a memorial service.

Perhaps that isn't a bad thing, though. In so many ways, it seems a gift for one who is passing to have their life flashed before their eyes by loved ones. I shouldn't be thinking of it in such terms. This is a celebration of life. It is a blessing. A gift. I have pressed my mental record button as we indulge in and savor this day.

But the time passes so quickly. The sun seems to race across the sky, and before I even realize, it has fallen below the horizon. Anxiety is a little whirlwind in my gut. I dig claws into the precipice of the day, focus on being purely present in this moment.

"Look, it's snowing," Jules exclaims. She nuzzles up to DeeDee's shoulder. "It'll be a white Christmas, Grann."

DeeDee pats her shoulder. "Oh, I do so love the first snowfall."

I look out, see the cotton ball fluff of big flakes meandering to the ground in the calm dusk of the day. It is beautiful. Magical.

I stand abruptly. "Let's go."

Raymond gives me a curious look. "Go?"

"Let's get you in your wheelchair, DeeDee."

"Oh, dawlin', I don't know—" Her gaze drifts to the window, eyes glistening. "Jules, dear, grab me that afghan." She looks up at me with a big smile. "Wheel it over, *mon cygne.*"

Raymond stands, a dubious grin across his concerned face. He gives me a shoulder shrug and, together, we help her into her chair and wheel her outside, into the small parking lot of the complex, and under a cone of golden light below a halogen lamp. The air is cool and still. Only the occasional car on this holiday weekend disrupts what is otherwise a quiet and serene evening.

I dash to my car, turn on the radio to the jazz station I've just started listening to and trot back to her. While Raymond and Jules stand close by, I gently spin her chair around. Her head goes back, eyes close as the flakes land on her cheeks and melt to winter tears. Her hands reach for the sky, her arms wave and slink in sultry dance. Jules laughs, steps up and dances with her grandmother around her chair. DeeDee takes her hand, and they move and sway to the smooth run of upright bass, the jangle of piano keys, the muted cry of trumpet that wafts in the air like an echo of the past.

I look to Raymond, nudge him with a head nod. He shakes his head, smiling, and steps over to take his mother's other hand. In this snow globe moment, we spin and dance and love and mourn and rejoice.

She is under the street lamp of ethereal light that cuts through the eternal night in the forever of their Tremé neighborhood. The snow falls, each flake a spark faintly ringing like a delicate chime. Music that sounds like all the songs she has ever heard resonates through every surface, through her very being.

And she dances.

Tall, lanky George steps out from the darkness into the light, looking so sharp in his gray suit, top hat, and white gloves he wore on the Mardi Gras float. He puts his arms out and she embraces him, laughing. He spins her around and around and they dance.

Alfred steps into the light, wearing the tuxedo from his wedding. He gives a big, devilish grin and she laughs, holds out a hand to him, and together, the three of them dance.

Maman and Papa come in from the dark, holding each other's hand. They reach out to their children. The three of them bound over, parents and children hug each other fiercely, and together, they dance.

Slowly, imperceptivity, the lamp light begins to dim. Above her, in that eternal night, a star begins to shine. And they dance.

The music fades as the starlight above flares brighter and brighter. Maman, Papa, George, Alfred. One by one, each of them break away, move to the edge of the diminishing light. They look up to that star, shining ever more brilliantly. Each of them in turn smile, beckon, and step out from the last remnants of lamp glow and vanish in the darkness.

And the dancer follows.

The End

AFTERWORD

Deborah Deneaux never existed, but her story is told within the rich, complicated backdrop of American history, particularly of Black America in 1960s New Orleans and 1970s San Francisco.

The Dancer and the Swan is a work of fiction, but the Tremé Neighborhood of Seventh Ward New Orleans and the once-prosperous Claiborne Avenue business district is real. The destruction and systematic erasure of Creole culture in New Orleans' Seventh Ward, and of minority populations in San Francisco's Fillmore District, represent the consequences of urban renewal that happened in countless neighborhoods across the country in the twentieth century.

In this novel, I merely skim the surface of the challenges minorities have faced even after the myth of the great American melting pot led many to believe that the equal rights movement of the 1960s had vanquished the atrocities of western civilizations' past.

I did not set out to write a novel about social injustice and the challenges of our minority populations, but that became an unavoidable and pertinent element to DeeDee's story. Certainly, DeeDee and Raymond can be seen as representative of those who managed to overcome the obstacles put forth by society and country—even now in the 21st Century—from the oppressions of western civilization well into the nineteenth century, to the failed promises and resistance of post-Civil War United States society. Unfortunately, DeeDee and her son do not represent a majority, and should not be seen as an example of how the "American Way" is a success. Anyone who comes away with that idea from this story has a very different interpretation of history than I.

The point of this story is to focus on the indomitable strength of will and power demonstrated by women who, unsung, have shaped so much of our society and our world—whether as inventors, entrepreneurs, scientists, leaders, caregivers, or in the most powerful role of all—as mothers. They have done it despite facing, at best, bias against their gender, and at worst, physical and emotional abuse because of it.

I also need to make clear that this novel is not an attempt to glorify the porn industry. In truth, although it had been, and perhaps continues to be, a means for some women to find financial success when they were otherwise shut out of other opportunities, and despite the fact that the moral and ethical implications are ambiguous and multifaceted, I feel it important to note that DeeDee is likely an exception within the world of porn. Many women in the porn industry—at least in the 70s and 80s, which is where my primary research was restricted—faced mental health challenges that led them to sexual and substance addiction. I do not mean to paint all professionals of the porn industry in that way, but enough of my research made it clear that it most certainly existed.

As for what in this novel is historical and what is fabricated, I will leave that to the inquisitiveness of the reader to motivate future learning. When it came to historical figures, for the most part, I kept them out of the main story and used them as a backdrop. If interacting with the storyline, I fictionalized them, but based them off real people and their historical relevance to the period (such as the Simon DeReznor character, very loosely based on Alex De Renzy, who was credited as establishing San Francisco as the porn capital of America and who made an estimated 200 adult films before dying at the age of 65).

For sake of story, select events have been manipulated. The bombing of the McDonalds did happen, and it was strongly suspected that the Black Panthers were responsible due to not supporting the BPP children's breakfast program or food pantry. It did not happen at that location, nor at that time. For the most part, however, historical events unfolded as portrayed in the work.

In regard to the Black Panthers, it must be clearly noted that my research was focused on the Oakland and San Francisco chapters during the end of the 60s and into the 70s. As I understand it, BPPs in other areas of the country did significant good for their communities without the stain of controversy that surrounds the Oakland leadership. My research across a wide variety of sources, however, made it impossible for me not to bring it into the story. Additionally, the more I learned about the positive impact made by female leadership compared to the violence and destructive natures of the male leadership, the more it simply became an allegory to our society as a whole.

I would encourage those interested to take a deeper dive into the histories of these events, as they are a crucial part of our America and must not be forgotten. I've included the sources to my research in the following pages. Explore any area that interests you. And, eternal thanks to my readers and their continued support.

- James L. Peters, April, 2025

SOURCES

"Behind the Mystery of Sarcoidosis: A Rare Disease That Can Cause Shortness of Breath, Chest Pain", The Balancing Act, 2022

"What is Sarcoidosis?", Dr. Stefan Cristian Stanel, www.youtube.com/@DrStefanCristianStanel, 2023

"Al Jackson - Growing up in New Orleans in the 50s and 60s", Ken McCarthy, Jazz on the Tube, www.youtube.com/@weshouldsharemusic7414, 9/19/2023

"Who Counts as Louisiana Creole? An Interview with Jeremy Simien", Danielle Romero, NYTN, www.youtube.com/watch?v=S-7F5qAQ_S8U, 2/12/2023

"Resilience and Hope 60 Years After New Orleans School Desegregation", KNTV - NBC Bay Area, www.nbcbayarea.com, 3/1/2022

"Some New Orleans Black History You Should Know", United Teachers of New Orleans, https://utno.la.aft.org/

"Rock Geography: Remembering 5 New Orleans Music Clubs!", Mind Smoke Records, www.msmokemusic.com

"What It's Like Growing Up Black in New Orleans", Growing Up Black on VH1, VH1, 2021

"The Seventh Ward New Orleans: We Will Rise Again", Ada James, www.Movoto.com

"Seventh Ward Neighborhood Snapshot", Greater New Orleans Community Data Center, 10/4/2002

"The Monster': Claiborne Avenue Before And After The Interstate", Emma Long, et al, WWNO New Orleans Public Radio, 5/5/2016

"As a highway looming over a historic Black community in New Orleans faces renewal", Tom Seymour, The Art Newspaper, 2/1/2022

"Where San Francisco's Black population stands — and where it goes from here", Greg Wong, San Francisco Examiner, 2/27/2024

"Fillmore Revisited — How Redevelopment Tore Through the Western Addition", Rachel Brahinsky, San Francisco Public Press, 9/23/2019

"A History of the Fillmore Neighborhood in San Francisco", KQED, 11/6/2023

"The Dawn of Black Power", David Hoffman, www.youtube.com/@DavidHoffmanFilmmaker, 2/14/2013

"The Black Panther Party: Challenging Police and Promoting Social Change", The National Museum of African American History & Culture, Unknown

"The Black Panthers Revisited", Laurens Grant & Stanley Nelson, *The New York Times*, 1/23/2015

"Sisters of the Revolution: the Women of the Black Panther Party", Sean O'Hagan, *The Guardian*, 9/4/2022

Bright Lights Lonely Nights: The memories of Sernena, Porn Star Pioneer of the 1970s, Serena Czarnecki, BearManor Media, 2014

"A Behind-the-Scenes Look at the Porn Industry in 1970", Eliza Berman, *Time Magazine*, 7/28/2015

"History and Theory of Feminism", *UGWAnet*, http://gender.cawater-info.net/

"The Dark Side: An Oral History Of Black Porn", Keith Murphy, *Vibe*, 6/25/2012

"[Talk Like Sex] The History of Black Porn Actresses", Feminista Jones, *Ebony*, 2/27/2014

"The Rise and Fall of Pornography", Rod Bastanmehr, City on a Hill Press, 2/5/2009

"The Unethical History of 1970s Porn", Alyssa Morterud , Sexual Health Alliance, 8/14/2021

"Meet the man who made San Francisco the porn capital of America 50 years ago", Greg Keraghosian, *SF Gate*, 2/1/2020

"Porn Star and Feminist: On Jane Kamensky's 'Candida Royalle and the Sexual Revolution'", Fred Turner, *LA Review of Books*, 3/28/2024

"The Deuce and the Real History of Why the Porn Industry Flourished in the '70s", Olivia B. Waxman, *Time Magazine*, 9/8/2017

Franchise: The Golden Arches in Black America, Marcia Chatelain, Liveright Publishing Corporation, 2020

"An Early History of Blacks on Madison Avenue", Michael Pollak, *New York Times*, 3/13/2015

"Madison Avenue: The failure of integration in advertising— and what it says about race in America", Tanner Colby, *Slate*, 2/27/2014

"Inside McDonald's Fraught History With Black America", Patrick J. Sauer, *Medium*, 2/6/2020

"Thomas J. Burrell", The HistoryMakers: The Digital Repository for the Black Experience, www.thehistorymakers.org

"Thomas Burrell", www.encyclopedia.com

"Tom Burrell, Ad Legend", David Burn, www.adpulp.com, 10/18/2021

Legal Services Director for Eau Claire County DA office, Eric Hufe

ACKNOWLEDGEMENTS

There are so many people for me to thank for their support and encouragement.

First and foremost—always and forever—my wife, Melanie, for being a widow to my silly creative pursuits, and for being my first and most important reader of anything I write.

To my cousin, Mary, whose eager demands for new chapters to read during this novel's creation spurred me on, and her feedback and contributions helped make the novel more accurate.

To my brother, Mark, for being the social justice warrior that was always in the back of my mind as I worked through this novel. Many of us talk the talk, but you, brother, have walked the walk. Thank you for being so dedicated to fighting for fairness and equality to all.

To my brother Dan, who for some reason continues to be one of my biggest supporters, and one of my most avid readers. It means a ton to me, brother.

To my brother Bob, who has been a best friend for most of my life, and beyond the tremendous support, is my go-to person to share so many of my passions—from movies to music to science.

To all my book club leaders of my previous books—Erin Swanson, Mary Sheetz, Jacqui Fedie—and all your club members. What pure joy to be invited to your groups and meet such wonderful people!

To my advanced readers—I can't thank you enough for your early attention and honest reviews.

To Lori Chilefone and her amazing work capturing the spirit and essence of Pauline's and DeeDee's stories with her cover art.

To my editor, Diana Sigler Peterson, and her passionate pursuit of proper punctuation (which I probably still broke in final edits), as well as her encouragement and support.

Special callouts to supportive organizations and businesses: the Local Store at Volume One, The Chippewa Falls Public Library, Wisconsin Maker's Market, Dragon Tales Books, and the Chippewa Valley Writers Guild.

A shoutout to fellow writers Drew Seveland, Dan Lyskett and Elan Mccallum for helping make this novel's opening far more effective than it originally had been.

And, to all friends and family who have taken the time and interest in my endeavors—far too many to list, but I sure hope you know who you are.

Finally, my continual thanks to all my readers. It's all about you, after all. It's just not worth it without you, so thank you.

BOOK CLUB MEMBERS

Find reader aids and discussion points at:
www.jameslpeters.com/book-club-resources

←——————→

If you'd like to read more about
Pauline Swanson's backstory, check out
the other novels she appears in:

Shrugging

Fortune Falls

Learn about these and other books at
jameslpeters.com.

ABOUT THE AUTHOR

James L. Peters isn't interested in heroes or villains. He does his best to write about realistic people with real problems. His characters are flawed, lack certainty, and make mistakes. Just like James.

James wrote his first "novel" at age seven. His mother typeset and bound the ten-page masterwork. By his teenage years, he was coming home from school, locking himself in his bedroom, abandoning his backpack stuffed with textbooks and homework into a corner, to sit down at his Smith Corona XD6500 Word Processing Typewriter. He clacked away at keys into the midnight hours while chain-smoking Camels and trying to be the next Stephen King.

Which never happened.

But college introduced him to contemporary fiction, to critical approaches to literature, and the joys of fully exploring nuanced characters and themes. He lost his taste for horror and supernatural thrillers, and instead discovered the thrill of letting complex characters guide him through the complications of living.

He has been published in collegiate literary journals, and most recently in the Midwest literary magazine, *Barstow and Grand*. He lives in northwestern Wisconsin with his best friend, soulmate, and wife, Melanie.

www.ingramcontent.com/pod-product-compliance
Lightning Source LLC
Chambersburg PA
CBHW020538120726
47903CB00001B/27